The Ones Who Got Away

RONI LOREN

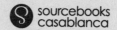

sourcebooks
casablanca

Sourcebooks and the colophon are registered trademarks of Sourcebooks, Inc.

Published by Sourcebooks Casablanca, an imprint of Sourcebooks, Inc.
P.O. Box 4410, Naperville, Illinois 60567-4410
(630) 961-3900
Fax: (630) 961-2168
sourcebooks.com

Printed and bound in United States of America.
OPM 10 9 8 7 6 5 4 3 2 1

To my readers—thanks for giving me a reason to keep writing stories.

chapter
ONE

NOTHING CAN SAVE YOU. OLIVIA ARIAS RUBBED GOOSE BUMPS
from her arms as she read the words scrawled on the
sign taped under a maniacal-looking wasp painted on
the wall of the gym. NOTHING CAN SAVE YOU FROM THE
STING! More hand-drawn posters hung crookedly around
the ridiculous mascot, bubbly cheerleader handwriting
declaring that the Millbourne Yellowjackets were going
to take down the Creekside Tigers. Some smart-ass had
drawn a tiger with a swollen face and an EpiPen with an
X through it.

Nothing can save you. The level of artistic skill on the
cartoon should've made Liv smile. Back when she was
in high school, she wouldn't have been the one making
school spirit signs, but she would've appreciated the art
and the sarcasm. Today, she couldn't find enthusiasm
for either. Because it all felt off. The new name for the
school. The weird, too-smiley mascot. Her, being there.

This wasn't the gym where it had happened. That
building had been knocked down within months of the

tragedy. Spilled blood covered with dirt. A memorial courtyard was in its place now on the other side of the school. She'd taken the long way around and had avoided walking past it on her way in, afraid it would trigger all the stuff she'd fought so hard to lock down. Even after twelve years, she couldn't bear to look at a list of names that should've been in a graduation program instead of etched onto a memorial. People she'd sat next to in class. People she'd been friends with. People she'd thought she hated until they were gone and she'd realized how silly and superficial high-school hate was. Now they were just names on stone, memories painted on the walls of her brain, holes in people's hearts.

"You said you weren't in the gym when the first gunman came in."

The interviewer's calm voice jarred Liv from her thoughts, and she blinked in the bright camera-ready lights. They'd been talking about the tragedy as a whole, but hadn't gotten into the details of the night yet. "What?"

Daniel Morrow, the filmmaker putting the documentary together, gave her an encouraging nod, making his too-stylish hair flop across his forehead. "You weren't in the gym…"

Liv swallowed past the rubber-band tightness in her throat. Maybe she'd overestimated her ability to handle this. She'd agreed to it because the proceeds were going both to the families of the victims and to research that could help prevent things like this from happening. How could she say no to that and not look heartless? But in that moment, she wished she'd declined. Old fear was creeping up the back of her neck, invading like a thousand spiders, the sounds and memories from that night threatening to overtake her. She closed her eyes for a second and focused on her breathing.

She wasn't that scared girl anymore. She *would not* be.

"Do you need to take a break, Ms. Arias?" Daniel asked, his voice echoing in the dark, empty gym.

She shook her head, the lights feeling too hot on her skin. No breaks. She needed to get this over with. If she took a break, she wouldn't come back. She opened her eyes and straightened her spine, rallying her reserve of calm, that place where she went and pretended she was talking about things that had happened to someone else, to people she didn't know, at a school she'd never heard of. "No, I wasn't in the gym. I'd gone into the hallway to get some air."

Not entirely true. She'd left the prom to sneak into a janitor's closet with Finn Dorsey. But she and Finn had never told that part of the story because he'd been there with a "proper" date, and he would've never wanted his parents or anyone else to know he was sneaking off with someone like Olivia Arias. She'd first dragged him into the closet to fight with him, to let him know how she felt about being passed over for his student-council-president date. But fighting had only stoked the fire that had burned between them back then. Young, misguided, completely inconvenient lust. They'd been rounding second base when they'd heard the first shots fired.

"What happened when you were in the hallway?"

Liv didn't want to picture it again. She'd wrestled with flashbacks for so long that it felt like inviting the devil in for another stay. Her only reprieve since that awful year had been one hundred percent avoidance, cutting herself off from everything and everyone from back then. Letting the scene run through her mind could be too much. But there was no helping it. The images came anyway.

"When I heard the shots and screaming, I hid in the janitor's closet." She and Finn had thought it was some kind of prom prank until they'd heard Finn's date, Rebecca, shout the word *gun*.

Gun.

A tiny, three-letter word that had knocked their world off its axis and punted it into a different dimension forever.

"So you never saw the shooters?"

Liv gripped her elbows, trying to keep the inner chill from becoming visible shivering, and ignored the pine scent of the janitor's disinfectant that burned her nose as if she were right there again. She still couldn't buy a real Christmas tree because of that smell. "I didn't see anyone until Joseph opened the door."

Because Finn had left her. The second he'd heard Rebecca scream, he'd bailed on Liv. He'd said something to her, but she could never recall what. All she remembered was him leaving. And in his rush to save his real date, he'd inadvertently alerted Joseph to Liv's presence.

"He pointed the gun at me and yelled at me to stand up." Her voice caught on the last bit, snagging on the sharp memory, bringing back that all-encompassing fear that she was in her last minutes. She'd learned to mostly manage the panic attacks that had plagued her after that night, but that moment was always the image that haunted her most—when she saw the barrel of that gun pointed at her, the scared but determined eyes of her former lab partner drilling into her like cold steel.

"But Joseph didn't pull the trigger?"

Liv looked down at her hands, turning her mother's wedding band round and round. "No. He knew who I was. I…wasn't on his list."

"Meaning?"

There was no way Daniel didn't know what that meant. The media had latched on to the killers' manifesto like ants on honey. Joseph and Trevor had chosen prom night for a very particular reason. Not to take out the popular people or people who'd wronged them. They wanted to take out the *happy* ones. *If you can be happy in a fucked-up world like this, then you're blind and too stupid to live.* That'd been the motto of their mission.

Liv hadn't been deemed a *happy one* and had been spared. But she wasn't going to say it and open herself up to the question of *why* she hadn't been happy. There'd been enough speculation in the press back when it'd happened. What was *broken* with all those lucky survivors? Were they the mean kids? The depressed kids? The damaged kids? *Friends* of the killers? "Joseph and I had worked together on a project in chemistry. We weren't friends, but I'd been nice to him."

And he'd been nice to her. But she'd also seen part of him that would haunt her later. When she'd worried that their project wouldn't be up to par, he'd assured her that the rest of the class was filled with idiots, jocks, and assholes, so they'd look like geniuses in comparison. He'd smirked at her and said, *I mean, seriously, someone should just put them out of their misery. Save us the trouble of having to deal with them.*

Back then, she'd already been a subscriber to the church of sarcasm and had no love lost for many of her classmates, so she'd taken his comment as such and agreed with him. Now the memory of that conversation made her sick. She'd reassured a killer that he was right. Given him more fuel for his bonfire.

"He cursed at me, told me to stay put, and wedged a chair against the outside of the door." She rubbed her lips together. "After that, I heard more shots."

"Presumably when he and Trevor shot at"—Daniel checked his notes—"Finn Dorsey and Rebecca Lindt."

Liv reached for her water and took a slow sip, trying not to hear the sounds of that night in her head. The gun going off in that steady, unrelenting way. The cries for help. A Mariah Carey song still playing in the gym. Her own rapid breath as she huddled in that closet and did—nothing. Frozen. For five hours. Only the chair against the door had alerted the SWAT team someone was in there after everything was over. "Yes. I didn't see any of it, but I know Finn was shot protecting Rebecca. You'd have to ask Rebecca about that part."

"I did ask her. I plan to ask Finn, too."

Liv's head snapped upward at that, the words yanking her out of the memories like a stage hook. "What?"

"Mr. Dorsey is my next interview."

She stared at Daniel, not sure if she'd heard the words right. "Finn's *here*?"

She barely resisted saying, *He exists?* The guy had become a ghost after the awful months following the shooting. He'd gotten a ton of press for being a hero, and the media had played up the story to the nth degree. The star athlete and son of a local business owner taking a bullet for his date. But within a year, his family had rented out their house and moved out of town, running from the spotlight like everyone else. No one wanted to be that brand of famous.

Liv hadn't heard anything about him since, and he never gave interviews. She'd decided that he had probably moved to some remote tropical island and changed his name. She would've skipped town back then, too—if she'd had the funds to do it.

"Yes," Daniel said, tipping his head toward the spot over her left shoulder. "He got here a few minutes ago. He's declined to be on camera, but he's agreed to an interview."

With that, she couldn't help but turn and follow the interviewer's gaze. Leaning against the wall in the shadows of the darkened gym was a man with dark hair, a black T-shirt, and jeans. He looked up from the phone in his hand, as if hearing his name, and peered in their direction. He was too far away for her to read his expression or see the details of his face, but a jolt of bone-deep recognition went through her. "Oh."

"Hey, we should invite him to join you for this part since you were both close to the same place at the same time. We'll get a more accurate timeline that way."

"What? I mean, no, that's not—"

"Jim, can you turn off the camera? I think this will be important. Mr. Dorsey," Daniel called out, "would you mind if I asked you a few questions now? The camera's off."

The cameraman went about shutting things down, and Finn pushed away from the wall.

Liv's heart leapt into her throat and tried to escape. She'd avoided Finn after everything had happened, not just from hurt, but because seeing his face, even on television, would trigger the flashbacks. But she wasn't that girl anymore. Seeing Finn after all these years shouldn't concern her. Still, she had the distinct urge to make tracks to the back door. She slid out of the director's chair she'd been sitting in. "I think I've probably given you everything I have to add. I wasn't in the gym, and my story is really just me cowering in the closet. Not that interesting—"

Her words cut off, her voice dying a quick death, as Finn got closer and some of the studio lights caught him in their glare. The man approaching was nothing like the boy she'd known. The bulky football muscles had streamlined into a harder, leaner package. The smooth face was now dusted with scruff, and the look in his deep-green eyes held no trace of boyish innocence. A thousand things were in those eyes. A thousand things welled up in Liv.

Finn Dorsey had become a man. And a stranger. The only familiar thing was the sharp, undeniable kick of awareness she'd always gotten anytime the guy was around. Time had only made the effect more potent. Without thinking, her gaze drifted to his hands. Big, capable hands that had once held her. When she'd known him, he'd always worn his football championship ring from junior year. The cool metal used to press against the back of her neck when he kissed her. Now he wore no rings at all. She took a breath, trying to reel in that old, automatic response to him, and smoothed her hands down the sides of her now-wrinkled pencil skirt.

Daniel held out his hand. "Mr. Dorsey, so glad you could make it."

Finn returned the offered handshake and gave a brief nod. "Not a problem."

Then, his gaze slid to Liv. His brow wrinkled for a second, but she could tell the moment he realized who she was. Something flickered over his face. A very distinct look. Like she caused him pain. Like she was a bad memory.

Because she was. That was all they were to each other at this point.

"Liv."

She pushed words past her constricted throat. "Hi, Finn."

He stepped closer, his gaze tracing over her face as if searching for something. Or maybe just cataloging all the differences time had given her. Gone were the heavy kohl eyeliner, the nose piercing, and the purple-streaked hair. She'd gone back to her natural black hair color after college, and though she still liked to think she had a quirky style, she'd chosen a simple gray suit for today's interview. Something teen Liv would've made snoring sounds over.

"It's good to see you," Finn said, his voice deeper and more rumbly than she remembered. "You look…"

"Like I've been through a two-hour interview, I'm sure." She forced a tight smile. "I'll get out of your way so that you and Daniel can chat. I'm sure you'll be able to offer a lot more detailed information than I can. I was just the girl in the closet."

Finn frowned. "Liv—"

"I was hoping I could talk to you both," Daniel interrupted. "May provide extra insight."

Liv's heart was beating too fast now. Part of her

wanted to yell at Finn, to demand why, to spew out all those questions she'd never asked, all those feelings she'd packed away in that dark vault labeled Senior Year. But the other part of her knew there was no good answer. In the end, all three of them had survived. Maybe if he hadn't left the closet, Rebecca wouldn't have made it. Then Liv would have that on her conscience.

She turned to Daniel and plastered on an apologetic look. "I'm sorry. This has wiped me out. I'd rather wrap things up here. I really don't have more to add."

"What if we took a break and then—"

"She said she's tired," Finn said, cool authority in his voice.

"It would only be a few more questions. The viewers would—"

Finn lifted a hand. "Look. I know you're doing this for a good cause, but you have to remember what this does to all of us. To the outside world, this was a tragedy. Something people discuss over dinner, shake their heads at, or get political about. To us, this was our life, our school, our friends. Asking us to come back here, to talk about all these things again…it requires more than anyone realizes. It rips open things that we try to keep stitched up. So let her go. She doesn't owe anyone more of her story than she wants to give." Finn's gaze caught hers. "She doesn't owe anyone anything."

Liv's chest squeezed tight, and Daniel turned her way, apology in his eyes. "I'm sorry. You're right. Ms. Arias, if you need to go, please do. I appreciate all the time you've given me."

He held out his hand for her to shake, and she took it. "It's fine. Knowing that the proceeds are going to the families helps. I know you'll do a good job with it. I just don't have any more to add."

She released Daniel's hand and turned to Finn, giving him a little nod of thanks. "I'll get out of here so y'all can get started. It was good to see you, Finn."

Finn's focused attention held hers, for a moment kicking up old memories that had nothing to do with gunmen or violence or the way it all ended. Instead, her head filled with snapshots of stolen minutes and frantic kisses in the library stacks and his big, full laughter when she'd tell him her weird jokes. Before Finn had abandoned her that night, he'd saved her each day of that semester, had given her something to look forward to, something to smile about when things were so awful at home. He'd made her hope.

But even before the shooting, she should've known there was no future for the two of them. The signs had been there the whole time. She'd just been too dazzled to see them.

"It's been too long," he said quietly. "We should have a drink and catch up. Are you staying in town?"

She was. But she didn't feel prepared for that conversation. She didn't feel prepared for *him*. All those years after he'd disappeared, she'd had a thousand questions for him, but now she couldn't bring herself to ask one. This interview, the twelve-year anniversary, and seeing him had left her feeling too raw, exposed. And what difference would his answers make, anyway? The past couldn't be changed.

She wanted to lie and tell him she was heading out tonight. But she was staying at the Bear Creek Inn, the only decent hotel in their little Texas town, which meant that was probably where he was staying, too. If she lied, she'd run into him because that was how the universe worked. "I'm meeting up with some friends for dinner. I'm not sure I'll have time."

He watched her for a moment, his eyes searching, but then nodded. "I'm in Room 348 at the Bear. Call my room if you change your mind, and I can meet you at the bar."

She forced a polite smile. "Will do."

"Great." But she could tell by the look on his face that he didn't believe her.

This was all just a formality, and maybe his offer for a drink was the same. No matter what had happened between them before the night of the dance, all they were to each other now were bad memories and even worse decisions.

She told both men goodbye and turned to head to the door, forcing herself not to look back. This place, this story, were her past. *Finn Dorsey* was her past. She didn't need anything or anyone reminding her of that time in her life, of how fragile she'd been. She'd worked too hard to lock all that stuff in a fail-safe box so that she could finally move forward. She couldn't linger here.

She picked up her pace. Her high heels clicked on the gym floor at a rapid clip.

But instead of hearing her footfalls, all she heard were gunshots. *Click, click, click. Bang, bang, bang.*

Anxiety rippled over her nerve endings, and she tried to breathe through the astringent pine scent that haunted her. *No.* Screams sounded in her ears.

She walked so quickly that she might as well have been running. Finn might have called out her name.

But she couldn't be sure, and she didn't turn back.

The faster she could get away from this place and the memories, the better.

She was not that girl anymore.

She would never go back.

chapter
TWO

Finn needed a stiff drink, a warm bed, and a long-ass vacation. He gratefully accepted the first from the waitress at the hotel's only restaurant and ordered another before she could leave.

"You want to add a little food to that, hon? We've got a great chicken-fried steak tonight with homemade white gravy and mashed potatoes. That'll make any night better."

Finn fought back a grimace. Nothing could improve this night except a pass-out-in-bed kind of drunk. But Janice, who'd been working there since he was a kid, looked way too eager for him to crush her with a snide comment. This was why he'd moved away from here. The whole town always wanted to *do* something for the Long Acre High survivors. But there was nothing anyone *could* do.

Even he had found himself trying to do something today when he'd seen Olivia Arias. Beautiful, quirky Liv all grown up. Seeing her had hit him like a hundred fists to the gut. Had jolted him back to a time when what he'd looked forward to most each day was sneaking away with Liv to steal a few kisses and share a few sparring words. A bittersweet ache like he hadn't felt in longer than he could remember had tightened his chest and stolen his breath.

He'd wanted to reach for her. He'd wanted to fix things. Apologize. *Do* something to take that haunted look out of her eyes. *Do* something to show her how goddamned sorry he was for how spectacularly he'd let her down. But he'd seen it in her face. There was nothing to be done. The past was locked in stone. He knew that better than anyone. The scars were deep and permanent, and he'd left an extra vicious one on Liv.

Now this lovely woman was trying to fix it with deep-fried beef. He found his voice, the words like gravel in his throat. "Sounds great."

Her smile brightened. "You betcha. I'll get one going for you right now and bring by that second drink."

Finn laced his fingers around his glass of Maker's Mark, staring into the liquid, watching the amber light play along the ice cubes. He should've gone straight to the lake house. The interviewer had asked all of them to stay in town an extra night in case he needed more information or more footage, but Finn felt exposed here and out of place. He wasn't the kid who'd left Long Acre. And after years of undercover work, he wasn't sure he knew who the man he'd become was either. Two weeks ago, he'd killed a guy and almost gotten killed himself. Tonight, he was supposed to be the hometown hero who'd shielded his date. The shift was enough to give him whiplash.

Even his name felt like an ill-fitting shirt. He found himself forgetting to answer to it. For almost two years, he hadn't been Finn Dorsey, former high school running back and school shooting survivor, he'd been Axel Graham—employee of Dragonfly Industries, a company that owned strip clubs officially, but trafficked drugs and guns by the shit ton while the pretty ladies danced.

He'd done what the FBI had needed him to do, even though he hadn't found what *he'd* ultimately been looking for. On that front, it'd been another false trail. One of many he'd tracked down over the years. But he'd uncovered high-level criminals and turned them in. Mission accomplished, though he wasn't sure at what cost. Pretending to be a bad guy for two years, seeing all the things he'd seen, and being part of those things, had seeped into him like tainted water. He wasn't sure when or if he'd ever feel clean again. Even his boss was concerned about him. But a summer alone at the lake house would hopefully be a start—if he could ever get there. He just needed to make it through one more night in Long Acre.

He lifted his glass and drained the liquor. The alcohol turned to smooth fire at the back of his throat right as Liv Arias walked in. He stilled and almost choked on the bourbon.

Liv didn't look his way. She'd have no reason to. He'd grabbed a corner booth in the dark restaurant to do his drinking, and she was already in conversation with someone. But he definitely couldn't take his eyes off her. She'd walked in with three other women, all around the same age, and he vaguely registered that the redhead was Rebecca Lindt. The others were probably classmates of his, too. The reporter had told him that he'd managed to get eighteen of the survivors for interviews and the mother of one of the shooters. But Finn hadn't considered that he'd be running into anyone. He'd been too focused on making sure the guy understood Finn couldn't be shown on film.

He needed to bail. The last thing he wanted to do was make small talk with anyone. But he couldn't seem to move from his spot. Liv was smiling at one of the women, a simple tilt of glossed red lips that illuminated her entire face. He remembered that smile. He used to be able to put it there.

She'd changed from her business suit into a pair of figure-hugging black pants and a simple white shirt that emphasized her bronze complexion. Her hair was pulled back into a curling ponytail, and his gaze snagged on the delicate tattoo on the back of her neck. That little detail had heat building in him that had nothing to do with the alcohol. That was the Liv he remembered. The girl who'd had a rebellious streak, the girl who'd dyed her hair crazy colors that skirted the edge of school rules, and the girl who had trusted him with her secrets. The girl who'd put up with *being* his secret.

God, he'd been such a spineless coward with her. He hadn't dated Liv publicly because his family would've had a shit fit. The daughter of the man who took care of their lawn, she was from the part of town his parents had told him not to drive through at night. On top of that, she was artsy and weird and foul-mouthed. She wouldn't have known the right fork to use at his mother's dinner parties. And she wouldn't have cared. So he'd kept their relationship hidden, and she'd put up with it.

She should've kicked him in the soft parts and told him to go screw himself. He had a feeling grown-up Liv would know what to do, based on her quick dismissal of his earlier offer to meet up tonight. She didn't look like a woman who would be walked on. Which, of course, only made him want to talk to her more, to discover who she'd become. But he didn't deserve her time. She'd pretty much made that clear, and he didn't blame her. He'd lost that right on so many levels he couldn't name them all.

Janice stopped at his table with another drink and set down a fried slab of meat as big as his head. White gravy sloshed off the side of the plate and onto the pine table. "Hot sauce and ketchup are by the sugar caddy if you need them. Can I get you anything else right now?"

"Lipitor?"

She laughed and patted him on the shoulder. "Strapping young man like you? I think you'll handle it just fine. I'll check on you in a few."

Finn took a half-hearted bite of his food as he watched Liv and her friends. They headed to a large round booth in the corner, and the bartender brought over two giant pitchers of margaritas. Apparently, Finn wasn't the only one ready to get hammered after the day of interview questions and hellish memories.

Liv was smiling still, listening to something one of the others said, but she was the first to reach for the pitcher, and she poured her glass to the top. When she lifted it to her lips, she drained half in one go, telling him exactly how much of a facade that carefree smile was.

He lifted his glass in silent camaraderie. *Here's to drinking away the dark, Liv. Let's hope we can outrun it for another night.*

The sounds of the restaurant and her former classmates blurred at the edges, everything becoming a little more fluid, a little less crisp. Liv set down her glass, knowing that three margaritas were more than her limit. She didn't drink like this anymore. College Liv could've taken down twice this much and still been on her feet—well, before she ended up off her feet in some random dude's dorm room. She wasn't that girl anymore. And she wasn't going to let this rocky hike along memory lane resurrect that train-wreck version of herself. But dinner with these women needed a little boozy fortitude, so she'd allowed herself a few.

"Need a refill, Liv?" Kincaid asked as she poured another glass for herself, her bangle bracelets clinking against the pitcher. Somehow the woman still looked put together after a long day of interviewing, not a lock of her golden hair out of place—a Texas beauty queen if ever there was one. "We can make a toast and then open the jar."

Liv lifted a palm. "No, I'm cutting myself off. If I drink any more, I won't be able to read what's inside that jar. Plus, I'm too old to be hungover."

"I'm not," Taryn said, lifting her glass and shaking it. The ice cubes caught the light, illuminating her brown skin with a disco ball effect and flashing off her dark-rimmed glasses. "If any night deserves a hangover, it's this one. I want to pretend that I'm here with friends I haven't seen in years because I missed them, and we're doing some fun little time capsule thing. Not because we had to recount the most horrible night of our lives in traumatizing detail, mm-kay?"

"I'll drink to that," Rebecca said from her spot across from Liv before taking a big gulp of her margarita, somehow managing to look prim while she did it. "And I'm not sure we should open the jar anyway. Let's just get drunk and move on. The notes inside are irrelevant. We aren't those teenagers anymore."

All four women stared at the dirty mason jar they'd placed in the center of the table as if it were going to detonate. Taryn had retrieved it a few hours ago from beneath the lemon tree in her mom's backyard where the four of them had buried it the summer after senior year. None of them had reached for it yet.

Kincaid tapped a bright-pink fingernail against the worn wood of the tabletop. "We had a pact, ladies. We were supposed to open this two years ago. We're finally all together. Now is not the time to chicken out."

"We also made a promise to stay in touch," Rebecca said between sips, her wry tone at full throttle. "That worked out well."

Taryn frowned, brown eyes shifting away. "Come on, it's not like that. We've…Facebooked. We've just been busy."

Rebecca arched a brow like she was still on the debate team and her opponent had just made a bullshit point. "For a decade? Yeah, okay."

Taryn opened her mouth to respond, but Liv cut her off. There was no reason to argue or pretend like this was something that it wasn't. "It's not because we've been busy. We all know that."

"We do?" Kincaid asked, looking genuinely curious.

Liv wiped salt off the rim of her glass and rubbed it between her fingers until it disappeared, not wanting to be the one to say it but knowing someone had to. "It's because we want to forget. We say we want to keep in touch, but it hurts to remember. And what else do we do for each other but remind ourselves of the bad stuff? We were never friends in the Before, only in the After."

Silence fell over the table, everyone looking as uncomfortable as Liv had felt since sitting down with them. The four of them didn't have good memories together because they had never been friends before the shooting. Kincaid Breslin had been friendly with all of them on some level because she was the type to be chatty with everyone. She could talk a tree stump into having a conversation and liking her. But it was a saying-hi-in-the-hallway kind of acquaintance. She'd been head of the dance team—gorgeous, popular, and sparkling in a sphere not many could touch.

Taryn Landry had been the honor student and athlete, playing three different sports and not having time for friends besides the other jocks and her younger sister, who had been one of the victims. And Rebecca Lindt, student council president and Finn's date the night of the dance, had been the goody-two-shoes redhead Liv rolled her eyes over, her nemesis. None of them would've ever been friends.

But after prom night, the four of them had ended up in a support group together. Overnight, they'd become members of the same club—a club no one would ever want to join. After what they'd been through, their differences and cliques had fallen away, leaving nothing behind but the bond of knowing no one outside the group could ever understand them like the ones in it. They'd made a promise to keep in touch. And they'd made a pact to live their lives to the fullest to honor those who wouldn't get the chance. Then they'd stuffed those promises into that freaking time capsule, outlining exactly how they would do that.

Liv didn't remember what she'd written on that piece of paper that was all folded up and tucked inside the jar, but she didn't really care. Whatever dreams she'd scrawled on that page were silly teenage fantasies of what it'd be like to be grown up. Easily dismissed. But as much as she'd been tempted to, she hadn't been able to turn down the invitation to meet up and do this. She didn't know these women anymore, but they'd gotten her through the worst year of her life and she wasn't going to break her word to them.

"I think we should just open the thing," Liv said finally. "Get it out of the way so we can relax the rest of the night."

"Amen, sister. I'm with you. It's ruining my buzz." Kincaid reached for the jar. "Let's open it, and we can each read someone else's letter out loud."

"Wait, what?" Rebecca's blue eyes went wide, her faint childhood freckles seeming to flare in opposition. "No way. It's private. It's—"

"If we read our own, we'll edit. This is about honesty." Kincaid grabbed her napkin and draped it over the rusty metal lid. "No one outside of this group is going to share anything about the letters. And we can burn the things afterward if we want, close the past for good."

The sound of the rusted lid grinding against the glass gave Liv a layer of goose bumps, and her palms went clammy. Visions of the night they'd buried the thing flickered through her head, dragging her back in time. The night had been humid, the scent of lemons and fresh-cut grass heavy in the air. None of them had cried. They'd been out of tears by then. They'd kneeled in the dirt and lowered the little jar into the ground together like it was some kind of religious ritual. Four lost girls making a plea to the universe, begging for the future to be better than the present, burying seeds of dreams and hoping they would grow.

Now they would see if they had.

Liv fought the sudden urge to reach out and grab the jar, throw it into the creek out back, leave that stuff buried. Her fingers curled against the table. But none of the women stopped Kincaid as she set aside the lid and fished out the pages.

Without ceremony, Kincaid looked at the names on the letters and then handed one to each of them. Liv ended up with Rebecca's. Kincaid kept Liv's.

The paper felt brittle in Liv's fingers, the blue lines of the loose-leaf faded. But when she unfolded it, the writing was still clear. Neat, looping green handwriting filled half the page.

"Liv, why don't you go first?" Kincaid suggested. "Put Bec out of her misery."

Rebecca winced at the suggestion, and Liv hesitated. "Hey, if you don't want me to read it, I won't. Seriously. It's up to you."

There was no love lost between her and Rebecca, but she wasn't going to torture the woman. These were her secrets to keep or share.

Rebecca stared at Liv for a moment, a few different

emotions flickering over her face. Bec was an attorney now, and Liv imagined she was having some sort of courtroom battle in her head, but finally she pressed her lips together and nodded. "No, go ahead. It'll be embarrassing, but I'll just make sure y'all drink enough not to remember this in the morning."

Liv smirked. "That may happen all on its own. But okay, let's do this." She smoothed the paper on the tabletop and began to read. "On this day, August first, I, Rebecca Lindt, promise the Class of 2005 that I will not waste the second chance that I have been given, that I will honor all the people we lost by living my life to the fullest. Professional goals: I will get a law degree and graduate at the top of my class. After practicing law for a few years, I will run for political office and will fight for better gun control laws and more mental health interventions for teens. I will make a difference in the world. Personal goals: I will stay a virgin until I'm married. And I will marry Finn Dorsey in a Paris wedding. We'll have two kids, preferably one boy and one girl, and a dog named Bartholomew, after my grandpa. I will be a good friend, wife, and mom. I will be happy."

"Oh God." Rebecca put her reddened face in her hands and groaned. "That was worse than I remembered. I hate you, teenage Rebecca."

Taryn pressed her hand over her mouth but couldn't contain the snort.

Rebecca turned and sent her an oh-no-you-didn't look.

Taryn grimaced and lifted her hand. "Sorry. The dog name got me."

"Not the virgin thing?" Kincaid said with a grin,

bumping Rebecca's shoulder with hers. "You really were rocking the good-girl life, Bec. You don't do things halfway."

Rebecca shrugged and took another sip of her drink. "Well, I never said I didn't go *halfway*."

The others burst into laughs at that, the margaritas and awkwardness of it all making everyone a little silly. But Liv only gave a distracted smile as her gaze ran over Finn's name again. Rebecca had never known about Finn and Liv's secret relationship or where he'd been that night before he'd jumped in to save her. Finn had said there was nothing between him and Rebecca but friendship, but clearly Rebecca had felt differently.

"Finn, huh?" The words slipped out before Liv could stop them.

Rebecca looked up, her smile faltering a bit. "Yeah. He'd been my neighbor since we were little. And after my mom left, things at home were…not great. So he'd let me escape to his house to get away from my real life. I think I loved him from fourth grade on, and I got pretty close to his family. So when he saved me at the school, I figured it was fate." She stared down at her drink, a far-off look on her face. "But I don't think he ever saw me that way. It was all very *Dawson's Creek* in my head. I just didn't realize I was Dawson."

"What happened with him?" Kincaid asked.

"We kept in touch for a few years after he moved away and I went to college, but eventually the emails stopped coming."

Liv felt a petty kick of jealousy, the old rivalry ghosting through her. Finn had kept in touch with Rebecca for *years*? But then the second part settled in. They'd been close friends but nothing more. Maybe Finn hadn't been lying to her.

"Well, some of the stuff worked out, right?" Taryn said, a hopeful note in her voice as she adjusted her glasses. "You're a lawyer."

Rebecca nodded, her expression going thoughtful. "Yeah, a divorce attorney. But I'm not the political warrior Teen Me wanted to be. I've never run for office. And I wouldn't have time for a dog, much less a husband or kids."

Even though Rebecca had a lot of be proud of, the undercurrent of disappointment in her voice was hard to miss. But Liv couldn't tell if that was Bec's overachiever gene kicking in—I'm *only* a successful attorney—or if it was something more than that. Liv frowned. "Maybe we shouldn't do this if it's just going to bum us out."

Rebecca's attention snapped upward. "Oh, no you don't. My dirty laundry pile is stinking up the joint. The rest of you aren't going to keep yours hidden." Her wry smile returned, and she rapped the table with her knuckles like a gavel. "Bring it on, ladies."

"I'll go next," Kincaid said, lifting Liv's letter. "Let's see what dark-and-broody goth Liv had planned."

Liv groaned. "To get the hell out of town. I think that's as far as I'd thought."

"Let's find out." Kincaid unfolded the letter and cleared her throat as if she were going to give a speech. "On this day, August first, I, Olivia Arias, promise the Class of 2005 that I will not waste the second chance that I have been given, that I will honor all the people we lost by living my life to the fullest. First, I will move anywhere but here."

Liv sniffed. "Told ya."

But Kincaid ignored her. "I will find a job I like that will make me enough money and give me enough time to do my photography. Then, when I get good enough, I will turn art into my job. I won't play it safe. I won't be practical. I'll live a passionate life and date passionate guys and see the world so I can take pictures of it. I promise, Class of 2005, to live the life that scares me."

Kincaid's eyebrows popped up, and Liv's heart sank as each word hit her like drops of cold rain. She could almost see her eighteen-year-old self climbing up on her soapbox and making all those declarations. That girl who was racked by panic attacks and nightmares, who had a family who didn't—*couldn't*—get it, a girl who was trying to look her fears in the face and give them the finger.

Too bad it hadn't worked out. "Boy, I certainly was dramatic."

Taryn put her chin in her hand, the dim light over the table making her brown eyes sparkle and her riot of black curls look like a halo. "I think it's beautiful. I mean, damn, I want that life, too. Minus the art part. I suck at art. But passionate guys and seeing the world? Sign me up."

"Right? Seriously," Kincaid said. "So did you get to do any of that? The travel? The guys? If it's a yes to the guys, we need to get more drinks so you'll tell us the sordid stories."

Liv laughed. "I'm definitely not drunk enough for that."

Not that there was much to tell. There'd been more guys early on than she wanted to remember. That'd been her go-to way of dealing with the anxiety that had stalked her at college. Drink too much. Find a guy to distract her. Anything to forget what she was going through for a few minutes—even if that meant waking up with a bucketful of regret in the morning. But passionate love affairs? Romance? The things she'd imagined when she wrote that letter? She'd never had that. Not even close.

"Are you still doing photography?" Rebecca asked.

Liv stared at her melting ice cubes, absently stabbing them with her straw. "Not really. I had this project I started, but I don't know. I haven't looked at it in a while."

Or in years.

"Was that the project with survivors of other tragedies?" Kincaid asked, curiosity lighting her hazel eyes. "I remember reading a story about you, and it mentioned that."

Liv rolled her lips inward, a pang going through her. "Yes. It was just an idea at the time. I thought I could take stripped-down portraits of survivors of different events to show their range of emotions, their strength and vulnerability. Somehow show the world that we weren't just the one thing they'd labeled us as. I was going to donate the proceeds to the Long Acre fund."

"Wow. I'm sure that'd be amazing," Taryn said. "And intense."

Liv glanced up. "Yeah. Too intense. At least for me." She'd made it through two sessions before she'd realized she couldn't handle it. Hearing other people's stories, seeing their scars…it'd been too much, too close to home. It had set off her PTSD like fireworks. "I put the photography aside and got a job doing web design. Eventually, all my time got sucked up as I moved up the ladder at work. Now I barely have time to squeeze in a workout, much less a hobby. I guess my just-to-make-money job became my career." She rolled her shoulders, trying to shake out the tightness gathering there. "Photography was never going to pay the bills anyway. I wasn't that good."

Taryn's expression soured. "No way. Your photos were gorgeous, Liv. Don't sell yourself that line of crap."

Liv took her letter from Kincaid, half wanting to ball it up and toss it across the room. But she forced herself to fold it neatly, creasing each line just so. "It's better than admitting that I got practical, right? That I've become some boring nine-to-fiver—or nine-to-niner—that teen Liv would've hated."

"I don't know," Rebecca offered. "Maybe that's just a consequence of being a grown-up. Dreams are called that for a reason. They usually don't happen."

"Oh, that's uplifting," Kincaid said, her East Texas twang turning dry. "Put that on a motivational mug, y'all. *If you can dream it…you probably can't do it.*"

Taryn snorted. "Let's call Oprah. She'd love the hell out of that one."

Rebecca gave both of the women a *gimme a break* look. "Just being realistic."

"Realistic?" Kincaid straightened, her nose wrinkling in derision. "Screw that. We need to do better."

"Kincaid—" Liv began.

"No. Realistic? Practical? What in the hell is wrong with us?" she demanded, her gaze alighting on each of them. "We made these promises to people. People we lost who will never get the chance to chase their own dreams. We're not eighty. We still have time."

"I don't think time's the issue," Liv said, giving in and

pouring herself another drink. Maybe she didn't drink like this anymore, but if there was ever a time to have earned being drunk, it was tonight. "Once you're on one path, it's not easy to take a hard left. Like Rebecca said, we're grown-ups. We have bills to pay, responsibilities. Jobs. We can't just chase whims."

"Why not?" Kincaid asked, in full bulldog mode now. "Does it have to be an either/or thing? There's got to be a way to do some of both—the practical and the exciting, right? Why couldn't you pick up your photography project on the side? Or travel? Or have a passionate affair?"

Liv shifted in her seat and frowned. "It's not that easy."

"Exactly," Rebecca said with a curt nod. "And how about you wait until we read your letter, Miss Rah-Rah-Siss-Boom-Bah, before you start making battle cries for us?"

Kincaid lifted a haughty brow. "If that's a cheerleader joke, it doesn't work. I was dance team. Totally different."

"I was referring to your cheering now," Rebecca said. "And how were you *not* on cheer?"

"Dance team had better outfits, and I didn't have to trust other girls not to drop me from great heights." Kincaid flicked her hand at Rebecca, giving her the cue to read her letter. "Bring it on, lawyer. I don't remember what I wrote. But either way, I'm definitely adding 'have passionate affair' to my to-do list."

"Agreed," Taryn said. "That's going on mine, too. Good suggestion, Liv."

"Thanks," she said distractedly.

The conversation moved on. But Liv had trouble focusing on any of it. Kincaid's challenge had landed on her with a thud. *Why can't you? Why not?*

Those questions poked at that long-ago rebellious girl who thought she could do anything. And they weighed on her as the other letters were read and as the night started to wrap up. She and the other women weren't doing badly. Kincaid was a successful real estate agent, Rebecca a lawyer. Taryn hadn't kept up with sports or moved away from town like she'd wanted, but she'd gotten a doctorate in forensic psychology. More than a little impressive.

From the outside looking in, they appeared just fine. Successful, even. They'd all managed to get good jobs, make a living. But it wasn't lost on Liv that none of them were in relationships. None had started families. No one had taken any risks. And none had lived up to the women they'd wanted to be in those letters.

They were still young, just entering their thirties. But they'd already settled. They'd been given this second chance when others hadn't, and they'd settled for *good enough*, for getting by, for not making waves.

Teen Liv had been racked with anxiety and nightmares, but still, she'd craved adventure. Art.

Passion.

She'd believed she could still have it.

What did grown-up Liv believe? Want?

Did she even know?

Her attention wandered from her friends as her thoughts tangled around themselves, and her gaze lingered on a booth in the far corner. The waitress was dropping off the check, but Liv caught the profile of the

man taking it from her, the big, capable hands. Hands
that never dropped the football. Hands that had once
held Liv close.

Finn.

He didn't look her way, just accepted the check and
fished some bills out of his wallet. But as she watched
him move, something stirred in her, something old and
familiar and dangerous.

Suddenly, she was back in the library, hiding from
Mrs. Wentz—the eagle-eyed librarian—and trying to
keep quiet. She was supposed to be tutoring Finn in history. But instead, Finn's hands were in her hair, his scent
in her head, and his lips on her neck. They'd always
known exactly how many minutes they had before the
bell rang. They'd used every second.

As if hearing her thoughts, his gaze drifted her way.
Their eyes locked, and a still quiet filled her. This was
the part where she was supposed to do something. But
she didn't turn her head, didn't offer a wave, didn't do
what any normal, polite person would do. She just let it
go on. The staring.

Let herself remember how he used to look at her. How
that made her feel. There'd been steel gates between
them in public, but alone, there were never any walls
with Finn. He'd made her feel wanted. Dangerous. Alive.

She realized right then how long it'd been since she'd
felt that brand of high, that flavor of reckless abandon.
That *good*. She wasn't supposed to think of that, wasn't
supposed to imagine the *before* because there was no
going back. She certainly wasn't supposed to let herself entertain how things used to be with *him*. But she
couldn't stop staring.

Without looking away, Finn lifted his half-empty glass in a silent question. *Drink?*

This time there was no hesitation with her answer. It was as if her body were on autopilot. She tucked her letter in her back pocket, grabbed the margarita pitcher to top off her glass, and then wished her friends a good night, saying that she needed to get some air and would see them in the morning.

She didn't look to see if Finn followed. She just kept moving forward, her heartbeat a steady thump in her ears. She stepped out onto the unlit porch that overlooked the creek behind the hotel and leaned against the railing, letting the heavy night air cloak her and the smooth soundtrack of the water and the singing crickets surround her. She shouldn't be out here.

Footsteps sounded behind her.

She thought of the words on the little rectangle of paper tucked in her back pocket, giving a little nod to teen Liv.

She was only here for one night.

Maybe it was time to keep some promises. And bury some ghosts.

Maybe tonight she wouldn't play it safe.

"Hello, Finn."

chapter
THREE

THE BOARDS OF THE RESTAURANT'S BACK DECK CREAKED somewhere behind Liv. She didn't need to turn and look to know it was him. Her senses seemed attuned to his presence. She kept her eyes on the water, letting her greeting drift between them. "Hello, Finn."

"Liv."

The quiet tenor of his voice hit her harder than she'd expected, the volume too close to how it used to sound against her ear in those stolen make-out sessions. Funny how even after all the years and the men who'd cruised through her life since, that voice still sounded so bone-deep familiar. She didn't turn to face him, not trusting her expression to stay neutral. "I guess it turns out I have time for that drink after all." She lifted her glass. "But I'll warn you, I'm a few drinks in and all out of energy for polite chitchat."

"Good. I don't chitchat."

He stepped a little closer, his scent drifting her way— some combination of cedar and mint. Like a man who chewed gum while chopping wood. The thought made her want to giggle.

"Are you okay?" he asked.

Liv scrunched her nose. "You mean, am I drunk?"

She wasn't sure what the answer was on that one. Probably a little. She doubted she could be this close to him without anxiety bubbling up otherwise.

"No. You ran out of the gym today. I mean, are you *okay*?"

Okay.

Was she? She hated that question. That was the question she'd probably heard most since that night—and then again when her mom passed from cancer two months later. That was what everyone always wanted to know. *Are you okay?*

But people asked, wanting her to say, *Yes, I'm fine. I'm going to pull up my bootstraps and not make you uncomfortable with my messy feelings.* No one wanted the real answer. But she got the sense Finn did. After all, he'd probably gotten asked that question just as much as she had. She released a breath. "Today sucked."

"Yeah."

She took a sip of her drink, the sweet liquid cool on her dry throat. "Being in the school got to me, but I'm okay now. Just a little panic attack—shitty but brief. Drinks and friends helped distract me."

She could hear him shift behind her, skin against fabric, maybe tucking his hands in his pockets or crossing his arms. "Distraction's good."

She finally stole a glance at him, but he was shrouded in shadows, just a broad-shouldered silhouette. "You could've joined us. You didn't have to eat alone."

"Y'all looked involved in something," he said, the gruff drawl in his voice making her think of steamy-windowed moments in the back of his car. She used to tease him that the more turned on he got, the more his country-boy accent showed. "You were reading papers. Seemed kind of intense."

"Oh, that." She turned back to the water, her shoulders curving inward and the sexy memories icing over. "We were opening this time capsule thing we did a long time ago. It's probably good you didn't come over and hear that part."

"Time capsule?"

She picked at a splinter in the wood railing. "Just something we did that summer after everything happened—promises we made to the Class of 2005 about our futures. Kincaid decided we should open the letters tonight to see what our teenage selves hoped we'd become. I decided we should get drunk after."

He made a throaty sound—like a laugh that didn't quite make it out—and moved closer. He settled next to her along the wooden rail, his gaze fixed on the dark water. "Sounds like a solid plan to me."

"I thought so." She rattled the ice cubes in her glass and dared a peek at him. But all she got was his familiar profile, the slight bump in his nose from when he'd broken it sophomore year, and the unfamiliar scruff as he took a sip from his drink. It was hard for her not to stare and catalog all the little differences, all the changes time and experience had given him. The harder angles. The dark mess of hair that looked at least two haircuts past neat. Expression that didn't reveal a thing. He was still Finn somewhere in there, but gone was the boy with the wide smile and the playful attitude. There was a sharpness to him now, jagged edges. Like if she met him in a dark alley, she'd have trouble determining if he was friend or foe.

He lifted his drink in agreement and turned, his green eyes gray in the darkness. "That was my plan, too. Minus the time capsule part."

"Ha. Lucky you." She shifted her stance and accidentally bumped her shoulder against his, sending a tendril of awareness down her arm. She wet her lips, ignoring the shiver. "Now you'll never know if you lived up to teen Finn's expectations."

He was quiet for a moment, and she wondered if he was having the same push and pull inside as she was. On one hand, this felt comfortable. They'd always talked easily with each other. But at the same time, they were strangers now. Strangers who had this big, breathing beast between them.

He took a long swig from his drink. "Teen Finn didn't have expectations. He just wanted to play football, not work for his dad, and get the hell away from here."

"Guess you lived up to that last part at least. I was convinced you'd changed your name and moved to a foreign country."

His jaw flexed. "Something like that."

"You'll have to give me your off-the-grid tips," she said, trying to make light of a completely un-light situation. "I had to change all my legal stuff to my mom's maiden name because I got tired of the phone calls from reporters and weirdos, but people still find me. Some dude cornered me at the grocery store last fall, convinced that I was part of a conspiracy with Joseph. That he'd been my boyfriend."

Finn frowned her way, his grip flexing against his glass. "You need someone to do a security evaluation for you, lock things down tighter and give you better protection. There are sick people who get obsessed with news stories like ours. You're too easy to find."

She gave a half-hearted shrug. "I told the cops what happened, and I keep my stuff unlisted. I'm sure the guy just got lucky. He didn't try to hurt me. He was just an asshole who wanted fodder for his conspiracy website."

Finn considered her, his hair ruffling in the breeze and his expression serious. "You work as a web designer at MCT Design and live in Austin—renting not owning. You're not married. You drive a Honda. You're a member of an online book club, and you've registered an LLC for a photography business that, from what I can tell, you never opened."

Her stomach flipped over and reared back. "And you know that, how?"

"How do you think?" He tapped the phone tucked in his back pocket. "The internet. If someone wanted to find you, they could."

Unease curled through her. Finn knowing that information wasn't a threat to her, but hearing that real stalkers could find her that easily was more than a little unsettling. She'd thought she'd put in protections both online and off. "Why the hell were you looking?"

He was stoic for a moment, but then his lips kicked up at the corners, some of the old Finn peeking through. "What? You never looked me up?"

Her spine drew straight, and she sputtered for a second. "I... Well, obviously, I wasn't as successful.

What am I supposed to do if you're not on Facebook? My hands were tied."

His smirk went to a full smile, and he chuckled. "Your online detecting skills are top-notch, Arias."

Hearing him call her by her surname sent nostalgic warmth through her. She'd always loved when he referred to her like she was one of the guys on the football team. For some reason, she'd found it unbearably sexy. "Hey, I'm a website designer, not a security specialist. I make things beautiful and functional. Someone else at the company worries about making them safe, all right?"

He lifted his hands in defense. "Duly noted. And to answer your question, I looked you up because I wanted to make sure you were doing okay."

Okay. There was that damn word again. Her mood soured.

"I'm fine." She turned to face him and swept a hand in front of herself like she was Vanna White revealing a new puzzle to solve. "As you can see. Fully functioning human and contributing member of society. Much to everyone's shock, I'm sure."

His gaze slid over her at that, accepting the unintended invitation for a slow head-to-toe appraisal. "Not mine. You were always the one going places. The one with big plans. I loved that about you."

The way he said it wasn't suggestive, but his attention sweeping over her made her skin tingle anyway, a slow-burning awareness that spread across her nerve endings.

She used to murmur all her crazy ideas to him when they got too worked up. They'd kiss until they were mindless, and then he'd slow them down with *Tell me where you'd go next, Livvy.* She'd lean into him and close her eyes, rattle off exotic locations and the photos she imagined taking, weave the fantasies until they were both presentable enough to get back to class or home or wherever they were supposed to be without revealing what they'd been doing. He used to tell her that nothing killed his hard-on quicker than hearing about her leaving.

The memory tightened her throat, and she set down her drink. "What about you? Are you okay?"

He ran a hand over the back of his neck, weariness there. "Depends on your definition of *okay*, I guess."

She cocked her head, the world tilting a bit and revealing that maybe she was a little tipsier than she'd thought. "Meaning?"

He broke eye contact and glanced out at the line of trees on the other side of the creek. He was quiet for a while, pensive, and she found herself focusing on his forearms, on the way the hair dusted over his tanned skin, on the obvious tension in the muscles beneath. He wasn't nearly as relaxed as he was trying to appear.

She wasn't sure he was going to answer, but after a few seconds, he bowed his head. "Meaning I'm back in the town that thinks I'm a hero when I wasn't, talking to some reporter about stuff I wish I could forget, and standing here with the girl I almost got killed—and I still don't know what to say to her."

The words fell like stones between them. Heavy words that would sink in the creek and pull them both under.

She swallowed hard, her *everything's cool* bravado faltering. "Finn…"

"No." He set his drink on the railing and turned fully to her, apparently ready to dive into the murky waters of their past. "I don't know what to say because nothing will undo it. I *know* nothing can fix it. But how about I start here?" He met her gaze, anguish there. "I'm sorry, Liv. I'm so. Fucking. Sorry. There hasn't been a goddamned day that I haven't thought about what I did to you."

She closed her eyes. Breathed.

"I know those are just words, but they're the truth. I was no hero that night. You know it, and I know it. It's time everyone else did, too. And if you give me the go-ahead, I will call Daniel tomorrow and tell him everything. He can put the truth out in the documentary."

Liv's lungs compressed, too many things rolling through her to pinpoint one emotion. She'd imagined this conversation many times before. She'd been so angry and devastated those months following and had thrown all this blame at him in her mind.

No, she hadn't been killed, but she'd blamed her PTSD squarely on Finn. If he hadn't left, she'd never have had that gun pointed at her face. That image wouldn't have haunted her for so many years. That feeling of aloneness, of knowing she was going to die, would've never imprinted on her psyche. But the words that spilled out of her weren't the ones from that script. "You can't tell."

His brows bunched. "What?"

"That's not what I want. You *were* a hero." She reached out and touched the spot in his left shoulder where he'd been shot. "You took a bullet for Rebecca. You earned that title."

He put his hand over hers, flattening her palm against him. His heart pounded beneath her fingers, hard and strong. "And I led Joseph right to you."

"And it is what it is," she said, moving her hand away and looking down. "You think some sort of public declaration or apology is going to make anything better?"

"I—"

"That's not what I want at all." She took a deep breath, trying to rein in her emotions and focus through the fuzz of alcohol. "You know what that would set off in the press? It's going to be bad enough when the documentary comes out and stirs up interest again. If new information comes to light, they'll be all over us again. *How do you* feel, *Ms. Arias? What were you two doing in the closet? What do you think of him choosing to save his date instead of you? Did you two have some sort of sexual relationship?* I can't deal with that." She shook her head, haunted at the thought. "It won't change what happened. *Nothing* changes what happened. It's like a rerun we're forced to live over and over again."

"Liv—"

"I'm serious." She pressed her lips together, searching for the right words. "I'm tired of being Olivia Arias, the Long Acre survivor, the girl in the closet, the goth Latina, or whatever gem they'd choose to call me this time around—which would probably be something horrible like the slutty chick who was making out with someone else's date." Anger flashed through her, remembering all the crap that had made it through the media, all the misinformation. "I'm done. Everyone else gets to decide who we are. They get to name us, label the boxes. The Girl in the Closet. The Jock Hero. The Wounded Valedictorian. It's why no one in my life outside of my family knows who I really am. I got so tired of all the bullshit. I'm not a character in some bad thriller novel or inspirational story."

"Of course not."

"And neither are you. You *were* a hero for Rebecca. You also left me behind that night, which hurt. But you were a seventeen-year-old kid who was scared shitless and reacted. And before that, we were totally different things, but we're stuck with how they branded us. Everything that we were before that night got erased." She snapped her fingers in front of his face. "Gone. Just like that."

"Not everything, Liv," he said softly, lifting his hand like he was going to reach for her but then lowering it to his side again. "They can't take everything."

"You know, I'm not so sure." She pointed toward the door to the restaurant. "Tonight, I had to sit at that table and listen to what my teenage self wanted. That girl you remember? *She* knew who she wanted to be. And all it did was remind me that those sick assholes stole not just my friends' lives but the *could be's* from us. We'll never get to find out who we would've been otherwise. Before we were aftermath."

"Aftermath." He rubbed the spot between his eyes, shadows crossing his face. "That's exactly what it feels like sometimes."

She tipped her head back and sighed, her frustration on a roll now. She always got ranty or reckless when she was drunk. Those margaritas had been a bad idea. But she couldn't staunch the words now that they were flowing. "And I hate that I'm out here with you and have to dredge this stuff up again. Other people have reunions where they drink punch and play retro music, do stupid line dances, and talk about when they were two sizes skinnier." She looked at him. "We have ones where we have to discuss our friends dying, how we let each other down, and our failed dreams.

"And if we did drink punch and play music for some get-together, people would look at us like *How could they?*" She was talking too loud now but didn't care. "If I'd rather just sit down with you and remember the good times, who we were before, there must be something *wrong* with me. We're supposed to move on, but not too much. Be happy but not *too* happy. I'm tired, Finn. I'm so sick of it being like this. I thought I was past it, but then I come here and…I don't know. It's like it's all just sitting there, waiting to remind me how we can never really escape it. How the ones who got away never really get away. Those sick bastards *changed* us—have their fingerprints all over our lives—and it pisses me the hell off. I don't… I can't… I don't know."

All her words fell into a jumble and her fist balled, ready to punch something that wasn't there. But she didn't have anything left.

"Livvy."

The softly uttered endearment undid her. Popped the pin in her balloon of righteous indignation and deflated her. She was trembling and drunk, mad and…lost. Like she thought she'd been following the right map on her way to a place where she wanted to be, only to find out that she didn't just have the wrong map, she was traipsing around the wrong goddamned continent. And now she had no idea where the hell she was or where she was supposed to go.

She closed her eyes, willing herself not to break down. She didn't want to cry. She didn't *feel* like crying. She didn't know what she felt like. There were too many options to pick from, and that made it hard to breathe.

But then big, warm hands landed on her shoulders, a gentle hold, a simple *I've got you*, and she couldn't fight against it. Her muscles surrendered to the touch and her body moved on instinct, her brain shutting off. She stepped into his space, didn't ask permission, and wrapped her arms around his waist.

He stiffened in her hold, his entire body going as rigid as the boards under her feet. But when she didn't back off, he released a breath and wrapped his arms around her, pulling her fully into an embrace. She pressed her cheek against his shoulder and breathed in the earthy scent of him, the familiarity of the minty shampoo he'd always used. Her guards fell away for a minute as he simply held her.

"I'm tired and pissed off, too," he said quietly. "And I'm sorry. I didn't mean to upset you. I won't say anything to the filmmaker. Just know that if there's anything I could ever do to make things up to you, anything you need, you just have to tell me."

She squeezed him a little tighter, not wanting to get dragged back into the memories, the apologies, the regrets. "You can stop talking about that night. That's what you can do. At least for now," she said against his shoulder. "I didn't come out here for that. I wanted to come out here and prove that the killers don't get a say in this. We haven't talked because of them. They're winning. I don't want them to win. So maybe we can just pretend for a little while that we're old friends from high school reminiscing about the good times."

"The good times," he said, his breath ruffling her hair. "Yes."

He set his chin on her head. "Like when all I was worried about was if our landscaper's daughter was going to be outside helping him that day."

Liv smiled, the words digging beneath the layers of all those bad memories, unearthing some of those simple, sweet ones. Ones she hadn't let herself think about in a very long time. She leaned back to look up at him. "Yes. Like that. Like how you were such a perv, watching me from your window. You weren't even sneaky about it. Just standing there and staring."

Some of the tension left his expression, and a droll look replaced it. "You wore a tank top, short shorts, and combat boots. I was sixteen and not that noble."

"It was a hot day."

"Oh, it was hot, all right," he teased. "And don't pretend you didn't know exactly what you were doing to me."

She stepped back from his hold with an innocent *Who, me?* smile.

Liv had only tutored Finn once before the day she'd helped her dad put in an herb garden at Finn's house, but she'd already developed a mad crush. He'd been nothing like she'd expected from all those years of catching glimpses of him from a different social circle. He'd been funny and friendly. Much smarter than people gave him credit for. And way, way too good-looking.

"My dad couldn't for the life of him figure out why I was volunteering to help out. I hated yard work. But free labor was free labor, so he didn't question me. If he'd realized I was trying to shamelessly flirt with the son of his customers, he wouldn't have been so accommodating."

Finn chuckled. "Best surprise ever when you showed

up. And confession: the dog didn't dig up half the garden a few days later when my dad had to call y'all back out."

She narrowed her eyes. "So that's why the next time I helped him, you brought out lemonade and cookies. You knew I was coming and were trying to butter me up. I thought it was very Martha Stewart of you."

He smirked. "Until you broke out in hives because I didn't know there was peanut butter in the cookies."

"God, I still remember your face when you realized what had happened. You were so horrified. It was kind of adorable." She leaned against the railing behind her, happy to be talking about something else, something good. "And the hives were no fun, but at least Dad let me go into the house to let the meds kick in and take a break from the heat. We watched some random movie that sucked."

"And then I made an ass of myself and tried to kiss you."

"Yeah, with my swollen lips and tingling tongue. Very suave."

His mouth curved, revealing the dimple hiding beneath the scruff.

Damn. Still unfairly good-looking.

"I remember you saying something like, *Now? You're going to try to kiss me* now? Like I had broken every rule in the *How to Impress a Girl* handbook. Any game I thought I had was effectively squashed."

"Well, your ego could withstand a few dings," she said, poking him in the chest. "Luckily, you were very pretty and I forgave you. Multiple times. In the library. In the back of your SUV. Wherever we could find."

He ran a hand over his hair, chagrined and boyish. Memories assailed her. Eager lips and whispered words.

All that building need. They'd never gone all the way
because she'd still been a virgin. But Lord, she'd wanted
him to be her first. She'd told him that on prom night in
the closet before everything had happened. If he had asked
her to be his date, she would've given him everything.

But just kissing him, being touched by those capable
hands, still held a spot as some of the hottest encounters
of her life. "Our make-out game was strong."

"Olympic level," he said, dimple ablaze again.

She wet her lips and had to remind herself that they
were just joking around, reminiscing, trying to forget
the bad stuff for a few minutes. This was not flirting.
Because that would be inappropriate. And ill-advised.
And fucked up.

"My tutoring game, not so much," she added.

"Hey, I passed, right?" he teased, wistfulness filling
his gaze. "God, it's so easy to let that stuff slip away, to
remember that there were good things." He reached out
and pushed a stray lock of hair behind her ear, letting his
fingers linger. "*Great* things."

Her mouth went dry, and electric awareness traveled
down her neck from the spot where he'd touched her,
lighting up nerves along the way. She bit her lip, searching for something innocuous to say, but no words would
come. All she could see was Finn. Not the one who'd
left her. Not the stranger he was now. The one who used
to make her feel good. *Her* Finn.

She couldn't turn away. She recognized that look, the
sharp edge of yearning in it. She had a feeling she was
giving the same one back.

She needed to stop, step away. Save them both. But
instead, her hands reached out and flattened against his

chest. She stepped closer, too close for friendly. She did all of it without saying a word, and then she pushed up on her toes and pressed her mouth to his.

—∽∾∼—

Finn's muscles locked the moment Liv's hands slid up his chest. He'd seen her shift forward but hadn't expected her to actually touch him again. He'd still been reeling from the earlier hug. But the feel of her hands splayed over him, moving up along his body, was far more erotic than the embrace had been, and his body was so starved for touch that it took everything he had not to groan.

But this was Liv. And she'd been upset. And drinking. He needed to warn her away. Stop this before anything happened. That was the right thing to do. This was not what he'd come out here for.

But then she kissed him.

Salty sweet lips and soft curves melted against him, blowing his noble plan to bits. Every cell in his body caught fire at the contact. It'd been so long—So. Damn. Long.—since he'd had a woman pressed against him. But more than that. This was Liv. Sexy, grown-up Olivia Arias. Subject of his teenage fantasies. His thoughts scattered like shrapnel, making it impossible to piece any together. He was supposed to be doing something. Stopping this. But he didn't say a goddamned word. He couldn't. Instead, he did the absolute worst thing.

He kissed her back.

His hands went to her face, and a needy groan escaped. The taste of her was like adrenaline to his blood—the tartness of her drink and Liv's own unique

flavor mixing together. She had started softly, tenta-
tively, a *Hey, how about we try this for a second?* But
soon he couldn't help himself. When she parted her lips,
he took the invitation and deepened the kiss, the starved
man taking over. He hadn't been with a woman in over
two years, but this was more than that. He hadn't kissed
this woman in what felt like a lifetime.

Liv gasped into his mouth but didn't pull away.
Instead, she took his cue and shifted closer, torturing
him with the feel of her curves and the heat of her against
him. His hand slid to the back of her neck, gripping that
soft place and holding her where he wanted her. But as
the kiss went on, he craved more, every male cell in his
body making demands. He wanted to tip her head back
and work his way down her neck, take that salty skin
between his teeth, fill his hands with her lush curves and
follow with his tongue until she moaned for him. Until
she begged and fell apart in his arms.

Maybe she wanted that, too, because this was not a
fumbling teenage kiss in the library stacks. This was
the kiss of a woman with experience, one who knew
what kisses like this led to, one who lit matches because
she wanted the fire. So when she fully aligned her body
against his, all that soft heat grinding against the increas-
ingly un-soft part of him, he was ready to set her whole
world ablaze.

His brain switched off completely. Gone were logical
thoughts, rational explanations, or wise decisions. He
just wanted the oblivion right now. He wanted Liv.

She gasped between kisses, grabbing a breath, her
eyes dazed. "*Finn.*"

His name was a plea, a prayer, a goddamned benediction.

He wanted to answer it.

"I've got you." He took her mouth again and backed her up against the porch column, the wood creaking in protest. Screw good decisions. Screw it all. He'd figure that shit out later. This felt too good to stop.

Her hands slipped beneath his T-shirt, her touch like a firebrand on his skin, and another groan escaped them both. He grabbed her thigh and dragged her leg up, pressing himself against her, liking the noise she made at the contact. Loving the way her nails dug into skin. *Yes. This.*

Tonight they'd finally—

"Whoa, uh, *oops*."

Finn froze at the voice, and Liv turned to stone in his hold, her eyes going wide as she looked over his shoulder at their visitor.

"Tell me it's staff," he said against her ear. "Tell me they're turning around and leaving us be."

"It's Kincaid," she whispered. "And she's not going anywhere."

Shit.

Finn grimaced and instantly released Liv, giving her space to straighten her clothes, but he didn't turn around to greet the unwelcome guest. He adjusted the front of his jeans instead and gave Liv a pointed look.

Blessedly, she got the message and stepped around him, giving him cover while he let the ice water of being caught cool his arousal.

"Um, hey," Liv said, her voice a little wobbly.

"Hey, yourself," Kincaid replied. "Everything all right?"

"Just fine," Liv said quickly. Too quickly.

After one more breath to calm himself, Finn rolled

his shoulders and turned to face the firing squad. Two of his old classmates stood there in the glow of the open door, Kincaid Breslin and Rebecca Lindt. Rebecca was owl-eyed, her gaze jumping back and forth between Liv and Finn. But Kincaid looked nonplussed.

"Sorry," she said brightly. "Didn't mean to interrupt, uh, things. We just got worried about you when we saw you didn't come back in. Wanted to make sure you hadn't fallen into the creek. Apparently, you fell into something else." Kincaid strolled forward, pinning her interrogating gaze on Finn. "And you are?"

Finn had forced himself back to stoic mode, but before he could respond, Rebecca stepped forward, her limp barely detectable. "*Finn?*"

Kincaid's brows went up. "Finn Dorsey?"

He nodded and glanced at Rebecca. "Hi, Bec."

He didn't have much to say beyond that. His body was still too revved to focus on much else besides Liv. A chat with a classmate and a childhood friend was not on the agenda. Now. Or ever, really.

"Um, can we have a minute, please?" Liv said finally.

Rebecca was still staring at him like she was trying to figure out an equation. But Kincaid smiled a smile that could cut right through a person, her Southern belle accent like a sugarcoated knife. "Sure. A minute. And Finn, it's great to see you, but our dear Liv here has had a lot to drink tonight, so I'm sure you'll understand that after I give you a few minutes to say good night, I'll be walking her to her room."

Finn stared at Kincaid for a moment and then nodded, keeping his expression smooth and feeling like a world-class dick. "Of course."

"Great." Kincaid patted him on the shoulder. "And don't be a stranger. We're all having breakfast at nine tomorrow. You should join us."

Hell no to that. But she didn't wait for his answer. He wasn't her concern. Liv was. Kincaid strode away from him, giving Liv a speaking look as she passed her. Rebecca remained silent as Kincaid grabbed her elbow and led her back into the restaurant.

Liv sagged back against the railing and made a face. "Well, *that* was awkward."

Finn laced his hands behind his neck and blew out a breath, trying to slow his heartbeat and the unrepentant lust that was still coursing through him. He'd almost hauled Olivia up to his room. Taken her to bed like she was some random woman he'd picked up at a bar.

When she was drunk and vulnerable on top of it. What the fuck was wrong with him? "I'm sorry. I don't know what… I shouldn't have done that."

She crossed her arms, looking grim. "What are you apologizing for? You didn't do anything. *I* kissed *you*."

"And I let it go too far. You're drunk. And you're…" He almost said *Liv*. "You were upset."

She pinched the bridge of her nose and gave a humorless laugh. "It's nice of you to take the chivalrous route, but don't fall on a sword about it. This was…"

"This was what?" he asked when her words trailed off.

"What I do," she said flatly. "Or what I used to do at least. Alcohol makes me…" She looked up and then shook her head. "Let's just say I have a two-drink limit for a reason."

Part of him was dying to know what word she would've filled in there. *Reckless. Stupid. Horny.*

The last one made him feel like an even bigger jerk for thinking it. He tucked his hands in his back pockets, trying not to let his thoughts show on his face. "It's been a long day and a lot of memories. I think we both just got carried away. We can't do that."

"Kiss?"

"No. Pretend we're the people we used to be. Those people don't exist anymore. They're ghosts."

She winced.

There was no denying the heat that had arced between them. He'd bet everything he owned that having her in his bed would be nothing short of spectacular. But it would be a lie. Drinking or not, she was seeing the guy he used to be. And he was seeing the girl he used to know. This was a grab at the past. Nothing more. Neither of them could afford to forget that.

She gave him a little smile. "Maybe we went traditional high school reunion after all. Getting drunk and having ill-advised hookups with classmates you never got to bed back then."

Just hearing the word *bed* from her was almost too much for him. "It's good that we were interrupted."

"Yeah." She smirked and pushed away from the railing. "Saved you from my drunken mauling."

Finn sniffed. "Saved you from mine."

She reached back and tightened the ponytail he'd loosened with his roaming hands. He wet his lips. How he'd love to drag his fingers through that glossy hair, wrap his fist in it when he…

"Do I need to be saved from you, Finn?"

The question yanked him back to the moment. He

gave a curt nod. "Yes. You don't want this. You don't even know me."

"Don't I?"

Grim reality filled him. He reached out and took her hand. "No, you don't. When you woke up in the morning and your head cleared, you'd be disappointed by what you found."

She stepped closer and tipped up her chin, their hands linked by just the fingertips. "And what would I find?"

Nothing she was looking for and nothing that she deserved. He could guarantee that.

"That making you feel good for a few hours was all I had to offer."

Her expression flattened.

He leaned over and kissed the top of her head. "I'm sorry I stepped over the line tonight. Go get some rest, Liv."

With a sigh, she stepped away from him, letting their hands stretch out until the hold broke. When she was a safe distance from him, she put her hand to her hip and cocked a brow. "A few hours, huh? Is that your ego talking, Dorsey, or a promise?"

The little jab made him smile. He leaned back against the rail so he wouldn't reach for her again and shrugged. "Rough estimate depending on your level of endurance."

Her grin was broad, full of sass, before she turned and strolled away, calling back over her shoulder. "Hell, that might've been worth the regret."

His fingers curled against his thigh, the need to haul her up against the nearest wall a real thing. "Go to bed, Arias."

"I'm already gone."

The door shut behind her, and he rested his head against the porch column. "And so am I."

He'd come back to do his part and help the charity by giving an interview, but that was over now. There was no reason left for him to hang around. He'd already been taking a risk by being there. He'd taken a bigger risk by kissing Liv.

First thing in the morning, he was getting the hell out of there.

chapter
FOUR

KINCAID WAS THE ONLY ONE LEFT WHEN LIV WALKED BACK into the restaurant. She was spinning the overturned mason jar round and round on the table, chin in hand, obviously lost in thought. Liv reached out and tapped her. "Hey."

Kincaid startled and then turned, looking disoriented for a second before a smile touched her mouth. "Oh, hey there, Hot Lips."

Liv groaned. "Guess we're not going to pretend that you didn't see anything?"

"Nope." Kincaid got up from the table, letting the spinning jar slow to a halt. "I have a photographic memory." She tapped her temple. "There's no erasing that."

Liv crossed her arms. "Fantastic. And everyone else?"

"Taryn went home, so she doesn't know what happened. Rebecca went to bed."

Liv shifted in her shoes and glanced toward the door that led to the hotel lobby. "Is Rebecca all right? She looked kind of freaked out. I mean, she mentioned Finn in her letter…"

Kincaid's smile dipped. "She's okay. Confused, I think. She told me she didn't think you two knew each other. At least not like that."

"We don't."

Kincaid gave her a look. "Sure you don't."

"I—"

Kincaid held up a hand, bangle bracelets clinking. "Hey, you don't need to explain anything to me. But, honey, I know the difference between a let's-get-to-know-each-other kiss and a reunion. Either way, it's not my business. My only business is following the girlfriend rules."

"The girlfriend rules?"

"Yes. Friends don't let friends bang drunk," she said sagely.

Liv snorted, mainly because debutante Kincaid had said *bang*. "Sounds wise."

"It is. It's bad for regrets and all that crap. But also, if you're going to bed a guy that hot, believe me, you'll want to be sober enough to remember it. Because *damn*. That boy grew up nice."

Kincaid gave her a *you know what I'm saying* look, and Liv laughed. "I think I'm not the only one who's a little drunk."

"You're telling me." Kincaid put her arm around Liv and used her for balance as she took off her heels. "Which is exactly why we're going to walk up to our rooms together. I'll keep you safe from Mr. Dark and Broody, and you keep me away from that adorable bartender who keeps calling me *ma'am* and making it sound dirty."

Liv glanced over her shoulder at the college-aged guy behind the counter, and he gave them a wink. She choked down her laugh. "Come on. I think that one's out past curfew. We both need to get some sleep."

They walked toward the lobby as Kincaid declared, "Yes. Sleep. Great idea."

"I'm full of great ideas tonight," Liv muttered.

"Oh, don't be like that." Kincaid gave Liv's shoulder a bump. "Your idea wasn't terrible. I mean, even though we're both ending our night like this—*drunk and alone*," she said with a dramatic flourish, "gold star for being the first to take the plunge. I didn't expect it from you."

"The plunge?"

Kincaid glanced over at her as they made their way through the small lobby. "We read those letters, and you went immediately into action. *Bam*." She opened her fist like a firework exploding. "No hesitation."

"No I didn't. I went outside and drunkenly made out with a guy." Liv pressed the button for the elevator, and the doors slid opened. "It's an old bad habit of mine. Not a plan of action."

Kincaid gave her a sly look as she stepped inside and turned to Liv. "That's not what I saw. You said you wanted to date passionate guys. I think that was a helluva good start. That's why I invited him to breakfast. You should try it sober with him."

Liv cringed. A good start? With Finn? *Yeah, right*. She got in the elevator and hit the button for the third floor. "I appreciate the gesture. But there are no starts with Finn. What you saw—that was just wrapping up unfinished business. The period on the end of a run-on sentence."

Kincaid was quiet until the elevator dinged and the

doors whirred open. She stepped out, her shoes dangling from her fingertips and a knowing smirk on her face. "Hmm, I don't know, sweetie. That didn't look like a period to me. That looked like a big ol' dot-dot-dot."

"A what?"

But Kincaid was already strolling down the hallway and wiggling her fingers in a backward goodbye. "'Night, Peaches."

Liv stared after her. A dot-dot-dot. A *to be continued*.

"An ellipsis," Liv said finally, but Kincaid's door was already closing. "It's called an ellipsis."

But it didn't matter what the hell it was called because Kincaid was wrong. Finn wasn't going to come to breakfast. There was no start. Tomorrow, Liv would go back home to her job and apartment in Austin. He'd go wherever he lived now. And this would just be another memory filed away. Closure.

Tonight had been her falling into her old, dangerous ways. Feel sad, stressed, anxious? Find a lot of alcohol and a cute guy to forget with. But Finn wasn't just any cute guy, and sleeping with him would risk a lot more than an awkward goodbye in the morning. They weren't strangers. They were worse than that. They had guilt between them, and regrets. Ugly stuff. You could hook up with a stranger and walk away with a dose of shame but not much further thought. Something like this could inflict wounds. She didn't need any more of those.

She grabbed her key card out of her pocket and headed to her room, trying to push away the knowledge that one of these doors she was passing was Finn's, that soon he'd be inside, undressing for the night, sliding beneath the covers. Pent-up. Alone.

Stop.

She let herself into her room and shut the door behind her, trying to block out the rogue thoughts. Even if things with Finn weren't so complicated, she was in no place to be with anyone tonight. Alcohol and stress were stirring up all these crazy urges. Her brain was seeking oblivion, no matter the type. She'd been down that road before. *No más.*

She flicked on the light and winced. A tequila headache was pulsing at her temples, and at the sight of the bed, what little energy she had left drained out of her. She dragged herself to the bathroom, stripping out of her clothes along the way, and put on a comfy T-shirt before brushing her teeth. One more night, and she'd be back to her normal life.

The thought didn't soothe her as much as it should. Goddamned time capsule. A few days ago, she would've told anyone who asked that she was content. She lived in a great city. Had a decent apartment. A job that supported her. Even though she worked a lot of hours, she was good at what she did and made more money than she ever would've from photography. She had a few friends and a couple of guys she saw casually when she had the interest or time. If she got lonely for family, her dad and older brothers weren't too far away.

From the outside looking in, everything was in place. Nice and neat and stable. Her former therapist would've been proud. Her mother would've called her a success. But after tonight and hearing all the declarations in the letters, her life suddenly seemed enormously mundane.

Teen Liv would be disappointed in her. All those big dreams she'd whispered to Finn had been neatly filed away and dismissed, the stories ending before they began. No photos. No travel. No passionate affairs. She'd survived when so many others at Long Acre hadn't gotten that luxury, and this was what she was doing with her life. Doing a job she sort of liked, living in an apartment she'd never decorated, and just…marking time.

The thoughts were like a growing itch, a restlessness moving through her. She couldn't get the notion out of her head that *they* were winning. Those pathetic cowards who'd taken so many lives were succeeding at messing with her life—still. She sighed and stared at herself in the reflection above the sink. The circles under her eyes told her she was tired, but the fine lines at the corners told her more. Time was passing. Not in minutes. But years. Twelve years since she'd walked away from the school. And what did she have to show for it? She'd moved away from things. She was a pro at that. But what was she moving *toward*?

She was still living like a college student—just with less booze and fewer one-night stands. Living in a state of perpetual waiting. But waiting for what?

Her mother had died at forty-three. What if Liv only had thirteen years left? Would she look back and be happy with what she'd done in life? Proud? Satisfied?

The thought made her stomach churn.

She grabbed her phone from where she'd left it on the bathroom counter, ignoring the crushing number of unread work emails, and lifted it, putting it in camera mode. She stared back at her image, making sure to catch the light just right, the shadows slanting across her face, wanting to capture herself exactly as she was in the moment, and clicked.

She lowered the phone, and the picture filled the screen. It was the same woman she saw in the mirror, but the camera always captured that other thing. The thing mirrors or the naked eye never seemed to catch. Cameras could tell a thousand lies, or they could tell the bald-faced truth. It was what she loved about them most. And staring back at her was the truth.

She was lost.

She didn't know who she was anymore. Liv Arias— that terrified, passionate girl from Long Acre. Or Olivia Moreno—the put-together web designer who, as far as anyone in Austin knew, had a typical past where nothing of note had happened.

The latter was the role she'd played for almost eight years now. The person both her parents would be proud of.

The former was the person who'd gotten drunk and kissed Finn Dorsey. The former was the one who'd run out with a panic attack today. The former could lead her back down the road to a ten-car pileup of problems.

Maybe Olivia Moreno was boring. But at least she was stable.

If her mother were still around, she'd tell her to be Olivia 2.0. Before her mom had gotten sick, they'd clashed regularly over Liv's rebellious nature. Why did she have to fight everything? Why couldn't she be more like her two older brothers who were practical to the core? Why did she have to make everything so hard on herself and everyone around her?

Both her parents had grown up with less than nothing, and they'd seen her attitude as a consequence of being spoiled. Not that they'd been well off. Far from it. But they could pay the rent on their house and had a car and food on the table, which was more than either of her parents had growing up. So Liv wanting to do impractical things like taking off a year before college to travel or becoming a photographer had seemed ludicrous to them.

Her mom had told her in those last quiet weeks that all she wished for Olivia was to find contentment in the simple things. *A good job, a safe place to live, and the love of a good man. That's all you need. That's my wish for you. Please don't break your papá's heart. I'll break it enough when I leave.*

Liv sat on the edge of the bed with a sigh and rubbed her hands over her face. Instead of listening, she'd gone off the deep end after her mother passed. She *had* broken her dad's heart. She could still remember his face when she'd had to call him from county lockup to bail her out after she'd gotten picked up from a party and caught with pills. He'd paid the money—money he probably hadn't had to spare—and then had looked at her with her smeared makeup, purple hair, and party clothes and told her with sad eyes, "You're not the daughter your mamá raised."

He'd left her there without a ride, and they'd stopped speaking for almost a year. If nothing else, it'd been a wake-up call. She'd agreed to get back into therapy as part of her probation, and that had helped her get her shit together. The next Christmas, she'd gone home and mended fences with her dad. Now he smiled when she came to visit. Now he looked proud when she told him how well she was doing at work.

She imagined what he'd say if she told him what she'd been feeling tonight, the things that were tempting her. Her dad would be terrified of her trying to recapture that girl she once was.

She should be terrified.

She groaned and rolled her shoulders, trying to chase the tension out of them. She needed to get out of this place. It was seeping into her skin and making her think crazy thoughts. The tequila wasn't helping either.

She couldn't trust herself right now.

She needed to sleep and sober up. She'd deal with the rest in the morning.

She climbed into bed, turned off the light, and gave into exhaustion, hoping for the oblivion of dreamless sleep.

Finn flipped the folded rectangle of paper in his hand, the loose-leaf brittle beneath his fingertips, as if it'd been dipped in water and dried in the sun. He'd found it on the deck on his way back into the restaurant and had brought it up to his room. Liv's name was in scrawly letters on the outside.

He shouldn't open it. He knew that much. He could guess what it was. But he found himself unfolding the page carefully in the lamplight of his room anyway, the investigator in him too curious to resist. The words on the page were faded but still easy enough to read.

On this day, August first, I, Olivia Arias, promise to the Class of 2005...

He scanned the page, hearing Liv's voice in his head as he read each word, taking them in.

I will turn art into my job. I won't play it safe. I won't be practical. I'll live a passionate life and date passionate guys and see the world so I can take pictures of it. I promise, Class of 2005, to live the life that scares me.

He let out a long breath, his brain snagging on the word *passionate*. That had always been the word he'd associated with Liv back in high school. Unlike him, who'd been going through life without much thought beyond the next day, Liv had dialed into things deeply. Her photography. Her views on life. The music she chose. Her future plans. They all had layers of meaning for her. She'd had big thoughts and big dreams. When he'd told her what bands he liked, she'd wanted to know *why* he liked them. What did their songs make him feel? He'd never thought about it before her.

Being around someone like that had been heady, had made him start thinking about things in a different way. He'd wanted to find that passionate part of himself, too. He'd wanted to be like she was—brave and bold and paving her own way—instead of following the prescribed path his parents had laid out for him. And he'd never had any doubt that Liv would do exactly what she set out to do.

But Liv had said tonight that they'd read the letters and that she hadn't lived up to her plans. Knowing that these things hadn't happened for her, that the night in the closet had stolen those dreams from her, made his chest ache.

He couldn't help but wonder if things would've

turned out differently if he'd stayed with her that night. If she'd never had to face down Joseph's gun. If they'd had each other to lean on afterward.

Would they have saved each other?

His cell phone buzzed on the bedside table, breaking him from his morose thoughts. He set the letter aside to grab the call. "Hello."

"It's Billings. You in a place you can talk?"

Finn tipped his head back against the headboard, not up for a call with his boss but knowing he didn't have a choice. When Billings wanted to talk to you, you talked to him. "I'm good."

Even though he'd known it was overkill, he'd swept the room for bugs when he'd arrived out of habit and had booked the room under a different name.

"Where are you? Wallace said after your psych eval, you didn't show up to get the key for the apartment we set up for you in Richmond."

Finn sighed. "I made my own arrangements for my break. I don't want to be in Virginia. Plus, I need to take care of some personal things. I have a place to lie low."

"You mean you don't want to be where all the resources to help you transition back are."

Finn didn't respond. His boss already knew the answer. They'd set up a "support network" for Finn after he'd taken what they considered too big a risk on the last job. He'd taken out the second-in-command in Dragonfly, which had been a victory, but he'd done it without approval and in a way that had nearly gotten him killed. Now they were worried the assignment had messed too badly with his head. Finn wanted to tell the powers that be that it had little to do with that and much more to do with the fact that he believed certain things were worth risking to rid the earth of scum like that. Dragonfly hadn't been the organization that sold Joseph Miller the guns for the Long Acre shooting—something Finn had believed when he'd sought out the assignment—but it could've been. They would've—and had—put weapons in kids' hands without blinking an eye. Finn had made sure that wouldn't happen again.

But now he was paying the price. And the thought of weekly appointments with the shrink, and everyone he worked with eyeballing him to make sure he wasn't screwed up after being undercover so long, made him want to punch things.

Billings grunted. "This line's secure. Where are you?"

Finn squeezed his temples. "Near my hometown. I've rented a lake house from an old friend. No one from Dragonfly ever made the connection to my identity, and they all think I'm dead anyway, so I'm good here. All I plan to do is rest, fish, and work on some projects. That's what I need to recuperate, not a bunch of therapy appointments. I need to be in my own space for a while."

Billings was quiet for a long moment. "I get that. And I'm not going to stop you. You've earned your break. But you've been under for two years. The transition from that can be a hell of a jolt. I want you checking in with Doc Robson at least weekly by phone. That's not a request."

Finn closed his eyes. "Got it. But I'm all right. I know the difference between me and Axel. I'm not going to do anything crazy. I just need some breathing room. I'll be ready for my next assignment by the end of summer."

Billings sniffed. "We'll see. I know you're champing

at the bit to go back out, but don't get cocky. Pretending to be a criminal for that long leaves a mark. It can alter you in ways you don't realize until you're knee deep in shit. Believe me. I've been there. So if you're home, spend some time with your family, your friends, people who know you and can remind you of who you really are."

"Right."

"I'm serious, Dorsey. You're one of my best agents, and I know these missions are personal for you, but I can see that this last one took a toll on you. I don't need you pulling some hermit bullshit and getting unhinged when all the crap you've seen and done in the last few years starts sinking in. I've lost agents who've taken the aftereffects too lightly. Don't be one."

"I understand, sir."

Billings let out an annoyed sigh. "Sure you do. I'll be checking in with you and the doc. And I want proof."

"Proof?"

"If you want back on the job, you need to send me a weekly update. Pretend I'm your great-aunt Mildred who's just dying to see what you're up to. I want notes and pictures of you doing the things you say you're doing."

Finn tapped the back of his head against the headboard. "You've got to be kidding."

"I don't kid, son. If I think you're not taking care of yourself, I'll send someone down there to get you. Or worse, I'll send Murray down there to babysit you."

Oh, hell no. Jason Murray had been in training with him, and he was the chattiest son of a bitch Finn had ever met. Good guy, but Finn might flee the country if he had to share his vacation with the dude. "Got it. Pictures. Active, social Finn."

"You better convince me, Dorsey."

Finn rubbed his brow where a headache was brewing. "Yes, sir. And keep me up to date on the case. I'm on leave, but I need to see this thing through."

"Of course. I'll keep you in the loop."

Finn ended the call with his boss and scrubbed a hand over his face. Part of him wished he was back in Virginia, working, going through the mountain of evidence he'd collected with the team. The operation had been his baby. He wanted to see those bastards who ran Dragonfly rot in jail. He wanted to look them in the face, knowing all the horrific crimes they'd committed, and tell them, "Gotcha, assholes."

But he'd known what would be awaiting him back there. He'd already gone through all the therapy and shit after high school. He couldn't face another round.

He could bury the ghost of Axel here. Be Finn again. Even though that persona felt like a ghost these days as well. Only when he'd kissed Liv had he felt a thread of that guy he used to be.

Liv.

His fingers flexed as his thoughts shifted from work back to what had happened on the deck. The way Liv had melted into him. The sounds she'd made. Had they not been interrupted, he could have her here in his room right now, drawing those needy noises out of her, tasting her skin…

No.

He needed to stop thinking about the woman. His mind and his quickly stiffening dick couldn't take it. He and Liv had made the right decision. The smart one. With a grunt, he pushed himself off the bed, tossed his phone onto the nightstand, and stripped down to his boxers, ignoring the half-hard state of his cock. He'd become a pro at taking care of things on his own, but he knew his hand wouldn't satisfy him tonight. It would just torture him more, remind him of what he didn't have.

So instead, he focused on doing his nightly routine. One he couldn't seem to shake even on break. He tucked his gun into his boot next to the bed, within easy reach, and then he double-checked the locks on the doors and windows, making note of all the escape routes.

Once that was all done, he finally let himself settle into bed, Liv still on his mind.

In the morning, he'd leave a note under her door with his number in case she ever needed anything. Then he'd head to the lake house before anyone else got up. Billings wanted him to socialize and re-acclimate, but he'd just have to figure out a way to send the right pictures to get by. Because what was the point? In a few months, he'd be back on assignment. A ghost again.

He didn't know how to be anything else anymore.

chapter
FIVE

THUMP.

Liv rolled over in bed and blinked in the darkness, the unfamiliar room jarring her for a moment. She rubbed her eyes, trying to clear the cotton from her head.

Thump. Thump. Thump.

The soft knocking that had disturbed her sleep came again. *What the hell?* She sat up and flicked on the lamp, squinting in the sudden light. The knock sounded again but became more insistent.

"Liv?"

The voice was muffled. One of her friends? Hard to tell. But the knocking didn't stop.

"Okay, okay, hold on." She climbed out of bed and made her way across the room, her feet moving as though she were walking through marshland, each step slow and cumbersome. She peeked through the peephole, but didn't see who she'd expected. She frowned and opened the door. "Finn?"

He stood in the hallway, looking just how she'd left

him on the porch—black T-shirt, worn jeans, and thick-soled boots. But his hair was mussed and the look on his face intent. "I couldn't sleep."

"Okay," she said carefully.

"I couldn't stop thinking about you."

"Oh." The words sent a wash of warmth through her. "That's…interesting."

He braced a hand against the doorjamb, leaning in, his voice low and dangerous. "I shouldn't be here. You should tell me to go back to my room. Right now. Tell me, Liv."

"Hmm." She wet her lips, her heartbeat picking up speed. "You're right. I definitely should."

But instead, she stepped back and let the door open wider. His gaze slid down, slowly, slowly, taking in the Long Acre Crusaders T-shirt that barely reached her thighs and her bare legs beneath. He stepped inside. "You should put some clothes on, too. Some pants and maybe a parka."

"Yes. Good thinking." She bumped the door shut behind him and moved closer, putting her hands on his chest. "Wouldn't want to give you the wrong idea."

He hissed out a breath at the contact and let his hands slide over her waist, making her T-shirt gather up higher, revealing her cotton panties beneath. She got the sense that she should be more worried about that or question how quickly things were moving, but she couldn't grab on to either feeling. And when he leaned in and kissed her, she didn't want to.

She moaned into the kiss, her fingers curling into his shirt and her body going from simmer to boil. One of his hands slid into her hair and he gripped her, tilting her head back and taking the kiss deeper. Breath and lips and tongues mingled, hungry, desperate. He murmured her name in between, and she responded in kind with a panted *please*. That was all she could manage, but he must've gotten the message. They moved across the room in an awkward tangle of kissing and touching until the backs of her legs hit the edge of the bed.

They tumbled onto it, his big body pressing into hers as he continued to worship her mouth and then moved down to her neck. She tipped her head back and arched against him. "Liv," he said, scraping his teeth along her shoulder. "Tell me you want this."

It'd been so long. Not just since she'd been with a guy. But since she'd felt like this. This pulsing, all-encompassing need for a man's touch. For *Finn's* touch. "I want you."

With that, he shifted and tugged his shirt over his head, revealing finely honed muscles and a dark dusting of hair. No sign of the scar she'd expected from the gunshot. She let her fingers trail over the spot. "There's no—"

"Shh." He cut her off with a quick kiss. "Now you." He reached for her and pulled off her T-shirt, leaving her in only her panties. He gazed down at her with hungry eyes and brushed the back of his hand over her breast, sending hot shivers along her skin and bringing her nipple to a tight peak. "You're so goddamned sexy, Livvy. I just want to touch and taste you everywhere. Lick every inch."

Her heartbeat pounded, her body aching to grant him that wish. "Yes. That. Let's do that."

His hand traced down slowly over her ribs, across

her belly, marking a trail of intention and driving her out of her mind with anticipation. His fingers played at the edge of her panties, and she fought not to arch into his touch.

"I can see how much you want me," he said against her ear. "We've waited so long." He tugged at the waistband and let his hand slide beneath, touching her where she needed it most.

She moaned when his callused fingers found her slick and wanting, her whole body going aflame. Her eyelids fell shut. *Yes.*

He nipped at the lobe of her ear, his fingers stroking her deep and slow, and whispered. "But we're going to have to be fast, or we'll miss that test in chemistry."

"The—" Her eyes popped open, her thoughts scrambling. "What?"

But now instead of seeing grown-up Finn, the fresh-faced high school version was looking down at her, all eager and urgent. His skilled, sensual touch from before turned fumbling and less sure. She froze, trying to figure out what was happening, but then the banging on the door started again, this time loud and threatening.

Teen Finn yanked his hand back and turned his head. "Dude, what the hell? Give us a second."

Liv tried to back away, the panic rising. "No."

"Livvy, it's okay—"

The scent of pine cleaner burned her nostrils. "*No!*"

The door to the hotel room swung open, and Joseph Miller stepped in with a satisfied smile. Seventeen. Angry-eyed. Deadly. "Well, look what I found. My favorite jock and another desperate girl trying to get his attention. Hope you had fun because time's up, asshole."

Joseph lifted the gun, the barrel looming huge in Liv's vision.

A scream ripped through her, trying to warn Finn, trying to do something. But her voice wouldn't come out. Her hands wouldn't move.

A click. A smile. An explosion of sound.

Then the blood.

Finn collapsed on top of her, his entire body going limp, eyes vacant.

The scream escaped now. Over and over, racking her body with its force.

Joseph stalked toward her, finger on the trigger. "Good news is, no one will care that you're gone." He put the gun to her head. "Bye, now."

<hr />

The shrill scream tore through Finn's sleep and jolted him awake. He sat straight up in bed, heart pounding, and blinked into the darkness, sure that he'd woken from a nightmare.

But then the sound came again. First the horrible scream and then someone banging on a door. Calling for help.

Shit.

Finn's body jumped into action before his brain caught up. He reached into his boot for his gun, hopped out of bed, and ran for the door. His brain kicked into gear when he hit the hallway, all his senses dialing up and calculating things. Which direction the sound was coming from. Places someone could be hiding. If any civilians were in the immediate area. The hallway was empty, but the screams turned louder, with barely a pause between them. He hurried toward the racket and turned the corner at the end of the hallway, gun poised. Rebecca was two rooms down, frantically pounding on the door. "Olivia! Open up! Please."

He lowered his gun and ran the short distance down the hall, the screams tearing at him. Someone was hurting Liv. "Out of the way."

Rebecca stepped back, a stricken look on her face. "She won't answer me. I called Kincaid and told her to find a manager with a key. The front desk isn't picking up the phone."

The sounds of gut-wrenching terror came again. *Liv*.

Screw waiting for a manager. Finn jerked the door handle, and when it wouldn't give, he rammed his shoulder into the door. The handle was new, but the door had seen better days and protested under the jolt.

"Finn, wait, you don't have to—"

He gave another hard shove, and the frame splintered. That was all he needed. He gave one more good push, and it released the lock and let him inside. He charged in. Liv's screams were twice as loud in the dark. "*Get away from me! No!*"

He raised his gun.

He couldn't see a damn thing but could hear the mattress squeaking, and Liv continued her desperate pleading. But no one jumped at him or moved in the dark. He reached out blindly and found the light switch.

"Police! Freeze!" He flicked on the switch, prepared to go to battle, but when light flooded the room, all he saw was Liv bolting upward in the bed. Terror was on her face, her gaze sweeping around the room like a cornered deer.

No one else was in sight.

"Liv."

But she didn't see him. Her focus zeroed in on his gun, and her eyes went wide. She scrambled backward against the headboard. "*Gun!*"

He immediately lowered the weapon and put a hand out. "Liv. It's me. Finn. It's okay. Is anyone else in the room?"

She squeezed her eyes shut.

"Shit. Okay. Hold on." He did a quick check of the closet and bathroom to make sure nothing was amiss. All the windows were locked. No signs of any struggle. No signs of intrusion. Under the bed was clear.

He let out a breath.

A nightmare. She'd had a nightmare.

He set his gun on the TV stand and moved toward the bed, keeping his hands out in front of him so that if she opened her eyes, she'd see he was unarmed. His gaze swept over her, checking for any obvious injuries.

There was nothing he could see, but she was gripping her elbows, soaked with sweat, and in a full-body tremble.

Very much not okay.

"Liv, baby, are you all right?" he asked, trying to keep his voice gentle. "Talk to me." He reached out to touch her shoulder, and she jerked away from his touch like he'd burned her. "It's Finn. You're okay. It's over now."

"Finn," she whispered.

"Yes. That's right. Just me." He eased down onto the bed, being careful not to jostle her. "You had a nightmare. Just take a few deep breaths. You're okay now."

She opened her eyes, tears spilling over and making damp trails down her cheeks. "It's really you."

"Of course."

Her gaze jumped to his face first, scanning, wary,

and then her attention went to his shoulder. She reached out and touched the puckered scar where the Long Acre bullet had exited. "You have a scar."

The words seemed out of context, but they seemed to offer her some relief. "Yes."

She looked down at her sweat-soaked Green Day T-shirt. She gripped the worn fabric like it was a life vest and nodded, whispering, "*Okay. Okay.*"

"Yes, you're okay." This time when he reached for her, she came to him, letting him put his arm around her. Her body still trembled, but her breathing had eased down from hyperventilation mode.

Rebecca and Kincaid, who'd been standing in the hallway, stepped inside, both looking at Liv with worried eyes.

A guy Finn hadn't seen before—presumably the night manager—came in behind them. He had to be all of eighteen but had a walk like he was going to go Wild West sheriff on them. "What's going on here? Is everything all right?"

"I need a minute," Liv whispered, turning her face away from the door. "Please."

Finn turned, blocking the view of Liv. "Everything's fine. False alarm."

"False alarm?" the guy said with a frown. "Look at the door. My boss is going to be pissed. And y'all woke up half the building. What the hell happened?"

"I'll pay for the door," Finn said.

"I need to make a police report for property damage. And someone yelled the word *gun*. If there's a—"

Rebecca had taken a few steps inside, and she shifted over in front of the table where Finn had placed his weapon. "There's no gun," she said. "Our friend just had a nightmare. We'll cover the damage."

"Sorry for any trouble," Finn said. "Everything's under control."

"Doesn't look that way." The guy tried to peek around Finn and get a look at Olivia. "You sure your friend's not high or something? Because we can't have that kind of thing—"

"Look." Finn gritted his teeth, fighting the urge to grab his gun, point it at the guy, and inform him he needed to leave—now. But that was Axel talking, the guy who ruled by ruthless intimidation. Finn took a breath, pushing that dark impulse down. "Look. It's just been a rough day for us all. She had a nightmare. A bad one."

"And we'd appreciate a little privacy," Rebecca said, taking a no-bullshit tone. "This hotel assured us we'd get it."

The guy's attention moved to each of them like he was connecting some dot-to-dot puzzle. Awareness dawned on his face. "Oh, you're the ones here for the *anniversary*. So she had a nightmare about…you know?"

Kincaid had been standing off to the side, watching Liv like a worried mother, but she turned at that. She pulled the pink robe she was wearing more tightly around herself and offered the manager a tight smile. "Sweetheart, I appreciate you rushing up here with me to intervene. That was real helpful and brave of you. But now that we know everything's all right, we'd all just like to get back to bed. No one wants to be seen by God and all the world in their nightclothes."

Kincaid's sweet-as-pie approach seemed to soften

him. He nodded. "Oh, right. Sure. I mean, I guess as long as no one's hurt, we can just deal with the rest in the morning."

"Good plan," Finn said.

"Such a smart plan. I'm sure that's why they put you in charge. Good head on your shoulders." Kincaid ushered him to the door like she was seeing him off after a dinner party—all smiles and sugar. The guy had no shot against that level of brutal Southern hospitality and offered no further protest. Once he was out in the hallway, Kincaid shut the mangled door behind her and turned around, dropping the Miss America smile. "Jesus H. Christ. Some people can't take a damn hint."

She strode over to the bed. "Liv, are you all right, honey? That sounded like a helluva nightmare…Liv?"

Rebecca frowned. "Uh-oh. She doesn't look so good."

chapter
SIX

"Olivia?"

Her friends' concerned voices were like safety ropes dragging Liv out of the terrifying in-between place she'd been stuck in. Kincaid. Rebecca. Both were staring at her. Finn's arm was around her. Everything was okay now. This was real. Finn had his scar. She wasn't wearing a Long Acre T-shirt soaked in his blood. Joseph wasn't going to walk in and shoot them all. She licked her dry lips.

"I'm sorry." Her voice scraped raw against her throat, and she slipped out of Finn's hold, suddenly self-conscious about her friends seeing her in this state. "I didn't mean to scare everyone. I'll be fine. I'm okay."

"Do you need us to get you anything, sweetie?" Kincaid asked, sitting on the opposite side of the bed from Finn. "Water? A pill? A former football player in his underwear? Because we've got the last one covered. And I can make the first two happen."

Liv looked up at that, registering the fact that Finn

was shirtless and his thick hair was sticking up every which way. Her gaze drifted down to his black boxer briefs. "You're in your underwear."

"'Fraid so," he said. "Good thing I don't sleep naked."

"In his underwear and running through the hallways *with a gun*." Rebecca stood at the foot of the bed, her knuckles white from the grip she had on her elbows. "What the hell was that?"

A gun. A shudder moved through Liv, the image burned into her retinas. Seeing the gun pointed at her when the lights came on had catapulted her into a panic where she couldn't tell real from flashback, the images superimposing on each other.

"I thought she was in trouble," Finn said calmly.

"You just have a gun at the ready? You pick up that before pants?" Rebecca insisted. "You scared me half to death."

"I'm sorry." He glanced back at Rebecca, and even in profile, it was clear he meant it. "I didn't mean to scare anyone. I thought there was trouble. I'm...a cop."

"A cop?" Liv asked, frowning.

He ran a hand over the back of his neck like he'd rather have any other conversation. "Yeah."

Rebecca seemed to have the same reaction as Liv based on the what-the-hell look she gave him. "Your parents told my dad you were working in Europe."

"Is that what they're telling people now?" He sniffed. "Sounds fancy."

"Well, that explains the Captain America routine at least," Kincaid said, waving them off like she couldn't care less what Finn had chosen to do with his life. She turned back to Liv, laser-focused. "You sure you don't need anything, hon? Want me to stay in here with you? Go slumber-party style. We can braid each other's hair and talk about boys in their underwear."

Liv sagged against the headboard. She appreciated Kincaid's offer, but there was no way she was going back to sleep, and she didn't have the energy to put on a happy face. It was mortifying enough to have them all see her like this. Even when her panic attacks had been at their worst, she'd been a pro at finding a way to have them alone, to hide. "Thanks, but it was just a nightmare. Probably from too many margaritas." She tried to offer a smile. "Y'all get some sleep. I'll be all right."

"You sure?" Rebecca asked, rubbing her arms like she couldn't warm up.

Liv met her gaze, hating that she'd also stirred up bad memories for Rebecca with this middle-of-the-night drama. "Yeah. I'm good."

"Okay," Kincaid said, reaching out and patting Liv's knee through the blankets. "But you let us know if you change your mind."

"Will do."

Kincaid circled her finger in the air and got up from the bed. "All right, troops. Back to your bunkers. Let's leave the woman be."

Finn didn't move, only glanced distractedly at Kincaid. "You two go ahead. This door won't be secured tonight. I'll help Liv move her stuff into my room, and I'll sleep in here."

Liv straightened. "You don't have to—"

He turned his head, giving Liv a look. "You're not sleeping with an unlocked door. Not an option."

His green-eyed gaze left no room for discussion. She sighed. "Fine."

She didn't bother to tell him she wouldn't be sleeping regardless.

"Liv?" Kincaid asked, eyebrows lifted in a way that said, *If you need me to escort this bossy boy out for you, I will grab him by his ear and make it happen*.

The concern warmed her. "Yeah, it's all right. Y'all go on."

"Okeydokey," Kincaid said, her tone too bright for this late at night. "See you two for breakfast in a few hours. Don't try to get out of it."

The two women headed to the door, Rebecca glancing back once with an odd expression before stepping out into the hall. They wedged the mangled door shut as best they could and left Liv alone with Finn.

Finn looked back to her, concern lining his face.

She ran her fingers through her knotty, damp hair, wishing she could just crawl in a hole or rewind time. "You don't have to worry about the room thing. I'm not going back to sleep anyway."

"You still shouldn't stay with a broken door."

He got up, giving her a view of his backside as he crossed the room and grabbed the hotel robe she'd tossed over a chair. Normally, she'd be able to appreciate the scenery—all those finely honed muscles and broad shoulders, and the way the boxer briefs clung to everything beneath. The guy had always been nicely put together and seemed to have only improved with time. But all she could focus on was the corresponding entry scar on Finn's back. That smooth, raised mark gave her comfort that this was real, that the nightmare was over.

Liv rubbed her eyes, trying to erase all traces of the images from the dream. "I'm sorry I woke you and scared everyone."

Finn's expression darkened as he shrugged on the robe and belted it. "Don't apologize. Not your fault. Stuff happens."

Sure. But most people's "stuff" didn't wake up half a hotel and get a door busted in. They didn't require a freaking intervention. She pointed to her open suitcase on the floor. "Can you throw me those shorts I have sitting on top? I'm feeling a little underdressed here."

His gaze briefly jumped to the sheets that covered her, something unreadable in his expression. "Yeah. Sure."

She caught them when he tossed them her way.

"I'm just gonna…" He jabbed a thumb to the left and stepped into the bathroom to give her some privacy.

Her face heated. Leave it to her to figure out a way to make things even more awkward with Finn. Throwing herself at him on the porch had apparently only been the opening act. She got up, wiggled into the shorts, and then snagged the bra she'd left on the floor so she could slip it on beneath her shirt. She needed all the armor she could get. "I'm dressed."

Finn came back out and handed her a cup of water, somehow looking businesslike and official despite wearing a hotel robe. Maybe it was a cop thing. All business all the time.

"Thanks." She accepted the water, sat back down on the bed, and took a long gulp.

He didn't move away. "Sounded like a pretty rough nightmare."

She eyed him over the rim of the cup. "Alcohol and

being away from home do weird things to my brain, I guess."

"Want to talk about it?" His voice was quiet, but his eyes were shrewd. "Sometimes describing the dream gets it out of your head so it won't come back."

The first part of the dream flickered through her mind, and her face went hot again as the images filled out in full color. The kissing. The roaming hands. His fingers… "Not even a little bit."

God. Leave it to her to have a sex nightmare. Was that even a thing? Apparently her mind was going to invent new ways to torture her. *Hey, here's a nice little sexy dream, a bit of X-rated fun—nope, just kidding! Demented, gory shit on the way!* She shivered and set the cup on the nightstand.

"You still look flushed." He sat on the edge of the bed, the springs squeaking, and pushed a lock of damp hair away from her face. "You sure you're all right?"

"Just peachy." She gave an exaggerated thumbs-up. "Can we go now?"

He tilted his head, giving her the not-buying-it face. "It was a nightmare about the shooting."

She looked away. "I didn't say that."

"Come on, don't bullshit me," he said, no ire in his voice. "You looked at me like I was a ghost and seemed relieved to see my scar. You're obviously shaken up. I just want to make sure you're all right. Tell me what happened."

Great. So they were going to talk about this. *Yay.* She pulled a pillow onto her lap, needing some kind of buffer between them. "Fine. It was about that night, but I'm okay. It's just something that happens sometimes."

He nodded in a *go on* fashion and scooted back a little, not letting her get away with a pat answer but giving her some space.

Ugh. She hated this, hated having these conversations, hated anyone seeing this fragile side. Especially Finn.

"I used to get them all the time. Sometimes nightmares. Other times flashbacks. Wasn't pretty and made college super fun, but I've learned what to avoid. Being here just set me off."

"Understandable. Today's been...difficult." His eyes scanned her, a line appearing between his brows. "Any tricks you have for calming down afterward? You're still shaking."

She glanced down at her hands, the slight tremor visible against the pillow. She grunted in frustration and flexed her fingers, trying to will them to cooperate. "Not really. It's kind of a suck-it-up-buttercup thing once it's passed. I have to let the adrenaline burn out and distract myself. Take a shower. Watch some TV. Read. Not go back to sleep—like I'm a character in a Nightmare on Elm Street movie." She smirked. "It'll pass. Just ignore the crazy lady over here."

There. She'd said it. *I used to be messed up. Still am sometimes. Now you know.* She braced herself for the oh-you-poor-thing face.

"I used to run."

She looked up. "What?"

He shrugged. "You're not crazy. Or if you are, I guess I am, too. I've been there. Had the nightmares. The panic attacks. For a while, anything that sounded like a gunshot or even the click of a gun being cocked would set me off. I'd freak out and then go running afterward to shake the feeling. Even if it was the middle of the night." He raked his hand through his messy hair. "I'd run until I physically couldn't anymore, until my legs would just give out. It made me feel nuts. So, I get it."

She stared at him, caught off guard by the confession. When she'd known Finn in high school, he'd been the poster child of laid-back—if anything, purposely chill to piss off his high-strung father. So imagining him crushed by anxiety was hard to picture, especially seeing the man he'd become. A man who'd bust through a door and run toward danger. A cop. She glanced over at the nearby table and rolled her lips inward. Even the sight of the gun made her heart pick up speed. "But you're a cop now. You *have* a gun."

"Yeah, well, I don't like things that can control me." He followed her gaze. "Sorry, let me take care of that."

In one smooth movement, Finn got up and went to the table. He picked up the gun, checked the safety, and then tucked it into the drawer and out of sight.

She swallowed past the tight feeling in her throat. "Meaning?"

He settled back onto the bed. "Meaning, one night I was on one of those middle-of-the-night runs after a panic attack. I usually stuck to a regular path, but that night, I was at a friend's house. I ran without any set direction. I wasn't paying attention, just trying to run as fast and hard as I could. I ended up on my knees, near passing out, in some random park. Some dude snuck up on me and put a gun to my head to rob me." His jaw flexed.

"I completely froze. Even if I'd had the energy to defend myself, I was useless. And when he found out I didn't have anything on me except my phone, he stole that and then beat the shit out of me with a piece of pipe." He looked up, lip curled in derision. "I survived one of the deadliest school shootings in history, and there I was, bleeding on the sidewalk at the hands of some punk kid out for kicks."

"Jesus." She hugged the pillow tighter, picturing the scene, knowing she would've reacted the same way.

"But it flipped some switch in me. Instead of getting more scared, I got *pissed*. Not just about that night, but about it all." He glanced up at her, those green eyes haunted but earnest. "I remember sitting in the hospital afterward, giving a statement to the police and thinking, *Never again*. Like *fuck that guy* and *fuck that gun* and *fuck the assholes who put that panic in me in the first place*. I was done." He rubbed a hand over his scar in what looked like an absentminded gesture. "I signed up for a gun-safety course as soon as I healed so I could deal with the fear."

Liv rubbed the chill bumps from her arms. "That must've been ridiculously hard."

He gave a humorless laugh. "The first few weeks, all I could do was sit there and watch other people do target practice. Listen to the sounds. Let the panic come and force myself not to run. It sucked. But then I met this cop who offered to help me. She pushed me, and I started to get used to handling the gun and began to train." He focused on a spot somewhere over her shoulder like he was seeing the memory play out on a screen. "She taught me how to switch off the emotion of it. It's going to sound ridiculous, but it became like football used to be for me. One mission. No emotion attached to it. Get the ball into the end zone. But this time it was hit the target. It was the only thing that helped."

"Jumping into the fire."

"Yeah. But it was the best thing I could've done. Learning from Eileen, the officer I met, seeing how confident and dedicated she was, made me want to do the same thing. When I eventually went into the academy, I was ready. I had to go through simulations where people would attack me or come at me with a weapon over and over again, in a hundred different ways. It diluted the power of my fears because now I had the skills to protect myself and the people around me."

She leaned back against the headboard, impressed and a little awed. "So no one is going to catch you off your game again."

His lips kicked up at the corners, some of that old arrogance breaking through. "Let's just say it's probably not going to go well for them if they try."

She laughed, his playful smirk helping some of her jittery feelings dissipate. "Now I see it. I couldn't picture you with a badge, but there it is. Cocky Finn does law enforcement."

"What? Afraid I couldn't pull it off?" He lifted an eyebrow, his face stern. "Ma'am, can you please step out of the vehicle? Hands where I can see them."

She bit her lip. Of course with his authoritative tone, her mind put him in a uniform and some aviators. She'd never had a particular fetish for men in uniform, especially after her own run-in with the police. But the thought of Finn wearing a uniform and manhandling her a bit had her reconsidering. She would definitely get out of the vehicle. Maybe even let him cuff her.

And as inappropriate as the thought was, considering the circumstances, it was a welcome respite from her nightmare. She cleared her throat. "I think you pull it off just fine."

His dimple appeared beneath the stubble. "You're blushing, Arias."

"I am not." She tipped up her chin. "I'm just...still flushed from all the adrenaline."

"Uh-huh. Or you've got a secret cop fetish."

"Stop flirting." She pointed a finger at him.

"Am I flirting?" he asked innocently.

"Yes. And that's not allowed. You yourself said that kiss was a mistake. So don't come prancing around here half dressed with your Batman abs and talking about where to put my hands. No one likes a tease, Dorsey."

His grin turned roguish. "I said that kiss was a mistake, not a regret."

"Finn."

"And Batman abs?" He grabbed the lapels of the robe like he was going to open it and check. "These old things?"

She stretched out her leg and kicked his thigh. "Stop it. You're terrible."

He lifted his palms in surrender and laughed. "At least you're smiling now."

"Yeah, well, there's that."

Even after all the years that had passed, Finn still seemed able to get her mind off things. When her mom was going through chemo and everything was doom and gloom at home, Finn could somehow figure out ways not just to make her laugh, but to do so in a way that didn't make her feel guilty for feeling a moment of happiness.

She leaned forward, bracing herself on one hand, and planted a kiss on his cheek. "Thank you."

"For what?"

She looked up, meeting his gaze, and realized how close she still was. Close enough to see the flecks of gray in his green eyes, close enough to kiss him. She wet her lips. "Being you. I've missed that guy."

His Adam's apple bobbed, his attention flicking to her mouth before sliding upward again. Her heart picked up speed, and his hand closed around her upper arm. "Liv..."

"I..." Whatever she was going to say died on her lips, because the way he was looking at her made her forget her words. There was want in those green depths— lust—but there was something else. Something that made her breath stall. Need mixed with something more dangerous. A wildness.

A curl of heat went up her spine, twining with unease. So much of her wanted to give in to it, to see what exactly was simmering between them. Just grab him and say to hell with it all and make the sheets even sweatier than they already were. But as much as he was drawing her in with that look, he was also warning her off. She didn't know how she got that sense, but it was there, loud and clear. *Push me away. Run.* He wanted her to stop this.

He'd told her outside what he had to offer—nothing but a one-night stand. And though right now that sounded all kinds of enticing, she wasn't going to go there. He didn't want this. Plus, even sober, it would be too close to how she'd handled her anxiety in college. She didn't need to chase away her nightmare with a hookup she'd regret in the morning. She wasn't that girl anymore.

"Finn." The word was strained.

"Yes?"

She swallowed past the dryness in her throat. "We should get my stuff moved. It's late."

He stared at her for a moment, and then his grip on her arm softened. His breath tickled her hair. "Right. Of course."

He released her, and she climbed off the bed with shaky limbs. She wouldn't let herself look at him. She needed a task—something, anything, to get her mind off the man sitting on her bed. She packed in record time, and Finn retrieved his gun from the drawer, tucking it in the pocket of the robe. No words were exchanged. When she was done gathering her things, he helped her roll her bag down the hallway to his room.

He let her inside and quickly rounded up his own stuff. He moved with quiet efficiency, awkwardness creeping into the silence between them and spreading into every corner of the room.

She leaned against the dresser, watching him, hating the growing divide. "Hey, Finn."

He looked up, his hands full of computer wires.

"I know the kiss was a mistake, and things have gotten a little weird and a lot personal tonight. But this—you and I having some time to talk—was good. I think that's what I missed the most when everything happened. Losing you as a friend."

His stance relaxed. "Yeah?"

She crossed her arms and shrugged. "Yeah. We were

good at the kissing, but we were better at the talking. I never had to fake stuff with you."

His eyebrow arched.

She laughed. "That's not what I mean, Mr. Mind-in-the-Gutter. I mean that things were easy between us. That's hard to find with people. I'm realizing that now. I don't...have that."

He tucked the computer cords in his bag and straightened, his watchful gaze making her fidgety.

"And that's not your problem, obviously." She was rambling now and couldn't bring herself to stop. "But I opened that time capsule tonight and got to see a big, long list of things I wanted to accomplish in life and haven't. I was supposed to do this. I was supposed to do that." She rolled her eyes. "I'm going to name my freaking autobiography *Supposed To*, by Olivia Arias."

He frowned. "Liv."

She shook her head. "It's fine. It is what it is. But all I'm saying is that I don't want another regret added to the list. So I just thought you should know that you meant— mean—something to me. And maybe you could give a flying flip about me. I have no clue what your life looks like now, but I would rather not leave Long Acre later today and go back to being strangers. Because people you don't have to fake it for are hard to find. So... Yeah, that's all I wanted to say. I'd like us to stay in touch."

His mouth twitched. "That's all you had to say?"

"Hey, I'm a photographer, not an editor."

"I thought you were a web designer."

Her lips parted, closed.

He smiled. "Maybe you're already making more changes than you think."

She let out a breath. "Maybe I'm just tired."

Finn stepped around the bed and held out his hand. "Give me your phone."

She was confused for a second, her brain running on too much adrenaline and too little sleep, but eventually his request registered. She reached into her bag to pull out her cell.

He took it from her, typed a few things, and then handed it back to her. "You can always call me, Livvy. For anything."

She took her phone back, her hope sinking a bit. "Right. Thanks."

He kissed the top of her head and then grabbed his stuff. "I'm going to get out of your way so you can shower and rest. If you need anything before breakfast, give me a holler."

"Thanks."

He stepped out into the hallway without a backward glance and headed to the room they'd left, obviously more than a little eager to get the hell away from her. She didn't blame him. She'd apparently become the queen of awkward conversation tonight.

With a sigh, she locked her door and made her way over to the bed and collapsed onto it. Spent. Exhausted. And a little frustrated.

Finn had taken her words to mean she wanted someone to call when she needed help, but she wasn't in the market for a therapist or a savior. She was in the market for a friend.

But maybe she was grasping for something that didn't exist with Finn anymore. Maybe she was just being nostalgic. They weren't in high school. They didn't live in the same place. They couldn't just *hang out*. The time for that had passed. She needed to be okay with that.

If he wasn't interested in keeping in touch, she wasn't going to chase him.

She checked the time on her phone to see how many hours she needed to kill before breakfast. But instead of seeing the time, she saw the address book entry Finn had made.

His phone number.

Filed under Batman.

And a note beneath: You will never be a stranger to me.

chapter
SEVEN

FINN SLUNG HIS COMPUTER BAG OVER HIS SHOULDER AND rolled his suitcase toward the front desk so he could drop off his key card. The early-morning sun squeezed through the blinds of the hotel's windows, and the smell of cheap coffee wafted down the hallway. His mouth watered at the scent. Cheap caffeine was still better than no caffeine. But he didn't have time to visit the continental breakfast. He'd already cut it close enough, lingering a little longer than planned to make sure Liv didn't call and need anything.

He hadn't really expected her to reach out. Even if she did need help, she'd be too stubborn to admit it. He'd seen the look on her face when he'd told her she could call him if she needed him. He hadn't meant it to sound like charity, but he also didn't have anything else to offer. He didn't know how to be someone's friend beyond that anymore. Plus, he'd be undercover again in a few months, so why bother?

He peered around the corner at the end of the hallway

to eye the setup of tables and chairs in the breakfast area. Only one table was taken—an elderly man eating pastries and reading the newspaper. Finn let out a breath and headed to the front desk. The night manager was still on duty, face in his phone, scrolling through something and completely ignoring Finn.

Finn cleared his throat. "Checking out of 348. Just charge the amount to the card on file."

The guy looked up and then frowned when he recognized Finn. "What about the door? My boss—"

"Put that on there, too, when you get it fixed." Finn tossed the key card on the counter.

"Cool." The guy took the key and went about printing the receipt, but his attention stayed on Finn. "What about that lady? Is she all right? I mean, she looked pretty freaked out last night. Is it because—"

"She's fine." Finn's fist curled at his side. If the kid had been asking about Liv out of concern, that'd be one thing, but Finn had been reading people long enough to recognize morbid curiosity masking as kindness.

"I went to the same high school, you know?" the kid said, as if Finn had given some indication he wanted to engage in conversation. "Different name, obviously, but it weirded me out every time I passed the remembrance garden. I can't imagine—"

"Forget it." Finn grabbed his bag. "I don't need a receipt."

The last thing he had time for was this kid's gawking. But before he could turn and get the hell out of there, a soft voice hit him in the back.

"Finn?"

The familiar sound of her saying his name made him wince. "Shit."

Desk Guy's eyebrows went up at Finn's under-the-breath curse.

Finn sent him a warning look and then turned to find Liv staring at him with questioning eyes. "Uh, morning," he said, none too gracefully. "You're up early."

"Yeah, I never went back to sleep. I figured I'd get some work done." Her gaze shifted to the bag over his shoulder and the suitcase. "You're leaving?"

"Just checked out," Desk Guy offered. "He's going to take care of the door for you, ma'am, so you don't have to worry about it."

Finn gritted his teeth and shot a look over his shoulder at Mr. Helpful. When he turned back to Liv, she still had the *Care to explain yourself?* head tilt. Finn sighed. "Let's grab a table."

Frown lines bracketed her mouth. "Yeah, okay. I already have one by the window. Come on."

She led him to a table a few to the right of the elderly man. Her laptop was open, and a cup of coffee sat next to it. She'd probably been away from her table when he'd glanced that way the first time. Plus, in her business suit and heels, her sleek silhouette was something altogether different from the casual version he'd seen last night. Some undercover agent he was.

She leaned over to click a few things on her keyboard and then shut her laptop with a tired sigh.

"I didn't mean to interrupt your work," he said, his tone gruffer than he'd planned.

She shook her head and sat. "It's fine. It's not

something I'm going to have time to fix this morning anyway. I should've never opened my email."

She indicated the chair across from her. Finn took a seat and ran a hand over the back of his head, trying to decide what to say and how to say it. Getting out before everyone woke up had seemed like a good idea at the time.

She stared at him, her eyes tired but her lips smirking. "We didn't sleep together, you know. You don't have to wear the morning-after, got-caught-sneaking-out look."

"I'm very aware we didn't sleep together." Painfully aware as he let his attention sweep over her. She'd pulled her hair into a low knot at her nape and had lined her eyes dark and glossed her lips red, making her look like a 1950s pinup version of herself. Gone was the vulnerable woman from last night. In her place was a confident, beautiful businesswoman. Liv had her armor on.

Her brows quirked as she sipped her coffee. "So what's with the cloak-and-dagger routine?"

"There's no cloak or dagger," he said, guilt washing through him. "I just—"

"Would rather take a fork to the eye than have breakfast with four old classmates?" She sat back in her chair with a knowing look. Feisty. Ball-busting. That was the girl he remembered.

His attention strayed to how her white-collared shirt gaped, revealing the smooth expanse of her throat, the curve of her neck—the neck he'd almost kissed last night.

He grimaced. *Focus, man.* "Being social really isn't my thing. I wouldn't be good company."

"Hmm," she murmured, setting down her coffee. "When I knew you, you could talk to anyone—would've been happy to hold court with four women."

He grabbed her coffee and took a swig. "Yeah, well, people change."

He could still hold court when he needed to, slather on the charm and bullshit, but now it was a role, a game, a way to get people to trust him with their secrets. He didn't know how to be genuine about it anymore and didn't want to go to breakfast and fake it.

"So I'm learning," she said, glancing at her cup. "You know, stealing a woman's coffee this early in the morning is grounds for a beating."

He smiled and sipped again, keeping his eyes on her. "Worth it. But I'll make sure to get you more before I leave."

"So what exactly does leaving entail? I forgot to ask you where you…" Her words drifted off as her attention shifted to a spot over his shoulder, her brow furrowing.

"Liv?"

Her eyes narrowed. "What the hell is he doing?"

"Who?" Finn glanced back to whatever had caught her attention. Front Desk Guy was looking their way from the other side of the breakfast bar, his phone lifted but half hidden between a display of mini cereal boxes and a juice dispenser. Even from a few tables away, Finn heard the faint click of the camera phone. Every muscle in his body tensed.

"*Hey!*" Liv barked. "Is that shithead *taking our picture*?"

Finn was already in motion, the chair falling backward behind him as he jumped to his feet and stalked across the room. The guy's eyes widened at Finn's approach, and he quickly swung his arm around, tucking his phone in his back pocket.

Finn didn't slow down. Red edged his vision, the

snap of the camera playing over and over in his head. He had nightmarish memories laced with that sound. All the cameras in his face. All the questions. No secrets, no privacy. All the false accolades. He stepped around the breakfast bar and crowded the guy. "What the fuck do you think you're doing?"

The guy lifted his hands, his blue eyes full of faux innocence. "What's your problem, dude? I was taking pics of the food."

"Because cereal boxes are so interesting?"

"Maybe they are."

"You were taking our picture." Finn took another menacing step forward, making the guy back up against the wall. "Give me your phone."

"Screw you, man. It's my property. And a free country. I can take a picture."

Finn growled. "Give. Me. Your. Phone."

The kid swallowed hard. "What's the big secret? Cheating on your wife or something? Or don't want the world to know you've got issues?"

Finn grabbed the front of the kid's shirt and shoved him hard against the wall, fury coursing through him. The guy's breath popped out of him, the impact rattling the nearby pastry table.

"*Finn.*" Liv called out somewhere behind him, but it was just background noise. He needed that phone. His photo couldn't be released. But more than that, how dare this piece of shit think it was his right to invade their privacy? To take their photo like they were fucking zoo animals?

"Get your hands off me," the guy said, trying to break the grip.

"Not until you give me your phone."

"Fuck you."

Finn grabbed for the phone, and the guy tried to take a swing at him, but Finn was too quick and too well trained. Instinct took over. He ducked and swung at the guy's unprotected side, landing the punch in his gut and bringing him to his knees.

"*Finn! Stop!*" Liv was shouting now, but he was moving too fast.

He knocked the kid onto his belly and put a knee in his back, ripping the phone from his pocket.

"Why were you taking pictures?" Finn demanded, keeping the guy pinned. "Did someone put you up to it?"

"No, man."

Liv grabbed at Finn's shirt. "Please. Let him go."

Finn couldn't process her plea. All he could hear was that damn snapping camera, the shouting voices, all the people vying for a sound bite, a candid photo, a glimpse of a tragedy that wasn't theirs.

Finn pushed the guy's cheek into the carpet. "How can I believe you, you piece of shit?"

Liv yanked at Finn's shirt, frantic and feeling helpless at the immovable force of Finn's wrath. He was going to demolish the kid if he didn't stop. The older man who'd been a few tables over from her was standing off to the side, phone to his ear, no doubt calling the police. But Finn was in some sort of zone. She'd never seen him like this. Scary. Out of control.

Deadly.

He shoved the guy's face against the rough carpet, demanding more answers, and she looked around for something—anything—that could help. Her yelling wasn't working. She didn't exist to him right now. When she spotted the pitcher of ice water, she ran over and grabbed it. As Finn was pulling the guy's head up by his hair, she dumped it over them both. Ice and water spilled everywhere, earning her a string of curses from the two men.

But it got Finn to turn his head. When his gaze met hers, it was as icy as the water dripping down his face—steely and cutting through her like a winter chill. *Mean*.

Goose bumps chased over her skin.

"Finn," she said, putting every ounce of command she possessed into her voice. "Stop. You've got the phone. He's just a dumb kid."

He stared at her for a long moment, fury burning in his eyes, but then finally he blinked, her words seeming to register. He glanced back at the manager, who was whimpering now, and abruptly let go, as if the kid's hair had burned him.

Finn climbed off him and sat back on his knees, the phone in his hand. "Shit."

Liv let out a breath and hurried over to the guy. He rolled over onto his back, panting hard, his face blotchy. She put a hand on his shoulder. "Are you okay?"

"I think that crazy fucker broke my rib."

She winced. "Okay, just lie here. I think someone called for help."

Finn was still where she'd left him. He'd set the phone down in front of him and had his hands laced behind his neck, breathing hard.

Sirens blared outside, and Liv's heart picked up speed. She took a breath, willing the panic away. She'd gotten used to sirens in the city, but for some reason, they sounded different here. Too familiar. She didn't have time to freak out, though, because Finn was going to need her to do some fast talking.

But when the two cops walked in, Finn didn't give her the chance. She thought he'd explain that he was a cop or tell them what the guy had done to set him off. Instead, he stood, still dripping wet, and put his hands up. "Just take me to the station. I don't want to discuss anything here."

Even though he was going willingly, one of the cops insisted he be cuffed. Finn turned and put his hands in position without protest. When the cuffs snapped shut, he finally looked her way, resignation there. "I'm sorry. Just go to breakfast. I'll handle this."

"Finn—"

The officer turned to lead him out before Liv could say anything else.

"The hell you will," she said under her breath as she grabbed the kid's abandoned phone. She'd just seen what Finn handling things looked like. With renewed resolve, she stalked over to the table where he'd left his bags and keys. She grabbed all of it, along with her own things, and eyed the kid—Adam.

The other officer had spoken with him, and now he was slumped in a chair, holding his side, while the officer interviewed the older man. Liv made her way over to the kid as she opened his phone. Sure enough, he had a number of close-ups of her, the back of Finn's head, and a picture of the broken door from last night. She deleted them as she went, but then an Any luck? text popped up, opening an excited text trail between him and what she guessed was his girlfriend, detailing the events of last night.

> **Adam:** I don't know which one she is, but she was totally freaked out
> **Claire:** Srsly? Still?
> **Adam:** Inorite? Like 10 yrs have passed & they're still messed up
> **Claire:** Sad. Would make a great story. Can u get me pics? Confirm which ones they are?
> **Adam:** What do I get in return? ;)

A string of sexual promises and suggestive emojis followed.

Ugh. Liv wanted to kick the guy herself. But even with this, he hadn't deserved a beating from Finn.

Adam looked up, his jaw tight. "Give me my phone back. That's private."

"Private? I wasn't aware you were familiar with the concept."

He put out his hand. "Your whackjob boyfriend better not have broken it."

Liv's teeth clamped together. She glanced at the other cop, making sure she was still occupied with her interview, and then crouched down next to Adam's chair. From a distance, her posture would look like she was making sure he was okay, but the words that were about to come out of her mouth were nothing of the sort. She pressed his phone into his hand, and when he grabbed it, she gripped his hand hard and pinned him with a stare.

"Now you listen to me, you smug little shit. I'm sorry that you're hurt, but you don't get to slap labels on us

like you know us. You don't get to take pictures like
we're some sideshow attraction. You think you know
what's what, but you have *no idea*. That cute little girlfriend you're sending eggplant emojis to? Yeah, imagine
if you'd taken her to prom, and while you were dancing,
her brain got blown up with a bullet in front of you."

His mouth went slack.

"Imagine if along with that, all your closest friends,
the people you cared about, ended up dead, too, bleeding
out on the floor around you. Oh, and maybe you got a
gun pressed to your head, and you had to beg for your
life. Then imagine years later someone photographing
you because—wow, cool, someone who was in the
news. And man, aren't they screwed up? Ha-ha."

His throat bobbed. "I didn't mean... I'm sorry."

She let go of the phone and stood. "Yeah, well, show
you're sorry then. Don't press charges. And thank the
universe that you're so freaking clueless and have no
idea what we've been through."

He looked up, eyes haunted, and gave a quick nod. "I
will. I really didn't mean it like... I didn't think."

"Everything okay over here?" the female officer
asked, stepping up behind Liv.

Liv tilted her head, her gaze still on him.

Adam cleared his throat and looked to the cop. "Yes,
ma'am, everything's fine. It was all just a dumb misun-
derstanding. I provoked him."

Liv gave him a tight smile and then turned to the officer. "Can I give my statement at the station?"

"Sure, you can head over. I'm going to wait for the
medic to show up to make sure he doesn't need to go to
the hospital."

Liv nodded, gathered the luggage, and headed toward the parking lot without looking back. One issue down, another much bigger one to go. Because Finn *had* been provoked. But his reaction had been over the top and…scary.

He'd helped her last night, but maybe she wasn't the only one who needed it.

chapter
EIGHT

FINN STEPPED OUT OF THE HOLDING ROOM AT THE POLICE station to find Liv sitting in an orange plastic chair, her foot bouncing with impatience or nerves and her attention on her phone.

He let out a breath. Olivia Arias—forever hard-headed. Of course she hadn't listened to him and had let his dumb-ass behavior ruin her morning with her friends. Frustration filled him. But when she looked up and he saw the wariness in her face, it broke something inside him. She was here. But not the same version he'd kissed last night. She'd seen who he was. Now she was guarded. Scared of him.

As she should be. He'd acted like a goddamned lunatic. This was exactly why he'd planned to keep to himself while he was here. But seeing that look on her face was like watching a shiny thing rust before his eyes—the only shiny thing he'd been allowed to touch, and he'd tarnished it.

"You didn't have to come here," he said, trying to

keep his voice quiet despite the ringing phones and noise of the station.

"I know." She stood and gripped her elbows like she was cold. "You left your keys, so I drove your SUV here. I figured you'd need it. The officer said I could get a ride back to the hotel with him, but I wanted to wait to make sure you were okay."

Finn glanced at the officer manning the front desk. "Do you want to ride with one of them?"

She gave him a once-over, a wrinkle between her brows. "I don't know."

"I understand if you do. I know I scared you."

"You didn't—" She bit the inside of her lip and glanced at the desk. "Are you free to go?"

"Yeah." He cocked his head to the side. "Come on. Let's talk outside. If you decide not to ride with me, you can come back in."

"All right." She grabbed her purse to join him but kept enough distance between them that he felt like they were miles apart.

He pushed the door open and let her walk out into the bright sunshine first. She pulled a pair of sunglasses from her purse and slipped them on, hiding her eyes from him. When they were out in the parking lot, away from the controlled chaos of the station, he stopped and faced her. "You okay?"

She frowned. "Are *you*?"

"Yeah. The guy isn't pressing charges. Not sure why, but he gave a statement saying he provoked me."

Her lips lifted at one corner, the effect more grim than amused. "I had a little heart-to-heart with him. Glad he listened."

Finn blew out a breath and squeezed the back of his neck. "You didn't have to do that. I deserved whatever they were going to charge me with. I…" He squinted at the road behind them before looking at her again. "I lost it."

She crossed her arms, tough in stance but worry creasing the corners of her mouth. "You did. You were…scary."

He wanted to reach out to her, take that troubled look off her face, but he hooked his thumbs in his pockets to keep his hands to himself. "I know. I'm sorry. I could tell you reasons why it set me off, but that doesn't excuse how I acted, so it doesn't matter. I should have more control than that."

She rubbed her arms, even though the temperature was probably already in the nineties. He hated that he'd put that chill in her. "Can you drive me to my car? The girls moved breakfast to brunch, so I'm going to try to meet up with them."

He shouldn't have felt so much relief, hearing that she was willing to ride with him, but it untwisted something tight inside his chest. He took the keys she offered. "Of course."

They climbed into his black SUV, the interior baking in the heat even with the tinted windows, and he put the air conditioning on high. Liv had tossed his bags into the back seat, along with her laptop case, and had set his cell phone in the cup holder. She'd taken care of him even when he'd scared her.

He turned out of the station. "I'm really sorry you're going to be late to your breakfast. I could've gotten a cab back to the hotel."

She clicked her seat belt closed and pushed her sunglasses to the top of her head. "I doubt Long Acre has a cab company. You'd have to wait for a car from Austin, and that'd take forever. Plus, if the guy didn't retract his statement, I was going to give one of my own. He was in the wrong, too."

"I should've handled it better."

"You think?" she said.

The tension in his shoulders eased a bit, her sarcasm comforting him somehow.

"And you're right, it doesn't change what you did to know why, but maybe you should clue me in. You went after that guy like you could kill him." She turned to him, her gaze full of questions. "What happened?"

He looked back to the road, picking through what he could and couldn't tell her. But before he could get anything out, his cell phone rang. *Private Number* flashed on the screen and he cursed, knowing who it was. The cops had made him get his boss on the line to confirm he was FBI. Billings had been brief and all business with them, but Finn had known that wouldn't be the end of it. Billings's response had been the equivalent of Finn's mother saying, *Just wait 'til we get home*, when he'd acted up in public. If he didn't pick up the call, he'd make it worse.

"I need to answer this," he said, reaching for the phone, but the car's Bluetooth picked up the call first, responding to the answer command.

Before he could switch the phone off Bluetooth, Billings's voice boomed through the speakers. "Goddammit, Dorsey, you just started your break, and you're already getting yourself *arrested*?"

Liv reared back at the yelling and looked Finn's way.

"Sir, just give me one second—" Finn tried to get the call onto the cell so Liv wouldn't hear all of it, but his boss was already on a roll.

"I am not giving you a damn thing. I trust you to keep a low profile and acclimate back to society, and a few hours after our talk, you're beating some guy for looking at you the wrong way?"

"It was a photo—"

"I don't care if it was a goddamned film crew. You could've handled it by flashing your badge and confiscating the phone. Think, Dorsey." Billings sighed heavily. "This just tells me I should've trusted my instincts. You were under for too long. I want you back in Virginia. We've got people here that can help you reset. I don't need you accidentally killing someone because they tick you off."

Liv's eyes had gone wide, and Finn gave up on trying to make the call private. Too late.

"I'm not... I don't need to come back, sir. It was a momentary lapse in judgment. I wouldn't have taken it any further than I did. It was just a little scuffle."

Liv's brows went up, silently calling him out on his lie.

"That's not what the witness said. He said you looked like you wanted to kill the guy. He said—"

"He was protecting me, Mister... Uh, sir," Liv said, boldly jumping in.

Finn stiffened.

"Hello? Who's that?" Billings barked.

"Olivia Arias. I'm"—she glanced at Finn—"an old friend of Finn's. We were having coffee together, and I freaked out when I saw the guy taking pictures. Finn was…protecting me. It wasn't as bad as the police made it sound."

Billings went dead silent on the phone. "You have a woman in the car?"

Finn winced, slightly horrified that Liv had talked to Billings, but smart enough to capitalize on the obvious opportunity. "Yes, sir. Liv picked me up from the police station. Like she said, we were having coffee together before we were supposed to meet some high school friends for breakfast."

Billings was quiet again and Finn glanced at Liv, unsure why she was helping him.

"Miss?" Billings asked finally. "I need your honesty. Did you see Agent Dorsey as a genuine threat to anyone this morning?"

Liv gave Finn a tense, questioning look but then wet her lips. "Well, sir, no, not exactly. I mean, he's a cop, so always capable of being a threat, but this was just a minor dustup. That guy was being an absolute douche canoe. I wanted to hit him myself."

Billings was silent for a long moment and then made a noise that might've been a chuckle if it had escaped his throat. "I see."

He doubted Billings had ever heard the term *douche canoe*, but something unlocked in Finn's chest, and he was able to take a breath. "It won't happen again," Finn assured him. "My plan for the rest of the summer is very low key, like I told you. Staying at a lake house, reconnecting with old friends, and tackling a few minor projects. If anything else happens, you have my word that I'll return to Virginia. But this was just a one-off, an unfortunate incident."

Billings didn't rush with his answer, leaving Finn worried that he was about to get yanked back to headquarters anyway. But when Billings finally spoke again, he was as direct as usual. "Okay. I'll take your word, Dorsey. For now. But I want yours, too, Miss…"

"Arias," she filled in.

"Ms. Arias. Dorsey is under strict orders to take a vacation and be around friends and family to recuperate after his last assignment. If you know him at all, I'm guessing you know he's got a head made of brick."

Liv sent Finn a wry smile. "I'm aware."

Finn sniffed as he rolled to a stoplight. *Takes one to know one, Arias.*

"So if you really are an old friend, keep an eye on him and make sure he does that. He doesn't just deserve a break. It's a requirement that he takes one."

Liv gave Finn a questioning look. "Of course."

"And Finn, any other screwup, and I'm ordering you back. No questions asked."

The fact that Billings used his first name only amplified the order, like a parent invoking a middle name. It didn't mean Finn was in trouble. It meant Billings was worried. He probably should be, but Finn wasn't going back to spend months being observed in a fishbowl. And he'd be damned if he'd mess this up and end up a desk jockey back at headquarters. "Yes, sir."

"Good." The phone cut off without a goodbye, and Finn pressed the gas, rocketing forward and feeling the burn of Liv's gaze on the side of his face.

He cleared the knot from his throat and focused on the road. "Thank you for that. Billings can be…intense."

He didn't dare hope that Liv wouldn't ask questions.

She'd never been one to not poke the bear, so he wasn't surprised when she immediately started firing them off.

"*Agent* Dorsey?" she asked. "So not a regular cop."

"No. FBI."

Silence.

When he dared a look her way, her expression was unreadable, her eyes revealing nothing. "The FBI. And your boss is worried you're some sort of live wire—which, from what I saw, you might be, and I just covered for you. I lied to a federal agent."

He didn't like the flat sound of her voice. Liv had always been free with her thoughts and emotions. It was one of the things that had drawn him to her. Big brown eyes that weren't afraid to convey *You're an idiot* when he was being one, or *I'm into you* when he wasn't. He'd rather she was yelling at him.

"Yes, but it's okay. I'm not going to do anything like that again. I just need to get to the lake house to clear my head. It's too early for me to be around people."

"Why? That's not what your boss said. He thinks being around people is exactly what you need." She gave him a pointed look.

"Being around people got me into this position in the first place."

She scoffed. "And by that, I'm guessing you mean being around me. I didn't ask you to go all *Die Hard* on that guy."

"My reaction had nothing to do with you. It was a reaction to having my picture taken." He squinted at the road, trying to choose his words carefully. "I've hated being photographed since all the Long Acre stuff, but it's more than that now. My picture can't be released in the press. It's why I wouldn't be on film for the documentary and checked in under a different name at the hotel. I've been working undercover with some dangerous people—people who would not react so well to finding out I'm not dead like they think I am."

"Hold up. You have *dangerous* people after you?" She peeked out the back window as if expecting bad guys to roll up behind them. "What the hell?"

"No, like I said, they think I'm dead. As far as they know, I was going on a trip to get my girlfriend out of jail, and I got killed along with another guy in a car wreck along the way. As long as they think that, I'm good. But my picture can't be out there. Even though we arrested the major players and I've changed my appearance, there are still people who could recognize me."

Liv sagged against the seat. "Jesus, Finn."

"I'm sorry," he said, meaning it. "I'm not trying to scare you."

"Well, you are." She gave him an exasperated look. "You were out of control this morning. You didn't hear me calling you or feel me grabbing at you. It was like you were some other person. A dangerous person."

"I'm sorry." His teeth pressed against each other, memories of the things he'd witnessed over the last few years flashing through his mind. The torture. The beatings. The killings. He'd been instructed not to break cover unless he needed to protect an innocent. But bearing witness to some of the things he'd seen had left its mark, had taken a piece of him. To survive ruthless people, you had to learn how to be ruthless yourself. "It's only been a couple of weeks since I got out. I haven't had time to decompress yet."

She was quiet for a moment after that, but he could almost hear the wheels grinding in her head as she parsed everything. "Are you still at risk? Shouldn't you be holed away in some safe house or something?"

The sign directing them to the main highway came up on the left, and he hit his blinker to merge. "I'm not under direct threat at this point. They don't know who I really am or where I'm from. I was wearing my hair long, had contacts and a full beard. Different accent. And the only person who figured out who I really was is dead. I've covered my tracks, and I'm hundreds of miles from where I was based."

"So you're on leave. That's what your boss was talking about."

"Yeah. I've rented a lake house in Wilder to take a few months off before I go on assignment again. I only came into Long Acre for the documentary interview. I never planned…"

"To speak to anyone. Make out with me. Get in a fight. Get arrested."

A smile fought its way through his sour mood. "Right. Though I only regret three of those."

"Don't flirt. You don't get to flirt right now." She jabbed a finger his way. "I'm worried about you."

"Duly noted." He reached out and gently lowered her hand, giving it a squeeze before letting go. "But you don't need to waste worry on me. I'll handle it."

"Uh-huh. Sure you will."

Another five minutes passed, Liv staring out the window, her fingers lightly drumming on the seat. Thinking. Or brooding. He couldn't tell.

But finally she looked his way again. "So you met

your demise picking up your old lady from jail, huh? Hell of a way to go."

Her unexpected teasing lifted the weight pressing down on his mind. He put his hand over his heart. "Yes, I'd been waiting years for my one true love to get out after serving time for the assault of an ex-boyfriend. Bridget didn't deal well with men who stray."

"Nice. You like 'em feisty."

He smirked. "Feisty's good. Violent, not so much. But it was a necessary cover. I needed a girlfriend who I had good reason not to cheat on. There were expectations otherwise."

"Expectations?"

He peeked at her out of the corner of his eye, her attention on him like the heat of a spotlight. "Their cover for the gun-and-drug smuggling was a strip club chain, so there were women in the group who provided services to the guys. If I had turned that down just because, it would've been suspicious. So I acted like I'd made a promise to a woman and planned to keep it. Got me a lot of ribbing from the others but saved me all kinds of fun venereal diseases."

Liv let out a sharp puff of breath, the humor draining from her face. "God. I can't even imagine. How long did you have to live like that? I thought I was living a double life just changing my last name and not telling people about Long Acre, but you took it to the next level."

"Just part of the job. I was under for a little over two years this time."

"*Two years?*" She shifted on the seat to face him fully. "Did you get any breaks? To see your family? Friends?"

"No. Not on this one."

She shook her head. "That's insane. So no being Finn for two years? No real friends. An imaginary girlfriend." She smoothed her hands over her skirt and then stilled. "Wait. So does that mean when you kissed me…?"

He cleared his throat. "Now you know why it might have gone a little too far too fast."

Her lips parted. "I… Oh. Wow."

Internally, he cringed. *Yes, Olivia. I've been celibate for over two years and am in a meaningful relationship with my own hand, so sorry I fell on you like a rabid dog. And please ignore that just the scent of your shampoo filling this car has potential to make me a little hard even though I spent the morning acting like an animal and scaring you.* "It's been an intense two years."

"So that's why your boss is worried about you."

He ran a hand over his jaw, weariness bearing down on him. His boss was worried about the usual things— the transition back to normal life—sure. But he was more worried because Finn had taken what everyone else saw as too high a risk, worried that Finn had some sort of death wish. But he couldn't tell Liv that. "Right. Some people have trouble transitioning back to the civilian world after being undercover. You get used to…not following the rules. Taking what you want. Treating other people like they're there to serve you. Solving issues with your fists or a weapon."

"Like today."

He nodded. "Like today. If you hadn't been there, I'm not entirely sure I would've been able to stop myself from hurting the guy worse. That's why I need to get to the lake house and be alone."

She sniffed.

There was so much in that one little derisive sound that he had to look her way. "What?"

Her expression went deadpan. "You realize that is a completely ridiculous plan, right?"

He frowned.

"Come on, Finn." She pursed those red-glossed lips like she could barely tolerate his foolishness. "That is such a man plan."

"A man plan."

"Yes. You don't know how to be among the living anymore so you're going to…go live alone in a cave. Right. Good thinking. That will pop your how-to-be-human skills right back into place."

He made a frustrated sound and pulled into the lot of the hotel to park so he could face her, make her understand. "You saw what happened today. I'm not fit to be around other people right now. I beat a guy down for taking a picture. And I was…aggressive with you last night."

"Aggressive?" Her mouth flattened, and she put a finger to her chest. "*I* kissed *you*. I was the aggressor. You were just…complicit in the aggressiveness. And you're lucky I haven't gone two years' celibate, because had I been in your shoes, I would've convinced you to go up to my room and used you eight ways to Sunday and back again by now. You'd be limping."

His libido gave a hard kick and knocked the logical thoughts out of his head for a moment. "I—"

"You need to be around people."

That snapped his attention back to where it needed to be—mostly. "No."

"You promised your boss you'd be around friends. You made *me* promise your boss that I'd make sure you did that. You made me lie to the FBI. That's got to be a federal offense or something."

"*Made* is a strong word."

"Finn."

He groaned. "What would you have me do? You want to babysit me, Livvy? Come stay at my lake house and make sure I don't turn into a deviant?"

She stared at him, her gaze way too sharp, and then tipped her chin up in challenge. "Is that an invitation? Because you know you shouldn't test me. I could babysit the hell out of you, Finn Dorsey. I know who you used to be. You don't get to become a bad guy. I will make you do slumber-party things like play charades or watch crappy nineties movies or incessant reruns of *Friends*. You won't be able to fight your old goofy side. It will emerge like a freaking butterfly and smother scary Finn."

He blinked and stared, and then he couldn't help it—he laughed. "A freaking butterfly?"

She smiled triumphantly. "A goofy freaking butterfly."

He let out a long breath, some of the tension from the morning draining out of him. "You're weird."

"So are you."

He rubbed the spot between his eyes. "Why are you trying to help, Liv? You should be running in the other direction."

A hand touched his shoulder. "The same reason you busted down my door last night and then took care of me when I was panicking. That's what friends do." She

sighed and let her hand fall away. "Last night, I was
mortified that y'all saw me like that. But having Kincaid
and Rebecca there…you there, it ended up making it
better. I didn't have to hide or lie about it because all of
you get it. I think I'd forgotten what it felt like not to be
alone in that."

She paused like she was figuring out her own feelings
about it.

"I don't know," she continued. "I have friends. I'm
sure you do, too. But maybe there's something to be said
for being around people who knew you before you were
a grown-up, before everything changed. You don't need
a babysitter, but maybe you could use an old friend who
knows the original color of the paint beneath all those
layers life has slapped on you. Maybe I could, too."

He lifted his head at that and found her gaze stripped
down and honest. Vulnerable. Despite what she'd seen
today, she wasn't afraid of him. Maybe afraid *for* him,
but nothing beyond that. There was trust in her eyes—
something he hadn't seen from anyone in a long damn
time. No one trusted anyone in the world he'd just left.
Everyone had an angle. And even his coworkers and
boss were wary of him right now. So seeing Liv so open
and earnest made warmth curl up the back of his neck
and spread through his chest. Warmth and something
else he chose to ignore. Something very, very specific
to this woman.

Specific and dangerous.

He should walk away. Stick to his original plan and
leave her out of it. Tell her he didn't need her help or
want her company. But the words wouldn't come out.

He swallowed past the thickness in his throat, and a

different kind of honesty came out instead. "I read your letter. You dropped it on the deck last night."

Her expression went slack. "What?"

"I know I shouldn't have, but I did. You had an original paint color, too. You wanted to be a photographer and artist more than anything." He glanced down at her business wear. "You weren't going to be a nine-to-fiver."

Her spine stiffened, and her gaze turned guarded. "What does that have to do with anything?"

He took a breath, felt the *Don't do it* anxiety well up in him, and pushed past it. "If you're serious about this—us being in each other's lives again—I may have an option to benefit us both."

Her brows lifted.

"The place I have by the lake has a pool house that could work as a studio, and it has an efficiency apartment above it. If you wanted somewhere to spend a few weekends and work on your photography, you could stay there while you did it. I know it'd be a commute for you, but it might help to get out of the city and have a change of scenery. Plus, you're right. I don't need a babysitter but...I could use some crappy nineties movies. And maybe you could get something out of it, too."

Her lips parted, closed, parted again. "You're asking me to stay weekends at your lake house with you?"

"It wouldn't be like that." Though his mind wanted to go there. It wanted to go there and stay there and roll around in that sexy, sweaty thought for a while. "You'd have your own space."

She stared at him like she couldn't quite figure him out. *Join the club.* He had no idea where this was coming from. He'd planned a few months of solitude, and now he was inviting a regular weekend guest. No, not a guest. *Olivia Arias*. But when she'd talked about movies and making him laugh and just hanging out, it had leached into his blood like morphine. He couldn't remember the last time he'd had those kinds of simple pleasures with someone. It sounded almost as tempting as sex.

Almost.

And ultimately, he needed to get back on the job. That was his life. He had a mission that he hadn't completed yet. One that had fueled him to join the FBI in the first place. He wouldn't rest until he'd taken down whoever was responsible for the guns getting into the hands of the Long Acre shooters. He had to prove to his boss that he was ready for that kind of assignment again, or Billings would plant him at some desk to push papers around. So if Billings wanted to see him acting like a normal human again, what better way to do that than to tell his boss he was spending weekends with an old friend?

Liv glanced toward the hotel, maybe looking for an escape route.

"No pressure," he added. "Just an idea."

Liv ran her hands over the front of her skirt again, smoothing it, keeping her gaze on her lap. She was going to say no. She was coming up with a way to let him down nicely. He didn't blame her.

"I don't have a lot of space at my current place to deal with my camera equipment." She peeked over at him. "And being outside and seeing new things always helped spark my creativity."

Finn sat up straighter in the seat, trying to look unaffected. "Okay. So…"

She rolled her lips inward, gears obviously turning. "This sounds a little crazy."

"I'm aware." Painfully aware. He'd just invited his high school girlfriend to stay across the driveway from him. Beautiful, sexy Liv. Liv, who'd kissed him like she was ready to get naked last night. Liv, who he wasn't allowed to touch.

Liv, who he wouldn't hurt just because he was hard up and fucked up and wanted her in his bed more than he wanted air.

It wasn't crazy. It was goddamned masochistic. She needed to say no.

Her lips curved into a tentative smile. "So…I guess maybe it's time I take a few weekends off."

"Great."

Fuuuuuuck.

chapter

NINE

LIV WALKED INTO THE BROKEN YOLK, HER BODY ON AUTO-
pilot and her brain on blender mode after her talk with
Finn. *What the hell did I just do?* Clearly, it had been an
insane decision based on lack of coffee and low blood
sugar from not eating. She couldn't possibly have just
agreed to stay at Finn's on the weekends. That was
some other Olivia in some alternate universe who was
living a different life from her—one where she didn't
have responsibilities or a crazy, busy job or a shred of
common sense.

One where she wasn't ridiculously attracted to the
man she'd be staying near.

She groaned inwardly and tried not to show her distress as she found her friends at a booth in the back. A
spread of food that could feed twice as many of them
filled the table. Stacks of pancakes, a waffle the size of a
dinner platter, and enough eggs and bacon to kill a man.
"Wow, y'all aren't messing around."

Taryn looked up. She'd wrangled her natural black

curls into a cute style with a colorful headscarf today, and she'd clearly gotten more sleep than Liv because her brown eyes were bright behind her dark-rimmed glasses. She beamed at Liv. "Hey, you made it." She scooted over and patted the spot beside her. "Sit. Kincaid is doing research for her food blog. We have graciously volunteered as tributes."

Liv slid into the booth, tamping down the nervous, electric feeling running through her. She could freak out later. Alone. Like a proper introvert. She forced a smile. "I'm so hungry I could eat the napkins."

"No need to resort to that. Plenty of tastier carbs to chow down on." Taryn slid a plate of pancakes her way.

Liv didn't hesitate. Food. She could focus on food. She grabbed the syrup and doused her plate. "So what did I miss?"

No one jumped in with an answer, and when she took her first bite, she realized everyone had stopped eating and was looking at her expectantly.

"What?" she mumbled, mouth full.

"Um, well," Kincaid said, giving her a pointed look. "How about starting with... Is Finn in jail? Do we need to rustle up bail money? Why did he attack someone in the first place? Pick anywhere to start, sugar, but start talking."

Liv swallowed her bite and sighed. "Sorry. No, he's not in jail. No bail money needed because the guy dropped the charges. And what happened is that the desk guy is an asshole who was snapping pictures of us to give to his journalist girlfriend."

Rebecca set her fork down with a clink, her cheeks flushing the color of her red hair. "Are you kidding me?"

"Disgusting," Taryn said with a grimace. "Some people have no home training."

But Rebecca wasn't done. She looked ready to take her own swing at the guy or drag his ass into court. "If he gives anyone those pictures, we can file a complaint. The hotel assured us privacy, and he's an employee."

"I don't think it will come to that." Liv grabbed the coffee carafe and poured herself a cup. "I threatened the guy, deleted the photos, and laid on a guilt trip that only a sociopath could ignore. By the time I left, he was stumbling over his tongue to apologize."

Kincaid nodded her approval, her lips pursed. "Good for you. And good for Finn for punching that little twerp. What in God's name is wrong with people? I'd say *kids these days*, but then I'd feel old and I am not."

Taryn frowned. "So Finn's okay? Why didn't he come to breakfast?"

"He's okay. He dropped me off at the hotel." He'd waited for her to get inside her car before he'd taken off—like he wasn't sure she'd be safe without an escort. But living among criminals for two years would probably make anyone a little paranoid. "He's had a rough morning and had some things to take care of, so he's heading out to Wilder to the lake house he's renting."

"Oh." Rebecca didn't bother to hide her disappointment. "That's too bad."

"Yeah." Liv shifted on the booth seat, desperate for the other women to stop grilling her. She didn't want to blurt out, *Holy shit, I just agreed to stay with my high school ex-boyfriend for a few weekends to make sure he doesn't lose it again. Someone slap me with a pancake and knock some sense into me.* "So blog research? I didn't know you blogged."

Kincaid shrugged like it was nothing worthy of discussion—which was weird because with Kincaid, almost everything was worth discussion.

Taryn swiped at her mouth with a napkin, losing all her coral-colored lipstick, and gave Liv a conspiratorial look. "Kincaid blogs about the best local eats in the Hill Country and then re-creates the dishes for the home cook. This will be her next post."

"That's cool," Liv said. "I do a lot of web-design work for bloggers."

"It is cool, but she's secretive about it. I found the website by accident," Taryn said.

"Yes." Rebecca dropped another pat of butter on her pancakes. "And we can all hate her because she eats her way through Texas and can probably still fit into that dance team outfit from high school."

"Oh, I so cannot." Kincaid said, wrinkling her nose. "I've tried."

Liv almost spilled the cream she was pouring into her coffee. "Wait. You tried to wear the *blue glitter leotard*?"

"I cannot be blamed," Kincaid said, raising a finger. "There was spiked eggnog and a dare involved at an after-hours Christmas party. What was I supposed to do?"

"Um, say no?" Rebecca suggested.

Kincaid gave her a look like she'd spoken a foreign language. "You don't say no to a dare, especially when it was issued by some know-it-all coworker who thought he'd make me look ditzy. I promise, I came out on the better end of the deal. I made him agree that if I tried it on, he had to as well." A wicked grin emerged.

"Leotards aren't meant to wrangle all that boy business, so things…escaped. The rest of the guys called him Glitter Balls for about a year afterward."

Liv laughed. "Nice. Remind me to never play Truth or Dare with you."

Kincaid did a mock half-bow. "Wise decision."

Liv didn't doubt it. Kincaid had developed a reputation in high school as a firecracker—pretty to look at but someone who could burn you if you got on her bad side. One of the football players had dated her, gotten caught cheating, and ended up with his brand-new convertible filled with Kibbles and Bits and *Dawg* written on the window in greasepaint.

Liv had secretly wished to be Kincaid's BFF that day. A woman who could pull off a master prank on a master prick scored an A for Awesome in Liv's book. But she and Kincaid had only been friendly, not close. Plus, Kincaid had intimidated the hell out of her. Still did sometimes.

"So is the blog like a job? I thought you were doing real estate," Liv asked.

Kincaid waved a piece of bacon like it was a pointing stick. "Nah, it's just a thing to do in between the day job. Food blogs are crazy competitive. You have to be able to cook, have a unique angle, be a writer and a world-class photographer. Promote your pants off. Preferably have a hot husband and cute kids to smile in pictures around the table so you look super wholesome. I can't take a good picture to save my life. I'd have to hire the cute husband and kids. And wholesome is a ship I never wanted to sail on. So I just dabble."

"We can't get you the husband or make you Betty

Crocker, but maybe Liv can give you a few tips on the photography if you want to do more than dabble," Taryn suggested between bites.

"Or I could take some pictures for you." Liv's words were out before she could stop them.

"Ooh," Kincaid said, perking up. "Really? I would love that. I can never get the lighting right. The deep-fried mac and cheese that I made last week looked like something a dog leaves on your lawn." She took a bite of her bacon. "But do you have the time? You said you work insane hours."

"I do." Liv frowned. "But I'm thinking of firing up the camera again on weekends, maybe taking on a few projects."

"Really?" Kincaid's expression lit—dangerously.

"What?" Liv asked after Kincaid continued to beam at her. "Why are you looking at me like that?"

Kincaid clasped her hands together like a happy child. "Oh my God. You're doing your letter!"

"I—"

"You are, aren't you?" Taryn said, her smile spreading wide. "Damn. Now I'm going to look like a slacker. One day in, and you're all in mission mode. Get it, girl."

"I'm not in mission mode. I'm just…dipping a foot in. No, not even a foot. A toe. I'm dipping a toe."

"No, no, this is good," Kincaid said, shoving her plate aside, pancakes forgotten. "It's not a toe dip. Don't downplay it. This is like…a call to action. You're throwing down gauntlets and shit. Go, Liv!"

Liv rolled her eyes. "There are no gauntlets. How were you not in drama club?"

"I have a hard time being anyone but myself,"

Kincaid said with a dismissive flick of her hand. "But I'm serious. We should all make a vow to do something from our letters."

Rebecca snorted and stabbed a piece of waffle like it had personally offended her. "Yeah, okay, let me get right on that. Any big political jobs just dying to have me? Any hot guys with husband potential wandering around? No? Okay."

"The cook looks pretty cute," Taryn offered. "I mean, if face tattoos are your thing."

Rebecca grabbed a blueberry off her plate and chucked it at Taryn, who laughed and batted it away, almost knocking her glasses off her face in the process.

"No, I'm serious," Kincaid said. "A husband or job change might be tough right out of the gate, but what about the dog you wanted? You could get a dog."

Rebecca's expression went deadpan. "I'm not getting a dog."

Kincaid shook her head with a *tsk*. "There is a dog somewhere in a shelter who will go to a mean family with kids who will torment him if you don't adopt him this weekend. Think about that, Rebecca. Bartholomew is waiting for you. Looking for a nice, calm house and a woman he can cuddle with. Are you going to let him down? Are you going to break his little, orphan doggy heart?"

Rebecca gasped and turned to Kincaid. "That is beyond messed up. You are laying dog guilt on me—about an *imaginary* dog."

"Doesn't have to be imaginary."

"Kincaid, stop," Liv said. "No guilt trips. If we do stuff in our letters, it's because we want to. We can't be forced into it."

"Fine." Kincaid lifted her hands and tipped her chin up. "I will leave sweet, orphaned Bartholomew out of this."

Rebecca's blue eyes narrowed. "I hate you so much right now."

Kincaid leaned over and smacked an air kiss next to Rebecca's cheek. "It comes from a place of love, Becs."

"Uh-huh."

Taryn sipped her coffee. "Outside of dog guilt, I think it's a good idea, but I'd need some time to think through what I'd want to do."

Liv nodded. Taryn's letter had been a lot more academic than theirs. She'd promised to figure out why the tragedy had happened so she could help with prevention. Out of all of them, she'd gotten the closest to following that path by becoming a forensic psychologist. But she was asking a question that might not have a real answer—at least not one that could be uncovered.

"Maybe it doesn't have to be about tackling some letter," Rebecca said, drawing all their attention. "I mean, my life is fine. I don't need a dog or to turn my world upside down or to switch jobs. I don't need the husband either. But maybe what I could use is…this."

Liv leaned back in the booth. "This?"

"You three." Rebecca shrugged, her gaze shifting downward like her plate had become super interesting. "I'm not going to lie. This still feels a little weird since we haven't seen each other in so long, and I'm not exactly a Ya-Ya Sisterhood kind of girl. But y'all are different from the friends I have now. They're mostly coworkers and mostly men, and there's all this competition wrapped up into it. Being around you three is much more…relaxed."

"You mean with the busting into hotel rooms and the cops being called? We're super low drama," Kincaid teased.

Rebecca tilted her head in a come-on-now look. "I just mean that I don't have to be *on* all the time, watching what I say, how I say it, how I come across. I don't have to be professional with a capital *P*. It's nice."

Liv considered her. Rebecca had been the over-achiever as long as Liv had known her. Rebecca had cried in fourth grade when she'd gotten a B on her report card. And it was no secret that her dad was some high-falutin' attorney and didn't accept less than the best from his kid. Liv had her own brand of pressure from her family, but she couldn't imagine how it must've been to feel like a failure if you didn't knock it out of the park every time on every play.

Kincaid leaned into Rebecca and bumped shoulders with her. "Are you saying you miss us, Becs?"

She rolled her eyes. "Some of you."

Kincaid grinned.

"It's not just that, though. That year afterward, we had each other's backs. There was no judgment. No bullshit. It was just...space to be whatever we needed to be right then. People who wouldn't bail on you even when you were messing up. I miss having that."

Liv's chest tightened, memories of those months after pressing down on her. The night after her mother's funeral when they'd dragged Liv out to see a midnight movie marathon at the dollar theater and didn't judge her when she snot-cried at the funny parts. Or the morning she and Taryn had picked up a banged-up Kincaid from a police station in Austin after she'd gotten in a fight at some frat party where she wasn't supposed to be. The day they'd gotten Rebecca drunk on cherry wine when her father had told her she had to go to his alma mater instead of the college she wanted most. They'd let each other see the ugly stuff—the thing best friends did for one another even though they'd never declared themselves as such.

Liv swallowed past the growing knot in her throat, the memories driving home the realization that she didn't have people like that in her life anymore. She had friends, people she liked and had fun with, but none she'd trust with her secrets. None who would've offered to braid her hair after a panic attack like Kincaid had last night. Even her dad had conditions on their relationship. She'd found that out in college.

"I think you're right," Liv said, tapping Rebecca's foot beneath the table to get her to look up. Liv gave her what she hoped was an encouraging smile. "Step one needs to be not letting another decade pass with us being strangers. I miss this, too."

Kincaid sat up straighter, eyes bright. "Is it weird that I just had the deepest urge to put our hands together at the center of the table and do some 'All for one' cheer?"

"Yes," they all said in unison and then laughed.

"No cheering." Rebecca gave Kincaid a look and used her lawyer tone. "I have my limits."

Kincaid was unfazed. "Fine. But y'all realize this is a binding agreement now? I will hunt you down if you three disappear on me again."

"I believe you," Taryn said and leaned over to Liv and mock-whispered, "That bitch is crazy."

Liv nodded. "And that from a licensed professional."

Kincaid beamed. "Stop going on and on about how much y'all love me." She pulled out her phone. "Now, let's start by getting something set up for pictures. I have an epic pancake blog I need to plan now. You ladies can eat the spoils of war if you want to join me and Liv."

Liv's phone vibrated on the table, and she glanced down at the screen where the word *Office* flashed. She silenced it and frowned. She'd sent an email to her boss telling him she wouldn't be in until late afternoon. "We'll set something up soon. I have to get into the office and see what's on my docket, but hopefully I can free up this weekend or the next."

"No problem. I can be pretty flexible unless I have a showing or open house scheduled. Would you want me to come to your place and cook? I live on the other side of the lake, so it'd be a drive for you. I don't mind going into Austin if that makes it easier."

"My place won't work. I have a shoebox kitchen in my apartment, and I need a change of scenery to get out of my creative rut." Liv shifted her gaze to her food. "I plan to…stay in Wilder on the weekends. So, I can come to you."

"Wait. You're staying in *Wilder*?" Taryn asked, dark brows lifting.

Liv shoved a bite of food in her mouth and shrugged.

"Like the same Wilder Finn's heading to?" Kincaid's voice had a little bit too much lilt in it. "Neighbors?"

"Something like that," Liv mumbled. Thankfully, her phone buzzed again before Kincaid could push, and this time Liv grabbed for it like the lifeline it was. "Sorry, I have to take this."

She excused herself from the table and put the phone

to her ear. But not before she heard Kincaid say to the others, "We've got to up our game. Liv's about to tackle a letter item *and* her football player. She's officially become my patron saint."

Liv didn't have time to respond. Her boss's voice making demands in her ear drowned out everything else.

"Pres—" She'd tried to say she was not in Austin and that she'd be there later today, but Preston wasn't hearing any of it.

Office. Now. That was the only option he gave her.

She sighed and agreed to be there as soon as she could.

Apparently, she'd muted her real life long enough.

It was getting restless.

chapter
TEN

Finn dumped a load of sheets into the washer, music blasting from his phone, and poured in detergent. The mundane task was a soothing ritual he'd performed a number of times over the last few days while making the lake house livable. Livable first, and then he'd start working on the minor repair issues. He'd told his friend who owned the place that he'd get the house in shape so that it could go on the market in the fall. The guy thought Finn was doing him a favor, but Finn needed that kind of physical work to keep from going stir-crazy. Hopefully, it would work.

After two years of always being on the move, of being in life-or-death situations, of needing to be on alert one hundred percent of the time, he was having trouble getting used to the quiet solitude of the lake house. Logically, he knew he needed the downtime, but his body craved the adrenaline, the challenge. In between chores, he'd tried to substitute punishing workouts and long runs around the lake to feed that part of him. But he still couldn't fully settle down.

Finn turned the knob to get the sheets going, and the loud rock music he'd been playing cut off, interrupted by a text message notification. He grabbed his phone from the laundry room shelf, expecting a check-in from his boss or a reminder to call in for his weekly chat with Doc Robson. Instead, he saw a different name lighting the screen: Olivia.

> **Liv:** How goes it, Batman?

The simple message curved his lips, the sight of Liv's name an odd relief, like taking a full breath after a long run. He flipped off the light and stepped out of the laundry room. He hadn't heard from her in days beyond a brief *chat soon* message, and he'd started to wonder if their conversation in the car had been all talk, if she'd come to her senses. His thumbs moved over the screen.

> **Finn:** Is this u checking on me to make sure I haven't mounted the head of a desk clerk on my wall?
> **Liv:** Basically

He chuckled in the quiet kitchen, the setting sun's rays cutting orange stripes over the granite countertops.

> **Finn:** His head is still attached though I suspect there's not much in it
> **Liv:** Good job. Everything else ok?

He hated that she was worried about him, hated that he'd given her reason to be. That was not who he was.

He was the one who took care of things, the one who handled whatever came at him no matter the circumstances. Not the guy who couldn't be trusted to control his actions.

> **Finn:** Yep. Haven't left Wilder. Just getting the place ready for habitation. My friend hasn't stayed here for a while, so lots of freshening up to do. And now I sound like my grandmother...
>
> **Liv:** U should get some potpourri & needlepoint throw pillows
>
> **Finn:** Hush, Arias
>
> **Liv:** What about a creepy Jesus painting? My grandma might've cornered the market on those, tho
>
> **Finn:** Creepy Jesus might be awesome
>
> **Liv:** No! *Still has nightmares of his eyes following me around* Jesus is watching, man. WATCHING.

Finn laughed as he grabbed a beer from the fridge and then made his way to the living room. He opened the bottle and stretched out on the couch, his mood lifting at the image of Liv reacting to his last comment, eyes big and smile wide.

> **Finn:** Fine. No creepy Jesus. U have no sense of style. So R U going 2 B seeing my needlepoint pillows soon?
>
> **Liv:** Is that flirting?

Was it? Probably. Even though he wasn't supposed to be doing that with her. For some reason, he couldn't help it with Liv. It didn't even have to be sexual—though who was he kidding? That was always there. But she made him...playful.

No one who knew him now would describe him as playful.

> **Finn:** I get all the girls w/ my needlepoint. Just wait til I show u my crochet.
> **Liv:** My eyes just substituted a totally different word for crochet
> **Finn:** Now who's flirting?
> **Liv:** Am not! UR a bad influence

Finn took a long pull on his beer and smirked.

> **Finn:** Truth. But I promise best behavior when u visit. I turned u down the other night, remember? This isn't an attempt to get u in a compromising position.
> **Liv:** So now I'm not worthy of compromising? Whatever, Dorsey. *Flips hair*

Finn groaned despite knowing she was only playing the game and joking around. Just the thought of her on the other end of the line had warmth gathering low. Liv curled up on her couch after work, legs tucked under her, hair loose around her shoulders. Was she laughing at his jokes, picturing him in her mind like he was picturing her? How would she be if he were there next to her having this conversation? Would she still flirt so boldly? Would she blush when he teased back? Would her body react to his words the way his reacted to hers?

He shifted on the couch and adjusted his jeans, painfully aware of just how easily her words could get to him, but he didn't want to make it awkward. He could play this game. He could pretend this wasn't affecting him.

> **Finn:** I would compromise u so hard, Arias, u wouldn't be able to compromise w/ anyone else for weeks
> **Liv:** Weird. I found that oddly hot.
> **Finn:** Oddly Hot is my FBI code name

There wasn't a response for a few seconds, and he wondered if he'd taken it too far. But just when he was about to type something else to shift the conversation, her message appeared.

> **Liv:** Sorry, just spit water on my screen & my coworkers are looking at me like I've lost my mind. I shouldn't text w/ u at work. UR going to get me in trouble.
> **Finn:** UR still at work?
> **Liv:** I'm always at work.
> **Finn:** How's the weekend looking?
> **Liv:** Not great. Been nuts here. Crisis w/ a big account & my boss has been out most of the week so had to pick up slack. I can't see getting caught up by Friday. But next weekend is a good possibility.

Finn frowned. Three days had passed since he'd dropped off Liv at the hotel. He'd been worried that it'd been a bad idea to invite her to stay across the driveway. But now that the possibility seemed to slip further away with her back in her real life, he found himself itching to make it happen.

> **Finn:** Sounds good. No pressure. Just need to know if I should clean out the room over the pool house next.

There. That sounded neutral enough, he hoped.

> **Liv:** Outlook is good. Freshen away. I expect mints on my pillow.
> **Finn:** Don't have mints but do have a Costco-size bag of Starbursts because…priorities.
> **Liv:** Score! Leave me the pink ones. Burn the lemon.

He laughed again and rested his head against the arm of the couch, feeling better than he had in a long-ass time.

> **Finn:** Get back to work & stop slacking. I want u here next weekend & those websites aren't going to build themselves.
> **Liv:** Websites are lazy bastards. And u get back to not working, which for Recluse Dude means what? Beer & porn?
> **Finn:** You. Don't. Want. To. Know.

He said it as a joke. But based on the suddenly tight fit of his jeans, it was more accurate than he wanted to admit. He was turning back into a teenager where just a few flirty words from the beautiful Liv Arias had him pent up and hard.

Pathetic. He needed to get that shit under control before she got here, or he was going to embarrass himself.

Liv: See u soon, Batman.

The screen went dark, and Finn blew out a breath, staring at the ceiling and willing his body to behave. If a PG-rated text conversation did this to him, what was it going to be like knowing Liv was just across the driveway? He closed his eyes and drained the rest of his beer.

Masochist. He was a goddamned masochist.

A week later, Liv stared at her screen, her eyes trying to close as she adjusted the aspect ratio on a header for the hundredth time. One of her most important clients had changed her mind ten different times on how she wanted the home page to look, and now nothing was looking right to Liv. She'd worked twelve-hour days, including last weekend, and now her brain was staging a protest, marching around with signs and blocking any solutions.

It hadn't helped that she'd barely slept the last few days. Since agreeing to spend weekends at Finn's, she'd felt a constant hum of anxiety, which was making her wonder if she was doing the right thing. A whisper of unease could quickly turn into an all-out panic fest if she wasn't careful. She could feel that old monster breathing down her neck, just waiting for a crack in the curtains so it could slip back into her life and take over.

She reached for her water and took a long drink, trying to tamp down the infiltrating thoughts. She didn't have time to sit here and worry. She needed to focus. Work. That was what had saved her in the first place. That was what she was good at.

Texting with Finn was a fun distraction—a really fun distraction—but her life wasn't set up to be away every weekend.

She leaned back in her squeaky office chair and sighed. Lying to herself wasn't going to get her anywhere.

Yes, she was busy. Her job was important to her. But she was also scared.

Really freaking scared.

She'd avoided anything to do with Long Acre for so long that this felt like charging into the fire without protection. She wouldn't be in her hometown, but she'd be right by it. She'd be with high school friends. She'd pick up her camera for the first time in forever. She'd be with Finn.

Nerves rippled over her, making her hands tremble.

She swallowed past the knot in her throat and glanced down at her phone, reading through the conversation Finn had started with her over lunch today.

Finn: Got all the rats & pestilence out of the pool house. It *could* be haunted, but I doubt the spirits mean any harm.

Liv: So if I visit this weekend, I get 2 B a woman in a gothic horror novel? Do u have a sick recluse I'm supposed 2 take care of? Or maybe a child that stares at me & doesn't talk?

Finn: A recluse. But I'm not sick.

Liv: Just ur sense of humor?

Finn: Yes, that's definitely sick

Finn: So is my guest going 2 B checking in?

Liv: Preston's back later today, have 2 make
sure he doesn't need me this weekend.

If only she could feel as breezy and confident as she appeared in her texts. She sighed and glanced toward her boss's office. Preston still wasn't back from his meetings, and she had a feeling she knew what he was going to say anyway. He wasn't going to give her a pass on finishing this project. If it wasn't done by the end of the day tomorrow, she'd be expected to work on it over the weekend.

So she had two choices: use that as an excuse for Finn, or bust her ass to get her work done and go to Wilder.

Her fingers moved over her phone screen.

Liv: U sure u still want me there? Seems like
ur doing OK now.

The words glared back at her from the screen, calling her a coward as she waited for Finn's response. A few minutes passed before her phone vibrated again.

Finn: There's no obligation. I told u that. But
u weren't coming just for me.

She sighed.

Liv: Stop pointing out true things

Finn: I'll try to lie more

Liv: OK. Sorry. Will let u know what my boss says.

Another minute passed before his response came.

Finn: U don't have to do this, u know. I want u here, but if ur not ready, I get it. The last thing I want to do is force or guilt u into something. U can say no. I'm not going to hold it against u.

She stared at the words, at the easy permission. *You can say no. You can walk away. You can go back to your life and forget this happened. You were doing just fine. Why mess it up?*

She put her head in her hands and groaned.

"Hey, Ms. Moreno, you okay?"

After Finn calling her Arias for the last few days, the surname she'd used for years suddenly sounded odd to her ears. Ms. Moreno. Her mother's maiden name, not hers. She lifted her head, finding one of the interns eyeing her with concern. She forced a smile. "Yeah, I'm fine, Skye. It's just been a long week."

Skye winced. "Then maybe I shouldn't tell you that Mrs. Gill is here and she wants to chat with you in person about more changes." She glanced over her shoulder and then lowered her voice. "She brought color swatches for the redesign, and they are fugly."

"Fantastic." Liv pinched the bridge of her nose. "Bring her back."

Skye nodded and hurried off.

Liv glanced at her phone, at the message glaring back at her. She should respond to Finn. She owed him that. But she had no idea what to say.

chapter
ELEVEN

FINN JOLTED AWAKE, THE BUZZ OF HIS VIBRATING CELL PHONE loud against the coffee table, and his computer almost sliding off his lap to the floor. He got a grip on it, cursing, and moved it out of the way before sitting up.

He rubbed a hand over his face, trying to clear the fuzz in his head, and glanced at the clock above the television. Almost one in the morning. Messages at that time never brought good news. He reached for the phone and saw this one was from Liv.

Liv: Are u uninviting me, Finn Dorsey?

Finn let out a breath, the fogginess from sleep fading quickly with the sight of Liv's name on the screen. She'd never responded after his message earlier today. He'd figured that'd been answer enough. But now...

Was he uninviting her? He had, sort of. He could feel her stress and had relieved her of the obligation. If she didn't want to be here, he didn't want her to feel guilty about it. She didn't owe him anything.

> **Finn:** U seem 2 B buried at work. Didn't want this to interfere.

There was a long pause, and he wondered if he'd lost his signal, but finally the dots indicating an incoming response appeared on the screen.

> **Liv:** Have a project I must wrap up. But if the invitation stands, I can be there by late afternoon Sat., stay Sunday & take vacation Monday. If it doesn't stand, I'm calling ur mom & telling her how rude her son is & I'm calling ur boss to tell him u lied.

His lips twitched. She had no idea how to contact Billings, but he didn't put it past it her to give it her best shot. *Dear Someone Named Billings at the FBI, Finn Dorsey is a dickhead.*

> **Finn:** The welcome mat is still out. I'll even order pizza to celebrate ur arrival.
> **Liv:** Fancy.
> **Finn:** If u want fancy, I'll add hot wings to the order
> **Liv:** If u don't add hot wings AND beer, ur doing it wrong.

He chuckled, and the sound echoed through the silent living room.

Finn: Noted. So it's OK to take off Monday?

There was another long pause.

Liv: Should be. Unless that's not cool w/ u. I don't want to interrupt grumpy recluse time.

A ripple of warmth spread through him, catching him off guard with its potency. Two and a half days with Liv.

Finn: Works for me. I have the rest of the week 2 B a grumpy recluse.
Liv: U should start growing ur beard out now. No self-respecting recluse would walk around w/ just scruff.
Finn: I'll work on it
Liv: Sorry if I woke u. I thought u'd have ur phone off & would get the message in the morning.
Finn: I was working late too.
Liv: Ur not supposed 2 B doing that. Clearly, u need me there to keep u in check.

Finn glanced at his laptop. Imagined it was Liv sitting there instead. Didn't hate the idea.

Finn: Ur right. I can't be trusted.
Liv: No more work. Go get some sleep. I'll see u Saturday & I'll bring the beer.
Finn: Deal.

They ended the chat, and something restless settled

inside Finn, like a sleepy dog that had been turning
in circles and had finally lain down. It was done. She
would be here this weekend. Now he just had to figure
out how not to fuck it up.

———~~~———

On Saturday morning, Liv flexed her fingers against the
steering wheel and tried to will away the impulse to turn
the car around and head back the other way. She'd never
gotten a chance to talk to her boss, but late Thursday
night after listening to Mrs. Gill wax on about all the
changes she wanted, Liv had hit a wall. She needed a
break. She deserved one. And she decided she wasn't
going to let the fear keep her chained to her desk for
another weekend when Finn, the lake, and her camera
were waiting for her.

So she'd worked a long day on Friday and had let
Preston's assistant know she wouldn't be in this weekend and was taking a vacation day on Monday. Then,
she'd bailed without waiting for official approval. She
had a glut of vacation days. She should be able to use
them. But breaking the rules had dumped an edgy dose
of adrenaline into her blood. It was something old Liv
would have done. She wasn't sure if that was a good or
bad thing.

Either way, she was really doing this. Taking a risk.
Not just staying with Finn, but all of it—taking her
camera out, exposing herself to memories she'd locked
away in her past, putting her job stuff aside when she
really should be working all weekend.

Go, me.

Liv rolled her shoulders and took in the passing

scenery, watching the land swell and ebb in the rolling terrain of the Hill Country. Long Acre had gotten its name because it occupied a flat piece of land tucked into an otherwise hilly part of Texas. That kept the tourists out for the most part: *Yawn, flat land*. But it gave the residents the option of affordable housing still within commuting distance of Austin, albeit an inconvenient hour commute. And it gave the more well-off folk access to lake houses in nearby Wilder for the weekends and summer. It had been a best-kept secret. Until it was national news. Then no one wanted to move there at all. Like the town had caught the tragedy disease and was now bound to have another, so must be avoided.

Stupid.

Signs for Wilder Lake appeared, and Liv took the exit. The businesses switched from national chains to the more eclectic—an odd mix of rustic home-style restaurants, gas stations advertising Fresh Kolaches, and hipster joints (Vegan! Farm-to-Table! Tapas!) that proved the Austin weekend getaway crowd still rolled through here on their way to the sexier tourist stops. Mixed in were the essentials—a small grocery store, a bait-and-tackle shop, and a liquor store.

This was the area the wealthier kids used to head off to on weekends. Parties at parents' lake houses. Bonfires on the shores. Skinny-dipping. Getting drunk and camping under the stars. Far enough out that you felt like you'd escaped town, but really only a short car ride away. Liv had visited Wilder a lot growing up but had only been to one lake party in high school. Her sophomore year, she'd tagged along with a girl from her art class and had promptly regretted the decision when the girl had disappeared with her boyfriend and left Liv on her own with nothing to do and easy access to Jell-O shots.

Liv had gone on a drunken walk to get away from the heat of the bonfire and had stumbled upon one of the *Let's go find someplace more quiet* spots. That'd been the first time she'd seen Finn outside of school. He'd been laid out on a couple of beach towels, a senior girl draped on top of him. The girl's hands were up Finn's shirt, and Finn's fingers were in her hair. Making out like the other person owed them their air.

Liv's head had been swimming already, but seeing that, she'd just stopped and stared. She hadn't gotten past the awkward-kiss stage with any guy by that point, so the whole scene had seemed scandalous—but oddly fascinating. She'd had the urge to photograph it, all those angles and curves and hands. Until the girl caught Liv watching and called her a freak. Liv had apologized and had fallen down while trying to hurry away. Even in her drunken state, she'd known she'd broken some major social rule.

She'd hoped to escape unscathed. Everyone was drinking. No one would remember. But it wasn't meant to be. Finn had come after her, asking if she was all right. He'd found her bent over, vomiting in the bushes. Fun times.

But he'd held her hair. Like they were friends. Like he cared.

She hadn't been able to say a damn thing to him beyond a mumbled thanks, but she'd never forgotten the kindness.

Liv shook off the memory, ignoring the pang it caused in her gut, and turned on her blinker to take the exit that would lead to the lake. The main drag of shops and restaurants disappeared in the rearview. Next stop: Finn's. A knot of tension gathered between her shoulders as the road narrowed and trees tangled above.

When she rounded a curve, the lake came into view, glittering like cut glass from the late-afternoon sun. A few birds were diving into it to find their dinner. But the bucolic scene did nothing to calm Liv's nerves.

When she saw the address on the mailbox, she turned into the driveway of an impressive house of cedar and hand-cut stone and parked next to Finn's black Expedition. Blue and yellow wildflowers lined the path to the door, and the address numbers were carved directly into a fat rock at the end of the path, along with the name of the house—*Stillwater*. Because apparently rich people liked to name their homes. This was to be her humble abode for her summer weekends.

"Okay, maybe I am crazy," she muttered.

She had a moment where she considered turning around and canceling it all, but then the door opened. Finn stepped onto the porch in jeans and an army-green T-shirt, damp-haired and a little dirty, as if he'd be working on something. He leaned against the post, arms crossed and an unreadable expression on his face. Liv's belly did a flip, and she tried to tamp down her body's automatic response to the man.

"Shit." Did he always have to look so good? Maybe he *should* grow the scraggly recluse beard. For her own protection. As a damn public service.

He raised a hand in silent greeting. Liv climbed out of the car and lifted the six-pack of Shiner Bock in response.

He smiled and swept his arm toward the house. "You have brought the proper sacrifice to gain entry."

She gave an exaggerated curtsy. "I wouldn't dare enter without it."

He laughed and sidled down the walk, his gait casual. He was comfortable here. He swiped his hands on the back of his jeans and took the beer from her, saving her the awkward decision of to hug or not to hug.

"Damn, it's good to see you," he said, his voice genuine. "I'd greet you in a more appropriate way than stealing your beer, but I'm filthy."

"Yes, I know. You've been texting me."

He grinned, dimple appearing. "Different kind of filthy. I'm helping my friend get this place back in shape so he can sell it. I decided to rebuild the fire pit down by the shore, but it took longer than I thought. Or my skills are rusty. Probably both. I haven't worked with my hands in a while."

She bit the inside of her lip, remembering what other things he hadn't done in a while. Although based on their kiss at the restaurant, those skills weren't rusty at all. "No worries."

"I'll need to grab a shower before dinner, but I've got your room all ready." He cocked his head toward the property beyond. "Where's your stuff? We can get you settled in before dinner."

"Suitcase in the back seat. Camera gear in the trunk. I can get the equipment if you can grab my bag."

"Got it." Finn set the beer on the roof of her car, then pulled Liv's suitcase and backpack from the back seat. "I ordered the pizza. And wings, of course."

"Excellent."

Finn hoisted her backpack over his shoulder. "I'm glad you were able to get away. You sounded slammed."

Liv busied herself with her stuff and avoided his gaze, trying to ignore the pang of guilt she felt for bailing on work. "Yep. But I'm always crazy busy. The work will still be there on Tuesday."

"True. I've learned that's a well that never runs dry. Work always fills whatever space you give it."

"So it seems."

He jabbed a thumb behind him. "This way to the pool house."

Finn took most of the heavy stuff, leaving Liv with a shoulder bag, her precious camera, and the beer. She followed him up the drive, past a wrought-iron gate, and when she turned the corner, all her breath whooshed out of her. A small, dark-blue swimming pool sparkled in the middle of the backyard, but beyond that was the wide expanse of the lake reflecting back the orange-pink sky.

And the sound. She wanted to wrap herself up in the sounds. Gently lapping water, a breeze whispering through the trees, a few birds twittering happy songs. It was all so different from her normal soundtrack of passing cars and city noise. She'd forgotten how quiet the lake could be.

"Wow, this is gorgeous."

Finn looked back over his shoulder at her. "This is my favorite time of the day. The water looks like it's on fire." He squinted at the lake. "I remember sitting out here in summers, fishing off the pier, and watching the sun dip below the tree line as everything went dark.

I always felt like I was in another time when I came out here. Someplace that real life couldn't touch."

Protected from real life. She could use a big heaping dose of that right now. "Is that why you wanted to be out here now?"

She followed him up a set of wooden steps that led to the room above the windowed pool house and set her bags on the small landing. He shrugged, keeping his back to her as he dug out a key. "Maybe. It's definitely better than a random apartment in Virginia."

He swung open the door and flipped on a light, illuminating a one-room studio with whitewashed plank walls. She stepped inside behind him and looked around. There was a small living area with a navy-blue couch, an efficiency kitchen to the right, and the bed against the far back wall, made up with white sheets, a soft-looking quilt, and a big pile of pink Starbursts on top. A lamp glowed on the table beside the bed, painting the room in warm light.

"I know it's small but—"

"It's adorable," she finished. And it was. Cozy and welcoming. Like him—the man who'd picked out all the pink candies for her. She set her things down and walked over to the window across from the couch. It looked out on the south side of the lake, giving her a fantastic view of the hills on the other side. "And you can't beat the view."

"No, you can't," he said quietly.

She turned and found him watching her. She rubbed her lips together. "Bathroom?"

He pointed toward the bed area. "Pocket door in the back corner. No bathtub, but a shower and all the other necessities. If you prefer a bath, there's a jetted one in the main house you can use."

A jetted bath. At his place. She cleared her throat. "Showers are fine. I'm not here for a luxury vacation. Just need a place to sleep in between working and keeping you out of trouble."

He ran a hand over the back of his head. "Right. Okay, well, I'm going to grab a shower and wait for the pizza while you get settled. I'll let you know when it's here."

She nodded. "Sounds good."

He stared at her for another few seconds, as if he wanted to say something else, but then nodded. "All right."

He headed to the door.

"Finn."

He turned. "Hmm?"

"Thank you for this." She tucked her hands in her back pockets, feeling awkward. "I know this wasn't your plan—to have a guest. It wasn't mine either, but I appreciate it. I probably wouldn't have taken the plunge otherwise."

He shrugged. "Yeah, you would've. You wouldn't have let that letter go unanswered. Not the Liv I know." His gaze met hers. "But for what it's worth, I'm glad I get to be here to watch you do it."

With that, he stepped outside and shut the door behind him, leaving just his scent behind—a heady combo of fresh-cut grass and man. She moved to the window on the opposite side of the room and watched him walk up the stone path that led to the back door of the main house. She sighed and rested her forehead against the glass. She was in so much damn trouble.

chapter
TWELVE

FINN WATCHED HIS ROCK PLUNK INTO THE WATER AFTER ONE sad skip on the surface and cursed as the ripple circled out, marking his defeat. "That rock was defective."

Liv burst into a laugh beside him, the sound drifting over the dark lake and echoing. She turned to him, her expression dancing in the flickering light from the fire pit. "You are seriously the worse rock skipper I've ever seen. That rock was the perfect skipping rock. I gave you the best one. It could've won awards for Most Awesome Rock."

"Worst rock ever," he said with mock severity.

She bent forward and laughed harder, her beer clutched against her waist, and he allowed himself a moment to watch her. Jubilant expression, pale-blue T-shirt clinging to full, soft breasts, and long, tan legs making khaki shorts look like lingerie. Unfairly sexy. She'd been pretty in high school. Quirky cool. But now she was just flat-out beautiful.

And successful. And hella smart.

And off-fucking-limits.

He dragged his gaze away before his brain started weaving fantasies about sweeping her off her feet and carrying her into the house, spreading her across his bed, and making up for all the hurt he'd caused her with orgasms. For every second of pain he'd brought her, he'd pay her back with pleasure—with his mouth, his tongue, his cock—until she was limp and smiling and all his.

Stop.

"Aw, don't make that face," she teased, taking his grimace for something else. "It's okay to lose to a girl."

He sniffed and sipped his beer. "This isn't about you being a girl. This is about you stacking the deck."

They'd eaten their pizza and wings by the shore in a set of Adirondack chairs that flanked the new fire pit, and they were now each working on their second beer. Liv had been the one to propose the rock-skipping contest—apparently, because she was some secret rock-skipping champion. She'd managed a solid four skips with her last attempt. Despite his words, Finn didn't care that he was losing miserably. Seeing her so entertained at his ineptitude was worth it.

"If this were a fishing contest, I'd be kicking your ass, Livvy. Just wait. I'm putting that on the agenda tomorrow."

Her eyes crinkled at the corners, and she waggled her fingers. "Oh, I'm scared now. How many fish have you caught in the last few days, Big Talker?"

"Three."

"Ooh, three." She sipped her beer, still smiling. "I'm sufficiently intimidated now."

"You should be. I think all three times it was the same fish. I keep putting him back, but he has a death wish."

She snorted. "Poor guy. Not the smartest of the school, huh? *Ooh, it's that bright, shiny thing again! Oh. Damn.*"

He chuckled. "And now I won't be able to eat him. You've given him a personality."

"Mr. Tough FBI Guy is sympathetic to a fish?" Liv put her hand to her chest with a dramatic flourish, no qualms about teasing him. "I'm shocked."

Finn attempted a wry smile, but the effect of her standing there so relaxed was too distracting. How long had it been since he was able to be so unguarded with another person? Even outside his undercover work, he couldn't remember the last time things had felt so easy with someone. She made him feel like that kid he used to be. And like that kid, he wanted to reach out and pull her to him, taste the beer on her lips, feel her smiling against his mouth.

He looked away, pretending to stare at the lake. "Don't tell my boss. You'll ruin my street cred."

"Right. Street cred." She got quiet for a moment, and he sensed her watching him. "How did you deal with that kind of thing undercover? I imagine you had to be pretty ruthless."

Unease moved through him and he glanced at her, finding her expression curious but without judgment. He squatted down, busying himself with finding another rock. "Ruthless was the name of the game. Showing any emotion besides anger could be deadly. Showing sympathy was as dangerous as showing fear. I had to…turn off those parts of myself."

"Sounds tough."

He picked up a rock and squeezed it. "It was at first, but then it got easy. Too easy, probably."

When he'd put a bullet in Dragonfly's second-in-command, he'd barely felt a blip on his moral radar. Yes, the guy had been a threat and would've killed Finn without thought. But if Finn could do the same, how different were they, really?

"Which is why your boss is worried," Liv concluded.

"Yeah," Finn said, a familiar dread moving through him. A dread that whispered that he could never go back, that promised him he'd shut off machinery that couldn't be switched back on.

She crouched next to him, selected a different rock, and then gently pried his fingers open.

He lifted his gaze to meet hers. She placed her rock in his palm next to his rock and gave him a soft smile. "I'm not worried."

He curled his fingers around the stones, catching her fingers in the process. "Why not?"

"Because you mean it when you say you'd feel bad about the fish." She stood and pulled him up with her. "Now let's see if you can suck less at this rock-skipping thing. I'll show you my secret tips."

Finn didn't want to let go of her hand. Her easy certainty in him was more than he deserved…and dangerous. "Don't give me so much credit, Liv. I appreciate what you're trying to do, but you'd be horrified by some of the things I did while I was under. And more horrified by the things I looked away from and didn't step in to stop. The fish is just a fish. Don't absolve me over that."

Her jaw flexed, determination filling her eyes. "Did you kill anyone?"

"Yes."

She flinched, but the resolve didn't waver. "Who wouldn't have killed you?"

"No."

"Rape someone?"

He grimaced. "Of course not. I would never—"

"I know," she said and let go of his hand. "Don't you get that? I wouldn't be here if I suspected you'd really gone to the dark side. I get that you had to do what you had to for your job. If that meant numbing your emotions to survive, then that was the cost. You can't expect everything to snap back in place overnight. Believe me, I was a pro at numbing things. It takes a while to remember how to feel stuff again. I'm still working on it."

He let out a breath, still uncomfortable with her faith in him. "What do you mean?"

She set her beer down and shrugged. "I stopped getting wasted and getting high. I stopped sleeping around while wasted or high. That was a start. Then I focused on my career." She shook her head and frowned. "But I'm beginning to realize that the job thing has its own numbing effect. Workaholic still has *aholic* in it."

Finn rubbed his thumb over the smooth rock in his hand, considering her and honored that she'd trust him with that kind of personal information. But he could tell the admission had cost her something. He tried to think of a way to shift the focus away from such serious topics. "So this is your solution? Taking a break and agreeing to hang out with a dude who's exponentially more screwed up than you?"

She laughed under her breath—the soft sound getting devoured by the snapping of the fire—and put her hands on her hips. "Yes. Exactly. I am super brilliant."

"And super beautiful."

The second the words slipped out of his mouth, he cringed.

She blinked, her superhero pose sagging.

"Sorry," he said quickly. "I… The filter's dialed to low tonight. Ignore me and show me how to throw this damn rock."

She stared at him for a moment longer, the awkwardness tangling between them, and then nodded. "Right. Let's give it a try."

Liv's blood was thumping in her ears, almost blocking out the sounds of the night around her. The way Finn had looked at her and his words had blindsided her. But what should have sent her scrambling to reassert their boundaries had her skin heating in ways it shouldn't. Maybe it was the fire. Probably the fire.

She led him to the edge of the lake and picked up her own rock, trying to focus on the task at hand. Rock skipping. She could do rock skipping. "Okay, so I think your problem is that you're too erect."

There was a strangled sound next to her.

Shit. Shit. Wrong word. Now images were happening. Images she didn't need while trying to form words. "Uh, I mean, you're so tall, and you're standing straight when you throw. You have to crouch a little so that when you sidearm it, you're closer to the lake's surface. Like this."

She demonstrated and got her rock to skim the surface with three perfect skips. *Plink. Plink. Plink.* Plunge.

"See. Your turn."

Finn grunted. "You making it look so damn easy is only going to further injure my ego when mine sinks like an anchor."

"Positive thoughts, Dorsey. Be the rock."

He sent her a come-on-now look but shifted his stance, crouched, and threw. The rock skipped twice, then sank. Not great, but better than his previous attempts.

"Hey," she said, turning his way. "You did it."

But there was still a look of consternation on his face. "I need three."

"Maybe you should stop while you're ahead."

"Not my style." He palmed the rock she'd given him, a nice flat, smooth one, then got into position again.

The wrinkle between his brows was adorably serious, like he was trying to figure out a missile launch for NASA instead of rock skipping. He gave it a toss, and it tapped the surface. One, two, three times. With a shout, he raised his arm above his head. "Score!"

"You did it!" She whooped and joined him in the celebration, making a cheerleader vee with her arms. "Go team! I'd do a toe touch, but then we'd have to go to the hospital."

He turned to her, grinning. "Thanks, Coach. Obviously, I was too *erect*."

She choke-laughed and pressed her hand over her mouth.

"I mean, really? I slip up and say something I shouldn't, and you go with *erect* in the next sentence?" he teased. "Way to make it weird, Arias."

"Hey, *erect* is a perfectly proper word. I can't help it if your mind was in the gutter."

"I've been celibate for two years. Assume it's always there. I've set up shop and built a little gutter town. We're about to elect a mayor."

She crossed her arms and tilted her head, goading him. "So during this whole deep conversation about emotions and past trauma and recovering, your mind was really just thinking—"

"Sex, skipping rocks, beer, sex, maybe more pizza, sex."

She rolled her eyes. "Nice."

He smirked. "No, but seriously, I'll try to do better at not making this awkward. I'm not trying to make a move on you. I wanted you here for exactly the reasons I told you. No ulterior motives. I just slip up sometimes because you're...I don't know"—he swept a hand in her direction—"*you*."

She swallowed hard, trying to ignore the sizzle of awareness that sent through her. "And because you've been hard up for two years."

"Yes, that, but mostly the other thing." He shrugged, honesty in his eyes. "You hit all my buttons, Livvy. Always have. But I'm smart enough to know not to screw up what could be a great summer for both of us with something stupid like lust. I'm a big boy. I can handle myself."

"Did you just say *big* and *handle yourself*?"

He smirked, all male confidence. "Now whose mind is in the gutter? And yes on both. I'm a pro at handling myself. PhD level, in fact."

She pressed her tongue to the back of her teeth. "Okay, we need to stop."

"What?" he asked, eyes sparkling with humor. "Making embarrassing admissions?"

"No, making...hot admissions. That's too much information." Her gaze tracked down his body of its own volition, and she forced her attention away. "You said no lust. Talking about how you use your hands is not an effective strategy for that."

Lust. Like what was building up in her right now. Not just at the images he'd ruthlessly painted in her head—him going up to the house, slipping out of his clothes, and curling that strong hand around himself, stroking and taking his time, maybe thinking of her. Even more distracting was hearing him tell her that she hit his buttons, that she'd always done it for him. That something specific about her made Mr. Cool-and-in-Control slip up. She'd had guys tell her she was pretty or sexy or whatever, but she wasn't sure she'd ever heard something so...specifically personal.

She knew what he meant, though, because it was the same for her. Her reaction to him had always been visceral, an awareness that even in light moments forever hummed beneath the surface. Like power lines linked directly to her libido. She fought the urge to step into his space, to inhale how the smoke from the fire mixed with his scent, to feel the heat of him against her again. To offer to take care of any erect situations herself.

"Right, sorry," he said, his tone gruff. "This was probably safer via text. We can't let joking turn into more than it is."

"Because that would be stupid," she said, annoyed at how breathless the words came out.

"Yes."

He held her gaze for a beat too long, as if he could see her thoughts. Heat crept up her neck, but then he rubbed his hands on his jeans. "It's getting late. We should probably head back up to the house."

She nodded, mouth dry. "Sure. Good idea."

Without another word, he moved toward the fire, dousing it and tossing their trash into the grocery bag he'd hooked on the back of one of the chairs. She followed behind him, picking up what she could, but mostly watching him, her thoughts chasing each other around her head like angry cats.

Or horny cats.

She was here for a break. She was here to do photography. She was here to help Finn acclimate back to normal life. She was not here to get naked with him.

Naked.

Well, that word was the wrong one for her to think, because now she was watching how his pants slipped low in the back every time he bent to pick up a beer bottle, revealing the dips below his spine and the top curve of what was sure to be a muscular ass. She wet her lips, feeling like a pervert for ogling him, but she didn't look away.

What would happen if she walked over to him, put her hands on that exposed skin, and slid her palms underneath his T-shirt? Would he jump away? Would he lecture her about lust? Or would he let her slip his shirt off and touch her, too?

The image was almost too much, and a little grunt passed her lips.

Finn peered back over his shoulder. "You say something?"

"Uh, no."

He gave her an odd look. "If you want to go on to the guesthouse, you can. I can finish cleaning up."

"No, it's okay. I don't mind helping," she said, snapping out of her frozen state and emptying another cup of water onto the fire to make sure it was fully extinguished. She imagined that the ensuing sizzle was what her thoughts needed. Something cold and wet thrown on them.

Wet. Another word that bounded down the wrong path. Her body was more than ready for all that lust they were purposely ignoring. She stepped a little closer to him, like iron drawn by a magnetic pull. She could feel dangerous words—propositions—hovering on her lips. Recklessness welled in her, but then her foot kicked one of the empty bottles.

Alcohol. Her personal invitation to bad decisions. She hadn't had much tonight, but it was there, her old familiar pattern. Feel stressed. Drink. Get in bed with someone.

Only this someone wasn't a stranger. And there wouldn't be an anonymous *thanks for a great night, see you in the next life* in the morning. This was Finn.

She closed her eyes, inhaling a deep breath.

"Hey, you okay?"

Liv's eyes popped open to find Finn standing too close, his body heat wafting her way. He put his hand on her shoulder, and everything inside her went molten and wanting. *Kiss me*.

No. She needed to get to bed. Or into a cold shower. She was not going to act like that girl she used to be. She was not going to mess this situation up before it started.

"Yeah, I'm fine. But on second thought, I might take

you up on going to bed," she said quickly. "I barely got any sleep this week, and I'm beat."

His gaze held hers, and she got the sense he was seeing every conflicting thought in her head, but his expression turned soft. "Absolutely. Go and get some rest. I've got this."

"Thanks."

He let go of her shoulder and dug something out of his pocket. He held it out to her. "This is a key to the main house and the code for the alarm. I didn't know what to stock in your fridge or what extras you might want, so if you need anything—food, more blankets, extra towels, whatever—you're welcome to come in and grab it. Just make sure to turn off the alarm. It's on silent so it won't wake me, but it will go off if the code isn't entered within thirty seconds."

She took the key and the slip of paper from him. "Thanks, but I'm sure I won't need anything tonight. I've had more than enough."

He shrugged. "Well, just in case then."

She stepped to him, forcing herself to act like a normal human being, and leaned forward to give him a quick hug. "Good night. This was fun."

He stiffened at the hug, and she shifted to pull back, but then he let out breath, loosened his stance, and wrapped his arms around her. "Yeah. I'm glad you made it out here."

She liked the feel of him against her a little too much. He was warm and solid. Smelled vaguely of spicy chicken and campfire. So a win all around. She was lingering too long but couldn't make herself pull away. She let the side of her face press up against his shoulder. "People should hug more. This is nice."

"Liv." The word was strained, tense.

"Hmm…"

"You should go to bed."

The warning in his tone cut through her haze, and she quickly released him and took a big step back. "Right."

He grimaced and turned from her. "See you in the morning."

Her stomach tightened, his obvious need like a siren call. *Two years*. She wanted to touch him, to give him what they both craved, but he'd see it as charity and she'd wake up in the morning regretting it.

Before she could get herself in trouble, she turned on her heel and headed back up to the house, ready to plunge into an ice bath.

So much for a weekend of relaxation.

chapter

THIRTEEN

FINN SWUNG HIS FIST ACROSS HIS BODY AND LANDED A SOLID punch to the bag, relishing the force of impact that traveled up his arm and into the muscles. Exertion. A little pain. Just what he needed to get his mind off what had kept him up most of the night. Liv by the firelight, looking at him like she wanted him. Liv wrapping her arms around his waist, her body soft and warm as she hugged him. The scent of her hair in his nose, the memory of how her lips tasted still fresh in his mind. He'd gotten away in time before his dick could stand up and embarrass them both. But just barely.

Sweat dripped off him as he threw another punch, the chain holding the bag creaking with effort. He forced the images of Liv from his head and tried to picture an opponent there in front of him. A guy with a gun and a bad attitude. Just because he was on a break didn't mean he could afford to let his skills slip. He swung his leg out and landed a solid kick. Bad guy would be on the floor now, holding his gut. *Take that, asshole.*

Finn stilled the swinging bag and wiped the stinging sweat from his eyes. The early-morning rays were peeking through at the edges of the workout room's blinds and scattering across the wooden floor. He wondered if Liv was up yet. Doubtful. They'd stayed up late, and she'd had a long day. Plus, when he'd known her, she'd been a night owl, not an early bird. Images of her curled up in bed next door filled his head. What did she sleep in? A T-shirt like she'd been wearing at the hotel? Nightgown? Nothing at all?

His cock flexed in his shorts, and Finn adjusted himself with annoyance. *Focus, man.*

He'd been pent up and turned on when he'd gotten back to the house last night, but he'd refused to give himself any relief. He wasn't going to be some horny teenager, jerking off every time he hung out with a pretty girl. He had self-control now. He was a grown-ass man. He'd gone all those years undercover without sex and had survived.

But that was because staying alive and alert had been much more important. Hierarchy of needs. Staying alive trumped getting off. But now that he wasn't on constant vigilance, his libido had rushed back in with twice the force. And having Liv around was like waving a red flag at a cooped-up bull. He'd had dangerous thoughts last night when he'd gotten back to the house. Unacceptable ones. Not thoughts of romantically taking Liv to bed. But thoughts of bending her over one of those chairs, stripping her down, and taking her roughly, making her beg for her release.

He'd never force anything on a woman. He trusted himself on that. But he'd spent so many years watching sex intertwined with violence that his fantasies had taken on a much darker tone than what he'd ever been into before going under.

Liv didn't need him in her bed at all, but she certainly didn't need that rough version of him. He took another swing at the bag, his knuckles stinging with the impact. This. This would have to substitute. Wear himself down and get the frustration out on the bag.

Another kick.

But now his mind was running down a forbidden road without any help. Liv sliding down from that hug last night and getting to her knees. Those long, elegant fingers undoing his belt and jeans. Those big brown eyes looking up at him with seduction, offering him respite from his self-imposed monkhood. His fingers in her hair.

Arousal pounded through him, his erection sliding against the soft material of his shorts, his blood pumping hard.

Liv…

The morning was gorgeous. Warm but not the blazing heat it'd be in a few hours. The breeze rattled the leaves, and birds chirped happily in the trees. Liv had woken at six after a fitful night of sleep and had decided to take her camera out for an early-morning stroll along the shore.

The weight of her Canon in her hand felt like spending time with an old friend and catching up. She'd forgotten some of the quirks and settings of the camera, but after an hour of snapping shots and test-driving some of her lenses, her confidence was coming back. She braced herself on her elbows and focused her macro lens to catch a ladybug making a purposeful walk across a leaf. The quiet click of her shutter was loud in the peaceful surroundings but soothing to her. Before all the media storm with Long Acre, some of her favorite times had that sound in the background. It was nice to reclaim it as her own.

When the ladybug decided she didn't want to be a model anymore, scurrying under a bush, Liv rolled back up to her feet and brushed off her jeans. The sun's rays were getting higher, and the light pierced her eyes. She squinted and held up her hand. Her head protested in response, the dull pounding that had started a few minutes ago going into full drum-corps mode.

Ugh. She'd hoped to not disturb Finn if he wanted to sleep in, but she'd hit the point of must-have-coffee-or-perish. She was beginning to see dots in her vision, which meant a migraine threatened. If she didn't staunch it with caffeine and it hit her full force, her whole day would be a wash. She eyed the house and decided to take the risk. If she woke Finn, she'd fix him breakfast or something to make up for it.

She packed her camera in her bag and trudged up to the house. She'd tucked the key into her pocket and had memorized the code, so getting in was easy. She slipped in through the back door and found herself in an open-concept kitchen. She glanced around, taking in the living room and the small attached eating area. The house was all warm woods, stone, and glass—somehow pulling off modern and rustic at the same time. Beautiful. Elegant. And only a part-time home to someone, which seemed a damn shame.

She walked through the kitchen on silent feet and peeked down the hallway. Most of the doors were shut, and everything was quiet. Finn had to be sleeping. His SUV was still in the driveway, and the coffeepot was dry as a bone.

Trying to be as stealthy as possible, she rummaged around in the pantry to find coffee and set it up to brew. While she waited, she picked through the breakfast offerings. Cereal. Instant grits. Granola bars. Some eggs in the fridge. Her stomach rumbled in response.

Not wanting to choose anything that would require a beeping microwave or the banging of pots, she grabbed a granola bar and polished that off while the coffee percolated. But right when the brewing cycle was almost done, she heard her name.

She frowned and glanced down the hallway. The word had been muffled, but she thought she'd heard *Olivia*. Maybe the coffee had woken Finn. Or maybe she was imagining things. Cautiously, she took a few steps down the hall. Sounds came from the door at the end on the left, which was slightly ajar.

"Olivia."

Yes, definitely her name. But not calling for coffee. The grunting sound that followed it was definitely not meant for her ears.

Her breath caught, and she froze next to the door.

"Fuck." The word was utterly male, ground out in a hoarse plea, and so damn sexy that her skin flushed instantly.

Her stomach clenched, and she couldn't help but lean closer and peep through the crack in the door. There was a mirror on the wall that she could see, some sort of workout room reflecting back at her, but that's not what caught her attention.

In the reflection a broad, shirtless back filled her view. Finn. Glossy with sweat. Head bowed. Athletic shorts riding low on his hips. And arm flexing.

The view and the slick sound of what had to be a fist over flesh were almost too much for her brain to compute, but her body certainly got the message. She pressed her lips together, sensation assaulting her. Finn was braced against the wall, stroking himself mercilessly and saying her name.

Her heartbeat jumped into her throat and pumped blood to every erogenous zone. She was not watching this. Absolutely not. She shouldn't be here. She needed to leave. She needed to—

BEEP!

The coffeepot let out the shrillest, most obnoxious beep she'd ever heard, and her stomach dropped to her feet. The sound from the other side of the door stopped.

Shit. Shit. Shit.

Liv took off down the hallway, trying to get back to the kitchen before the worst happened. She skidded to a halt at the counter, heartbeat frantic, and pressed all the buttons on the machine, trying to get the thing to stop screeching.

Right when it silenced, the sound of a door squeaking open came from the end of the hallway. She cringed, trying to will herself into a calm state, trying to tame the flush heating her cheeks.

"Liv?" Finn called.

"Uh, yeah, it's me!" she said in an overly cheerful voice. "Sorry! Didn't mean to wake you! Just making coffee!"

She closed her eyes, chiding herself for turning everything into an exclamation. *No! I didn't see you getting off! I'm completely oblivious! Do you take cream or sugar?!*

The door shut again, and she managed to pour herself a cup of coffee before she heard the shower turn on. He took a few minutes, and she considered bolting but figured that would probably make her look even guiltier. When he finally stepped into the kitchen, she'd managed to down her first cup of coffee and cool her cheeks but not her too-fast heartbeat.

"Morning." The word was gruff.

She turned, pasting a smile on her face. "Hey."

He was in jeans and a white T-shirt, his hair wet and mussed from the shower. But she couldn't focus on anything but the flush of color riding high on his cheekbones. The glow.

"I didn't hear you come in. How long have you been here?" he asked.

She waved a dismissive hand, way too cheerily. "Oh, not long. Sorry if I woke you. I needed a caffeine fix but didn't realize the coffeepot doubled as a tornado siren."

His eyes met hers, evaluating. "That coffeepot's the slowest I've ever seen. You must've been here a little while."

Damn it. She kept her Stepford smile in place. "Guess I was good at being quiet and not waking you then."

She took a long sip of her second cup of coffee, wishing it were spiked with something.

"You didn't wake me. I was working out."

"Oh. Great!"

Stop. Exclaiming.

He leaned against the island and crossed his arms. "You know FBI agents are trained to spot lies, right?"

She closed her eyes. Breathed.

"How much did you hear, Liv?"

Hear. Well, at least he didn't think she'd seen him. She lifted her gaze to his and scrunched her nose. "Enough?"

"Fantastic," he groused and moved toward the coffeepot to pour his own cup. "Can we ignore that you heard anything?"

"Yep!"

"Can you stop using the cheerleader voice?"

"Yep!"

He turned and gave her a sardonic look.

"Sorry," she said, shaking her head. "I'm not sure why my voice is doing that. And I'm sorry I invaded your privacy. I really just needed some coffee."

"I should've been more aware. Usually I hear everything. I didn't think you'd be able to get in without me knowing." He took a sip of his coffee, but she didn't miss the wary look on his face.

"Well, working on that post-doc can be distracting."

He glanced up, confused for a second, and then her comment registered. "The PhD level I mentioned last night. Weren't we going to not talk about this?"

She gave him a sheepish look. "Sorry. I'll stop."

Though her thoughts didn't stop at all. Like wondering if he got to finish. Wondering what he was thinking right now. Wondering if that color in his face was from orgasm or frustration.

He gave her a look like a teacher would give a naughty student, like he knew. He nodded at her camera bag, which she'd set on the island, and blessedly changed the subject. "So you look like you've been up a while."

"Yeah, I couldn't sleep so I decided to go for a morning walkabout. Got some sunrise pics. Annoyed some wildlife."

He finally let a half-smile peek through. "That's good. Not that you couldn't sleep, but that you're already getting some camera time in."

"I'm on borrowed time, so I figured I should squeeze in as much as I can."

He nodded. "Have any particular plan of what you want to photograph today?"

She braced her hands on the island and pushed herself up to sit on it. "I don't know. I was thinking maybe I could go into town. There's an art park there. I've always preferred photographing people, but I need to flex my muscles a little first. Statues can make good subjects and don't complain that you're making them stay still too long."

Finn smirked. "They're helpful that way."

"Yeah." She shrugged. "If you're up for it, I could use the company. We could try out one of the new lunch places. Midday sunlight sucks for outdoor shots, so if we can kill some time until late afternoon, that'd be better. And I still have to grab a shower. I pretty much rolled out of bed and headed out this morning. Dawn is the magic hour. I didn't want to miss it."

He leaned against the counter, considering her over the rim of his coffee cup. "You should see yourself right now."

She tilted her head and patted her hair. "What? Am I scary bedhead or something? I've been crawling around on the ground."

"You do have grass in your hair." He laughed and leaned over to pluck out a blade. "But I mean you should see how excited you look, like a little kid preparing for Christmas. This totally does it for you."

She gripped the edge of the counter and swung her legs. "I am kind of excited. I got a kick-ass shot of a ladybug today. I know that sounds stupid—"

"It doesn't."

She rolled her lips together. "Thanks. I guess I still feel like this is kind of indulgent, putting work aside to futz around with my camera."

He pushed off the counter and tugged on a lock of her hair. "Nothing wrong with indulging sometimes."

Her lips curved. "Guess we both indulged some this morning then."

His expression darkened. "Arias."

She laughed and slid off the counter, feeling small with him towering over her. "If we can't joke about it, then it will just turn into another awkward thing. Let's not do that to ourselves. If it helps any, I worked on my post-doc last night, too."

She patted his shoulder, and his face went slack. "That doesn't help at all. That is the complete opposite of helping, Olivia."

She turned, grabbed her camera, and headed to the door, giving him a wicked grin. "Sorry. See you in a little while."

Before she stepped outside, he called out to her. "I don't remember you being this evil."

"Then your memory is failing you." She gave him a little wave and shut the door behind her, feeling lighter than she had in a while.

chapter

FOURTEEN

Finn sat on a bench in the art park, watching Liv in full concentration mode while she took shots of a bronze cowboy statue. The cowboy had his head down and his foot forever pressed back against the wall, James Dean style. Liv had the tip of her tongue sticking out between her lips and had pulled her hair into a messy bun on top of her head—all business. She'd probably forgotten he was there, which was just fine by him. He didn't mind playing audience. But the location had him on edge.

He couldn't help scanning the perimeter regularly. The art park was spread across an open stretch of land hemmed in by forest area on two sides. A running path wound along the edge of the trees and on the outskirts of the art displays. A few people milled about, and a group of runners looked to be gearing up for a race on the far side of the park. None of that should have concerned him. The neighborhood was fine. But if someone wanted a clear shot, they could just post themselves behind a tree and pick off people like in a video game.

Of course, he didn't expect anyone was out there to do it, but he couldn't turn off the internal checklist he'd learned to perform at every public location. Plus, having Liv so oblivious to her surroundings made him extra vigilant.

"Almost done with the cowboy, photog? He's looking like he needs a smoke and some beef jerky," Finn called out.

Liv glanced back at him with a smile. "Almost. I've got a few minutes of light left. Fading on me?"

He leaned back and stretched his arm over the back of the bench. "Nah, I can go all night."

She rolled her eyes. "Stop with the double entendre."

He chuckled. "Just paying you back."

Liv had set the bar this morning when she'd overheard him in the workout room. He'd been mortified that she'd heard him in such a weak moment, a moment where his body and libido had overtaken his plans to work out his frustration in the gym. But instead of making the situation painfully awkward or embarrassing, she'd teased him—and admitted she'd sought her own relief last night. Not that he was ever going to be able to get *that* distracting image out of his mind. But he appreciated her ease and openness around him. That was what had drawn them together in the past, too. No bullshit. Just being honest and playful and leaving the pretense out of it.

So even though it was a dangerous line to walk, he'd accepted that if you can't beat 'em, join 'em. She knew he wanted her in his bed. He didn't have to pretend that wasn't there between them. She also understood why they shouldn't act on that, which meant they could playfully flirt without the pressure of it having to mean something more.

He could handle that. Probably.

His phone buzzed against his hip. He pulled it out of his pocket. An email from Billings, checking in, and another from his mother, asking when he was coming to visit now that he was off assignment. He groaned, not wanting to deal with either.

The first he couldn't ignore. He lifted his phone. "Liv, turn around and strike a pose. I need my weekly proof for boss man."

Liv spun around and walked over, setting down her camera and plucking the phone out of his hand. She slid into the spot next to him on the bench and held up the phone in selfie mode. She put her head next to his.

"Say cheese."

"Nope."

"Fine." Right before snapping the pic, she reached over and pinched his nipple hard.

"Hey!"

Click.

The photo appeared on the screen. Finn's face scrunched and Liv sticking her tongue out. She laughed and set the phone on his lap. "There you go."

"Least professional picture ever."

She bumped shoulders with him. "You're supposed to be on vacation. Serious pictures aren't going to help."

He rubbed his chest and his abused flesh. "Damn, woman. You've gotten rougher in your old age."

She grinned. "I remembered how much you loved when I did that."

"Right. Such fond, sore memories," he said wryly. "Why did I invite you to hang out with me again?"

"Aw, don't be like that." She kissed her fingers

and gently rubbed the place she'd pinched. "There. All better."

Her hand on his chest was a different kind of jolt to his system, adept fingers stroking in a suddenly sensitive place. He cleared his throat, and she dropped her arm to her lap.

"So, ready to head out or want a few more?" he asked.

She glanced at the statue. "I—"

Bang!

The blast of the gunshot rent through the peaceful quiet and whatever Liv was going to say. Liv's eyes went wide and Finn leapt from his spot, grabbing her around the waist. He hauled them both to the ground and rolled her beneath him, covering her with his body.

A few voices sounded around them, but all Finn could focus on was Liv's trembling body and figuring out which direction the shot came from. Back left near the trees, from what he could tell. He cursed himself for leaving his gun in the car.

"Finn," Liv said, her voice shaking.

"Shh. Just stay down. I've got you."

He strained his ears, anticipating the next shot, calculating how he could get Liv to safety. There was a sculpture three yards away that could offer some protection. He turned his head toward the woods. But instead of finding what he expected—a park of people scattering—an elderly couple was standing there staring down at them, blocking his view.

"What are you doing?" he barked. "Get down!"

The man smiled, his fisherman's hat shielding his eyes. "It's okay, son. It was just the starting pistol for the race."

"What?"

The woman crooked a finger toward the far side of the park and gave him a kind look. "The charity relay. That starting shot was loud. Scared the biscuits out of me, too. But everything's okay."

"Oh." Finn let out a breath. *Shit*. "Thanks."

The woman smiled, looking more than a little amused, and the couple strolled off hand in hand.

Finn rolled off Liv and looked over at her, finding her in full scowl.

"Liv, I'm sorry. I thought—"

"A freaking starter pistol?" she demanded, cutting off his apology. "Christ, they should warn people. This isn't the goddamned Olympic games."

Her words were annoyed, but her voice and hands were shaking. Damn. If anything could set off a panic attack for Liv, it was this. Ten years ago, this would've had him in full freak-out, too. He grabbed her hands and squeezed. "Yeah, a warning would've been nice. You okay?"

She flexed her fingers in his hold and took a deep breath. "I'm all right. Just give me a sec. I think it's just an adrenaline rush making me shake."

He helped her to sit up and continued to rub her cold hands. "I'm sorry if I made it worse. I didn't mean to scare you. I just reacted."

"Not your fault." She gave him a quivery smile. "This anxiety thing can be a pain in the ass. But seeing you go all Rambo might've been worth it."

He sniffed. "You mean going all paranoid."

She tucked her knees beneath her and reached out to brush some dirt off his shirt. "No. That wasn't being paranoid. It was being brave. You protected me."

He shrugged, still keeping hold of her other hand. "That's my job."

She pinned him with a look. "No, it's not. You're not on duty right now. I wouldn't expect or want you to take a bullet for me."

The words dug into his skin, burrowed in deep. He didn't want that kind of pass from her. He reached up and cupped her chin. "You need to expect more of me then."

She frowned, big brown eyes holding even bigger questions.

"I know you don't need a protector. But if you're with me, you're getting one," he said, his voice coming out rough. "I'm never going to be that guy who left you vulnerable again. I can't offer much these days, but I can promise you that. I've got your back, Livvy. I can keep you safe."

She looked down and wet her lips. "You're making me forget to have a panic attack."

"Good."

"Finn?"

"Hmm?"

She leaned forward and put her face inches from his. "Don't make me be the one to kiss first this time."

His thoughts stuttered, ran into each other. "What?"

"Not asking twice."

He didn't need her to. Not letting himself think about how this was a bad idea or how they'd made an agreement, he shifted his knees wide, grabbed Liv's belt loop, and guided her to him. She slid into his space like she was meant to be there, and he took her face in his hands, closing his eyes and bringing her lips to his.

The minute they connected, every muscle in his body softened, like a snake that had been coiled for hours and finally let loose to strike. Her mouth was warm against his, eager, and sweet from the ice cream they'd eaten after lunch. She parted her lips on a groan and he took advantage, slipping his tongue against hers and deepening the kiss.

She gripped his shirt, shifted her legs to straddle his hips, and gently pushed back on him. He let her guide him back down to the grass. He was used to taking the lead with women, and she was letting him control the kiss, but he liked that she was just as hungry as he was. *More. More. More.* The word was a silent chant between both of them.

He slipped his hand around her and pressed her chest to his, loving all that soft femininity against him and the heat of her. He dragged his hand up to the back of her neck, murmuring her name against her lips like a prayer. He could do this forever.

"On your left!"

The shout startled him out of his erotic plans, and Liv broke away from the kiss, turning her head toward the voice. A group of joggers came pounding by on the running path next to them, their paper numbers flapping in the wind, and their attention on the sprawled couple making out in full view of everyone. Some expressing their disapproval. Some smiling. Most just gawking.

"On your right!" Liv called out and waved. "Lower right."

Finn closed his eyes and let his head fall back to the grass, laughter rumbling through him.

Liv flattened her hands against his chest once the group was gone and whispered, "Hey, Batman."

He looked up at her, finding her grinning down at him. "Yes, dear?"

"We suck at the stealth kiss."

"You think? We must have unresolved exhibitionist tendencies. Take off your shirt, and we'll find out."

She sniffed and got off him, letting him sit up. "I'll pass."

He climbed to his feet and helped her to hers. "Your loss. I would've taken off mine."

"We also suck at this boundaries thing. You can't..." She pressed her lips together and made some swirling motion with her finger.

"Can't what? Kiss you when you blatantly demand I do it?"

She flinched. "No. Say sweet stuff like you did. Flirting's on the table. That...that is not."

His brows lifted. "Okay, so say asshole things instead?"

"Yes. That'd be better. Be an asshole." She grabbed her camera, tucked it in her bag, and then slung the bag over her shoulder. "I know you've had a lot of practice at that."

"I really don't need to practice. That comes naturally. But fair warning, you might find that irresistibly hot, too."

She groaned.

"What? I'm following instructions. That was an asshole thing to say."

She bit her lip, and a small smile broke through. "Come on. Time to go home before we get kicked out for lewd behavior."

He grabbed her other bag. "If that's what you consider lewd, you haven't lived yet, Arias."

Her smile sagged and she turned toward the parking lot as he fell into step beside her. "Don't try to out-lewd me. I was *that* girl in college. My rap sheet is probably way more scandalous than yours. And here I am, basically throwing myself at a guy again when we've made an agreement to keep it platonic."

He glanced over at her, not liking how she said it, like it was some sort of damning sentence. He grabbed her hand, halting her. "Hey."

She didn't look at him. "What?"

"You're not throwing yourself at me. And this—us—is never going to be platonic."

Her gaze jumped to his.

"We may be able to keep from going to bed together because we're trying to be smart about this, but don't fool yourself into thinking that the thing we have between us is going to go away. The attraction is always there. Knowing we can't have it makes it worse. It's like being locked in a room with fresh baked cookies but only being allowed to smell them and not take a bite."

She frowned.

"But the difficulty of resisting is still worth the effort because I know that, at least for me, I haven't had fun like this in a really long time. I don't have rock-skipping contests. I don't get to relax and joke around with someone who I don't have to bullshit. I don't get to scandalize a group of joggers. And I know it's pretty obvious, but I live a lonely fucking life on purpose. I like it that way. But when you're around, you make me not want to."

"Finn…" She blinked, her eyes going shiny in the

fading sunset, and shoved him lightly. "You're not sticking to the asshole rule, asshole."

His lips curved, and he grabbed her hand. "Sorry. I'll try harder." He stepped back and gave her an exaggerated up-and-down look. "You also have a great rack. Like top-notch."

She smirked, then tipped her chin up. "That's not being an asshole. That's stating the obvious."

He laughed. "True enough."

She shook her head, tugging on his hand. "Come on. Now I'm hungry. Let's run by the grocery store, and I'll fix us a nice platonic dinner."

"So no hot dogs and buns?"

She pulled him toward the parking lot and grinned. "Or pigs in a blanket."

"See, Livvy, you get me."

And she did.

That was the most dangerous part of it all.

chapter

FIFTEEN

Liv and Finn had planned another night by the fire and a rock-skipping rematch. But on their way home, clouds had rolled in and rain had followed soon after. So instead of heading outside after dinner, they'd dug through the dusty DVD collection and had decided to watch *The Wedding Singer*. The main house had a screened-in porch with a TV, so they'd set themselves up out there, listening to the falling rain and laughing at Adam Sandler singing "Love Stinks."

Finn had dutifully sat on the opposite side of the couch from her, but Liv hadn't been able to stop herself from glancing at him throughout the movie. The easy way he draped his arm over the back of the couch and took up space. The deep, full sound of his laughter when a funny part came up. The way he kept peeking at her to see if she was laughing, too.

Today he'd kissed her, but more than that, she couldn't shake the memory of him blanketing her when he thought shots were being fired. For all the years since the shooting, she'd resented the fact that he'd abandoned her that night. But today, when she'd been pinned under him, thinking they were under attack again, she'd felt utter and complete panic…for him.

The thought of him taking a bullet for her hadn't comforted her. It had scared her to the core. She didn't want him sacrificing himself on her behalf. And, she realized, she wouldn't have wanted it back then either. She couldn't imagine living her life, knowing he'd given up his for hers. But beyond that, it was his job now. The man spent his existence risking himself for the safety of others.

Knowing he could be taken from this earth at any time as part of his job had bone-deep fear going through her—and gave her yet another reason why she couldn't let herself get attached to him. She couldn't take that kind of loss. Not again.

But even knowing that, she couldn't deny that what he'd said at the park was true. They could try to ignore the pull between them, but it wasn't going to go away. Not only that, but being together and not acting on it was making it worse.

She should probably walk away now. Call this weekend a one-time thing and create some distance. Protect herself. That was the smart thing. That was what had kept her sane and stable the last few years—keeping distance from everyone and everything having to do with her past. But instead, this growing sense of restlessness tugged at her.

"You want a decaf?"

"Huh?" Finn asked, glancing her way.

She untucked her legs from beneath her and got up from the couch. "I'm craving coffee. You want any?"

He shrugged. "Yeah, sure. I can make it if you want."

"No, I've got it."

Liv went inside, the sounds of the movie fading behind her, and made her way into the kitchen. She ignored the coffeepot and dug through the things she'd bought at the store, nerves making her hands shake a little. She found what she was looking for and popped them in the microwave. She didn't let herself think, just went through the motions—one step, then the next—until she was back at the doorway that led to the porch.

She peered in. Finn's gaze was on the TV, a hint of amusement on his face. The rain poured down behind him, pinging against the metal roof. He'd changed into black athletic pants and a Texas Longhorns T-shirt after dinner, looking like some high school fantasy of hers all grown up, making her mind drift down that what-if path. What if the shooting hadn't happened? What if that kiss had never been interrupted? Would they have figured out how to be together after high school? Would they have been sneaking into each other's dorm rooms in college? Would she have managed sober sex in college instead of creating the train-wreck version of herself? Or would they have parted ways anyway? Was the fantasy only enticing because she'd told herself they couldn't have it?

She'd slept with so many guys since she'd known him. Guys whose names she couldn't remember. Guys she hadn't given a damn about. Guys who'd treated her like she was something to use up and toss out. She'd given them her body without a second thought. And here was Finn, a guy she cared about, a guy who cared about her, a guy who hadn't touched a woman in two years but was keeping his hands to himself despite her slipups. A guy who'd protected her today without hesitation.

She couldn't stop herself. The words came out.

"Are you doing this for me or for you?" she asked loud enough to be heard over the rain and TV.

Finn turned his head, brows knit. "What? The movie?"

She rubbed her lips together, heartbeat in her ears, heat creeping up her neck. "No. The ignore-the-lust thing. Is that for my benefit or yours?"

"The lu—" He gave her a look, strain around his eyes. "Uh, I'd say that's obvious."

She swallowed past the tightness in her throat. "So you're trying to protect me."

He grabbed the remote to lower the volume and then scrubbed a hand over his jaw, wary. "Liv, I told you—"

"That you have nothing to offer. That you're leaving. That you don't want to hurt me." Her hand tightened around the doorjamb.

His mouth was a grim line. "Yeah."

She took a breath, steeling herself, and grabbed what she'd set on a table by the doorway. She took the plate, walked to Finn, and set it on his lap. He glanced down in confusion, but the scent must've hit him before his eyes caught up.

He made a sound in the back of his throat, his gaze jumping to hers.

The smell of warm chocolate chip cookies wafted up between them. "I think we're making this more complicated than it needs to be."

"Liv..." A thousand concerns were in his tone. Concerns and something beneath that...yearning.

"If you think it's to protect my feelings, take that off your list of worries," she said, her confidence building. "Sex doesn't have to be that complicated. I'm not wired that way anyhow. It's always been a strictly physical thing for me. Like eating a really good cookie." She glanced down at the plate and then up at him again. "And I'm really tired of only smelling the cookies."

Finn stared at her, his face flickering in the TV light and his eyes dark and unreadable.

"The things you want the most are the things you can't have," Liv said, her words soft. "I say if we want this summer to work, instead of ignoring it, why not take the power out of the forbidden thing? Indulge instead."

His throat worked, and he eyed the cookies. His silence made her shift on her feet, self-conscious.

She forced a tight smile. "Or you can just tell me to leave you the hell alone and we can eat the cookies."

He shook his head, his fingers curling around his knees. "I don't want to hurt you, Liv. Or walk away at the end of the summer and feel like I've used you. Because I have to leave. That's not a question."

She looked out at the pouring rain. "It's not using if we both get something out of it and know where the end is upfront." She rubbed a chill from her arms. "I won't fall in love with you, if that's what you're afraid of."

He jerked his head up at that, his face slack.

She gave him a flippant smile, though her stomach felt tight. "I just want your cookies, Dorsey. I'm not in the market for more than that—from anyone."

"Livvy…"

"But why don't you sleep on it?" she said quickly. "This is a no-pressure situation. You won't hurt my feelings.

You won't wound my ego. So if you need time, which it looks like you do, take it. I'll see you in the morning."

Before she could lose her nerve, she spun around and headed toward the screen door that led outside and to the pool house. She stepped out into the rain, thankful for the cold drops on her skin, and refused to look back. She'd said her piece. At least she'd had the nerve to do it. She could go to bed knowing that. Fear hadn't won today. The girl who'd made that list was still in there somewhere. Even if she didn't always make the wisest decisions, she had guts.

That would have to be enough for her tonight.

But when she was three steps from the pool house stairs and soaked to her skin, a hand wrapped around her arm and whirled her around.

Finn stood there in the downpour, shirt already plastered to his chest and water tracking down his face.

"You think *that's* what I need? Time to decide if I want to touch you?" he asked, disbelief in his voice.

The thunder rumbled above them as if to emphasize his point.

"Well, I don't know," she shouted into the rain. "I don't know what you need. You weren't saying anything. And I just put it all out there and there were cookies and—"

The next word never made it out because he grabbed her other arm and dragged her to him. His lips were on hers before she took her next breath. Hungry. Searching. Almost angry.

He cursed between kisses—at her, at himself... She couldn't tell. But then he was lifting her off her feet and carrying her up the stairs.

The door to the pool house banged against the wall as Finn hauled Liv inside, her legs hooked around his waist and his mouth fused to hers. Neither of them caught more than a gulp of air between kisses on the way in. And the only words uttered had been, "Inside?" by him and "Yes" by her.

She didn't care if he was asking to go inside the pool house or inside her body because the answer to both was a resounding *yes*.

Finn kicked the door shut behind them, both of them dripping water everywhere, and didn't bother turning on a light. All the curtains were still open, the windows streaked with rain, as he carried her past the small living room and to the bed. He set her down at the foot and grabbed an extra blanket off the couch, draping it over the quilt so they wouldn't soak everything through. Then he was back in front of her, invading her space in the best way.

"I want to lick all this rain off you," he said against her skin as he kissed her neck and guided her down to sit on the bed. "And then I want to get you messy again."

She groaned and grabbed for his shirt, wanting to feel him, wanting to get him naked as soon as damn possible, but he stilled her movements, gripping her wrists and pressing them down at her sides.

"No. You asked for this, now you take it how I want to give it. I'm in no hurry."

The little promise was enough to send shivers through her that had nothing to do with her wet clothes. He went back to licking rivulets of rain off her throat and trailed a hand down her calf. He slipped off her sandals one by one and then grazed his teeth along her collarbone.

She let out a soft moan, the feel of his mouth against her unbearably erotic. He'd always had a thing for her neck. She'd had to hide his little bites and marks from her parents after those illicit make-out sessions in high school. But she'd liked having those sexy mementos, even though she'd tease him mid-make-out with *You're going to leave evidence.*

He'd whisper. *I know. I like seeing you in class and knowing my mark is on your skin. It drives me crazy. Makes me hard.*

To her virgin self, that tidbit had been about the hottest thought ever. It'd made her feel sexy and powerful. It'd made her want to take things further with him, even when she'd vowed to wait.

But now she didn't have to bank her desires or keep her line in the sand. There was no innocence to protect, no parents to obey, no tender teenage feelings involved. She could have Finn and enjoy the moment without guilt.

He knelt on the floor in front of her, kissing down the hollow of her throat and holding her head in his hands to angle her just how he wanted her. She wanted to watch, to see him there between her knees, but the sensations had her eyes closing and her head tipping back in his hold.

"God, Livvy," he murmured against her skin, inhaling like he was trying to rein himself in. "Tell me you really want this. That this is real. Tell me I didn't fall asleep during the movie and am lying in there with a hard-on, having a dirty dream."

She smiled. "I think I've made it clear that I want this. But no guarantees on the sleeping thing."

"Don't wake me until this is done then."

He unbuttoned the first two buttons on her shirt and

slipped his hand inside her bra, cupping her breast with his big, warm hand. He grazed a thumb over her nipple, and needy awareness rushed straight downward. She arched into the touch and gasped, surprised by the intensity of the sensation.

"Fuck, you're sensitive," he said, illicit appreciation in his voice as he traced his thumb over again and then pinched lightly. "And I love your breasts. Love how heavy and hot you are in my hand."

She sucked in a breath at the sharp need and looked down at him again, gripping his shoulders, needing something to ground her. "I think you're turning me into my teenage self. I'm not usually so easily... I... *Oh*."

She couldn't finish her sentence because he slipped the cup of her bra beneath her breast and licked. Hot mouth on chilled skin. Her feet arched, her toes pressing into the floor.

He groaned, his breath tickling her. "The feeling's mutual. I feel like I'm going to have the staying power of a fifteen-year-old. Thank God for the cold rain. Otherwise, I would've come already."

She laughed, but the sound died when he put his lips fully on her and sucked. She may as well have had a wire attached to every erogenous zone with the way her body lit up—a circuit board of *oh, hell yes*. Her nails dug into his shoulders again, his wet shirt bunching beneath her fingers.

"But that just means I'll have to take my time with you first," he said, his voice dark with sensual promise as he rubbed his scruff against her breast. "Taste every little bit of you. I'm really disappointed about that."

"Me too," she whispered. "So sad."

She could almost hear him smile. He quickly relieved her of her shirt and bra, dropping them into a wet heap on the floor, and then eased her back onto the bed. She lay down and opened her eyes just in time to see the way he was staring at her. His green eyes had gone dark and dangerous. Hungry. He reached for her shorts and tugged them off, leaving her in just her plain, black cotton panties, which had mostly survived the rain but were damp for other reasons. He trailed his hand over her sternum, his gaze following his fingers down her body until they paused at the band of her underwear. He lifted his head to meet her eyes. "You're so damn gorgeous. You're testing all my willpower right now."

She licked her lips. "You don't have to go slow. I know how long it's been."

His jaw flexed, warning flashing in his eyes. "I'm not an animal. I can control myself."

She believed him, but she also saw the strain there, the fierce want. She encircled his wrist with her hand, boldly guiding it downward, until his fingers slipped beneath the band of her panties and he could feel the state of her arousal. "Maybe I can't."

Something broke in his expression, revealing a feral edge as his fingers curled against her most sensitive place, finding her slick and wanting and burning hot.

"Liv," he said through gritted teeth.

It was a warning. She'd poked a starved lion. Maybe it wasn't the smartest thing, but she knew down to her bones that he wouldn't harm her—and maybe part of her wanted the ferocity. There was something unbearably erotic about seeing such a stoic man lose his composure simply from touching her.

"You can do what you want, but I promise I'll tell you to stop if I want you to stop," she said, trying to keep her words steady despite his exploring fingers. "We've got all summer for slow."

His gaze locked on hers, the war in his head obvious in the lines of strain on his face, but in a flash, he slipped his hand from her panties and then ripped them off.

She gasped in surprise as she felt the fabric give way. She'd always wondered if panties could actually be ripped off. They seemed to be made of durable stuff. But this pair tore away like they were made of wrapping paper. He tossed them aside and then reached back with one hand and yanked off his T-shirt, keeping his eyes on her the whole time and giving her quite the view.

She took her own fill as he discarded his shirt. She'd seen him shirtless the night in the hotel room but had forced herself not to stare. Now she didn't have to bother. Broad shoulders and a sculpted chest, the scar she now found comforting—along with a few other scars she'd have to ask about later—and a dusting of dark hair that trailed down to the waistband of his black pants. Masculine in all the best ways and beautifully built.

He put his hands to his waistband, and she watched his battered fingers untie the drawstring. He didn't have smooth hands like the guys she'd dated in the tech industry. Finn's knuckles had been nicked and marred. Working hands. This was a guy who'd been through God knows what—football, police work, fights, life-or-death situations.

But she lost the train of thought when he shucked the pants along with his boxer briefs. Good Lord, the guy was sexy everywhere. She'd felt him through his pants a few times in high school during those steamy make-out sessions, had been fascinated and intimidated by what she'd found at the time. Seeing him now, though, made her body clench in response. At the shameless arousal. At the promise of pleasure. He took himself in his hand and stroked. "I like that look you're giving me. Like you're desperate for me to fuck you."

She smirked. "Are you calling me a slut?"

He climbed onto the bed, looming over her but not yet touching her. "I'm calling you sexy. And bold." He trailed the back of his hand over her breast, sending shivers through her, and then found the needy place between her legs and circled a finger over her clit, making her whimper. "And if being a slut means asking for what you want and not feeling bad about it, then I hope you are one. I hope you are selfishly using me right now to get off."

She laughed, breathless from his clever fingers. "Oh, I'm completely doing that. Have you seen you?"

His expression went old-school Finn—all cocky and sly. "I have. I've been in an exclusive relationship with myself for a few years. I'm amazing in bed."

"So I've heard. This morning, in fact. Glad I get to join in this time."

Instead of teasing back, he groaned—and not in a good way. His let's-do-this face switched to a scowl. "Shit."

Her muscles tensed. "What?"

"Condoms." He moved his hand away. "Dammit. I haven't done this in so long, I don't have any. I didn't think—"

"My purse is on the side table. I have one."

Relief flooded his features. "Thank God. You are the best girl ever."

She laughed, and he rolled over to grab her purse. She took it from him and fished out a packet, tossed it on the bed, and then dropped her purse to the floor.

He kissed her. "I love a woman who's prepared. I might've had a good cry if we'd had to stop."

She grinned. "Crisis averted."

"Now, where were we?" He slipped his hand between her legs again. "Oh, I remember. Right here."

She thought he was going to roll on the condom and go for it, but instead, he took his time working her up even more, bringing every nerve alive, making her writhe. Then, when she thought she was going to resort to begging or threats, he shifted down the bed, put his hands on the backs of her thighs, and opened her like a naughty book. Before she could even process what was happening, his mouth was on her and her thoughts blinked out of existence.

Oh. *God.*

The sound that escaped her throat was borderline embarrassing, but she didn't have it in her to care. Finn's scruff was brushing against her inner thighs, and his tongue stroked over her like he'd been waiting all his life to taste that particular delicacy. Her head thumped onto the pillow, and her hands went to his hair.

He grunted at her rough grip, but she didn't let go. If she did, she might break into a thousand pieces. The man might have been off the market for a long time, but his skills certainly hadn't suffered. He had radar for her hot spots—or maybe that was her tightening her hold on him when he hit pay dirt—but either way, it was working for her. Slow and sensual, like he was doing it for his benefit more than hers—like this was a seven-course meal and not just the appetizer.

That was probably the hottest part of all. This wasn't a serviceable *I'll scratch your itch first*. This was *I live for making a woman try to crush my skull with her thighs because I'm driving her out of her mind with my tongue*.

She was determined to enjoy every second of it, to not go over too fast, but when he slid two fingers inside her and dragged his tongue over her clit, light exploded behind her eyes, catching her off guard with the magnitude of sensation. She cried out and nearly levitated off the bed, her hands going from his head to the sheets and gripping hard.

He made a belly-deep sound of pleasure, the vibration of it against her sex driving her even higher, and she almost launched him right off her. But he wasn't having any of that. He placed a palm on her hip, pinning her in place, and shifted as his fingers continued to stroke her and push her higher.

"Finn, I can't... Please." The plea slipped out, but she wasn't sure what she was begging for—a reprieve, more, both.

Her eyes blinked open, and she found him watching her—watching her come, watching his fingers work, watching her fall apart. Then his gaze rose to meet hers. Another wave of pleasure overtook her, but she couldn't turn away. All the humor was gone from his eyes now. This was a man on a mission. A man who could tear her apart with one look.

"Finn," she begged again, but she let him see it. Let him see what he was doing to her. Her eyes fell shut, and she rode the wave of the orgasm, her body his to orchestrate and out of her control now. Surrendered. Fully and completely.

Finally, when she was limp and melting back into

the bed, he moved his hand away. But he swiped her inner thigh with the evidence of her arousal, and then followed the trail with his tongue, sending shivers to every part of her.

"Still with me, Livvy?"

She sighed. "So very with you."

"Tell me you want this."

She opened her eyes, finding him staring down at her, his jaw set, barely banked desire all over his face. That look said he'd die if she told him to stop. That look said he'd stop anyway.

"I want you."

"Thank God." He tore open the condom with quick fingers and rolled it on, his attention staying on her. "Tell me which position works best for you."

She blinked, her breath still coming in pants and her mind scattered. She'd never had a guy ask that before. They always just…did their thing unless she made a suggestion. "Hands and knees."

He hissed out a breath, clearly in full approval. "Flip over, gorgeous. I'm going to make you do that again."

Normally, she would've made a joke, a tease, something to lighten the situation and take the pressure off because she was a one-orgasm kind of girl, but she couldn't find the words. If he wanted to give it his best shot, by God, she was going to let him.

She turned over, strangely unself-conscious about baring herself to him in that way, and gave herself over to the moment.

Bring it on, Dorsey.

chapter
SIXTEEN

FINN'S HEAD, BODY, AND BRAIN WERE GOING TO EXPLODE. Subatomic particles. That was all that would be left. Every part of him had been screaming for relief since Liv had set that plate of cookies in his lap. But once he'd gotten her into the pool house, all he'd wanted to do was savor. The girl he'd known had grown into a bold, sexy, blessedly unashamed woman.

All lush curves and bronze skin and teasing smiles. Every inch of her begged to be kissed, licked, stroked, bitten. He'd wanted to feast on each bit laid out before him, have the taste of her on his tongue forever. Had wanted to hear those breathy, needy sounds she made when he put his mouth on her. But hearing her lose it, feeling her body grip his fingers, and now seeing her on her hands and knees waiting for him, all sense of patience or savoring the moment had left him. Instead, a wave of violent urgency rumbled through him like an earthquake.

His hands trembled with the force of it as he gripped

her hips. He'd promised to make this good for her, but he wasn't sure he could make it gentle. All he knew was that he wanted to hear her fall apart again, and he wanted to have it happen when he was deep inside her. He wanted to go over the cliff with her.

Taking in a deep, steadying breath, he positioned himself behind her and eased forward, watching her body open for him in the most beautiful, erotic way. The view and instant feel of her heat around him was almost enough to make him go off like a virgin, but he exhaled through it, using every bit of willpower he possessed to maintain his control. He'd once stayed up four days straight with no sleep and little food to do surveillance. He could handle this. But the *oh-God-yes* groan from Liv almost did him in. He loved that she didn't hold anything back. Loved that she owned her pleasure.

He closed his eyes and seated himself deep, determined not to rush it even though her body squeezing his cock made every other sensation he'd ever felt in his life feel worthless. His fingers dug into her hips, probably leaving bruises, but he couldn't let go. He dragged in another breath.

But when she rocked against him, begging with her body in a slow, teasing slide, his resistance shattered. He yanked her against him again, enveloping himself in her heat, and his hips pumped of their own volition. One. Two. A million times wouldn't be enough. The feel of her was going to drive him mad. "Fuck, Livvy. I can't go easy."

She glanced over her shoulder, her hooded gaze giving him the go-ahead before her words. "Then don't."

The words were like fire licking up his spine. *Screw*

patience. He did his best to angle just right for her, but he was beyond finesse. All the pent-up frustration he'd had since that first kiss on the restaurant deck morphed into pure, feral need for this woman. He took her hard as she made gritty, back-of-the-throat sounds that said she wasn't minding at all.

"Touch yourself," he commanded between panted breaths. "I want to feel you come around me."

She groaned and braced herself on one elbow while her hand slipped between her legs. Just the sight of that almost sent him past the point of no return. This was the image that had popped into his mind when she'd teased him this morning about indulging, too. Liv taking what she needed, showing him what she liked.

"Oh, right there," she gasped when he angled downward. "*Oh*."

He ate up her words, but she wouldn't have had to say anything. He could feel the reaction of her body. Tightening. Tightening. A vise grip. His eyes were going to roll out of his head and across the floor. "*Liv*."

"Finn!"

His name coming out in a desperate cry was the last straw. As she went over the edge again, he plummeted after her in a free fall. His hips pumping, his brain buzzing, and his release emptying in her with a force that made his knees go weak.

After few long, blissful moments, she collapsed onto her belly, taking him with her, both down for the count. He draped over her back, his fingers slipping from her hips, and panted like he'd run a marathon.

For a minute, he couldn't move and was sure he was probably smothering her, but just when he was about to ask her if she could breathe, she let out a voluminous, satisfied sigh. Like she'd just had the best meal ever.

A laugh escaped him. A not-so-subtle one.

She reached back and slapped his thigh. "Don't laugh at me, Dorsey."

But her muffled, face-in-the-pillow words only made him laugh harder. She smacked him again, but soon she was laughing along with him, the whole bed bouncing.

"Hold on. We're going to dislodge things." He grabbed the base of the condom and slipped out, rolling off her and tossing it into the trash before turning back her way. She had stopped laughing but was still facedown in the pillow, all that bronze flesh and silky dark hair on display. He mapped her spine with the tips of his fingers and traced the delicate flower tattoo on the back of her neck. "Sorry I was a little, uh, quick there at the end."

She turned her head on the pillow to look at him, a lazy smile on her face. "You know I wasn't judging you on your stamina, right? Anything I got out of it after round one was going to be a bonus."

He smirked. "Ironically, this is probably how our first time would've gone back in high school, too, only in half the time and I wouldn't have had a clue what to do with my mouth."

Her eyebrows lifted. "Mr. Big Man on Campus? I thought you'd had practice."

He propped his head up on his fist. "You assumed that. I was a virgin, too."

Her lips parted, and then she narrowed her eyes. "Liar."

"Nope."

"But I saw you with that senior chick here at the lake sophomore year. She was all over you."

He put his hand to his chest in faux wistfulness. "Ah, Leigh. She gave me my first hand job and a painful lesson in why you shouldn't let a girl with fake nails handle your business when she's been drinking."

Liv snorted. "Ouch."

"Yeah." He noticed goose bumps popping up on her skin so he dragged the wet blanket from beneath them and tossed it on the floor. Then, he grabbed the dry quilt and draped it over them. "After that, I fooled around a few times, but I didn't let anything go far."

"How come?" she asked. "Didn't feel ready?"

"Oh, I felt ready the first time I saw Mila Kunis in *That '70s Show*. But my dad had given me a talk in junior high about women trying to trap the guys who are going somewhere. He told me that once girls saw I was good at football and had money, they'd try to latch on and even get pregnant so that I had to keep them around."

Liv made a disgusted face and rolled over to prop herself up on the pillows. "Geez. That's a shit thing to say."

"Yeah, extra shitty considering my mom got pregnant with my older sister in high school. Like he wasn't an active participant in that and it was her fault." He frowned, old bitterness bubbling up. "But at the same time, the thought freaked me out. I didn't want to get stuck in Long Acre."

"So if I had asked you to sleep with me, you would've thought I was some scheming chick from the wrong side of the tracks trying to put my claws in you?"

He gave her a *yeah-right* look.

"What? There's no denying that we were from different sides of town."

"I would've never thought that of you. First, I pursued you. Second, no one wanted to get out of town more than you did. *I* would've been an anchor on *you*, not the other way around. But I never pushed because you deserved better than losing your virginity with a guy who was too chickenshit to date you publicly."

A little line appeared between her brows. "Is that why you kept us secret? Because if your dad found out, he would've seen me as a leech?"

"Partly." Finn flipped to his back and scrubbed a hand over his face. "He saw us together once. That day I invited you over when I thought my parents were going to be out overnight. My dad forgot something and had to come back to get it and saw us kissing by the pool. The next day, he cornered me and told me what he'd seen."

"Damn."

"Yeah, the things he said, the way he talked about you and your family… I've never come so close to punching my own father. But he threatened to take everything. My college fund. My car. Any support after high school if I didn't shut it down." He stared at the ceiling and blew out a breath, anger building in him anew. "I should've let him. I should've stood up for myself. For you. Instead, I let him think he'd won and got more careful with you."

Liv shifted to her side and peered down at him, her damp hair tickling his chest. "You were a kid. He was your dad. You can't blame yourself for being scared your father would disown you and throw you out. My parents had a lot of sway over me, too."

He stared up at her, old shame filtering through him.

"I wanted to tell him the real story of where I was during the shooting, but he was so proud to call his son a hero and I just…let him. It was easier to let him think what he wanted." He closed his eyes. "I'm sorry. I shouldn't have given a damn about his opinion. I was a coward."

The words felt jagged in his throat, but it felt good to finally say them to her, to admit what a selfish asshole he'd been.

When he opened his eyes, instead of seeing disappointment on her face, she bent down and kissed him lightly. "Stop apologizing. You were seventeen, and every kid has a part of them that wants to make their parents proud. Even if your dad's a dick."

"That's being kind."

"Okay, an überdick. But that's not news. I once overhead him refer to my dad as the illegal who does his lawn." Finn cringed, but she smoothed his forehead with her fingers. "Part of me knew all along that you could never bring me home. To be honest, I doubt my father would've been overly thrilled with me bringing that 'rich asshole's' son around either."

"The difference is you would've done it anyway."

She shrugged, conceding the point, and the quilt slipped down a little. "Well, to hell with them both because here we are again anyway. Doing unspeakable things to each other."

He traced the edge of the quilt, revealing the top curve of her breast, and watched goose bumps rise on her skin as his fingertip brushed over her. "Still in secret, though."

She smiled, letting her hand slide under the quilt and over his abdomen, and then she laid her head against the crook of his shoulder. "You're not my secret. You're an old friend who I might be having some naked fun with for the summer. I have no desire to hide that unless you do."

He gathered the quilt around them both, loving the feel of her, skin to skin. "No, I agree. No hiding."

"Good."

He let his fingers play idly in her hair for a few minutes, his brain working, his gaze on the ceiling. "I'm supposed to visit my parents on this break."

"Yeah?"

He let out a sigh. "It's one of Billings's and the psychologist's directives. I haven't been home in years, and when I called my mom to let her know I was off assignment and okay, she cried. She got me to promise I would stop by, and she's been texting me."

"Hmm. You sound really excited about that."

"I've been thinking of a hundred ways to get out of it," he admitted. "I don't know how to…be around them anymore."

She was quiet for a moment, her breath soft against his chest.

"I guess that makes me sound like a heartless jerk," he said finally.

"No, I get it. You've been through a lot, and family can be…intense. But you can't break a promise to your mom." She traced her fingers over his hip bone. "I'm sure she's been worried. And I know it's going to sound trite, but I wish my mom was still around for me to visit and get annoyed with."

His lungs contracted at that. "God, I'm sorry. I didn't think—"

"Don't. That's not why I'm saying it. I've had a lot of years to get used to my mom being gone. All I'm saying is don't lock out the rest of your family just because you and your dad don't see eye to eye. Life's short."

He let out a long breath, the words sticking to him with a thick layer of guilt. She was right. He knew that. But it didn't make the idea of visiting them any more palatable. He didn't know how to be part of a family anymore—particularly his. He would probably make things worse rather than better by being there. "Maybe you could come with me?"

The question popped out before he could evaluate the repercussions.

Olivia tensed in his hold. "Uh, are you drunk on afterglow? You want to take *me* to see your parents? Maybe not the best icebreaker. *Hey, Dad, remember that girl who did your lawn? The one you didn't want tarnishing your precious son's reputation?*"

He frowned. "I don't give a shit what my dad thinks at this point. In fact, part of me wants to stroll in there and lie, tell him we're going to elope or something. But you're right. I don't want you to go someplace where you're uncomfortable. And I couldn't promise that my parents wouldn't make you feel that way." He pulled her closer. "Sorry. I'm not sure where that idea came from."

She was silent for a long moment, and he thought maybe she'd dozed off, but then she let out a sigh, one that drifted over his chest with a warm gust of air. "If you want me to go, I'll go."

The offer made his breath stall. "No, I wasn't thinking—"

She lifted herself up and gave him a shut-up-and-listen

look. "I said I'll go. You're helping me with stuff. I'm helping you back. And I can handle whatever dirty looks your dad throws my way. I might tell him I'm pregnant with your triplets. I give exactly zero shits about his opinion of me."

He smiled. "Zero shits?"

"Exactly zero."

He pushed her hair behind her ear. "You're kind of amazing, you know?"

Her eyes flickered with some emotion he couldn't pinpoint, but it was gone almost as quickly as it was there, making him question if it had been there at all.

"I know. All the boys tell me that when I'm naked." She pecked him on the lips. "Now get out of my bed so I can get some sleep."

He chuckled. "Kicking me out already?"

"Yep."

"And into the rain, no less. I feel so used."

Her mouth kicked up at the corner. "You should. I used you well. But I can't share a bed. Sleeping quirk. All guests must exit by midnight, or I turn into an angry pumpkin."

"I'm thoroughly terrified."

"I can tell." She rolled off him, pulling the quilt around her. "But maybe I'll let you have breakfast with me tomorrow and help pack my camera gear for Kincaid's blog shoot."

"I'm honored." Finn sat up, hearing her teasing tone, but seeing the seriousness in her eyes. She wasn't kidding. She didn't want him staying overnight. Usually that was his move. He didn't do sleepovers either, but getting kicked out felt a little different than being the one leaving of his own volition.

He wasn't going to push, though. They had boundaries. This was a friendly hookup. Not let's play like we're dating. That was important. He wanted to spend this time with Liv, and goddamn did he want her in his bed again, but his one nonnegotiable was that he wouldn't hurt her. Pretending this was something that it wasn't would only tangle up what could be a fun respite for them both.

He climbed out of bed and pulled on his boxers, liking how she watched him. "Tonight was great."

"It was."

He hoped that was the truth for her, that she wasn't regretting anything. Liv was generous by nature, and she'd known how long it'd been for him. He didn't want to be her charity case. He turned to face her. "I just want it to be clear that this isn't some binding contract. I know this wasn't the plan. So just tell me if you need me to back off, and I will. Us doing this once doesn't mean I have any expectations that it's how things will go while you're here. Hopes but no expectations."

She gave him a get-over-yourself look. "Once again, *I* came on to *you*, so maybe I should be giving you that speech. No pressure, Dorsey."

The suggestion was ludicrous enough that he had to fight not to laugh aloud.

"Right. Like I wouldn't want to do that again. And again." He sniffed. "Have you seen you?"

She grinned at her words being thrown back at her. "I have, and I am spectacular."

He stepped around the bed and went in for one more kiss. "Understatement of the year. Now, get some rest. You've got pictures to take tomorrow."

She nodded and settled under the covers but stayed propped up on her elbows. "I'm thinking you in those boxers—or out of them—will be a good subject."

"Ha. Keep dreaming. I'm a strictly behind-the-scenes guy."

"Shame."

He shook his head and grabbed the rest of his stuff off the floor. There were no neighbors close, so walking to the house in his shorts wasn't going to cause a scandal, and he was just going to get rained on again anyway. "When'd you get so dirty-minded, Arias?"

She arched a brow and tapped her temple. "It's always been there. You have no idea the filthy things I did with you in my virgin mind back then. If only you'd dated me for real…"

The admission made his blood heat again. "Did I mention I was a stupid, stupid boy back then?"

Her lips curled into a playfully evil smile.

"I'm leaving now because otherwise you're going to get no sleep at all."

She leaned over and clicked off the lamp. "Good night, Finn."

Damn she was good at the tease. "Good night, Livvy."

He jogged back to the main house in the cold rain, fighting the urge to return to her room and launch into a campaign about how sleep was overrated. They would have time.

A summer of weekends.

With Liv.

That had seemed like forever when he'd first heard it. But now it didn't seem like nearly long enough.

When he got to the main house, he took a hot shower

and then went through his normal bedtime routine, checking all the locks, making sure nothing was tampered with, and slipping his gun in his boot. But for the first time in a long time, instead of lying there and going through the last two years or combing his memory for any evidence he might have missed, he went to sleep with a quiet mind and a grin on his face.

chapter

SEVENTEEN

L IV BLINKED AWAKE, THE LEVEL OF THE LIGHT IN THE ROOM unfamiliar and her ringing cell phone unwelcome. It took her a second to remember where she was. Not her bedroom with the blackout shades back in Austin, but in Finn's pool house. She squinted, letting her eyes adjust to the morning sunshine streaming through the windows, and flipped over in search of her phone. Her body protested the movement, sore in places she hadn't been sore in a long time.

"Shut up, shut up, shut up," she groaned, slapping her hand around the nightstand for the phone.

The ringing thankfully stopped and she sighed, pressing her face into the pillow. But before she could consider going back to sleep, the phone started up again.

"Oh, son of a bitch." She pushed herself up and leaned over the side of the bed. Her phone was on the floor, halfway under the nightstand, her work number staring back at her on the screen. She sighed and grabbed for it.

"Hello." She fell back onto the bed. "I'm on vacation."

"Unapproved vacation," Preston said into her ear.

"Huh?" she said, still groggy. "No. You weren't in. I gave my request to Greg. He said you'd let me know if it wasn't okay."

"I'm letting you know," Preston said. "It's not okay. I need you in today. We just got a big job from Butter and Brittle, a new chain of candy shops opening across the state. They're willing to throw big money at it, so I promised to put my best designer on it and to personally oversee it. They want multiple concepts and a preliminary design to look at by next Wednesday, so we're going to have to crash the schedule to get it done by then. Next ten days, you're mine. Nail it, and there will be a nice bonus involved."

She closed her eyes and rubbed the bridge of her nose. A nice bonus would be…nice, but she'd taken today off for a reason. "I'll get right on it when I get in tomorrow. I'm in Wilder for…a family thing."

"Did someone die?"

"No."

"Then you need to come back." The sound of a clicking keyboard filled the line. "If you leave now, you can be here before lunch. I can brief you on the phone once you're in your car. Their ideas are a little scattered, so we need to narrow the focus."

Liv sighed and scooted up the pillows, the warmth of the bed calling for her to snuggle back under the quilt. She *should* be able to snuggle back under. Today was supposed to be a vacation day. Plus, she had pictures to take for Kincaid later and a hot FBI agent to keep her company this morning. "Pres—"

A sharp knock sounded on her door, followed by a

booming voice. "Open up. I come bearing breakfast and sexual favors."

"Who was that?" Preston said into her ear.

Shit. She pressed her hand over the mouthpiece and called, "One sec!" Then into the phone: "No one."

She and Preston had had a casual thing once upon a time before he was the boss, but she knew that wasn't jealousy in his voice. Preston only had one love—the business.

"You've got to be kidding me," Preston said. "I'm telling you I desperately need you in the office, and you're with some guy?"

Liv gritted her teeth and flung the quilt off so she could climb out of bed. All she'd thrown on after Finn had left were a T-shirt and underwear, but he'd seen her in much less so she didn't bother finding something else to put on. "I have a right to a personal life."

"Not during work time."

"Hold on." She stalked across the living room and opened the door.

Finn grinned, a takeout bag and coffee in his hand. "Oh, pants optional. I'm fully on board with this plan."

She pointed at her phone.

He winced and mouthed, "Sorry."

Preston sniffed in her ear, his opinion clear. "I need you in the office now. I didn't approve this vacation day. Tell your personal life to keep his pants on. He doesn't pay your bills. Your job does."

Liv's fist clenched at the threat, but she swallowed what she really wanted to say. Preston was being a dick, but he was also stating the truth. He was her boss. And this was her job. What else was she supposed to do? Get fired? "Fine, I'll be there by eleven."

"Thank you." Preston ended the call without another word.

She tossed her phone onto the kitchen counter and cursed. Colorfully.

Finn's brows lifted. "Everything okay?"

"It's fine."

"You sure?" He glanced at her phone. "You'll be where by eleven? Kincaid's?"

Liv ran her fingers through her hair, trying to tame the bedhead and her annoyance. "No. Work. There's a crisis, and apparently, my boss never approved this vacation day."

"That sucks." He frowned and handed her one of the coffees.

"Thanks." She took a long sip, feeling weighed down all of a sudden. "It does suck. It's not a total shock. I was taking a risk asking for a Monday off, but I thought it was squared away. I should've known to double-check."

Finn leaned against the counter. "What about Kincaid? Isn't she cooking all kinds of things for the photo shoot?"

Liv's shoulders sagged, more stress piling on. "Yes, I need to call her, make sure she doesn't start cooking. Damn. Now all her ingredients might go bad by the time I can get back."

"They might last until next weekend."

She groaned. "But I won't be here. This project is going to go through the weekend."

Finn's frown deepened. "So I'm not going to see you for two weeks?"

Liv set down her coffee and rubbed the now-throbbing spot between her eyebrows. "Yes. Preston's not so aware that weekends and weekdays are different things. I was going to work extra hours during the week to make this summer work, but when big projects come up, I'm going to have to be there."

"So this could happen all summer then," he said grimly.

"Maybe." She forced brightness into her voice that she didn't feel. "Missing me already?"

"I missed you when I walked out last night," he said, no flirtatiousness in the tone.

The stark honesty jabbed her in her chest, made her feel things she shouldn't be feeling. "Oh."

He leaned against the counter. "I get it. Work is work. But you made a commitment to Kincaid. And to yourself. And I already emailed my mom telling her I'd be visiting next weekend."

She set down her coffee, guilt flooding her. "I'm sorry. Can you move it?"

He considered her, something closing off in his expression. "No, it's fine. This isn't about me. I'm a big boy and can go solo."

She rolled her lips inward and nodded. "Right."

"Well," he said grabbing one of the paper bags he'd brought in and handing it to her. "I got you a bacon-and-egg biscuit for the road. I'll head out so you can get ready."

He stepped past her, and she clutched the bag in her hand, feeling a chill in the room. "Finn?"

He gripped the doorjamb and looked back. "Yeah?"

"I'm sorry for the change in plans."

He shrugged a shoulder. "Not your fault."

"You seem mad."

He turned and folded his arms over his chest. "No, not mad. I'm just wondering if you didn't push back on your boss because it's easier to leave than stay."

Her stomach flipped over. "What?"

"Sometimes the devil we know isn't as scary. Here you have to deal with a friend's expectations. Here you have to figure out if you're still talented with your camera. Here you have to deal with a morning-after conversation when you've made it clear that you're a cut-and-run kind of girl."

Her spine stiffened. "You think I'm running out because I don't want to have the after-sex talk?"

"I don't know." He shrugged. "But I think your boss gave you an out from all of this, and you took it."

Heat crept up her neck. "I have to go to work because it pays my bills. I have to listen to my boss because that's how life is. I'm not a trust fund baby who has a cushion if it doesn't work out."

He didn't take the bait. "Right."

She made a sound of frustration. "I don't want to fight with you. That's not what this is supposed to be. We agreed…no complicated shit. We had sex. That doesn't mean you get to lay a guilt trip on me for leaving to do my job."

He stepped closer, his eyes not leaving hers, and cupped her shoulders. "I'm not fighting with you," he said softly. "We're supposed to be doing a job for each other this summer. This is me doing mine. I'm fighting *for* you. Remember why you wanted this. Remember why you came here. It wasn't for a good lay."

"Finn…"

He tucked her hair behind her ear, eyes serious.

"I'll still be here in two weeks, but don't forget the point."

He released her, and her breath whooshed out. Before she could say anything back, he walked out and shut the door behind him.

She gripped her elbows, feeling chilled and a little lost. He didn't get it. He'd lived a life where he always had a financial safety net. She wasn't running to work because she was scared. She was going because she had to.

Right?

She leaned against the wall and slid to the floor. Then why did she feel so damn shitty?

chapter

EIGHTEEN

"How is it possible that someone who can make such beautiful food can be so bad at photographing it?" Liv asked, chin in hand as she stared at her computer screen.

"I know!" Kincaid announced in her ear. "I told you I'm lighting impaired. Maybe it's my kitchen."

Liv frowned as she clicked through the photos Kincaid had emailed her. Her pancakes looked weirdly yellow and the sausages gray, so lighting was definitely an issue. But even if she could adjust the coloring in one of her photo-editing programs, the angles were all wrong, too. "Are you sure you didn't purposely take bad ones to make me feel worse about standing you up?"

Kincaid snorted. "Sadly, no. This is my best effort. I have similar trouble when I photograph houses for work. So there's no way to adjust them?"

Liv sighed. "I may be able to tinker with them a little when I get done with work tonight, but I think a reshoot would be better. When I get out there, I can train you to get better angles and show you where the best light is in your house or yard. Natural light is your friend."

"Thanks, but when do you think you're going to be able to get out here again? If you left Mr. Hot Cop's bed behind, you clearly had an emergency, because why else would you leave *that* behind?"

Liv grimaced and glanced up to make sure none of her coworkers were close enough to hear her. Oh, how she loathed the open-concept office model. "I never said I slept with him."

"Uh-huh. You were staying at his place—after that kiss I caught you in on the porch—and you're not sleeping with him?"

Liv rubbed her temple, a mild headache brewing. "I never said that either."

Kincaid laughed. "Ha. I knew it. You're my patron saint right now. Have I told you that?"

"Don't canonize me yet. Things have been so crazy here at work that I haven't talked to him since Monday morning when I left. I kind of accidentally one-night-standed him."

"Accidentally?" Kincaid asked, the *don't bullshit me* tone clear.

Liv closed her eyes, regret pressing down on her. "Okay, maybe work has conveniently gotten in the way. I just don't know what to say. He made it sound like he thinks I'm choosing work over following my letter stuff, but I can't help that I have a job to do, bills to pay. But I feel shitty because we'd made an agreement to be there for each other—not in the bedroom kind of way but in the friend way—and I've had to bail on him."

Kincaid was quiet for a moment. "Do you *want* to spend more weekends with him?"

"Yes. But…"

"But?"

Liv looked up at the ceiling, hating the relief that had rushed through her when she'd gotten back into the routine at work. When she'd left Finn, she'd had every intention of getting back to Wilder as soon as possible. She'd made a promise to him and to the other women. To herself. But when she'd stepped into the office on Monday afternoon, and everyone had been happy to see her because she could make things happen, all she'd felt was relief.

The chaos had felt familiar, comforting. Things made sense here. She knew her role. She didn't have to think about the past or ponder her letter or replay what had happened with Finn. She didn't have to worry about flashbacks or panic attacks. She could do what she always did—throw herself into work and get shit done. Be the go-to girl.

But every time she thought of that night with Finn, she got a pang deep in her gut, one that reminded her what she'd left behind. Long Acre, Finn, and her friends seemed like another universe when she was away from it. One that she used to be able pack into a vault in her mind and ignore. But now it wouldn't stay locked away. It tugged at her in a way that made her chest hurt. Even talking to Kincaid like this stirred an ache inside her. They'd grown so close those months after the shooting, and then Liv had just closed the door on her like everything else. She didn't want to do that again.

"I guess I'm scared," she finally admitted.

"Of him?"

"Of the fairy-tale trap." The words hadn't been what she'd meant to say, but once they were out, the truth of them resonated through her.

"You mean, falling for him?"

"No." She frowned. "I know better than to let that happen. But I've always been really good at creating a fantasy world when I want to escape. In high school, I was struggling with my mom being sick so I created this secret little world with Finn—one where I got to sneak away and forget who I was and pretend I was some other girl. And then after the shooting, I went to college and used alcohol and guys to pretend I was this carefree badass who lived on her own terms, even though I was a wreck inside. Now I've finally gotten my life together, and I'm sneaking away to a lake house to take pretty pictures and be with a guy while we pretend our real lives don't exist. It's dangerous and feels too familiar."

"Right," Kincaid said. "But you're not running away from anything right now, are you? I mean, what are you escaping? You have a good life, it sounds like."

Liv rolled a pencil along her desk, back and forth, back and forth. "My life is fine."

"So maybe this isn't a fantasy so much as an augmentation. A bonus. With a penis."

Liv laugh-snorted and one of her coworkers looked up from his desk. She faked a cough. "You have a way with words, Kincaid."

"All I'm saying is that we're all screwed up in some way, right? We're human. We're survivors. That all has its own baggage. God knows I have mine. But we all seem to be doing okay now. You're allowed to have fun.

You're allowed to have a fling with an old boyfriend and not feel like it's some big life decision or an unhealthy coping mechanism. Be smart about it, but don't deny yourself some simple life pleasures. Taking your photos. Hanging out with your awesome, amazing, super-wise friends. And hot cop penis."

A real laugh burst out of Liv this time, and she quickly pressed her hand over her mouth to staunch it. "He's FBI, for the record."

"*Federal* cop penis," Kincaid corrected. "That's top shelf. It has authority across state lines."

Liv shook her head. "You're ridiculous."

"And awesome, amazing, and super wise?"

"Obviously."

She could almost hear Kincaid's grin over the phone. "So when are you going to get back out here and take these pictures for me, woman? Because this whole pep talk has been a thinly veiled ploy to get your talented butt out here to help me not embarrass myself on my blog."

Liv glanced at the clock and then calculated the amount of work she had left. Too much. But her resolve had been renewed. "I'm going to do everything I can to knock the first part of this project out by Friday. If I can pull a few late nights, I can tell my boss I'm taking Saturday and Sunday off and will finish the rest next week."

"Yay, perfect. Let me know."

Liv told her she would, and they said their goodbyes. It was already close to seven, but Liv got up and made herself another cup of coffee. If she could pull this off, she'd not only be able to help Kincaid, but she'd get back in time to go with Finn to his parents' house.

With a smile and more resolve than she'd felt since leaving Wilder, she got back to work.

———

By Friday afternoon, Liv's eyes felt like they were going to melt out of her head. She'd worked every night this week until the wee hours of the morning, bringing the project home with her and doing little else. She'd thrown herself into all the details, making sure it wasn't a rush job despite the crazed schedule. The account was a big one, and she wanted to nail it to show Preston and the client that they could count on her to deliver great work.

The pace had taken its toll, and exhaustion was settling in. But it was worth it because she was now ahead of the proposed schedule and had gotten to the point that would allow her to take off the weekend without guilt. She could almost smell the lake air, hear the water lapping at the shore, feel the warmth of Finn's body against her in bed…

"Hey, Olivia?"

Liv looked up, startled out of her thoughts. Annabelle, one of the junior designers, stood in front of her desk with an apologetic smile. Liv sat up straighter and pasted an I-wasn't-thinking-about-X-rated-things look onto her face. "Hey, what's up?"

Annabelle held out her hand, a bright-pink sticky note attached to her fingers. "So I've been trying to build a members-only page for this client, but I made some mistake in the code somewhere and it's letting anyone get in and access paid features. I'd tried to figure it out, but it's going to take more time than I have. I'm playing a gig with my band tonight and really need to be there. Pres said I should let you take a look since you're ahead on your project and are a genius with these kinds of things."

"Pres said—" Liv frowned and grabbed the sticky note that had the client's account info on it. "Big show?"

Annabelle brightened. "Yeah. It's Battle of the Bands at Three Thirsty Roosters."

Three Thirsty Roosters, which held a Battle of the Bands every week and probably could hold, like, thirty people if those people didn't have issues with personal space or body odor. Not exactly a super-important gig when anyone could get onstage and take a shot.

Normally, she wouldn't have blinked. Her coworkers had all kinds of things going on that she chalked up to being young and in Austin—bands, throwback bowling leagues, street taco cook-offs, roller derby. She usually didn't mind picking up the slack where needed since she was a senior designer and worked late anyway. Her father had always told her the best way to maintain job security was to be indispensable. She'd taken that to heart, always filling in the gaps others wouldn't.

But the words *Pres said* and the assumption that she would take on more despite her already-crazy workload dug under her skin. She'd already sent him an email saying she was ahead. Instead of him thanking her for working fourteen-hour days and telling her to take her weekend, he now assumed she'd stick around and take on even more work? What if she wanted to go try her hand at Battle of the Bands? It could happen.

Okay, probably not, but she did have something on her schedule. No, *someone*. She put the note back in Annabelle's hands, aggravation pulsing through her. "Sorry. There's no way I can squeeze this in tonight, and I've got plans this weekend. You'll have to tell the client you'll handle it on Monday."

Annabelle's pierced brow arched. "But they want it ASAP."

"Then you'll have to work late tonight, come in tomorrow, or get Preston to deal with it. I'm not available."

"I—" Annabelle's lips opened but then shut when she saw the look on Liv's face. "Fine. I'll figure it out."

Annabelle stalked off, her knee-high boots clicking on the wood floors like a hammer, but Liv couldn't find it in her to care. She didn't have a band, but she had important things she needed to do. Like take photos of pancakes and irritate Finn's parents. And naked things. Lots of naked things.

With that surge of righteous indignation, she got up from her desk and headed to Preston's office. He'd told her he wouldn't be available to talk until later tonight when she'd show him her preliminary designs, but she'd heard that line a few times this week and was done with it. They would talk now.

Liv knocked on Preston's door but didn't wait for him to call her in. She stepped inside his office and shut the door behind her. "I need a minute."

Preston didn't look up from the papers he was flipping through. "I was just about to call you. Great job on fixing the Anderson Wines site so quickly last week. They said they're sending you a gift basket."

"Cool. Pres, I—"

"Are you making sure your designs for Butter and Brittle look great on mobile, too? The design you sent me yesterday wasn't converting well on my phone."

Liv shifted in her heels, swallowing down her annoyance at the interruption. "I figured out the issue. It's fixed."

He glanced up, smiled camera-flash quick, and jotted something down on a notepad. "Great. I told them we're running ahead. They're thrilled. Hopefully, we can get the designs to them early. That would look fantastic and would probably get us some referrals."

"What?" she said, forgetting to watch her tone. "You're not supposed to *tell them* we're ahead. I'm working with the original schedule, which was already fast. It's not going to be early."

Confusion flashed over his features. "But you're days ahead."

She smoothed her lipstick, steeling herself. "I'm days ahead *for me*. I doubled up my hours this week so that I can take the weekend."

Preston looked at his notepad again. "No way."

She blinked. "What?"

Jotting, jotting, jotting, like she wasn't even there having a conversation with him. "No can do. The client is now expecting early, and we deliver what we promise. Plus, Annabelle's out this weekend already. You know weekends are part of the deal here."

"Then I need to take vacation days. I have a thing."

He sniffed. "You mean your new boyfriend?"

Her ears went hot. "And in the category of things that are not your business…"

"We're too swamped."

"We're always swamped."

He glanced up, warning lingering behind his dark-frame glasses. "Which means business is going well, which is job security for you and me, which is what we're trying to do here, right? Plus, even if I was granting vacation requests, I need them six weeks in advance. And I can't grant you special favors. You know how that'd look."

Her teeth clicked together. She knew that wasn't true. Manny had taken a last-minute vacation two weeks ago when he won an entry to a Vegas poker tournament. Preston had been all back slaps and go-get-'em about that.

And the *you know how that'd look* comment burrowed right through her last bit of tolerance. Early on, before Preston had taken over the top spot from his brother, she and Pres had had a minor thing. A few hookups after working late together because it was convenient and light. Nothing dramatic and not the best decision on her part because he'd blabbed about it to a few coworkers. She'd ended it shortly after that. But now he inevitably brought it up anytime she asked for anything because other employees knew they had a history.

But this wasn't a special favor. She didn't ask for those. "I worked double hours this week. I brought work home to get ahead on the project. Everything will be delivered on the original schedule. The client can wait."

"No."

The response was so curt, so *I'm not even listening to you anymore* that she wanted to snap her fingers in his face to get his attention.

Liv's fingers curved around the back of the chair she was standing behind. Earlier in the week, she'd been debating going back to Finn's place, wondering if she'd made a huge mistake. But now that Preston was pushing back on her, she realized how useless the internal debate had been. He could pull the plug on it without her even having a say. "What about working remotely? Everything I need is on my laptop."

He let out a belabored breath, like she was officially annoying him now. He set his pen down. "Olivia, I'm sorry, but it's not going to work. I need you here. You saw what happened when you were gone for two days. We can talk about vacation near the holidays when things slow down." His gaze shifted to his computer screen, dismissing her. "And hit the brew button on the coffeepot on your way out. It's going to be one of those nights."

Liv stood there, anger making her freeze up.

She wasn't one to make waves at work. Even with her carnal knowledge of her boss, she was nothing but a professional here. She'd done the rebel thing in her teen years and in college and had been burned thoroughly. She'd learned that life was easier when you played along, did your job, didn't get labeled difficult. But something deep inside her was on fire, and the flames were gaining ground. She knew what she was supposed to do. Act rationally. Swallow her frustration. Go to her desk and suck it up. Get her work done. Get Annabelle's work done. Make Preston some fucking coffee.

But her legs wouldn't move.

When Preston glanced up and noticed her still standing there, he frowned. He didn't say it, but the sentiment was clear: *Why are you still here?*

She didn't have an answer.

Not for why she was still in his office. And not for why she was still *here*. In this job. In this place. In this life.

"I need the weekend, Pres," she said finally. "I'm taking it."

His eyebrows disappeared beneath his over-styled, messy-on-purpose hair. "That's not for you to decide."

She took a breath and released the chair in front of her. "It is, actually. Fire me if you need to."

That seemed to snap some of his bravado. He groaned and scraped a hand through his hair. "Olivia, what the hell is going on with you? You're my partner in crime when shit hits the fan here. I'm telling you I need you, and you're threatening to bail? This isn't you."

"Maybe you don't know me then."

He scoffed. "Don't know you? Come on." He got up from behind the desk and stepped around it to perch on the front, facing off with her. He gave her a confident smirk, the one the interns got all doe-eyed over. "I'd say we know each other pretty well. I know you have a cute birthmark on your inner right thigh."

Her nails curled into her palms. "That's not knowing me. That's fucking me."

His smile fell. "I know you're a perfectionist like me. I know your clients matter to you. I know that you don't go off on whims and leave a client hanging. I know you're like me."

"Like you," she said, her voice flat.

"Yeah." He stepped forward and put his hands on her shoulders. "We get each other because this job is our life. We know that's what it takes to get ahead. So don't threaten me with walking out when I know that's not what you want to do. If you don't have this, what do you have? Because I know what that answer is for me."

The words hit her like hot needles, each one a prick to her skin, drawing blood. If she didn't have work every day, what did she have?

A generic apartment. A few friends she occasionally met up with for lunch. A couple of TV shows she recorded. A family that loved her as long as she was their version of a well-behaved, contributing member to society.

She swallowed hard.

Preston smiled at her lack of answer. He gave her shoulder a squeeze. "Why don't you take the rest of the night off, and I'll take care of Annabelle's issue? Get some sleep and then come back with your head together in the morning. I'll be working all weekend, too, so we can keep each other company."

"Pres…"

His smile remained in place. "Yeah?"

She removed his hand from her shoulder. "You have no clue who I am."

"Olivia," he said, the word full of impatience.

"I quit."

His pretty-boy eyes went wide, and her stomach did a roller-coaster plummet.

I quit?

Had those words just come out of her mouth? *I quit?*

Before he could say anything else or she could sufficiently freak out, she turned and strode out of his office. Numb. Trembling. Ears buzzing.

"Olivia…"

She heard her name but didn't stop. She passed the coffeepot on the table outside and, in a daze, tapped the button. The thing sputtered to life as she went to her desk on autopilot. A few of her coworkers remained in the industrial-style open office even though the lights had been turned low. From the outside looking in, it

looked like it'd be a fun place to work—toys on people's desks, a basketball net above the trash can, bright
comic book artwork on the exposed brick walls. But she
glanced around at those who were still at their desk—
headphones on, eyes glued to their screens, Red Bull
cans on their desks—and just felt hollow.

Just keep moving. Just keep moving.

The words repeated in her head like she was channel-
ing that forgetful fish from the Disney movie. *Just keep
swimming.* She gathered a few personal things, dumped
them in a bag, and then walked out of the office. *Keep
moving.* No one even looked up. And Preston never
came out of his office to chase her.

Only when she hit the thick evening heat outside did
the reality of what she'd done smack her in the face.
She sat down on a bus stop bench, her bag o' crap at
her feet, and let the wave she'd set in motion crash over
her, splashing reality all around her and pooling anxiety
in her gut.

Her big risk this summer was going to be spending
time at Finn's and knocking the dust off her camera.
That was going to be her toe in the water. Instead, she'd
fallen off the dock into the ocean.

She'd quit her job. Her only source of income. A job
she'd dedicated years to. A job that was…

Her life.

Holy shit.

She'd just quit her life.

chapter
NINETEEN

"DID YOU GET THE PHOTOS?" FINN ASKED IN BETWEEN SIPS OF beer as he leaned back in the chair, the view of the lake black at this hour and his mood the same.

"I did," Billings said. "Barely recognized you."

"Yeah. I shaved off the beard and cut my hair. Didn't want to take any chances."

Billings sniffed. "It wasn't that. It was the goofy smile on your face. Not sure I've seen you with one of those before."

Finn grunted. "You usually aren't telling me things that inspire smiling."

"Well, that and I'm not half as pretty as your lady friend. What's her name again?"

"Olivia." Finn closed his eyes and rubbed his brow. He couldn't think about Liv right now. She'd been gone almost a week, and he hadn't heard a damn thing from her. He'd fucked it up and scared her off by moving too fast, by letting his dick commandeer his brain. "And don't fool yourself, boss. You're a beauty."

"Kissing up will get you nowhere. But I'm glad to see you looking human again. Keep the pictures coming, and keep up those weekly calls with Doc Robson. They'll help your case."

"My case?"

"Yeah. I have a big operation shaping up that I know you'll want to be in on, but I'll have to go to bat for you to convince the higher-ups that you'll be ready that soon."

Finn straightened in the chair. "What kind of operation?"

Billings didn't respond for a few seconds. "Can't give details yet. We're still in surveillance mode."

Finn frowned, frustrated that his boss insisted on keeping him in the dark. But if Billings thought Finn would want to be in on it, there was a chance it was a lead on the Long Acre guns. Finn's heartbeat ticked up a notch. "When would it start?"

"September is my goal. Would need you up here before that to get you prepared."

"Got it. If you send me the files, I can start—"

"No," Billings said firmly. "No work right now. This break is a requirement. You'll get everything you need when it's time. The only reason I'm telling you anything now is so that you're motivated to keep doing what you're doing."

Finn nodded, determination making his muscles go tight. "Got it."

"And Dorsey?"

"Yeah?"

"Do all you can to enjoy this break. Spend time with your lady. See your family, your friends. Do whatever it is that gets you smiling like you were in that picture because you're going to need those memories going into this assignment. It's an ugly one, and it's gonna take a while."

Finn swallowed hard. "Right. I'll be ready for it. And I'm visiting my family tomorrow."

"Good." Finn could almost picture Billings giving that curt nod he did when he dismissed people after meetings. "I'll check in soon."

Finn ended the call and leaned back in the chair, mind whirling. Something in Billings's voice was off. Whatever this next assignment was, his boss was more concerned than normal. He wanted Finn to be mentally sound—that was a given—but something else was there, too. Finn knew if he asked, he wouldn't get any answers, but at least he now had an end goal in sight. They'd let him back in the field if he could prove he wasn't irreparably damaged from the last job, that he wouldn't go rogue on them. That he was normal.

Or mostly. Because God knows he'd never be totally normal. He wasn't even sure what that looked like anymore. Seeing his family tomorrow would only high-light that. But bailing on the visit wasn't going to cut it. Billings would expect more photos, more proof that Finn was stable and ready for this job. He needed to keep up appearances, and Liv was no longer here to help. She didn't say she *wasn't* coming back, but she hadn't called or texted. He'd messed things up. He needed to call her, apologize for taking advantage of the situation, try to get things back on track…

But when he lifted his phone to call, he couldn't bring himself to do it. He didn't want to be someone's charity case. If she didn't want to be here, he wasn't going to guilt her into it. He'd figure it out on his own.

Dread curled in Finn's stomach as he rummaged through the pantry, looking for something to bring to his parents' house. His mother used to make comments to her father if a guest came to lunch or dinner without a hostess gift—like it was some egregious sin. He didn't know if he was considered a guest now or if he still qualified as family, but he wasn't going to take any chances.

He grabbed a dusty bottle of tequila that he found tucked in the back of the pantry. He frowned down at it. For a dinner with friends this would probably work, but he doubted his parents were planning a margarita lunch. That left him with canned corn or a sleeve of Ritz crackers. Neither was going to pass muster. He pulled his phone out of his pocket and checked the time. His mom used to love the macaroons from one of the local bakeries. It wasn't exactly on the way, but he could leave enough time before lunch to swing by and pick up some. If that failed, there was a wine store next door to the bakery. At least wine had the added bonus of taking the edge off the awkward meeting.

He set his tequila down, resisting the urge to take a swig of it to prepare him for this visit. Part of him wanted to text and say he'd gotten a flat tire and couldn't make it, but knowing his family, they'd just send someone to pick him up.

He shook his head. "Get it together, man."

He'd faced down criminals who wouldn't hesitate to cut his throat and ask questions later, but one family get-together and he was ready to bolt. What was the worst they could do? Make him feel guilty for not being around? That was a given. Comment on how he'd let the family business down by not following in his father's footsteps? No doubt.

He could survive all of that. If he wanted to get back on the job, this was part of the assignment. Billings wanted him to visit his family. Plus, Liv had made a good point. His parents were getting older and wouldn't always be around. He also had sisters he missed. This was the only family he had. He needed to do this, even though he didn't feel like he belonged in their world anymore.

With that internal pep talk complete, he grabbed his keys and headed toward the front door. But when he swung it open and saw someone standing there, he jumped back and cocked his fist, ready to use it as a weapon.

Liv lifted her palms in defense, her eyes wide. "Don't hit me!"

All the air rushed out of his lungs as he lowered his arm. "Shit, Liv. You scared the hell out of me."

She winced. "Sorry. I was about to knock, but you beat me to it. Um…surprise?"

The hopeful look and head tilt she gave him made him laugh despite his pounding heartbeat. "I'd say so. What are you doing here?"

She spread her arms out at her sides, revealing her flowered sundress, just enough cleavage to make his mouth water, and a smile. "If you're still looking for a sidekick for the parental gauntlet, I'm here to provide my services."

His lips parted. "Really?"

She shrugged and smoothed her hair behind her ears. "Yeah, if you still want me to go and if I'm not too late."

If he still wanted her to go? Like she wasn't doing

him a huge, uncomfortable favor. Like she wasn't the best damn surprise he could imagine. He wanted to sweep her up and squeeze her, he was so happy to see her standing there. "Of course I do, and you're early, actually. But are you sure you want to volunteer as tribute? I'm still not sure *I* want to volunteer."

She laughed and stepped into his space to give him a quick peck on the lips. "Yes. And tribute? You've been Netflix-ing."

He tossed his keys on the table by the door and gave in to the temptation to touch her. He wrapped his arms around her, the tension in his shoulders easing at the feel of her, at the grapefruit scent of her shampoo, at just... her, being there. After a week of radio silence, he'd been convinced he'd screwed the whole thing up, scared her off. He'd half expected her to never come back to the lake house. Seeing her standing there was like a potent drug injected straight into his veins. "Of course I'm Netflix-ing. I am properly recluse-ing and getting over being dumped by this girl who used me for my body."

She touched her forehead to his chest. "I'm sorry I didn't call. I didn't dump you, though."

"Just used me for my body then?"

She looked up with a sly smile and slid her hand up his chest, those gentle fingers sending hot awareness straight downward. "Yes. It is quite a body."

God, this woman. Even the simplest touch had him aching for her. He bent his head and kissed her, a little more than a peck this time. "I got the better end of the deal. And feel free to use me anytime. Right now, in fact. I'm very easy. Super-loose morals."

She grinned. "Ooh, I love a man with loose morals.

It's at the top of my checklist. Too bad we have a lunch to go to."

He ran his finger under the thin strap of her sundress and watched with fascination as goose bumps appeared along her skin and her nipples hardened beneath the cotton fabric. So sensitive. Sexy. "We have a little while until I'm supposed to be there. I was just leaving early to pick up dessert." He dragged the strap down, revealing the top curve of her breast, and leaned down to kiss the smooth, tawny skin. "Maybe we should just have dessert here."

Liv tipped her head back as he trailed kisses up her neck. She braced a hand on the doorframe, her body shuddering underneath his lips and his cock hardening in his pants. She let out a soft sigh. "I'm supposed to tell you no right now. That we'll be late, and that will be bad. And that I'll have after-sex hair, and that will be worse. But…"

"But?" he asked, sliding his hand into all that dark hair and cupping her neck.

"But…what was I saying again?"

He laughed softly and pulled her inside, shutting the door and then crowding her up against it. She didn't hesitate or resist. Instead, she reached for him and pulled him in for a kiss, one arm looping around his neck and her other hand sliding between them to stroke him through his jeans. His knees tried to give out at the feel of her hand on him, but he managed to keep them both upright, kissing her back with a frenzied need he couldn't staunch.

A throaty moan rumbled through her, like touching him was so damn satisfying, and his body went all systems go. He loved how responsive Liv was. No games.

No pretending she wasn't interested. Bold and brazen and hot as fuck.

It made his normal filters fall away. Flipped all his dirty switches.

"You want my cock, baby?" he said, moving her hand away and dragging her leg up to press his erection at the apex of her thighs. "You missed having me inside you?"

She groaned and rocked against him, sending jolts of pleasure up his spine.

He rutted against her slowly, torturing them both, and brushed his lips against her ear. "You should've called. I would've kept you company during those late work nights. Would've told you in filthy detail exactly what I was going to do to you when I saw you again, would've made you tuck your hand beneath your desk and stroke yourself between those pretty thighs while you came and no one else was the wiser."

A hard shudder rumbled through her. "Shit. *Finn*."

It was a plea. He reached beneath her dress and shoved her panties to the side. When he slipped his fingers inside, he found her slick and pulsing with heat. His erection pushed painfully against his zipper. "Christ, you're sexy. You need to come, Livvy?"

She tapped her head back against the door. "Please."

He released her leg and tugged her panties down and off. "Lift your dress for me, but don't take it off. Show me where you want me."

Her eyes blinked open, but her gaze was hooded, her cheeks flushed. Without hesitation, she grabbed the hem of her dress and slowly raised the skirt, joining in the dirty game. His heart pounded harder with each sweet inch she revealed. Long spread legs, high heels still on, and then all that pretty feminine flesh on display. His tongue pressed to the roof of his mouth, and he had to remind himself to breathe.

He dropped to his knees in front of her, gripped her thigh, and ran his tongue over her while sliding two fingers deep. She moaned, and her head hit the door again as she lifted up on her toes, offering everything she had to give.

He could spend hours there, worshiping at that particular altar. There was nothing more erotic to him than Liv Arias, dressed up like she'd just left a church luncheon but naked and spread for him from the waist down.

He kissed and licked and touched her, mapping her hot spots and committing them to memory because he planned to spend a lot of time this summer making Liv writhe and moan like this. Billings wanted him to take up a hobby. This was going to be it.

But when Liv started to gasp with the first throes of orgasm, his own body protested, screaming with arousal. She called out his name and rocked against his mouth, taking exactly what she craved and driving him wild with need. Blindly, he reached down and undid his jeans, freeing his erection and giving himself a stroke for relief as he continued to work her with his tongue.

Liv wasn't shy with the noises she made, and she pushed him away gently when she couldn't take anymore. He shifted to give her space, but when she opened her eyes and saw his hand working, she shook her head.

"Don't," she whispered.

"What?"

She slid down to her knees, her skin glistening with a

fine sheen of sweat. She grabbed his wrist and moved it away. "I didn't get a turn last time."

"Liv—"

But she was having none of that. She crawled over him, leading him down onto his back, and then she lowered her head. He knew what was about to happen, but he was completely unprepared for the feel of her hot, soft mouth sliding over his cock. His neck arched, and he said some sort of gibberish word that had only vowels.

She murmured something in reply, but the vibration of her mouth on him only served to blend his brain further. His hands went to her hair, gripping for dear life, and she swirled her tongue around the head. Goddamn, he'd forgotten what a blow job felt like. Or maybe he'd never had one like this. Maybe Liv had some magical skill at making a man want to explode into a million blissed-out pieces because...damn.

She worked him slowly but in a way that said she wasn't just marking time. Women who didn't like giving head didn't do the things she was doing, didn't run their cheek over his shaft, didn't nuzzle and lick and kiss every bit of him, didn't run their finger along...

Oh. *Oh.*

He'd planned to warn her, but it was too late. With that last move, his verbal functioning shut down and every ounce of energy in his body zeroed in on the point of contact. His shoulders lifted up off the floor, and his hands gripped her head as he came in a hard rush.

He expected her to pull away, to back off, but she continued to pleasure him, making noises of her own and softening the pressure as he rode the wave down.

When he was done, his head sank back to the floor, and his belly rose and fell with ragged breaths.

The air shifted and her dress brushed him as she leaned over him. He opened his eyes to find her smiling down at him with red lips and after-sex hair haloing her face. "You okay, Batman?"

He grinned back up at her. "No, you've killed me. I'm now speaking to you from the great beyond."

She laughed. "Is it nice there?"

"So nice."

"Are there unicorns?"

He reached out and brushed his thumb along her lips. "You're weird, Arias."

"I know. You can be Oddly Hot. I'll be Weirdly Sexy. We'll be a crime-fighting duo."

"Excellent. And sorry I didn't give you fair warning before I came."

"None needed." She leaned down to kiss him, letting him taste himself on her lips and her flavor still lingering on his. He could get used to that combination. She eased back, straddling his stomach. "I like seeing you lose it like that. It's a power trip."

He chuckled. "Feel free to assert your authority anytime then."

She fixed the strap on her sundress. "How much time do we have before we're late? I'm going to need a quick shower."

"You look perfect. Well-laid."

She rolled her eyes. "Smelling like sex is not the first impression I want to give your parents. Shower is nonnegotiable."

"Details, details. Fine. I will allow a shower." He

rolled her off him, and they both got to their feet, right-ing their clothes. But before she could escape him, he lifted her up and hauled her over his shoulder.

She yelped and slapped his back. "What are you doing?"

"I need a rinse, too. And if I'm going to pick up something to bring on the way there, we only have time for one shower. We're going to have to share it," he said, his tone gravely serious. "I'm being a responsible adult. Behave."

She snorted. "Somehow, I don't think this plan is going to work out."

He smiled. "Don't worry. All I'm going to do is make sure you're very, very clean."

"Good luck with that one."

He laughed and carried her upstairs. "That's okay. I like you dirty, Livvy."

"Yeah?"

"Definitely."

He liked her dirty. He liked her sweet. He liked when she got bossy and when she gave in. And he liked the way she'd made him feel when he'd opened up his door and realized she'd come back to him. He hadn't quite understood what that feeling was when it'd first hit him, but as they showered and she flicked shampoo bubbles at him, he knew exactly what that feeling was.

Happy.

chapter
TWENTY

LIV STARED OUT THE WINDOW, WATCHING THE SCENERY change, her mind busy but strangely content. Two orgasms could do that to a girl. No, Finn Dorsey could do that to a girl. It was a welcome change after her sleepless night.

Finn laced his fingers with hers and squeezed. "Maybe we should change plans. I feel a fever coming on."

She looked over at him. "Oh really?"

He nodded and gave her a serious look. "Yes. I think I need to call and tell them I'll be in bed for a week. It's bad. Want to play nurse?"

She pulled her hand free and pinched his arm. "Stop. There's no going back now. We're doing this. Plus, you're going to be fine. I'm here to run interference. They'll be much more likely to take jabs at me than you."

His expression darkened. "I'm not going to let them insult you, Liv. That's a deal breaker."

She waved a dismissive hand. "Let 'em. After the week I had, I can deal with whatever they throw at me."

He lowered the radio. "You do seem oddly calm about all this. You remember my dad, right?"

"Vividly."

"So is it just the sex relaxing you or something else?" He sent her a look of mock concern. "Have you been drinking? Eating mushrooms? Dropping acid?"

"Not exactly." She took a breath and looked forward. "Worse."

"Worse than dropping acid? I'm not even sure what that would be. Meth? Toad licking?"

She grimaced. "Ew, gross. Not as bad as licking toads."

"Well, that's a relief. We did just kiss."

"I quit my job."

"You—" The car jerked to a halt, the tires screeching as he almost missed a stop sign. "*What?*"

She bit her lip and glanced his way. "Yes. That look on your face. That's basically what I've been feeling inside since I walked out of work last night."

He stared at her, green eyes searching. "You're just telling me this *now*? Liv…"

She shrugged. "I was going to lead with that, but then you had to go and be all hot and seductive. *I just quit my job* is kind of a mood killer. Plus, I'm…okay about it."

He eased onto the gas, checking what was in front of them, but then looking her way again. "Yeah? You seemed pretty freaked out last weekend at the thought of losing your job."

She smoothed her dress and frowned. "Believe me, acceptance wasn't my first reaction. I didn't sleep. Pretty much was in full freak-out mode all night, strategizing ways to undo it. But then this morning, I typed up an email to apologize to my boss, to beg for my job back, for him to chalk my behavior up to temporary insanity, and…"

"And?"

She let out a breath and leaned back in the seat. "I couldn't send it. Beyond the fact that the reasons I quit were legit and the thought of crawling back and saying they weren't made me want to vomit, I realized that this job has been another version of a drug for me." She turned her head toward him. "You were right."

"I never said it was a drug."

"No, but last Monday you said I was looking for an excuse to run, and you were right. This—you, being back in Long Acre, the photography, all of it—scares the living hell out of me," she admitted. "At work, I don't have to think about the what-ifs or unfulfilled plans or friends I cut out of my life. I don't have to deal with the anxiety of any of that. I don't have to do anything hard or scary. That also means I don't get to do anything interesting."

He reached for her hand again, and she let him take it. "So you really did it? Just walked out."

She took a deep breath, one that lifted her shoulders and made her heart beat in her ears. "Yeah. I did." She wet her lips. "I said in my letter that I wanted to live a life that scared me. My job was my safety bunker, and I just burned it down. So…now I'm feeling kind of terrified." She turned her gaze to his and swallowed hard. "But at least I'm feeling something. *You* make me feel something."

Finn's expression flashed with something raw. Affection. Pride. Something else.

His undisguised reaction hit her in the chest and twisted, making it hard to breathe for a second. She'd seen glimpses of the boy she used to know, but for the first time since finding him again, she felt that tenderness from him.

And that stirred something much more dangerous in her. Something she wasn't going to stop herself from feeling but that scared her more than all the other stuff added together.

His throat bobbed. "Liv, I—"

She squeezed his hand. "Don't. Please. I'm not telling you all this for any other reason than that I'm tired of playing it safe. I don't want to play games with you or be coy. Here's the truth. I loved last weekend. Hanging out. Taking pictures. Sharing a bed with you. I've missed you this week, and I'm sorry I didn't call. I didn't call because you scare me. I know you're leaving, and it will hurt me when you do. But I'd rather have a summer with you and my friends and my camera than walk away now and never have had it happen. So here I am." A shimmer of nerves rippled through her. "Trusting that I'm tough enough to handle it all and that my savings account will keep me afloat until I figure out what I'm going to do with my life."

Finn pulled off on the shoulder of the road and brought their joined hands up to kiss her knuckles. "Not that you need my stamp of approval, but I am ridiculously proud of you. Here I was, dragging my feet all morning because I didn't want to deal with an awkward visit home, and meanwhile, you were setting a bomb off in your life and going balls out with all of your worst fears. You amaze me, Olivia Arias," he said softly. "And I missed the hell out of you this week, too."

The words sent curls of warmth through her chest. "Yeah?"

"Yeah." He leaned forward and kissed her.

She gave over to it immediately, her lips softening against his and opening, welcoming him in. His fingers slid into her hair, and he held her just where he wanted her, gentle and sweet.

When he eased back, he ran his thumb over her bottom lip and smiled. "I guess if you're going to be ballsy enough to quit your job, I probably need to grow a pair and deal with my family, huh?"

"You have a pair. I fully inspected them. But let's just get your family drunk and see what happens."

He lowered his head and touched his forehead to hers. "Bad things, Arias. Bad. Things."

Her lips hitched up. "How about for every classist, racist, or asshole comment your dad makes, you owe me an orgasm?"

Finn lifted his head and grinned. "I fear that you are going to be one very satisfied lady."

"I think I win either way," she declared. "So, what am I going to be? Fiancée? Knocked up with triplets? One of an illicit ménage relationship you're in?"

He laughed, settled his hand back on the steering wheel, and pulled out into traffic. "Let's not give my mother a heart attack. How about we go with the truth? We're dating."

Her eyebrows lifted. "We're dating?"

"Yes. If that works for you. I have no desire to share you this summer. I'm morally loose but very traditional," he said with a half-serious tone. "Plus, you're supposed to be helping me with my violent tendencies."

"Violent tendencies?" she said drolly.

"Yes, violent tendencies, as in I feel the deep inner

need to break things when I imagine some other guy touching you."

"I see. That is very caveman of you."

"I realize this." He checked the rearview mirror and exited the highway. "I apologize. I'm not as evolved as you."

She pulled her lip gloss out of her purse and smoothed it on. "Oh, I'd cut a bitch who came near you so...not that evolved."

A sharp bark of a laugh burst out of him. "Why do I find this vicious side of you weirdly sexy?"

"Duh, because that's my secret agent name now. Plus, you were dating an imaginary felon who attacked for love. Maybe you've developed a kink."

His dimple appeared. "Oh, I'm developing a kink, all right. Her name is Olivia."

"So, dating?" she asked.

He nodded. "Dating."

The word settled into a more comfortable place in her head than she expected. She knew that this was temporary, that they had an expiration date, and that it would hurt like vinegar in an open wound when it was done, but for once, she wasn't running from the thought.

If she'd learned anything from coming back to Long Acre and reading her letter, it was that you didn't know what tomorrow would bring. You had to live for today. Enjoy the moment.

Even when you knew that moment couldn't last.

Liv leaned back and gazed out the window. The familiar view registered for the first time. She'd been so wrapped up in her conversation with Finn that she hadn't even noticed they'd taken the Long Acre exit.

"What are we doing here? I thought your parents moved."

"No." Finn turned into the only swanky neighborhood in Long Acre, Briar Bend. "They rented a place in San Antonio until the media circus died down, but they came back home a few years later. They never sold the house."

Liv's stomach flipped over, her contentment from a moment earlier threatening to disintegrate. "Oh, I didn't realize."

He glanced over at her, worry marring his brow. "Is that a problem?"

She pressed her lips together and shook her head. "No, I just...I have memories there. Anything tied to that time in my life freaks me out a little. I never know what will trigger a panic attack."

"Damn, I'm sorry," he said, regret in his voice. "I didn't even think. If you don't want to—"

She lifted a hand. "No, don't even say it. This is new Liv. Brave Liv. The woman who just walked out of her job mic-drop style. I can handle it. If I feel any anxiety coming on, I'll find a quiet spot and get it together. I won't cause a scene."

"You can cause whatever you need to, but if you feel any signs, come get me," he said. "Don't be afraid to do that. I can help talk you down. I've been there."

She nodded and rubbed her palms on her legs. "It'll be fine."

She said the words, hoping they'd be true.

⌐∾∾⌐

Finn took a bracing breath when he and Liv strode up to the door of the house he'd grown up in. Not much looked like it had changed since the last time he'd visited. There were some new flowers in the front garden and a different welcome mat, but otherwise, it was the house he remembered—a sprawling three-story Texas-style home with stone, dark wood accents, and a wide porch across the front. Down the length of the porch, three rocking chairs that he'd never seen his parents use tilted back and forth in the breeze, creaking their greeting.

"That's creepy," Liv said under her breath when she followed his gaze. "I feel like we're being watched."

"The ghosts of the Dorsey family's past," he said in his best scary voice. "Do not enter if you want to live."

Liv punched him in the arm. "Shut up. You're making me want to do the sign of the cross or something."

He grinned. "You can take the girl out of the church but not the Catholic out of the girl."

Liv stuck her tongue out at him but then quickly did the sign of the cross, touching her forehead, sternum, and each shoulder. When he raised his eyebrows, she shrugged. "Going to visit your family. I'll take all the protection I could get."

He chuckled. "Hopefully it won't require divine intervention."

But when he turned to knock on the door, the spot between his shoulders tensed up like he was gearing up for a fight already. He sighed and tried to shake off the feeling. This was going to be fine. It was just a family visit. He gripped the neck of the bottle he had in his right hand and knocked.

There was noise on the other side, and he could hear shoes clicking against hardwood floors. He forced a pleasant look onto his face and snuck a peek at Liv, who looked like she was about to bolt.

The door swung open, and the woman on the other side let out a shriek. His younger sister, Jill, broke into a wide smile and then launched herself at him, a cloud of auburn hair and girlie perfume. "Finn!"

Finn nearly dropped the bottle as she wrapped him in a fierce bear hug. "Jills."

The tension he'd been feeling eased a bit at her enthusiasm. He'd had plenty of family drama in his life, but Jill had never been a part of it. Ten years younger than he was, she'd been the surprise baby and the one they'd all shielded. Even his father had doted on her instead of laying down the standard Dorsey family pressure to perform that Finn and his older sister, Katherine, had been subjected to.

Finn leaned back and smiled down at Jill. "I didn't think you were going to be here. Last I heard, you were studying abroad."

"I'm home for the summer." She gave him another quick hug, and then her attention snagged on Liv. "Oh, oops, I'm sorry. I didn't realize you brought someone. Here I am, being all kinds of rude."

Liv waved her off. "You're not. I know it's been forever since you've seen Finn. Don't mind me."

Jill disentangled herself from Finn and put out her hand to Liv. "I'm Jill, Finn's sister."

Liv clasped his sister's hand, genuine warmth on her face. "Liv Arias, Finn's...date."

Jill's eyes lit up. "Yay, a date." She turned back to Finn, her expression way too pleased. "You brought a girl. I'm super impressed. Dad told me you've been living in a cave or something. I figured you'd have adopted a volleyball for a friend by now."

Liv laughed and then quickly coughed over it.

Finn scoffed. "Dad has no idea what I've been doing or where I've been. I was adopting felons as friends."

Jill frowned, worry wrinkling her brow. "Caves and volleyballs would be safer."

He reached out and cupped her chin, giving it a gentle squeeze. "Hey, none of that. I'm here and fine. Okay? And yes, I brought a date. Who is not a felon."

Some of the light in Jill's face had dimmed, but she made an attempt to clear the frown. "Okay." She stepped back through the doorway and then turned her head and yelled, "Mom, Finn's here!"

Liv sent Finn a here-we-go look, and they followed Jill inside. She hurried toward the back part of the house, announcing to whomever would listen that Finn was there. Soon there were more voices drifting from the kitchen. His mom stepped into the hallway and clasped her hands to her chest at the sight of him. "Finn-Joseph."

The gentle drawl of his mother's voice using his first and middle name like one word hit him harder than he expected.

She hurried across the hallway, her silver bob bouncing and heels clicking until she stopped in front of him. Her eyes went shiny while she gave him a full head-to-toe perusal as if to make sure he hadn't been lying to her about being okay.

"Hey, Mom."

"Don't you *Hey, Mom* me," she admonished. "You come here and let me hug you, you stupid boy. Why have you made me wait so long to see your handsome face?"

He bent down and embraced his mother, feeling none of the awkwardness he had anticipated. He and his mom hadn't always gotten along because she'd sided with his dad by default on most things, but he'd never doubted her love for him and his siblings. And he could feel by the tight, almost desperate way she was gripping him that she'd been well and truly worried about him never coming home again. Or coming home in a box.

A ripple of guilt went through him. "I'm sorry it's been so long."

"You should be," she said matter-of-factly before releasing him. "It's not good for an old-*ish* woman's heart."

He lifted the bottle of tequila, which was all he'd been left with for a gift after his and Liv's predinner detour to the shower. "I brought this."

His mother took the bottle and read the label. "Interesting choice, Son. Expecting a need for hard liquor tonight?"

"Maybe?"

She laughed, her blue-eyed gaze flicking to Liv. "Well, now you've probably scared your friend. Hello, I'm Barbara."

Liv shook his mother's hand. "Hi, Mrs. Dorsey. Liv Arias. You probably don't remember me, but we met a few times when Finn and I were in high school. We were classmates."

His mother's lips pressed together in thought. "Arias? That name does sound familiar."

Liv released her hand and smiled. "My father also used to do your landscaping. I helped him out from time to time."

"Oh yes!" his mom said, face brightening. "Santos.

He did such a lovely job and was always so friendly. And oh"—she snapped her fingers—"you were his daughter with the purple hair. I remember thinking you had such a unique style."

Finn cringed at the word *unique*, but Liv laughed. "That's one way to describe it. I was going through a fashion-questionable phase."

His mother waved a hand. "Don't we all, darlin'. You should've seen my hair in the eighties. It was so big, it needed its own zip code."

Finn let out a breath he didn't realize he'd been holding. He'd never expected his mom to make Liv feel uncomfortable. She was the consummate hostess and, unlike his father, a whole lot less judgmental about where people came from or how much money they had. But it was a relief nonetheless to see Liv relax.

"All right, you two," his mother said, leading them down the hall. "I have appetizers in the kitchen. I went with a devilish theme."

"Devilish?" Liv asked.

"You'll see," his mom said proudly. "Finn will tell you. I love a theme. But don't fill up too much. The ham will be ready in a little while. I'm expecting a few more guests."

Finn and Liv followed his mom into the kitchen where she had set up a number of delicious looking plates of food. Deviled eggs with jalapeños on top. Her famous spicy, roasted garlic dip with crudités and crackers. These things she called devils on horseback, which were dates wrapped with bacon and stuffed with cheese. His stomach rumbled at the sight.

Most kids he'd known growing up had found his

mom's food odd, but it was comfort food for him. His dad had always been working, so she'd picked up new hobbies or projects regularly. But cooking had turned out to be her love. When she'd told his father that she was considering opening a small catering business, he'd squashed the idea instantly. They didn't need the money, and he'd be damned if his wife was going to be serving the neighbors food like hired help.

Finn had never heard his parents argue so loudly. His dad had won.

"This all looks fantastic, Mrs. Dorsey," Liv said, gazing at all the food.

"Oh, thank—"

"Barb." A booming voice came from the hallway. "Where the hell is my golf bag? You better not have—"

At the sound of his father's voice, the tightening of Finn's mom's lips was barely perceptible, but Liv's sharp intake of breath wasn't. Finn reached out and grabbed Liv's hand just as his father stepped into the kitchen, his sentence cutting off at the sight of them.

His mom's smile was forced. "Look, Carl, Finn's here."

His father straightened, his expression as dark as the hair on his head. "So I see."

"Hi, Dad."

His father headed over to them. He gave Liv a brief, confused glance and then turned back to Finn. He stuck out his hand. "Son."

The handshake was firm, almost painful, and Finn tried not to notice how much his father had aged in the years since he'd last seen him. The lines in his face had deepened, and he'd lost weight. Somehow the towering, intimidating man of his youth seemed tired and small. But the hard glint in his eyes was the same.

"Carl, this is Finn's friend, Liv Arias. Her father used to do the landscaping. You remember Santos?"

His dad frowned and turned to Liv. "Can't say that I do. We've had a lot of lawn guys. They all blend together. Names all sound the same."

Liv's grip tightened on Finn's hand as she offered a brittle smile. "He worked for you for five years. And you once caught me and your son kissing. Maybe that will jog your memory. Unless Finn was kissing more landscapers' daughters than I was aware of. Maybe we blend together, too."

Liv said it with a light tone, but the dig was obvious.

His mom's lips parted in surprise, and Finn couldn't help but grin. "No, I only kissed one daughter. That should narrow it down for you, Dad."

His father's face reddened a bit. "Yes, now I recall."

The tension was subtle but growing like a cancer. His mother stepped in, lifting a plate. "Bacon-wrapped thing?"

Liv bit her lip and took one with thanks.

"So, dear, how is your father?" his mom asked, making the men take an appetizer, too. "Is he still making yards beautiful? You should see the rose garden he planted out back all those years ago. It's thriving and the envy of all my friends in the neighborhood."

Liv gave his mother a gracious smile. "Yes, ma'am. But he doesn't do the frontline work anymore. He expanded the company and is now in charge of a number of crews throughout the Austin area."

"That's wonderful," Finn's mother said, her drawl

coming out in full force. "Running your own business is such a challenge. I'm opening up a little wine bar in town this fall, and I tell you, it's been the hardest thing I've ever done. But I've also never had so much fun."

His father grunted.

Finn paused, devil on horseback halting halfway to his mouth. "Wait, what? You're opening up a bar?"

His mother beamed. "I am. That's one of the things I wanted to get you out here for. I wanted to tell you in person."

"That's amazing, Mom." He gave her another quick hug. "I know you've always wanted to do something like that."

"I have, and I'm not getting any younger. Nothing makes me prouder than knowing I raised three wonderful children, but sometimes you just need something for yourself. Even if it's an utter failure, at least I can say I gave it a shot, right?" She laughed.

"Of course," Liv said. "You've got to take a risk sometimes."

Finn gave Liv's hand a squeeze and smiled her way.

But before Finn could say anything, his dad tossed his appetizer in the trash and left the room without a word. His mom glanced over her shoulder and then rolled her eyes.

"I guess Dad's not a fan?"

His mother let out a sigh. "That's the other thing I needed to tell you in person. Your father and I are getting a divorce. It'll be finalized in a few weeks."

"What?" Finn leaned back against the kitchen island, a little thunderstruck.

"I'm sorry to say this in front of your guest," she said,

sending Liv an apologetic look. "But yes. He hasn't lived here for a few months. I know it's probably hard to understand since you've been gone for a while, but things..."

He lifted a hand. "Mom, you don't have to explain to me. I always wondered why you stayed with him so long. I'm just shocked you're actually going through with it."

She shrugged. "Well, after a health scare last year, I got this idea for the wine bar in my head."

His chest tightened. "Health scare?"

"I'm fine. Turned out to be nothing. But it could've been bad. And afterward, I had this need to do *something*. Otherwise, what's left? Just counting out my years here in the house, waiting for him to get home from work? So I told him I was going to do it with or without his approval. He gave me an ultimatum. Him or the business idea." She pointed a finger at him. "Word of advice: don't give a woman an ultimatum."

Liv made a sound in the back of her throat and then quickly shoved her appetizer in her mouth.

"Wow, Mom. Good for you," Finn said, swelling with pride for his mother. "I mean, I'm sorry about the divorce. I'm sure that's hard, but maybe you two will be better off doing your own things."

She patted his arm. "I'm sure we'll both be just fine, honey. Now enough unpleasant talk. I want to hear about you. What have you been up to since you ended your assignment? And how'd you and Liv reconnect?"

Finn opened his mouth to respond, but before he could get anything out, Jill's voice drifted into the kitchen. "Mom, the neighbors are here!"

The neighbors? Why would the...

Oh. Shit.

"Oh, honey, I hope you don't mind. I invited the Lindts. I didn't realize you were bringing a guest, and I thought you could use the company of an old friend."

Before he could even attempt to warn Liv, Mr. Lindt walked in with his daughter following right behind.

Rebecca froze in the doorway, her attention on Finn and Liv, and looked to be just as shocked to see them as he was to see her.

He turned to Liv, who looked like she'd swallowed her devil whole, horse and all.

Welp. So much for the family visit not being awkward.

chapter
TWENTY-ONE

LIV NEARLY CHOKED ON HER BACON WHEN REBECCA appeared in the doorway. Bec was perfectly coiffed with a pretty cream-colored blouse and pale-blue capri pants. She looked like a perfect match for this garden party—the elegant southern debutante—but based on Rebecca's wide eyes, she was just as surprised to see Liv as Liv was to see her. Rebecca's father—who was dressed in shirt and tie, even though it was a Saturday—offered a stiff smile to Mrs. Dorsey and kissed her cheek in greeting.

"It smells wonderful in here, Barbara. Thanks for inviting us. It's been a while since I've had a home-cooked meal."

He handed her a box from the local bakery, and they exchanged more pleasantries. Finn's expression was mildly pained. But Liv shifted her attention to the woman who looked like she was ready to slowly walk out backward, hoping no one noticed her. Liv refused to let this be weird. She went straight to Rebecca with a smile. "*Hola*, *chica*. This is a surprise."

"Hey." Rebecca glanced at the others, nodded politely at Barbara, and then lifted her hand in awkward greeting for Finn. She lowered her voice. "And *surprise* is one word for it."

"Guess you didn't know the guest list either."

"Oh, these look delicious," Rebecca said loud enough for the others to hear, and then she grabbed Liv's elbow, guiding her away from the others. They parked on the far side of the kitchen island where they pretended to admire the deviled eggs. She gave Liv an earnest look. "Liv, I had no idea you and Finn were going to be here. Dad just said he'd got an invite and insisted I come with him. I wouldn't have—"

Liv lifted a hand. "Seriously, don't stress. I wasn't supposed to be here. It was a last-minute thing. I'm sure Mrs. Dorsey invited you to keep Finn company."

Rebecca cringed. "God, that sounds horrible. Like I'm some paid date."

Liv smirked and took an egg off the platter. "More like the victim of motherly matchmaking and good intentions. Take it as a compliment. You're a bright, successful woman whom she'd love to see her son with."

"Ugh, that might even be worse. Now parents think they need to help me with my dating life. That is a sad state of affairs."

"Ha, at least they think you still have hope." Liv plucked the jalapeño off the egg and popped it in her mouth. "My father gave up on me getting married and giving him grandkids years ago. And Finn's mother would've never picked me to set up with her son."

"You don't know that. Barbara isn't like Finn's dad." Rebecca glanced at her and then over at Finn, who was now chatting with Mr. Lindt and his mother. "If this is going to be weird, I can fake a headache."

"Don't you dare. Have you seen the food? This is the place to be. Plus, you can be my voice of reason and keep me from throwing a punch at Mr. Dorsey. Or you can hold his arms back so I can get a clear shot if he insults me or my family again." She bumped shoulders with Rebecca, who finally relented and gave a small smile.

"That guy is an ass," she said, grabbing one of the eggs and taking a big bite. "For some reason, he likes me—which means he insists on talking my ear off every time I come here."

"My condolences. We brought tequila if that helps."

Rebecca snorted. "Don't tempt me. A few hours with my dad, my former high school crush, and his blowhard father will be enough to drive me to drinking. But I've had a rough week and my filter needs to be in full force, or it's going to get ugly."

Rebecca said it with jest in her tone, but the wary look in her eye as she glanced at the group told a different story. Liv wasn't close enough to Rebecca to know what was going on in her life, but she knew how it felt to be on the edge of losing the socially acceptable mask. She put her arm around Rebecca's waist and gave her a quick side hug. "I've got your back, Bec. But I can't say that part of me isn't curious to see Rebecca unleashed. You look like you've got some *Girl, hold my earrings* in you."

Rebecca's mouth hitched up at the corner. "Oh, I've got fight in me. I wouldn't have become a lawyer if I didn't."

"I don't doubt it. Honestly, I'm learning that some-times it's good to get that stuff out, even if it sets some fires. You just have to trust that you'll be able to walk through them."

Lines appeared around Rebecca's mouth, her gaze scanning Liv's face. "That sounds ominous. Speaking from experience?"

Liv glanced at Finn, who raised a wineglass to her and offered a tentative *Everything okay?* smile. She raised an egg to say *cheers* and then sighed, turning back to Rebecca. "Well, this week I quit my job without another to go to."

Rebecca's lips parted. "Shit."

"And now I have somehow ended up dating my ex-secret-boyfriend and moving into his guesthouse for the summer even though he's going to disappear without a trace again. So"—she shrugged—"on second thought, maybe don't take advice from me until I test out this fire suit."

"Liv," Rebecca said, mild horror on her face. "That's...a lot. You sure you're okay? I know you're taking on that list, but..."

Her friend's obvious distress on her behalf had Liv's stomach flipping over. It was the look her friends had given her senior year when she'd said she was going to cut off her hair and dye it green. "I—"

"Time for the ham!" Mrs. Dorsey announced, cutting the conversation off. "Everyone to the dining room. I've got wine in there, and fresh bread. Place cards are on the table, but feel free to rearrange."

Finn headed over, giving Rebecca a hello and a quick kiss on the cheek, and then took Liv's hand. "Ready for Lunch of Awkward-Divorcing Parents with Disappointed-in-His-Kid Father leading the way?"

Liv laughed, Finn's easy warmth tossing a blanket over some of the anxiety that Rebecca's words had stirred. "Totally."

"Wait," Rebecca said. "Is Disappointed Father mine or yours? I lose track."

Finn smiled at Rebecca with a fondness Liv hadn't seen from him before—the sweet, genuine affection of old friends. "They could have a contest to determine who's more disappointed. Fight to the death with butter knives?"

"That'd take a while," Rebecca said. "Maybe they can just swing wine bottles. Knock each other out and save us all the trouble."

"My money's on awkwardness over violence," Liv said. "But as long as there's good food involved, I'm there."

"United in hunger we stand." Finn leaned over and kissed Liv quickly, surprising her with how natural the move felt. Like they'd done it a thousand times. An old couple. He touched his forehead to hers. "And thanks again for this. You have no idea how much it helps having you here."

Liv leaned in to him, his words moving through her and stirring pleasant feelings. She'd never had this comfort level with any guy she'd dated. Dating had always been a means to an end—brief companionship and sex. This felt richer, more layered. Like eating a piece of homemade chocolate cake when you'd only ever eaten Twinkies. But when she glanced over at Rebecca, the deep wrinkle in her friend's brow yanked the cozy feeling away and replaced it with a wash of cold unease.

Liv took a breath and shook off the feeling. *No*. She wasn't going to go there. She appreciated the concern.

But Rebecca had always been the worrier. The practical one. The safety-first one.

Yes, Liv was taking some leaps, but she wasn't being stupid about it. She had on her fire suit. She'd survived much worse. She'd be fine.

TWENTY-TWO

FINN SIPPED THE ON-THE-ROCKS MARGARITA HIS MOTHER HAD made him and watched from the back porch as his mom led Liv to the far end of the property where the rose garden was located. The air hung heavy with the scent of rosemary and thyme from the herb garden Liv and her father had planted all those years ago. Liv had marveled at how big the rosemary bushes had become after getting such a rough start, sending him a secret smile. He'd known what that look was for. His hands had smelled like herbs for days after he'd secretly dug up the first version of the garden so Liv would have to come back.

But now she was smiling and listening to his mother intently, her sundress and dark hair fluttering in the early-evening breeze as they made their way to the back of the property. Despite a rather stilted and uncomfortable meal with his father basically ignoring everyone but the Lindts, Liv seemed to be taking the visit in stride. And having her there had made everything infinitely more enjoyable for him. She was like a safe harbor in an ocean of pointed stares and expertly wielded digs hiding within polite conversation.

He hated to say he was happy about his parents' divorce, but if this was the last meal he'd have to share with the both of them in the same room, he wasn't sorry. Maybe now he could spend more time with his mom and sisters without the specter of his father looming in the wings.

Not that he'd get to see them that much anyway. Work would beckon again.

Footsteps sounded behind him.

Finn glanced back toward the house, expecting Jill. He'd told her he wanted to hear all about college and studying abroad and any gossip she had on their older sister who had moved out of state, but instead of Jill making her way toward him, there was an old friend. With a big glass of wine.

When Rebecca had first shown up today, he'd braced himself for awkwardness. His relationship with her had gotten complicated as they'd gotten older, and then he'd pretty much bailed on the friendship in college, keeping in touch in a haphazard way. But his parents had always seemed intent on getting them together, and with Liv there today, he hadn't put it past his father to highlight who Finn should be with and who he shouldn't. But thankfully, the only awkwardness had been moving her place card from next to him at the table to make room for Liv.

"Hey," he said, shifting on the couch to turn toward her.

She gave him a tight smile. "Hey. You busy?"

He rattled his glass. "Just having a drink while Liv and my mom *ooh* and *ahh* over rosebushes. What's up?"

She pulled her shoulders back, suddenly looking every bit the no-nonsense lawyer and nothing like the girl who used to be one of his closest friends. "We need to talk."

"Okay…" he said carefully. He didn't have a ton of experience with women, but he knew enough to know those words weren't tidings of joy.

Rebecca walked over and sat on the other side of the couch, turning slightly to face him. "First, I'm blaming this on Olivia. She let me drink and put ideas in my head about fires."

He eyed the wineglass. "Fires?"

"Yes." She smoothed a wrinkle in her pants. "You're one of my fires I need to deal with."

Oh boy. "I'm not sure I understand where you're going with this, Bec."

"Just bear with me for a minute." She pinned him with a mildly pleading look.

He nodded. "Shoot."

She rubbed her lips together and smoothed the wrinkle again. Nervous. "I thought I was past this. It's so long ago, it might as well have been in another life. But being here today, seeing you, being around your family again… It just brings back a lot of memories, and I don't know, it all hit me."

He frowned. "What did?"

She laughed under her breath and fiddled with the pearls at her throat. "God, I feel ridiculous saying this. I clearly didn't drink enough."

"Bec…"

"Okay." She set her wineglass on the coffee table and took a breath. When she met his gaze, she was all business again. "Look, here's the gist. I don't like things hanging over me, and these time capsule letters have been stalking me like some demented ex-boyfriend." She shook her head as if admonishing herself. "I thought I could brush mine off, support my friends if they wanted to do something about theirs, but chalk mine up to stupid things teenagers say and move on. But today proved that it won't be ignored. I need to deal with it. So"—she cleared her throat—"I need brutal honesty, and you're one of the few people I can ask these questions."

He took a long sip of his drink, not liking the sound of that. "We haven't talked in years. I'm not sure how much of a help I can be."

She met his eyes with determination. "Humor me."

Her back was poker straight, her posture making her look haughty and confident, but the lines around her mouth showed strain. This was hard for her. Whatever the hell this was. "Yeah, of course. Go for it."

She tucked a lock of hair behind her ear and glanced out at the greenery and flowers as if she needed a moment to compose her thoughts. The setting sun threw slants of pink-orange light over her profile. Finally, a little smile pulled up the corners of her mouth. "You remember that first time you found me hiding in this yard?"

He followed her focus to a tangle of bushes behind the birdbath, old memories tugging at his mind. "Hard to forget."

Growing up, having families that ran in the same circles had forced them together regularly, but they'd dutifully ignored each other because *eww, girls* and *eww, boys*. But then in fourth grade, after Rebecca's mom had taken off, Finn had found Bec hiding in the bushes one night, Hello Kitty suitcase packed and eyes red from tears. She'd been planning her escape route, how she was going to find her mother. But he'd overheard his own parents talking about the neighbors earlier in the evening. Rebecca's mom had left with another guy and had no plans to take her daughter with her. His mom had called Bec's mother a number of colorful names, which had let Finn know it was serious because his mom rarely swore.

"You thought I was crazy then, too," she said.

"I never said you were crazy…then or now."

She scoffed. "No, you told me that I was being stupid. That if I ran away, I'd get kidnapped, chopped into pieces, and made into sausage."

He laughed. "Sorry about that. I might've snuck into my uncle's horror movie collection that year. Gave me a vivid imagination."

"Yeah, well, it was a pretty motivating speech. Then you told me to stop sitting in the mud and to come inside so you could kick my butt at video games."

"Which pissed you off and made you come inside."

She glanced over, smug. "And I beat you. Badly."

Finn took a sip of his drink and raised his glass in salute. "My male pride was forever wounded. Thanks for that."

He'd been hella impressed, though. The girl knew how to play. They'd agreed from that point on that anytime she wanted to run away, she could come over to Finn's for a while. He'd had his own brand of loneliness going on at his house, and hanging out with Rebecca had been a fun distraction.

"You saved me from running away. I probably would've gotten myself into major trouble or, perhaps, been made into sausage."

He stretched his arm over the back of the couch and hooked his ankle over his knee. "You were never going to leave. You were smarter than that."

"I don't know," she said, looking out at the yard again. "I didn't have many friends back then. I was always...kind of intense. But I figured other kids just didn't get me. Then Mom left." She clasped her hands in her lap. "You have any idea how it feels to know that you're not even likable or lovable enough for your own mother to want to be around you?"

He winced. "That's not—"

She lifted a hand, cutting him off. "Then you and I became friends and it seemed like...oh, maybe things aren't so bad. *He* gets me." She gave him a wan smile. "I fell hard, Finn."

The words hit him like a soft punch to the chest. "Bec."

She didn't look away, though her eyes were sad. "I always knew it was a long shot. But after the shooting, my hope got even stronger, because you saved my life. I didn't remember how much hope I'd pinned on things working out with us until we dug up that time capsule. My letter is...ridiculous."

"I'm sure it's not."

She gave him a sardonic look. "I had us getting married in Paris, having kids, and had already named our dog. Bartholomew, in case you were wondering."

Finn lifted his eyebrows. "That's...specific."

"Well, you know me. Always making a detailed

plan." She waved a hand dismissively. "But that's not the point. That's not why I'm out here."

"Okay," he said carefully.

"I'm here because when I saw you and Olivia kissing on the deck that night at the hotel, saw how you looked at each other, it…knocked me on my ass."

His frown deepened.

"Not because I'm still hung up on you. I've thought through that. That's not it. I don't even know you anymore, really. But it made me realize that you never looked at me like that."

He didn't know where she was going with this, so he practiced what he did so often undercover—kept his mouth shut and let someone who wanted to talk, talk.

"How long were you together?" she asked.

"About a year."

She inhaled a deep breath and released it. "God, I was such an idiot. You must've thought I was pathetic."

"Of course not," he said emphatically. "I never thought that. I loved hanging out with you. And if I led you to think what we had was more than friendship, I'm sorry. The last thing I would've wanted to do was hurt you."

"Thank you." She sat up taller as if steeling herself for something. "But it doesn't really matter at this point. What matters is that I read my letter and realized I've been stuck in this same place. And if I want to get out of it, I need to ask the hard questions. So all I want to know is—why not me?"

The question was said matter-of-factly, but it sliced at him and drew blood, knowing that he'd hurt her, one of the few real friends he'd had in his life. Unease moved through him. "Bec…"

She pointed a finger at him. "And I don't want some sugarcoated version, Finn. I'm not that little girl anymore. I can handle it." She stared down at her hands, spun a ring she had on her index finger, before looking up again. "But I need someone to tell me honestly what it is about me that makes me…hard to like. I know I can be abrasive, but I wasn't that way with you. I showed you exactly who I was, and it didn't…matter."

The last word caught in her throat, revealing that she was holding back a lot more emotion than she was showing, but her face remained set, determined.

Finn's chest squeezed tight, and he set his glass on the coffee table, trying to find the right words. He reached out and placed his hand over hers. "You're not hard to like, Bec. You were one of my closest friends. I cared about you. You're brilliant and beautiful and tough. You were back then, and you still are now. I would've been lucky to have you as a girlfriend. My parents would've been thrilled. For a while I thought that might be the next step…"

"But?"

"But I fell for someone else," he admitted.

"Olivia."

He sat back, releasing her hand. "Yes, and that had nothing to do with anyone else's deficits and everything to do with how I felt when I was around her. I'd liked girls before. I'd had crushes. And I loved you as my friend. But she"—he glanced out at the yard, catching sight of Olivia's silhouette in the distance—"lit up everything inside me."

The quiet admission was out before he could evaluate it or edit it.

When he looked back at Rebecca, her eyes had gone shiny.

"I'm sorry, Bec," he said softly. "I'm not trying to hurt you."

She gave him a wavering smile and swiped at her cheek where a tear escaped. "It's not you. I think that's…a beautiful thing to say. Just hearing you say it makes me realize I've never felt that. About anyone."

He blew out a breath, feeling exhausted all of a sudden, and ran a hand over the back of his head. "In a way, that's probably a blessing."

She gave him a you're-an-idiot look and scoffed. "A blessing. That I've never fallen in love like that? Gee, yeah, sounds awful. Who wants to be lit up inside? Screw. That."

Her dry tone was classic Rebecca, and it stirred an old fondness in him, but he reached for his drink, mulling over his thoughts. "It was teen love—hormones mixed up with the thrill of firsts with a big dash of pie-in-the-sky plans that would never come true. It's idealized stuff that screws with your head and makes you reckless."

"So you don't still love her?" she challenged. "That woman out there doesn't light you up like that anymore?"

The words dug in and burrowed under his skin like sharp hooks, making him shift in his seat. He stared out at the fading light, knowing Liv was in the distance, wishing she were on her way back, but feeling Rebecca's stare on the side of his head. "I…care about her. But I'm not in a place that I can start a relationship. My job keeps me away."

Rebecca let out a gimme-a-break groan. "Really, Finn? You've become that guy?"

He turned. "What?"

"*I'm not in the place for a relationship* is guy-speak for *I really like sleeping with you as long you don't expect anything real from me*."

"I—"

"Look," she said, gracing him with what was probably her don't-mess-with-me lawyer glare. "I get that you have a job that doesn't make things easy. But there are people in the military who are gone for long stretches who have relationships and families. So that's a bullshit excuse."

"I'm not going to put her through that." His jaw clenched. "And it's not just the time away. Liv deserves better than what I could give her. You said it yourself. You don't know me anymore. I'm not the guy I was when I was seventeen."

"She must see something in you," Bec said, not backing down. "Sex with a good-looking dude is not that hard to come by. Liv's gorgeous and smart. She could get that at any bar on any given night. She could leave here tonight and find it."

He grimaced. "Thanks for that visual, Bec."

"Just speaking the truth." She shrugged. "And I'm not going to pretend Liv and I have always gotten along. Maybe subconsciously I sensed something going on between you two and got jealous. I don't know. But I got close to her and the other girls that year after everything happened, and Liv was there for me. She was a disaster. We all were. But she was strong and fought hard to get where she is now."

"I know she did."

"So don't do something to undo it," Rebecca said.

His stomach clenched. "I'm not trying to. I've told her where I stand with things. She's not looking for a relationship either. We both know this is just for the summer. She's okay with that. We're going into it with eyes open so that when we walk away, no one is surprised."

Rebecca frowned as if something had just occurred to her. "What happened the last time?"

"What?"

"If you were in love in high school, what broke you up? Going to different colleges?"

He squeezed the back of his neck and let out a breath. "No. The shooting."

Rebecca tilted her head. "What?"

"I didn't ask her to prom because I was such a chickenshit, but that night, we were in the janitor's closet. It started out as an argument—or her rightly telling me what an asshole I was. But by the time the shooters came in, we were kissing. I heard you scream, and..."

Her frown deepened. "And what?"

"I ran out to help. I left her in there, which led Joseph right to her. I almost got her killed."

Rebecca's expression fell into one of disbelief. "Jesus."

He lowered his hand and shook his head. "I know. I thought it was okay. I thought she'd be safe in there. But...I wasn't thinking straight. I left her vulnerable. And I put you at more risk because they weren't after you. They were aiming at me, and you were collateral damage. I'll never forgive myself for either."

"Finn." Rebecca reached out this time, taking his hand and forcing his attention upward. Her eyes were gentle, sad. "Don't do that to yourself. You saved me. Trevor was aiming *for me*."

"No, he—"

She shook her head. "I know he was, because I gave him good reason to."

He blinked, confused. "What?"

"It doesn't matter," she said, her expression closing off and her hand slipping from his. "But Finn, don't repeat the other mistake."

"The other mistake."

"You think Liv's safe," she said quietly. "She may even believe she's safe. But I saw the way she looked at you today. I know that look because I used to look at you that way, too. If all you're going to do is leave her again, she's not safe. You're leading the devil to her doorstep again."

Finn's skin went cold.

"You said it yourself. Falling for someone makes you reckless. Between you coming back into her world and our stupid letters, just…don't let her upend her life anymore than she already has. You know better than anyone how hard she's worked for hers. When you leave, she's still going to be here. Alone. And now without a job."

The icy feeling crawled up into his throat, making his mouth go dry.

"Hey, you two."

Olivia's bright voice jolted Finn out of the conversation, but the wash of dread remained.

"Wow, why so serious?" Olivia asked, carrying over a handful of rosemary sprigs and glancing between the two of them. "Everything okay?"

Rebecca was the first to manage a smile. "Yep. Just

catching up and letting my wine wear off so I can head out. I have a long drive back into the city."

"Yeah, it's probably time we head out, too," Finn said, trying to keep his voice neutral despite his darkening mood.

"Sounds good. Look, your mom let me steal some rosemary. I'm going to pot it and try to grow my own. I grabbed a few for Kincaid, too. You want some, Bec?" She held out a sprig.

Rebecca got up and lifted a palm at the offering. "Nope, I can't be trusted with a plant. I once killed a cactus."

Liv laughed. "Wow. That takes effort."

"I know. It's a gift." Rebecca leaned over and gave Liv a quick hug. "But I'll see you soon. Call me if you need anything."

Liv gave her a curious look, but her smile quickly returned. "Sure. Same here."

Rebecca headed out, and Liv turned to him. "Everything cool? She seemed in a hurry to get out of here. Did I interrupt?"

Finn cleared his throat and stood, tucking his hands in his pockets. "No. Just catching up."

She set the rosemary down and hooked her arms around his neck. "So, what's with the glum look then, Agent Dorsey? We should be celebrating. We survived. No panic attacks. No punching out your dad. I love your sister. And your mom is pretty great. I think she likes me."

He let out a breath, unable to resist the pull of her enthusiasm. He kissed the top of her head. "Of course she likes you. You're amazing."

"I know, right?"

He chuckled despite himself.

"But next time, we better show up with something better than a dusty bottle of tequila," she warned. "This isn't really a margarita crowd."

Next time. The words hit him right in the sternum. He leaned back and cupped her face, guilt spreading through him like an oil slick. She looked so happy right now, so confident and content. Hopeful.

What was he doing, dragging her into this? Bringing her to visit his family? Making her like his mom and vice versa? All when this would probably be the only time she'd ever have a meal here. There would be no next time.

He'd leave again. Leave his family. Leave her. This was a farce. Playacting. He'd been too much of a coward to face his family on his own, and he'd taken advantage of Liv's generous spirit. He'd used her. Made it seem like this was real, like this was going somewhere. Even let himself believe it for a little while.

Just like high school.

Yes, they'd said all the right words upfront. She knew it was only for the summer, *blah, blah, blah*. But then he'd shown her something different. Without realizing it, he was doing what he did in his undercover work. Acting as if this was the reality. But it wasn't. And this time, if he didn't do something to fix it, the people who could get hurt weren't the bad guys.

He was the bad guy.

chapter
TWENTY-THREE

Liv stepped out of the bathroom and found Finn standing at the bedroom window in just his pajama pants, looking out at the trees. Even in profile, she could see the dark look on his face. Since they'd left his parents' house, he'd been quiet and tense. She hadn't heard what he and Rebecca were talking about when she'd walked up on them, but she had a feeling it was responsible for his mood.

She stepped up behind him and pressed a kiss between his shoulder blades. He inhaled a slow breath and let her wrap her arms around his waist, layering his arms on top.

"Hey," he said quietly.

"Hey." She pressed her cheek to his back. "Ready to talk about it yet?"

His muscles shifted against her. "Talk about what?"

"Whatever it is that has you brooding. Did you decide you're really into Rebecca instead and need to dump me?" she asked, trying to lighten the mood. "Because I can go back to the guesthouse."

"Stop."

"Then tell me what's going on. I can't even enjoy this sexy view of half-naked man because I can feel sexy man is upset about something."

He rubbed his thumb over the top of her knuckles. "I've just been thinking."

"Ah, a dangerous venture. What about?"

He continued to stroke her absently, back and forth, back and forth, like he was a million miles away. "About how you're doing all this stuff from your letter."

She frowned, not sure where he was going with this. "What about it?"

"I know it's supposed to be about going after what you want. But what is it that you really want? Like have-a-magic-wand-and-make-it-happen want?" He paused, his heartbeat a steady thump against her cheek. "It can't be this."

She lifted her head, wary. "This?"

He extricated himself from her hold and turned to face her, his eyes searching hers. "Yes. This. Quitting your job and shacking up with some guy who's at best a temporary distraction and at worst someone who's going to hurt you and leave you worse off than he found you."

She flinched, even though the words were delivered quietly. "That's what you think you are?"

"What else could I be, Liv?" he asked in a resigned voice. "I'm a guy who goes on jobs and doesn't come home for years. That's not just what I do. It's who I am. The mission that got me into the FBI in the first place is still unfinished. That's what gets me up in the morning. I can't sleep if I think the bad guys are winning." He ran a hand over his face, the sudden weariness adding shadows to his features. "I'm not a guy who's husband material. I'm not going to be a dad. I'm not anything you want or deserve."

The warmth of the room faded as a chill crept over her skin. She swallowed past the dryness in her throat. "Whoever said I was looking for a husband or to have kids?"

His jaw flexed, his gaze finding hers. "You're telling me you don't want to?"

She wet her lips, trying to figure out her feelings and not betray them on her face. "I...don't know. If you'd asked me a few weeks ago, I would've said no without hesitation. I saw what losing my mom did to my dad. I saw all of those parents at Long Acre, how losing their kids destroyed them. Who wants to invite that kind of anguish into their life?"

"And now?"

She let out a breath and sank onto the edge of the bed. "Now, I don't know. A few weeks ago, I also didn't realize how sterile my life was. Empty of the sad, hard stuff, but also empty of the good stuff. I mean, today, Rebecca Lindt of all people was concerned about me, like genuinely concerned. I can't think of anyone in my life outside my family who would give a damn if I quit my job or not, if I was making mistakes or not. So even though it's messier, having someone care or try to interfere, it was also...nice."

"Rebecca's good at interventions," he said dryly. "She should've been a therapist. A bossy therapist."

Liv looked up. "Is that what she was doing with you?"

"She was warning me that I'm going to hurt you again." His Adam's apple bobbed. "She's right."

Liv's belly dipped, that familiar feeling of sorrow trying to bubble up, but she tamped it down and forced a small smile. She reached for his hand. "Don't you think I know that?"

His frown lines cut deeper.

"Come on, Finn. I'm not some wide-eyed seventeen-year-old anymore. I realize the high of the happiness I feel this summer with you will come with an equal level of sadness when you leave." She linked her fingers with his. "But it's two sides of the same coin. You don't get to have only one side or the other. You have to put the whole thing in your pocket and take both, or you get nothing at all. I don't want to live with empty pockets anymore." She pulled him closer until he was towering over her. "You asked what this is? *This* is worth both sides to me. *You* are worth both sides."

Finn closed his eyes, anguish there, and lowered himself to his knees in front of her. She took his head in her hands and pressed her lips to his hair.

"I don't want to hurt you," he said softly, "but I can't seem to stop myself from wanting you."

Her ribs cinched tight, stealing her air for a second. "Finn…"

He looked up, pushing her hair away from her face, apologies in his eyes. "It's selfish. I feel like a vampire, taking all I can from you, sucking up the light before I have to go back into the cave. I'm trained to evaluate worst-case scenarios. This scenario is only going to get worse the longer I stick around, but I can't stop, even when I know I should walk away now. I can't quit you. Tell me to leave you alone, Liv. Tell me you don't want me here."

The words wound through Liv like a song, a melancholy one that simultaneously made her want to smile and cry. She stared at him, at the earnest green eyes, the stubbled cheeks, the beautiful sweet boy who'd turned into a beautiful caring man. One who thought he was breaking his personal code by being here with her, putting her heart at risk. She slid her hands onto his shoulders. "I'm not going to lie to you. And what's the worst-case scenario? I fall in love?"

He winced and glanced away.

"Right." She leaned forward and brushed her lips over his cheek, bravery swelling in her. "I have good news then."

He met her gaze.

"You're already too late. Worst-case scenario achieved. So you might as well ride it out to the end now and make it worth it."

He inhaled a sharp breath, his expression going slightly panicked. "Liv."

She pressed her fingers over his mouth, her heart beating wildly but her voice staying steady. "Don't freak out about what's already done. When you leave, no matter what, you can know that you gave me a gift. You reminded me that I'm capable of feeling this." She looped her arms around his neck. "Now let me feel it, Finn. Don't take that away by trying to protect me. I don't need your protection. I just need you to be yourself with me. I love you. And you will leave. And I will be okay."

She said the words almost more to herself than to him. She had to believe that. Had to hold on to that. Because there was no putting the feelings back in a box. They were there. Maybe had always been there on some level, waiting to bloom again. They would come along with a broken heart, but for the first time in longer than she could remember, she felt fully present. Alive. *Real.*

For that, she would pay the price.

Finn slowly rose to his feet, taking her with him, and wrapped his arms around her waist, some of the tension melting out of him. "That much I can give you. You want me. Here I am. Selfish, wants-to-be-with-you-all-summer, damn-the-consequences me."

Her lips curved. "Excellent. Now can I get back to using you for your body?"

Finally, some light came back into his eyes, and he traced his finger along her lower back where her T-shirt was riding up. "Yes, on one condition."

She shivered at his touch. "What's that?"

"You're not allowed to sleep in the guesthouse any-more. If I can't hide, neither can you. You sleep with me." His hand slipped lower, beneath her sleep shorts, teasing at the band of her panties.

She closed her eyes and nodded. "Deal."

"And one more thing?"

She was having trouble focusing now. A hot, shirtless man with roaming hands could be such a distraction. "Hmm?"

He put his lips to her ear. "I love you back. Guess we're both screwed."

Her eyes popped open, the words sparking through her like lightning. "Finn…"

"No more talking." He lifted her into his arms and lowered her onto the bed, taking her mouth in a kiss on the way down.

She didn't protest.

What was there left to say?

Finn undressed her in between kisses, slipping off her T-shirt and tugging off her sleep shorts and panties. She was naked and warm beneath him in a matter of seconds, his hands mapping her, and his mouth following the trail. She dragged her fingers along his back, through his hair, not guiding him on where to go because he seemed to know exactly how to touch her. He slid a big hand along her thigh, opening her for him, and then he pressed a kiss right at the center of her. Gentle, almost reverent. Like he was thanking her for being a woman. For being his. His name fell from her lips like a mantra.

It was all she could manage to say. Her heart felt too big for her chest, and each touch was electric. She didn't know what to do with all that *feeling*. She'd slept with more people than she cared to admit, but she'd never made love to someone. Never had anything at stake. This felt different. More intense. More important.

And hotter. Way hotter.

She wanted all of him. His body. His smiles. His secrets. His fears. Those sounds he made when she did something to him that felt good. Wanted to be the one making him feel good. He laid a path of kisses up her stomach and between her breasts until he braced over her, muscles tensed and gorgeous, green eyes intent, erection brushing against her belly. She made a hungry sound in the back of throat.

He smiled a smile that set off firecrackers inside her. "What's that look for?"

"That's the *I hope he's not going to make me wait too long* look." She worked her other hand down his body and gripped his erection through his pants. "Apparently love is a potent aphrodisiac. I'm ready to throw you down and have my filthy way with you."

He gave her a wicked grin. "I'd like to see you try. I'm trained in hand-to-hand combat and restraint."

She let her fingers slide into the open fly of his pajama pants, finding the velvet heat of his cock. "I know how to do better things with my hands."

His eyes flared with interest. "Tell me about it."

She licked her lips and glanced down to where her hand was wrapped around him and gave him a slow stroke. She'd never been a dirty talker with other guys, had always felt silly even though she had X-rated commentary running through her head. But with Finn, the filters fell away easily. "I like how hot and smooth you feel when you're this hard. Like to think about how that heat will feel inside me, filling me. I'm wet imagining it."

His eyelids went heavy and he rocked his hips gently, taking the pleasure she was giving him. "Keep talking."

"I like when you're so deep that I feel these bumping against me." She slid her hand down further and cupped his balls, running the tip of her finger on the sensitive spot underneath.

He lowered his head and groaned, his arm muscles flexing. "I'm going to need to record you saying this. I'll never need to conjure up a fantasy to jerk off to again."

She grinned, loving that she was getting to him. "How about for your next birthday, I'll record all my filthy fantasies for you so you can have a library?"

He looked up with a sexy half-smile. "You have enough for a library? Did I mention I love you?"

She would never get tired of hearing those words.

"You might've mentioned that. I trusted it more when I didn't have your cock in my hands."

He grabbed her wrist and pinned the hand she'd been using on him above her head. He leaned down and kissed her. "I love you."

Warmth spread through her. "I love you back."

A soft look crossed his face, naked emotion on a normally stoic man, and she fell even harder for him. She'd been okay with loving him and not getting it back. But seeing it there on his face…it stole her breath. Built a place inside her just for him.

She reached up and cupped his jaw with her free hand. "Make love to me."

He touched the tip of his nose to hers. "That's the plan, gorgeous. I'm not letting you out of this bed until sunrise. Hope I bought enough condoms."

When he shifted as if to roll away from her, she grabbed his shoulder. "No condoms."

He raised his head, his gaze searching hers. "No?"

She wet her lips and nodded. "You've been celibate. I've been tested, and I'm on the pill. If you're okay with it, I don't want anything between us."

He lifted her hand to his lips and kissed her knuckles. "I can't imagine anything better." He smiled. "But you'll be my first without, so if I come in three seconds, I'm blaming you."

She laughed as she helped him take off his pants. "Good thing we have all night for do-overs if you screw it up."

He slid his hand behind her knee and positioned himself against her, the hard heat of him sending the laughter right out of her. "That sounds like incentive to mess up. Over and over and over again."

"That could definitely get messy."

"We've always been messy, Livvy. That's what makes it so good." He bent down to kiss her and guided her legs around his hips. When he entered her, it was like she'd been waiting her whole life for that moment of connection. Yes, this was messy and would get worse. It was temporary. But with him deep inside her, skin to skin, his lips on hers, and the words *I love you* in her ear, she'd finally found what she'd been searching for.

The woman she wanted to be.

She wasn't living scared anymore.

chapter

TWENTY-FOUR

Finn watched in silence as Liv positioned one of their former classmates against the fence of Long Acre High's baseball diamond. Reynaldo Lopez had been a junior and the catcher on the baseball team when he'd gotten caught in the crosshairs at prom. He'd been shot in the stomach and almost hadn't made it, but now he looked like he could bench-press a Toyota and model for *Men's Fitness*.

Liv had told Finn on the way to the shoot that Rey was playing minor league ball and helping run a charity that refurbished playgrounds at low-income schools. Perfect subject for Liv's revived photography project. Strength out of tragedy. That was the theme. Finn had told her she should just turn the camera on herself. She'd rolled her eyes.

But he had a feeling she knew how much of a badass she was. Hell, they were on Long Acre's campus again. She wasn't panicking. She wasn't avoiding. Instead, she was facing down her biggest fear and tackling the

project she'd had to abandon so long ago. His chest
swelled with pride. And love.

That feeling didn't get old. And still terrified him.
Even after weeks of *I love you's* and shared days, he still
got that tight feeling in his chest when he looked at her.
Still wondered if he'd done the right thing by staying the
summer. But when he pulled her into his arms and kissed
her, tumbled her into bed at night, and woke up to her
in the morning, he couldn't bring himself to walk away.

He was running out of time.

He shifted on the bleachers, bracing his arms on
his thighs, and tried to push away the dread that had
been plaguing him since he'd gotten the email yesterday morning. An email he hadn't had the guts to tell
Liv about yet. Billings was going to be in Austin for
meetings and wanted to see Finn this afternoon after
he was done.

> Flying in tomorrow. Let's meet up. I've
> got some news that will interest you.
> Send me a meeting place for later in
> the day.

Finn had told him where he'd be, but it wasn't a mys-
tery what the news was about. Billings wouldn't bother
driving all the way out here to tell Finn to his face that
he was going to be put on desk duty. They were going to
give him the all clear. Billings was coming to give him
the good news. Finn would be sent back into the field.

It was what he'd been working toward. What he'd
wanted. Why he was here in the first place.

He felt sick inside.

Laughter traveled across the field and made Finn look up. Rey had taken off his shirt and was doing a ridiculous strongman pose. Liv was laughing. A genuine laugh. Finn's teeth clenched. He wasn't surprised about the lack of shirt. Liv's project would show the scars, and Rey's were on his stomach. Finn had been with her on a number of shoots in the past few weeks. He knew the drill. But a sharp stab of annoyance went through him. The guy could take off his shirt. He didn't need to flirt.

Rey playfully tapped Liv on the arm with a faux punch, and the annoyance turned into a pit in Finn's gut. He stood up, ready to insert himself into the situation, show Rey that Liv already had what she needed. But before he took a step, he sat his ass back down, the old bleachers groaning beneath him.

Liv *didn't* have what she needed.

What right did he have to be annoyed? Liv was talented and beautiful and smart. He hadn't offered her anything permanent. Rey could be the type of guy she sought out after Finn was gone. She'd said it herself. She wasn't ruling out marriage and kids anymore. They weren't getting any younger. Finn would probably be gone for years again. And there were never any guarantees he'd come back.

Finn closed his eyes, images of Liv with someone else flickering through his mind like his own personal horror movie. Liv calling out some other man's name in passion. Liv in a white dress for someone else. Liv holding a baby who looked like some other dude. Liv *loving* someone else.

That was what he should want for her. That was what she deserved. But… He clasped his hands behind his neck, the pain going through him like a rusty knife, twisting, twisting.

He tried to breathe through it. This summer, he'd been so worried about hurting Liv that he'd forgotten she didn't just lose him—he lost her, too.

For good. Forever.

He couldn't breathe.

He couldn't do this.

"Dorsey." A hand tapped his shoulder. "You taking a nap?"

Finn startled and raised his head, finding T. J. Billings staring down at him, suit wrinkled but salt-and-pepper hair perfectly in place. "Boss?"

Billings curled his lip. "Well, I'm not the fucking tooth fairy."

"You're early."

"Yeah. Got out of the meeting earlier than expected, and you weren't answering, so I pinged your GPS." Billings thumped him on the knee. "You're losing your touch. I shouldn't be able to sneak up on you like that. Could've killed you before you even knew I was here."

Seeing his boss on the baseball field of his old school was causing a disconnect in Finn's mind. He didn't like being surprised, and his head was still spinning, but he managed to slip on a stoic mask. "I'd say this isn't the kind of town where I'd have to worry about that, but you're standing on the campus of one of the deadliest school shootings in history, so...guess I should pay more attention."

Billings glanced toward the school and frowned. "This is it, huh? The reason you signed up for this crazy gig."

Finn ran a hand over the back of neck where sweat had gathered during his mini-meltdown. "Yeah."

He'd shared his mission with Billings early on, wanting any chance at tracking down the suppliers of the Long Acre guns. Billings had understood that need for revenge and updated Finn when leads came up. They'd thought Dragonfly had been involved and that Finn would finally get a firsthand shot at his mission, but the group ended up having no link to Long Acre.

Billings cocked his head toward Liv and Reynaldo. "Is that your lady friend?"

Finn looked over, a hollow pang going through him. *Lady friend.* What did that term even mean? "She's more than that."

Billings glanced back at him, frown lines appearing. "Uh-oh. That sounds ominous."

Finn's jaw flexed.

"Dorsey, I told you to relax and have a good time, not get attached."

Finn's fingers curled against the bleachers. "I'm aware. I didn't exactly plan to fall in love. Things happen."

Billings snorted. "Well, word of advice from a thrice-divorced man: it's not love. Any pretty, willing woman who gives you attention after a long assignment looks like the answer to a prayer. It's your dick talking. It's the loneliness talking. And I promise you, after two months, that's all you're feeling. It'll pass once you're back out there."

The dismissive attitude raised Finn's hackles. "You have no idea what I feel for Liv."

Billings rubbed the spot between his eyes and sighed. "Look, Dorsey. I'm not trying to be an asshole, but I'm speaking from experience. You remind me a lot of myself when I was your age. And I did this. Came home from a brutal assignment and latched on to a girl I knew from college. It felt like I'd unlocked the key to happiness. It was *this* woman. So I took a gig pushing paper around and married her." He shook his head. "Most miserable year of both our lives. She was great and tried to make it work, but I got restless after a few months at home, started feeling like a caged animal, trapped. I made her life hell.

"And I didn't learn my lesson. Ended up trying two more times before I figured out I'm not wired for that life. Men like you and me don't do well being out of the action. The adrenaline is addictive. Knowing you're doing important shit, taking risks, saving people, that's what fuels us. And when you give it up, you end up resenting the person you gave it up for. It's not fair to you, and it's definitely not fair to her. You ready to sit behind a desk all day? Type emails?"

Finn's gut churned, and he glanced toward Liv. "I don't know. Maybe." If it meant coming home to Liv, seeing her face every night, waking up next to her every morning. Hell, he'd spend his life collating and alphabetizing if it meant he could have that. "The people behind the desks do important work, too."

"Of course they do," Billings said, his opinion clear. "But are you ready to walk away from the assignment you've been waiting for your whole life?"

Finn's attention snapped back to Billings. "What?"

Billings smiled and tucked his hands in his pockets. "We got 'em, Dorsey. We pinpointed the operation where the Long Acre guns originated from."

Finn rose out of his seat, a bolt of adrenaline rushing through him. "Pinpointed? Like, no doubt?"

"Yes. We've been doing surveillance for a while on a major operation out of Mexico. I flew in today to fact-check a few things and confirmed the details this morning," Billings said. "I wanted to be sure it was the one before I told you. And I wanted to make sure you got first crack at it. We're going to need a guy on the ground. That's why I've been pushing you to get your act together—so the higher-ups would give you approval to get back on the job. This is your baby. The operation has been around for decades and has brought in countless numbers of illegal weapons for the underground market. We nail these bastards, and it'll be the takedown of your life."

Finn's heart pounded against his ribs. This was what he'd been waiting for. All those late nights in between assignments, painstakingly going through leads. He wet his lips. "How soon would this start?"

"You'd fly back to Virginia with me tomorrow. You're going to need to go through a psych eval to clear you. Then you have to get caught up on intel pretty quickly. We've had some movement in the organization, which is why I'm calling you back early. It's an ideal time for them to bring new guys in. We need to get you down there, establish your identity sooner rather than later. We need to get these guys to trust you enough to hire you. That's going to take some effort. This organization is locked down tight and more volatile than Dragonfly."

Volatile. Code word for more deadly. Finn could feel the adrenaline already, the need to personally dismantle those responsible for taking so many lives. For ruining his. Liv's.

Liv.

The thought was like a punch to the stomach.

"Can I count on you, Dorsey?" Billings asked, his voice stern. "No one's going to go after these assholes like I know you will."

Finn peered over at Liv, who was crouched down to take a photo, her back to him, and he felt like he was being ripped in half. His stomach hurt. His brain was spinning. And his heart ached.

He forced his attention back to Billings. "I need to think."

To his credit, Billings didn't push any further. He nodded. "Let me know by tomorrow morning. I have our flights booked for late afternoon."

Finn nodded, numb. "Got it."

Billings reached out and gripped Finn's hand in a firm shake. When Finn moved to pull away, Billings held on for an extra second. "I'm glad to see you've got your head back together, Finn. I'm sorry you're going to have to leave someone you care about, but I'm grateful she dragged you back from the edge. I was worried about you there for a little while. Good work getting back into fighting shape."

Finn looked away. He didn't feel together at all. No, he wasn't flying off the handle anymore, but this...this may be worse. "Thanks."

Billings left with that, heading back across the short grass of the outfield. He passed right under the sign that said LONG ACRE MEMORIAL FIELD. ALWAYS IN OUR HEARTS.

Finn sank onto the bottom bleacher and put his face in his hands.

chapter

TWENTY-FIVE

L IV TILTED HER CAMERA AND LOOKED AT THE SCREEN. T HE angle she'd chosen had captured the rich oranges and pinks that reflected off the water from the sunset but didn't take away from the greens of the trees or the main focus of the shot. She'd caught Finn's silhouette in frame. A dark outline of a broad-shouldered man look- ing out at the water. Still. Stoic. *Wild Silence*—that's what she'd call the shot.

Finn didn't know she was photographing him. She'd told him that she'd be in the kitchen, throwing together a salad to go with the steaks he was going to grill tonight. But the sunset had been too good to miss, and when she'd seen him standing there, she'd been compelled to capture the moment. At first she'd assumed he was enjoying the view, but now looking at the shot in still frame, she noticed different details, sensed melancholy. A ripple of worry went through her.

She'd gotten that gloomy vibe from him off and on since the photo shoot with Rey that morning. He hadn't shown it when he knew she was looking. But his smiles had seemed thin, his jokes scarce—so unlike what she'd gotten used to. Since that night they'd said the l-word, Finn had gone all in. No more brooding. No more tense conversations. They'd been spending long summer days hanging out, taking photos, strategizing about her new business, and making love in between. But today, she'd felt a reserve in him, like she was seeing him through a thick pane of glass.

She'd asked about it over lunch, but he'd shrugged it off and said he was fine. Her gut told her otherwise.

After she snapped one more shot, she set aside her camera and walked down the path toward him. Her shoes crunching on the dry grass had ever-vigilant Finn glancing back. When he saw it was her, he graced her with a dimpled smile, but his eyes betrayed him. Whatever he'd been feeling lingered there for a moment before he turned back to the water. "Hey, gorgeous. You're just in time for our nightly sunset."

Our. The word settled in a place that felt far too comfortable. A place she liked far too much. They were developing routines, rituals. Shared things. Even though she understood this was temporary, being here with Finn had seeped into her psyche more and more, making this feel like…home.

"Yeah, it's a pretty one tonight, even though it's still eleventy billion degrees out here. We could probably cook dinner without the grill."

Finn grunted. "Texas in July. Where you can see beautiful summer sunsets and cook a steak on the sidewalk at the same time."

"That should be the Department of Tourism's new tagline."

"Definitely," he said, but his light tone seemed forced.

"But I'll take this. Before you know it, we'll be complaining about the ice storms."

Something wary flashed in his eyes, and she realized her mistake. She cleared her throat. "I mean, *I* will. You won't be around by the time the ice hits. Lucky you."

"Liv—"

She forced a smile, even though her throat burned. "What? I know we don't talk about it much. But it's not a secret that summer will end in a few weeks. You won't be here for the winter."

He turned to her, face unreadable. "About that. We need to talk."

"We do?" Hope swelled in her chest. She didn't want to jump to any conclusions, but for weeks she'd been secretly hoping he'd reconsider, hoping he'd push his leave out further, hoping he'd do something to stay. If he wanted to talk, maybe... "What's there to talk about?"

He shook his head, and his shoulders slumped. "A lot. Billings visited today."

"What?" she asked stupidly, the statement blindsiding her. "Billings...your boss?"

He nodded. "That's who I was talking to at the field. He had a meeting in Austin and drove out to talk to me."

Her heart picked up speed, her words tumbling out of her. "You said it was someone from the school."

His jaw flexed. "I wasn't ready to talk about it."

Wasn't ready to talk about it. As in this was not good news. This was bad news. *The* bad news. The guillotine that'd been hanging over them from the start. Her hands trembled, and she forced them into the pockets of her jeans. "Talk about what?"

He let out a long breath and looked to the horizon. "They've got my next assignment. Looks like I won't be seeing the end of summer here, much less winter."

She felt like she was hearing the words through water. Slow and distorted.

"They want me to leave tomorrow night so I can start prepping for it."

Her stomach plummeted to her toes, and her knees tried to buckle. "*Tomorrow?*"

He looked at her, regret in his eyes. "Yeah."

Her body had needles in it. Needles and glass. But she tried to keep a grip on her reaction, tried to be mature about it. She'd promised. "For how long?"

"Until it's done," he said, resigned. "Months. Years. Who fucking knows?"

"Right," she whispered. *Months*. *Years*. "How dangerous?"

"Liv." There was a begging note in his voice. The message clear. *Don't ask.*

She walked on wooden legs to the Adirondack chair and sank onto the arm of it. She needed to breathe. This was what she'd prepared for. Despite her fantasy of turning things around, she'd known it was a long shot. She'd known this was coming. Not this soon. But in a few weeks. This was the other side of the coin she'd bought. *Breathe.*

He turned and lowered himself to a knee in front of her. "I'm so sorry. This is tearing me up, too. I love you, and I don't know how to make this better."

Tears slipped down her cheeks, and she forced a

humorless smile. "There is no way to make it better, right? You told me this would happen, and I said I could handle it. Guess I overestimated my abilities."

He cupped her cheek. "Livvy, please don't cry."

She shook her head and her fingers curled into her thighs, her body hot all over, yet cold inside, all this feeling welling in her. Loss edged with panic. "I want to ask you to stay. I want them to find someone else. I don't want you to be in danger." She lifted her gaze to his. "*Tell them to find someone else, Finn.*"

She hated the desperate tone in her voice, but she couldn't help it. The words were falling out on their own. She was in that closet again, clinging to his shirt. He was leaving. Hurtling into danger.

"Sweetheart," he said softly, her face in his hands. "I'm so sorry. I was prepared to quit. I've been thinking about it for the last few weeks. Just walking away and figuring something else out."

Hope raised a flag in her, but it was a flag on fire. She could hear it coming. The *but*. She filled it in for him. "But?"

He let out a ragged breath and lowered his hands. "But this assignment is tied to Long Acre. I shouldn't be telling you that because it's classified information, but you have the right to know. This is the case I joined the FBI for, what I've been working toward for years. They found the people who got Joseph and Trevor the guns. People who bring illegal weapons in for so many terrible things. I can take them down. Stop them from doing it again."

All the air left her.

He shook his head, his eyes begging for understanding.

"I don't know how to walk away from that. I want to be here with you, but…I also made a promise to all the people we lost. A promise to myself. It's what's gotten me up every morning since I first joined the FBI." He pressed a hand to his chest. "It's *my* fight. I…need to see it through."

She wagged her head, tears flowing freely now and frustration building. "But why do *you* have to be the one do to do it? Why can't someone else be the hero this time?"

The question made him blink. "What?"

Anger welled in her, and she pushed to her feet. "Why does it always have to be *you*? Are you the only agent in the goddamned FBI? Is it because you think you failed? Is it because you have some hero complex? What is it?"

He stood. "Liv—"

"No, I'm serious. Whoever these people are, they had a hand in destroying all those lives. My life. Yours. But where does it end? What about the people who made the guns? Or whoever screwed up Joseph and Trevor along the way? Or the security guards who didn't pay enough attention on prom night?" Her voice was rising now, echoing off the lake. "Nothing's going to bring the people we lost back, Finn. You can't save them. Or anyone else. It's done. All you're going to do is go and get yourself killed and add another victim to the list."

His expression darkened.

"But maybe that's what you want," she said, unable to stop the deluge now. "To go down as a hero. Be the martyr. Pay some penance you think you owe. Leave the rest of us to deal with the loss of you."

His stance went mutinous, defenses up. "You think

I want to die, Liv? Or leave you? You think all these weeks with you have been a game?"

She looked away.

"*I love you.* I want to spend my life with you. If I didn't think it was the most selfish thing I could do, I'd ask you to marry me, to wait for me, to give me something to come home to. I'd promise you this was the last job. But you deserve better than that."

The admissions gashed at her heart, drawing blood. It was everything she wanted and nothing she could have. "I do. I deserve someone who would stay for me. Who would choose *me*."

He gave her a bereft look. "I told you from the start what I had to do."

She shook her head, feeling hollow inside. "You don't *have* to. This is a choice. Don't pretend it's not."

"I have a duty, Liv," he said, frustration filling his voice and his hands going out to his sides. "Everyone likes to walk around every day pretending the ugly stuff doesn't exist. But it does, and there are men and women fighting that fight every day. In the military. In law enforcement. First responders. Someone has to do it. I signed up for that. Maybe if someone else had done their job, those guns would've never been there on prom night. Maybe the guy in charge of that mission was at home barbecuing steaks with his girlfriend instead."

The words were like a stinging slap. An argument she couldn't refute without looking heartless and selfish. "I guess that makes your decision easy then."

He stared at her, his expression wounded. "If you think that, then you don't know me at all."

An utter, echoing sadness filled her, and she hugged her elbows. "Maybe I don't."

"Right." His expression closed off, and he pulled something out of his pocket. "I guess I should've left from the start after all. Saved us both the trouble."

The words hit her like icy rain.

He placed a key on the arm of the chair. "I bought this place two weeks ago. It's yours. Don't go back to your job."

She stared at the key. "What?"

"That way, when I see your photos in a gallery some-day, I'll at least know I did one good thing this summer." He tucked his hands in his pockets, and his jaw flexed. His gaze shifted away from hers. "Goodbye, Liv."

Before she could react or respond, he walked past her toward the house, shoulders hunched but gait determined.

She sank to the ground frozen. Numb. Her voice wouldn't work.

He went inside, and she had no idea how long she sat there watching the door. Eventually, he came out with his suitcase and laptop bag. He didn't look back. Instead, he turned, went toward the driveway, and got into his SUV. He was gone before she could say a word.

Out of her life just as quickly as he'd come back into it.

Gone.

She pulled her knees to her chest and took the key in her hand, rubbing her thumb across it and letting tears fall.

I didn't want a house.

I wanted to be home.

chapter

TWENTY-SIX

THE BANGING SOUND POUNDED THROUGH LIV'S HEAD LIKE the reverberation of a gong. She groaned and buried her face deeper in the pillow. How could she have this horrid headache when she hadn't even been drinking? Did crying do this?

Boom. Boom. Boom.

She blinked, squinting in the relentless morning light streaming through the windows, and tried to make sense of where she was. Not Finn's room where she'd been waking up for the last few weeks. And not her own place. She focused in on the thick wooden roof beams, awareness filtering through her half-asleep brain. The living room. Finn's living room. No, now hers. Finn was gone.

A fresh wave of despair washed over her, and she closed her eyes again, wanting to curl into a ball and stay there. But the booming returned and became more insistent. Not inside her head. The door. Someone was at the door.

Finn?

Her heart leapt at the thought. But why would he be knocking?

She pushed herself off the couch and glanced at the key on the coffee table. Maybe he didn't have a key anymore. Maybe he was coming back. Maybe he'd changed his mind.

She hurried to the door, though her limbs were still heavy with the kind of sleep you fall into after a long, hard cry. But she made it to the door in record time. She swung it open, and her hopes popped like soap bubbles.

Kincaid stood on the doorstep with a grocery bag in her arms, and Rebecca and Taryn were behind her, all three peering Liv's way. Kincaid gave her a good up-and-down look, sympathy crossing her face. "Oh, honey."

Liv frowned and pushed her tangled hair back from her face. "What are you doing here?"

"Triage." Kincaid stepped inside, moving past her without an invitation. "Rebecca got a mysterious text from Finn asking her to check on you, that he was headed out of town. I figured that could only mean bad things. I brought cake."

"And coffee," Taryn said, following her inside and balancing a tray of Starbucks.

"And liquor for the coffee." Rebecca cradled a bottle of Irish Cream.

Liv braced a hand on the doorframe, watching the women file past her, her stomach knotting up at the words *headed out of town*. "I appreciate the concern, but I'm really not up for visitors. I barely slept and—"

"Would rather wallow alone," Kincaid finished. "Believe me, I get it. But we made a deal. No more handling the hard shit solo. We're here for you. We've been preparing all summer."

"Preparing?"

Rebecca turned, auburn hair neatly tucked behind her ears but regret in her gaze. "We all saw what was happening between you two. It was hard not to see."

Liv sighed and shut the door—too emotionally exhausted to argue—and followed them into the kitchen.

"It was like watching two friends getting on a plane that you know doesn't have enough fuel," Kincaid said, setting her bag on the counter. "We couldn't tell you to not take the trip, but we knew there'd be a crash landing at the end."

Rebecca frowned as her attention skimmed over Liv's bedraggled state—wrinkled clothes from yesterday, and her face was probably a puffy mess. Rebecca let out a huff. "So he left."

Liv pressed her lips together, willing herself to hold it together, and nodded. But the tears wouldn't be denied. Her eyes filled up again, even though she would've bet good money that she had none left after last night.

"Oh, Liv," Taryn said, setting the coffee down and coming to her side. "Come here, girl."

Taryn put her arm around her, and Liv fought her instincts to lock all of the emotions up tight, to ask them to leave, to hide. Instead, she let herself lean into Taryn and be led to a chair. Her friends surrounded her, offering her tissues for her tears, shoulders to lean on, and cake.

Because that was what friends did.

And somehow Liv now had some to call her own.

In between sniveling, Liv relayed the story. Not

every detail but the basics. Love. Work. Fighting. Leaving. Gone.

When Liv had finally gotten it all out and regained some of her composure, the women took seats around the kitchen table with her.

Kincaid set the chocolate Bundt cake in the middle and pushed a cup of coffee and the bottle of Irish Cream Liv's way. "So you told him you were fine with a summer-only romance, and then you freaked out when he told you he had to leave?"

"Basically," Liv said miserably, taking the coffee to warm her chilled hands but ignoring the cake and alcohol. She hadn't eaten since lunch the day before, but she didn't have the stomach to handle food or liquor. "I totally reneged on the deal. I wasn't fair."

Kincaid shrugged and cut a slice of cake. "Nah, it sounds like a legit reaction to me. Those types of deals are null and void once someone says I love you. That's in the fine print."

"Agreed." Rebecca poured a shot into her own coffee. "That breaks the contract."

"But it doesn't." Liv ran her finger around the rim of her coffee cup. "I doubled down on the deal after the l-word. I was all *I'm a badass woman who can totally handle this. It's better to have loved and lost than blah-blah bullshit.* What the hell was I thinking?"

Taryn gave her a sympathetic pat on the shoulder. "You were thinking, *I'm in love, and we'll figure something out.*"

"Apparently figuring something out meant simultaneously asking me to marry him and announcing he was leaving."

"Shit," Kincaid said, forkful of cake stalling halfway to her mouth. "He asked you to *marry him*?"

Liv closed her eyes and pinched the bridge of her nose, her headache turning into the icepick-to-the-temple variety. "Sort of. He said if he didn't think it was selfish, he'd ask me to marry him and to wait for him to come home."

"Damn." Rebecca shook her head. "Maybe he *was* listening that night I talked to him."

"That *would* be selfish, though," Kincaid said. "That's asking a lot."

"But kind of crazy romantic, too," Taryn said. Their attention all flicked her way, and she gave an apologetic shrug. "I mean, a little bit, right?"

"No." Kincaid shook her head. "I'm all for romance, but waiting for a guy to come home from what's basically war is only romantic in the movies. In real life, that has to be horrible. Always wondering if he's okay, if he's going to come back, never getting to talk to him the whole time he's gone."

"Yeah, that's real stress," Rebecca agreed.

"But what if someone's worth the wait? What if that person is *the* person for you?" Taryn asked. "Like soul-mate stuff."

Rebecca gave her a skeptical look. "Don't tell me you believe there's only one person out there for everyone."

"I don't know," Taryn said, not backing down. "But what if there is? I mean, I can't imagine how hard it would be to wait for someone you love in that situation, all that unknown, but I also get why Finn wished Liv would. He thinks Liv's his one. He won't ask her to make that sac-rifice *because* he loves her so much. That *is* romantic."

Liv's muscles cinched tight and the words dug in, opening wounds.

For the first time, it hit her that Finn was going through this, too. She didn't doubt he loved her. He was choosing work, but that didn't mean he didn't feel the loss of her. He was going into a dangerous situation one hundred percent alone again, with no one to come back to. Would he be reckless again? Go back to that angry, isolated man he'd been? Cut himself off from the world?

The loving, playful man who had emerged over the last two months would be lost, maybe for good. Images of Finn flickered through her mind. The two of them skipping rocks on the lake. Him tossing her over his shoulder and making her laugh. Finn smiling down at her in bed and telling her he loved her back.

A fist of anguish gripped her heart. She groaned and put her head in her hands, all out of tears but stocked to the rafters with self-pity. "Why couldn't he just stay?"

Rebecca rubbed Liv's back in gentle circles. "This part will get better. It's fresh now, but I promise, it will get better."

Liv shook her head, wishing she could believe it.

"She's right," Kincaid said, reaching out to take her hand across the table. "If nothing else, Long Acre taught us some things. We know we've survived worse. And we're pros at saying goodbye."

Liv lifted her gaze, finding Kincaid's smile sad.

"That's right," Taryn said, adding her hand to the pile. "We are badass motherfucking survivors."

Liv smiled at that.

"And you don't have to go through this alone,"

Rebecca added, placing her hand on top their stacked ones. "We've got this. Together."

Liv glanced around the table, the determined and loving looks on her friends' faces seeping into her like sunlight on her skin. These women were fierce and tough and brave. And for the first time in longer than she could remember, she realized she was one of them. Those words applied to her, too.

Finn had told her he hoped she got something out of this summer besides heartbreak. He meant the house. A new job.

But she'd gotten so much more than that.

She'd found these women.

Her tribe.

And maybe, just maybe, her way back home after all.

She took a deep breath and slipped her hand from beneath theirs. "I've got to go."

"What?" Kincaid's brows lifted. "Where?"

Liv pushed her chair back. "There's something left in my letter that I haven't done."

chapter

TWENTY-SEVEN

LIV STARED BETWEEN THE FAMILIAR BUILDINGS, HER HEART-beat a rapid staccato against her ribs. She swallowed past the tension in her throat and gripped the crinkled paper in her hand. No one would be here today. If she panicked, at least she could do it in private.

She let her gaze fall to the sidewalk. This part of the school had never been redone. When the concrete had been laid, the original class of 1982 had pressed shoe prints into it, initials carved beside each one. A small plaque had been embedded at the start of the walk. THE FIRST STEPS TO YOUR FUTURE START HERE.

The message was supposed to be hopeful, but Liv knew it offered no guarantee. Many people's futures had started here. Many had ended.

It was a tradition as a freshman at Long Acre to see which shoe print fit yours best and then to try to guess via the initials which student of the original class was your match. Were you destined to be the next football star if you matched 1982's Michael John's giant print?

Were you going to be the class president if you matched Claire Connell's? Liv took a few steps and found her match. *V. M.*—she'd known for sure who her match was without checking the graduation pic on the wall. Valerie Moreno. Her *mamá*. Liv lined her foot up with the print.

Back then, she wouldn't have said she wanted to end up like her mother. A woman who'd gotten married young and who'd never left her small town. But after seeing what her mother had gone through, seeing her fight, how she kept her spirits and hope throughout, Liv knew she'd be lucky to have half the inner toughness her mother had. She squatted down and ran her fingers over the initials. Would her mom be proud of who Liv had become?

Liv thought she'd been doing right by her mom with her former job. Being practical. Staying out of trouble. But now she'd realized she'd been living in a protective shell the whole time. Her mom had probably been shaking her head. She could almost hear her voice in her ears. *Life is short and precious, Oli. Do something with yours.*

Liv stood, her eyes misty, and let her gaze travel down the rest of the walkway. The sunlight was streaming through the buildings, angling across the place she most feared. With a deep breath, she forced her legs forward, her sandals quiet as she crossed over the rest of the footprints.

The first steps to your future start here.

The sound of the small fountain that sat in the corner of the memorial courtyard hit her first. Her fingers tightened around the paper in her left hand. She straightened her spine, determined not to let the panic in, and took the last few steps. On the way to the documentary interview, she'd had to avoid this place. She would not look away this time.

The space was more beautiful than she'd expected. A garden of wildflowers lined the path, and there were benches of natural stone. The back wall had the names of the victims etched into it in a neat, square font. But what caught her eye was the wall adjacent to it. The entire wall was smooth concrete covered in blackboard paint. In the center, metal words had been embedded: LOVE NEVER ENDS. But it wasn't those words that had her drawing closer and holding her breath. Instead, it was what surrounded them.

Endless messages written in chalk on every inch of the board. And as she got closer, she realized they were not messages to those who had died, which had probably been the original intent, but messages to current students from other students. Compliments, encouragement, congratulations, thank-you's. Nice things about their classmates.

Jess Sands has the prettiest eyes.
No one rocks a spelling bee like Keisha Biggs.
Clay Rogers wears awesome T-shirts.
Love.

Messages of love in a high school environment where tearing each other down was the norm. In every way, it was a big, fat middle finger to the shooters who had walked these halls with guns and hate. They'd had a mission to go after the happy ones. Well, the happy ones were thriving here. Liv pressed her hand against the wall, her eyes watery but a swelling sense of pride inside her. This was her school, her town, her home. Not all had been lost that night.

Not all had been lost within her.

Her eyes went back to the message at the center. LOVE NEVER ENDS.

Vaguely, she remembered it was part of a Bible quote, but as she traced her fingers over the metal lettering, the truth of it settled into her.

She'd never stopped loving this place, her friends, or her mother just because they were gone from her life. And she'd never stop loving Finn.

Not back then. And not now.

Love just was.

She let her arm fall to her side and made her way farther down the path until she reached the wall of names. Panic tried to climb up her throat, but she swallowed past it. She was stronger than that instinct. She lowered herself onto the bench in front of the wall, and her eyes traveled over each name.

With each one, she tried to picture the person. Some were just glimpses, snapshots from passing people in the hallway or yearbook photos. Some she remembered clearly. Brenna Carlson who sat next to her in English and always read aloud under her breath instead of silently. Zoe Redmond who used to swap music magazines with Liv and introduced her to some of her favorite bands. Curtis Beacher who had asked Liv on her very first date, which had turned out to be playing video games followed by an awkward kiss that tasted like Twizzlers.

Tears tracked down her cheeks, but she smiled at the memories. If she had ended up on that wall, she wondered what people would remember of her. Crazy hair colors. Artsy. Shitty attitude.

Fortunately, she didn't have to know. She'd been one of the lucky ones. And for the first time, the full weight of what that meant settled on her. She could still change her story. There was no ending on her pages yet. No name etched in stone.

She opened the letter that Finn had returned to her and ran her eyes over it again, her gaze lingering on the last line. *I promise, Class of 2005, to live the life that scares me.*

Time to really keep that promise, not just pay lip service to it.

She wiped away her tears, stood, and walked over to the fountain. Her rippled reflection stared back at her— changed but not as far from the girl who used to walk these halls as she thought. She smiled back at herself, ripped up the letter, and tossed the pieces into the water, watching as the ink bled along the paper and the old loose-leaf disintegrated in the bubbling water.

Love never ends. But fear could.

She pulled her phone out of her pocket and typed.

chapter
TWENTY-EIGHT

FINN SHIFTED IN THE FIRST-CLASS AIRPLANE SEAT AND TRIED not to bump Billings's coffee out of his hand. The flight attendants had already closed the doors and were making the preflight announcements to make sure everyone's electronic devices were off and seat belts were fastened, but Finn's heart was pounding like he was a nervous flier. He couldn't get the image out of his head of Liv by the lake, begging him to stay. He'd almost called her a hundred times since he'd walked out, but he didn't know what to say to make this better. He had a duty. He'd made a promise.

He clenched his jaw, trying to force down that burning in his chest, and flipped through the file Billings had thrust into his hand for in-air reading. He needed distraction. Needed to remember why he was doing this.

The first few pages were write-ups of the crimes that had been committed with weapons traced back to this organization. He'd expected to see the standard list of gun-related crimes: robberies, street violence, domestic stuff. But instead the list had a distinct trend. Crimes committed by teens. The Long Acre shooting was one of the earliest ones. But others had followed. A fifteen-year-old in Kentucky who'd killed his family. A seventeen-year-old who'd shot his boss at the movie theater where he worked on weekends. Another school shooting in Florida.

Finn frowned. "These guys have a specific market."

Billings grunted. "Yeah, kids with enough money and smarts to find what they need on the internet. We haven't figured out the exact method, but somehow they find the kids using keywords and then offer to help. Of course, they do the actual deal and exchange offline. We haven't figured out the logistics of that yet. That's one of the things we need you for."

Finn flipped through a few more pages. "Have we posed as a teen needing that kind of help online?"

He nodded. "We've tried. No bites. They haven't been operating this without being exceptionally savvy. We suspect they know they're on our radar. That's what's going to make it so tough to get you in. We need to be very precise about how we do that, and I need you one hundred percent focused. Any chink in your cover, and they'll shoot first, ask questions later."

"Great." Finn ran a hand through his hair. There was nothing more dangerous than trying to infiltrate a group that already suspected someone was on to them. Normally, that wouldn't faze him, but for the first time in longer than he could remember, a thread of unease curled up his spine.

He'd lived in dangerous situations for years. One slipup, one wrong move, and your cover was blown—and so were your chances of getting out alive. He'd thrived on that adrenaline, on knowing he could outsmart criminals. If he died trying, that was part of the deal. He'd accepted that a long time ago. But now the idea didn't settle so easily in his head.

"Be honest, boss," he said, looking Billings's way. "Suicide mission?"

Lines appeared in Billings's face, his gaze serious. "If you had asked me that a few months ago, I would've said yes. You were looking for a reason to go down in a blaze of glory. This mission will provide opportunity for that. You could have the hero's death. *Agent avenges his classmates in one last heroic face-off.*"

The words made Finn's stomach hollow out.

"But that's why I forced you to take this break," Billings said, voice gruff. "You've earned this opportunity to go after them, but I need you to do it with your head on straight and your priorities in check. And from what I saw and heard over the last few weeks, you found the secret weapon that will help get you through this alive."

"Secret weapon?"

Billings patted Finn's arm, and his lips lifted at the corners. "You reconnected with your family and friends. I saw those pictures with you, your mom, and your sister. You're not going to want to break their hearts by going and getting yourself killed. You have people waiting for you to get back."

Finn leaned back in his seat, snapshots of the summer drifting through his mind. His sister throwing her arms around him. His mother telling him about her new business idea. Of course, that was motivation enough. He didn't want to hurt his family.

But his mind zeroed in on another part of that picture. The girl behind the camera in those photos.

Liv.

Smiling his way. Making him laugh. Curling up next to him at night.

A bone-deep ache settled into him. She wouldn't be waiting for him when he got home. He didn't blame her. It was too much to ask, especially when he didn't know how long he'd be gone. Or if he'd make it back. She'd been through enough hurt, and he didn't want to add to it.

But the thought of her living her life without him, moving on with someone else, making a home there by the lake filled him with grief. For himself. For the life he could have with her.

He flipped through the pages of the file again, the pictures of his classmates filling one of the pages. It was a newspaper write-up about the Long Acre tragedy. Victims' yearbook photos in one column. Survivors' names in the other.

Survivors:
Arias, Olivia
Breslin, Kincaid
Dorsey, Finn

Right there nearly next to each other on the page. Finn and Liv. They were survivors. They were the ones who got away, only to be chased for years after. By the memories. By the anger. By the fear. By the label the killers had given them. His entire life, he'd wanted revenge, wanted to fight back. Wanted to *win*.

He still wanted that.

Now was his chance.

Billings was talking again, but Finn wasn't listening.

His blood was pounding too loudly in his ears, like the panic attacks he used to have. But this wasn't panic. This was something different. This was...clarity.

He reached below the seat, searching for his phone. "I need to make a phone call."

Billings grunted. "They frown on that when we're rolling down the runway."

"Let them fucking frown." Finn found his phone in the outside pocket and powered it on.

The flight attendant was heading down the aisle, checking each row, his smile polite but his eyes hawkish. Finn pressed the power button, willing the damn thing to boot up quickly.

"Come on, come on," he cajoled.

The attendant paused at a row, asked a guy to put up his tray table.

The screen lit, and the phone searched for a signal. The plane rolled toward the runway. Finn hit a button and put the phone to his ear.

"Sir." The flight attendant's voice was sharp. "I need you turn off your phone or put it in airplane mode now."

"I just need to make a quick call. This is government business—"

"I'm sorry, sir. No calls allowed." The guy's tone had taken on an authoritative edge, which had made other passengers turn their way.

"I have to—"

Billings took the phone from Finn and quickly hit the button for airplane mode. "Sorry. We're good."

The attendant frowned and gave Finn a don't-try-me look before walking off.

"What the hell was that for?" Finn demanded.

Billings handed the phone back. "Don't draw attention to yourself. Are you that out of practice?"

Frustration welled in Finn, and he hit the unlock button on his phone again. But before he could attempt to make a call, a notification appeared on his screen. He hit the box and his eyes scanned over the message.

"Sir, I'm not going to ask you again…"

But he waved off the flight attendant.

There was a selfie of Liv at the Long Acre memorial. Her eyes damp but clear. Her smile small but genuine. And there was a message.

Go get them for all of us, Batman, and take care of yourself. The world is better with you in it. *My* world is better with you in it.

I'll be waiting for you when you get home.

However long it takes.

You're worth the wait.

chapter
TWENTY-NINE

LIV BALANCED A BAG OF TAKEOUT IN ONE HAND AND HER camera equipment in the other. After Finn had left town and not responded to her message, she'd needed to zone out and get behind the lens. Not think. Not obsess. Just be at peace with the message she'd sent him no matter the outcome.

She'd spent the last three days taking photos and working on building her website. Olivia Arias, artist and photographer. Seeing the heading on the site had given her butterflies but also filled her with purpose. She'd booked two more sessions with survivors. She didn't know if anything would come of that project, but she had to do it anyway. Even if no one would ever see it, she felt called to complete it.

This afternoon, she'd had lunch with Taryn and then snapped photos of the school until the sun had gone down and stolen her light.

Busy was good. Busy was keeping her sane. She wasn't shocked Finn hadn't responded. They hadn't exactly walked away from each other with the nicest words. But she had faith a response would eventually come. Probably not the one she wanted. He'd told her when he left that he wouldn't ask her to wait. He wasn't a man who easily changed his mind. But he wouldn't be cruel and leave her hanging indefinitely. She knew that much.

She frowned at the doorway, realizing too late that she needed to get the key out of her purse and had no available hand to do it. With a sigh, she set her food and equipment at her feet and dug into her purse, looking for the house key.

As soon as she got her fingers on it, her phone buzzed in her pocket. She groaned. At this rate, she was never going to get to eat her beef lo mein.

It had to be one of her friends checking on her. They were mother-henning her pretty hard-core. She had a feeling they were having nightly phone powwows to determine who would casually check on Liv this time. It was sweet. Exhausting, but sweet. She let the key fall back into her purse and grabbed for her phone.

The crickets sang around her, and she peered at the screen. It was bright in the dark, and it took a second for her eyes to adjust and read the notification on the screen.

But her brain registered the name first. Her heart gave a sharp kick. *Finn*.

Finn: I don't want you to wait.

She stared at the words, her hope plummeting and her lungs deflating in a crush of defeat.

She'd thought she prepared herself for this kind of response, knew in her heart Finn wasn't going to ask her to put her life on hold for him. But still, seeing the words in black and white was like a judge's gavel slamming in her ear. Decision had been rendered. Thank you for stopping by. Please leave the court.

Tears pricked her eyes and she dragged in a ragged breath, trying to keep the pieces of herself together. She'd be okay. She'd get through this.

Probably.

Maybe.

Her phone vibrated again.

She looked down through blurred vision.

Finn: Because I won't survive waiting for you.

She frowned, trying to process the message, but a noise drew her attention upward. She looked toward the house, instantly on alert.

The porch light came on, and the door cracked open. She shoved her free hand in her purse, grappling for her mace but grabbing a hairbrush instead. She held it out in front of her as if it could protect her. But then a man stepped out onto the porch. All six feet of dark-haired, sexy, familiar man.

The hairbrush and her phone slipped from her fingers and clattered to the porch floor. She stared, lips parted.

"Hey," he said softly.

"Finn." It was the only word she could manage. Her brain had forgotten how to work, but her legs managed to move her forward. She stopped in front of him, looking up, almost afraid she was imagining him.

He smiled, pain there at the edges, and cradled her face. "I got your message."

"You—" She licked her lips, tried to find her voice. "That was days ago. I thought…"

"I'm sorry I didn't respond." He swiped his thumbs over her cheeks where earlier tears had tracked. "I didn't want to do this by phone, and I had a few things I needed to work out first."

Her breath had quickened, every cell straining to touch him. "Work out?"

"My job, my duty… I take it seriously."

She rolled her lips inward. "I know that. I told you… I'm willing to wait for you. What you do is important. I reacted selfishly the first time. I didn't mean—"

He pressed his fingers over her mouth, quieting her attempt at an apology. "You reacted honestly. I should've, too." He slid his hand down to her shoulder, regret on his face. "I didn't want to leave you either. I should've told you that. Every day of this summer has been better than the next. I've never felt so…content. And that scared the hell out of me because there's this part of me that tells me I'm not worth anything if I'm not out there fighting the fight. That I'm giving up. A coward."

She frowned and shook her head. "Finn…"

"But it hit me on the plane that the only cowardly thing I was doing was running from the very thing that would make me happy."

She closed her eyes and rested her forehead against his shoulder, the words falling over her like warm rain.

"I don't need this mission to get revenge or to prove my worth." His hand coasted over the back of her head, his fingers sifting through her hair. "I already have the best revenge I could ask for. Trevor and Joseph wanted to take out the people who they thought were happy. They figured the rest of us would mess up our lives on our own."

She lifted her head.

"I've done a pretty good job of it. I've done their bidding. And I was about to do it again. Turning away from something great and spending another few years of my life focused on *them*, on their legacy." He brushed her hair away from her face. "But that's not what revenge would be. Revenge would be happiness."

She swallowed past the apple-sized lump in her throat.

"And you, Olivia Arias"—he stepped back and took her hand in his—"are my happiness."

She'd been trying not to cry, but he wasn't playing fair. Her eyes filled, and she choked out the words she couldn't keep in any longer. "You're staying."

"I'm staying," he confirmed. "If you'll have me."

Before she could process what he was doing or say anything else, he lowered himself in front of her. On one knee.

Oh God. All of the starch left her, and she nearly dissolved into a puddle on the porch. She reached out for a column to steady herself.

He held her other hand. "I love you. I did back then. And I love you even more today. I don't need a mission to get me up every morning. I already have my mission right here—to wake up every day and spend my life with you." He pulled a gold ring from his pocket, one she recognized, one she'd secretly coveted all those years ago but could've never worn publicly. His high school ring. He held it up. "I know it hasn't been long, but in some ways it feels like we've waited a lifetime. Will you marry me, Liv?"

Liv slid down to her knees, no longer able to hold herself up. All those years she'd told herself she wasn't looking for this. Relationships weren't for her. Marriage wasn't for her. That day by the lake, she'd told him she couldn't wait for him. But that was a lie.

She'd been waiting for him all along—twelve years of trying to find what she'd only gotten a taste of in high school. She'd found the one on her first try and had spent all the years afterward with an empty place in her heart that she didn't know how to fill. A place fit just for this man. That part overflowed now. Hot tears tracked down her cheeks as she nodded. "Yes. *Sí. Ja.* All the yeses."

The dimpled smile that broke out on Finn's face could've lit the whole front yard with its brilliance. His hands trembled as he unfastened her necklace and slid the too-big ring onto the chain, proving that at least one thing could shake his nerves of steel. "This will have to hold a temporary spot until I can get you a real one. I didn't think you'd want the airport jewelry special." He kissed her ring finger. "Plus, I always wanted you to wear my class ring."

She smiled, her heart almost too full for her to form words. But instead of some brilliant declaration of love, a non sequitur burst out. "They sell engagement rings at the airport?"

"Yep." He smirked. "Next to the Cinnabon."

A laugh tumbled from her, and she launched herself at him, toppling him and kissing him on the way down. *I love you, I love you, I love you.* The words poured out of her in between kisses, and he said the same thing back. She ran her hands through his hair, over his stubbled chin, mapping him, proving to herself that he was really here, that this was actually happening.

His hands went into her hair, and soon the kisses turned from sweet to heated. Every part of her craved him. This week, she'd thought she'd lost him forever. Tonight, he was here, safe, hers, loving her, offering her forever. She didn't want to let him go.

But they were on the porch, it was hot, and the mosquitos in Texas were no joke. He groaned into her kiss. "Maybe we should take this inside. Getting arrested for public indecency will really put a cramp in my celebrating-our-engagement-by-giving-my-girl-multiple-orgasms plan."

His girl. A hard shiver of happy, yummy things went through her. "Yes, let's not interfere with that plan. That sounds like an excellent plan."

Finn helped her to her feet and quickly gathered the things she'd left in the walkway. The scent of her food drifted between them. "You were about to eat dinner. Do you want to eat?"

The appetite she'd had earlier had shifted into an entirely different hunger. "Food can wait."

"Thank God." As soon as the door shut behind him, he tossed everything on a table and was reaching for her again. "I need you. It feels like it's been years."

"Eons," she said, breathless.

He tugged her shirt over her head and then followed the path with his mouth, kissing her throat, the space between her breasts, her belly. Urgent. Hungry. "You really would've waited for me?"

"Yes." She dug her nails into his biceps, trying to hold herself up while he weakened her with every hot, openmouthed kiss to her bare skin. "Impatiently. Anxiously. But yes."

He unhooked her bra and tossed it to the floor. His big, warm palm cupped her breast, and he dragged his thumb over its peak, sending sparks to the now-throbbing spot between her thighs. "Damn. I must be really good in bed for you to be willing to wait indefinitely."

She groaned as he teased her sensitive skin with his stubble and then took her nipple in his mouth. She leaned against the wall and threaded a hand in his hair, her thoughts slowing and her senses taking over. "You've ruined me for other men, Dorsey. You suck."

He lifted his head and gave her a roguish grin. "Your other-men days are over. I would apologize, but I'm not at all sorry."

"Neither am I." She shifted her hips to help as he tugged off her shorts and panties. "I've heard you're a great lay."

A gleam came into his eyes as he took in the sight of her naked against the wall. "Is that right?"

He looked like an avenging angel, all dark looks and darker promises. This was a man who'd seen the stuff of nightmares and faced it down anyway. Strong. Brave. Sexy. The fact that he loved her was frosting on an already irresistible cake. "Yeah."

He dragged his T-shirt over his head with one hand, his hungry eyes staying on her. "And I've heard you have a reputation."

Her lips curved, heat fluttering low and hot. She cocked a brow. "All true. Better bring your A game."

He stripped out of his jeans and took himself in hand, giving his erection a leisurely stroke.

"That's the only game I have." Without warning, he grabbed her and spun her, pressing her against the wall like he was about to search her for weapons. The wall was cool against her cheek, and the heat of him rubbed against her backside.

He slid his hand over her hip and then downward, clever fingers finding her wet and wanting. She groaned at the touch.

His lips brushed the shell of her ear. "Are you using me for my body again, Arias?"

"God, yes." She tipped her hips back and brazenly rocked against him. "Get used to it. I'll be thoroughly using it for the rest of my life."

His own groan filled her ear, and he grabbed her hip, tilting her just how he wanted her. "I love you so god-damned much."

He angled forward, pressing the hard part of him against the softest part of her, and she sighed in plea-sure, taking him inside her body and letting him own her heart. Joined. She was his and he hers. In every way. She closed her eyes and gave herself over to the moment and to him. They were rutting against a wall like some illicit hookup in an alley. Sweaty and rough and both saying words that would make a hooker blush.

But she'd never had a more romantic moment in her life.

The fractured pieces of her world had finally landed in just the right place, creating a picture she'd never imagined. One that took her breath away.

Broken glass still made art.

Sometimes, the most beautiful kind.

I love you back, Finn Dorsey. I will always love you back.

epilogue

SIX MONTHS LATER

THE VOICES ECHOED OFF THE GYM WALLS, THE HUSHED TONES becoming a dull roar because of the number of people who'd shown up. Liv's stomach rolled with nerves, and she forced herself to take a deep breath. *I can do this*.

Warm fingers closed around her hand. "You've got this, Arias."

Liv pressed her lips together and glanced over, finding Finn wearing an encouraging smile. "What if it all sucks? What if people are only here because it's a news story and something to gawk at and not because it's good? What if they're here to *humor* the poor, pitiful survivor? Oh God, are they humoring me?"

Finn chuckled and turned her toward him, looking dashing and calm in his tux. Her own James Bond. He pushed a finger under her chin, tipping her face up and locking her in his firm gaze. "Stop. This. What you created is beautiful and special and amazing. No one is paying lip service. The money it's raising is going to charity, and the accolades are anything but."

She nodded, making herself hear it. "Okay."

"You're talented. Accept it, Livvy." He leaned down and kissed her. "Sleeping with me has clearly freed up your creative genius. Thank God I showed up when I did, or the world would be denied your art."

She snorted. "Oh, it's the sex, huh?"

He gave her a *well, duh* look. "Obviously."

She shoved his shoulder, and he caught her hand. He brought it to his mouth and kissed her knuckles.

Warmth tracked up her arm and filled her chest. And other places. Finn looked damn good on her arm. But she tucked that particular urge away for later. She had work to do. "So are you ready to get the personalized tour by the artist herself?"

"Yes, and then I'd like to take a personalized tour of the artist herself," he said, green eyes sparking with mischief as his gaze traveled over her sleek black dress.

"That can definitely be arranged." She slid her arms around his waist, her heels giving her just enough height to kiss him without getting on tiptoe. "Do you have to work tonight?"

"Nope," he said triumphantly. "Took the whole weekend off. Billings is covering for me. It's been a quiet week anyway."

Liv smiled. After Finn had backed out of the undercover assignment, Billings had offered him lead on the operation. Instead of being on the ground and infiltrating the organization, he was the main contact for Jason Murray, his colleague who'd gunned for the undercover job when Finn bowed out. Finn worked from home and the local FBI field office, coordinating the operation, deciphering the information coming in from the field, and developing strategies to keep Jason safe and bring the criminals to justice. He couldn't give her details on what he was doing, but based on his mood lately, she got the feeling they were making significant progress.

"All right, let's get this going before I chicken out," she said, reluctantly sliding from his arms and taking his hand.

Finn let her lead him to the other side of the gym where the bleachers had been removed and temporary white walls had been erected to hold the art pieces. People milled around, stopping in front of each display to look. Liv tried to keep her eyes forward, not wanting to see people's reactions. Afraid of what she might find.

She'd never attempted mixed media art in any big way like this before. Photography had always been her go-to. But when she'd gathered all the photos she'd taken of the survivors over the last few months, she hadn't been satisfied. No one shot captured what she was trying to convey about the person and their experience. If she'd learned anything, it was that being a survivor was layered and complicated and painful and beautiful.

Liv had found herself with photos spread around the pool house and no way to tell the story she wanted to tell. But then one day in late summer, Taryn had told her she'd found boxes of old newspapers and magazines in her mother's storage units—all with stories about Long Acre that her mom had kept. The idea had hit Liv like a punch to the gut.

She'd taken the boxes off Taryn's hands, and then she'd dug out her old yearbooks. Soon, images had started to come together in pieces. Strips of newspaper stories for someone's hair. Pieces from the photos she'd taken mixed in with enlarged yearbook photos and splashes of paint. Snippets of follow-up stories, accomplishments, and quotes. The heartbreaks and the triumphs intertwining until they formed a portrait of the person. A riot of colors, printed words, and photographs. Real people. Messy. Layered. Perfect in their imperfection.

But she feared she'd be the only one to find the pieces beautiful. She leaned over to Finn and whispered, "I can't look. Do people seem to like it?"

"You're kidding, right?" Finn squeezed her hand and smiled at her, pride on his face. "Baby, look at them. Enjoy your moment."

Liv swallowed past the constriction in her throat, her heart ready to pound out of her chest, but she forced herself to look as they walked through the crowd.

What she found had her heart picking up speed for a different reason. Emotion. There was emotion on every face. Some faces were somber, others thoughtful. Some held tears. Some had smiles. And instead of the quiet that everyone observed at the memorial outside, people were talking, pointing things out, hugging one another.

Liv's chest filled and expanded, making everything feel lighter inside her. She'd done it. She'd done what every artist sets out to do every time they lift a camera or put brush to canvas or pen to page. Her work was making people *feel* something.

Finn wrapped his arm around her. "See? You've made something beautiful and important."

She spotted Taryn sitting on a bench with her mother in front of the piece Liv had done on Taryn. Liv had portrayed Taryn as the strong woman she'd become, but had created her heart out of news clippings and photos of her younger sister. Because that was what drove Taryn. Every day she went to work, researching what made people commit crimes like the Long Acre shooting—all as a tribute to her sister. The piece had been one of the hardest to get through, and the canvas contained some of Liv's tears as well. But seeing the two of them sitting there made her want to cry again. Taryn's mom was clutching Taryn's hand in hers and there were tears, but both women were smiling.

Liv's voice thickened. "I'm not sure I'm going to get through this without becoming a weeping disaster."

"Don't do that. Documentary guy wants a quick interview after to add to the film."

She groaned. "No more documentaries."

Finn laughed and lifted her left hand, the engagement ring sparking like fire in the overhead lights. "Oh, I don't know. We may owe him a few minutes of our time."

She stared down at the ring and then looked up at the man who'd given it to her. Over a decade ago, she'd walked off this campus with a shattered life. This past summer, she'd walked into this gym alone, afraid, and lost. Tonight, she'd walk out the woman she'd always wanted to be with the man she'd always loved. A smile touched her lips. "Yeah, I think I might owe him my life."

～～～

Finn waited in the hallway for Liv while she finished the short documentary interview and said goodbye to the people who'd come to the event. He'd loved seeing her art on display after all those months of work she'd put into it, but he'd had to take a break from the crowd. He'd gotten better at being around people again. He'd even managed to make regular visits to his family's house. But too much socializing still wore him out. Plus, he'd felt the pull of the school. Needed to take this walk.

He hadn't been in this part of the school since he'd had to come back with the police right after the shooting to walk them through what he'd seen and experienced. Unlike the gym, this part hadn't been demolished, only redecorated. Seeing it now with blue lockers instead of gray, with different floors, almost let his mind trick him into thinking he was somewhere else. But when he saw the janitor's closet, the same crooked No Students Allowed sign on the front, his mind rushed back to the past. Liv in a glittery red dress, him in a tux just like tonight. He'd dragged her by the hand down this hallway, knowing she was pissed at him and wanting to fix it.

Finn stopped in front of the closet and took a bracing breath. He pulled the knob. Locked.

It hadn't been locked that night. He'd stolen glances down the hallway and then pulled Liv inside with him. He'd wanted to tell her he was sorry. He'd wanted to tell her he loved her. He'd wanted to tell her that he didn't care if his parents cut him off. He'd figure it out. Instead, he'd kissed her.

Then he'd left her.

He laid his hand against the worn wood of the door, trying not to think of what could've happened.

"You know you probably saved her," said a quiet voice. The slow click of high-heeled footsteps sounded behind him as his visitor came closer.

He turned and found Rebecca standing there in a

dark-green dress, purse clutched in her hand and sober look on her face.

Finn cleared his throat, his words coming out like gravel. "No. I left her here. Exposed her."

Rebecca peered down the hallway, her gaze going distant, like she was seeing that night, too. "You have to forgive yourself for that. Trevor led the way, and Joseph opened every door in this hall. Every classroom. He would've opened this one whether you'd left or not." She wet her lips. "If he had seen her with you, he would've shot you both. Being alone saved her. He liked her."

Finn stared at Rebecca and blinked, the words unexpected. "He liked her?"

Her lips kicked up at the corners. "Who didn't? Liv was the girl who was too cool to want to be cool. And she never went out with anyone, which made her mysterious. Guess we know why she wasn't dating."

He grimaced. "I was an asshole for keeping it secret."

She shrugged. "Maybe, but once again, maybe that saved her, too. She was under their radar. That's my point. No use in looking back and wishing you'd handled it differently. We survived. Whatever we did got us here."

He nodded and tucked his hands in his pockets. "So you're not mad at me for running out and making you a target?"

She shook her head and gave him a sad smile. "You saved me. That part I do know. I was on their list. Maybe at the top. And not because I was happy." She glanced down the hallway again, her shoulders sagging. "I'd earned that spot with one of them."

He frowned. "Bec, you—"

But she raised a palm, cutting him off. "You better get back to the gym. Liv was looking for you."

The simple mention of Liv's name lifted some of the cloud of gloom hovering in the hallway. He turned toward the gym. Away from the past. Toward his future. "Want to head back together?"

She rubbed a chill from her arms. "No. I think I'll take a few minutes down here."

He closed the distance between them and gave her shoulder a squeeze. "You sure you're okay?"

She lifted her head and gave him her signature smirk, though melancholy lingered in her eyes. "Stop trying to save me, Finn. Your job is done here. I don't need a hero anymore."

He smiled and leaned over to kiss the top of her head. "I don't know, Bec. We all need saving sometimes. I know I did."

With that, he left Rebecca to whatever demons she needed to slay in the hallway and made his way back to the gym. Liv stepped through the double doors when he was a few steps away. The smile that broke over her face at the sight of him lit up every cell in his body. He would never get tired of seeing this woman, of knowing she was his, and he, hers.

"Where'd you sneak off to?" she asked, stepping close to him and looping her arms around his waist.

"There were some doors left open that I needed to close."

Her attention drifted past him and toward the hallway, a small line appearing between her brows before she looked up at him again, quiet awareness there. "All done?"

He smiled down at her and slid his hand beneath the dark curtain of her hair, feeling her pulse against his thumb, seeing his life stretch out before him. His life with this woman. A life with love and laughter and all the messy stuff in between. He brushed his lips over hers. "All done."

She stepped back and held a hand out to him. "Ready to go home, Mr. Dorsey?"

Home.

"Always."

He took her hand, and through the doors where the shooters had once walked, he stepped out with the woman he loved into the cool, starry night.

No longer aftermath.

Happy.

We win.

The One You Can't Forget

chapter
ONE

THERE'S A REASON WHY ROMANTIC MOVIES ONLY SHOW THE beginning of people's love stories. That's the exciting part, the thrill, the magic. There is something undeniably enticing about the ripe sense of possibility. What will their life become now that they've found each other?

Well, Rebecca Lindt could tell them. They had about a one-third chance of maintaining their happily ever after, a one-third chance of staying married but being miserable about it, and a one-third likelihood they'd end up in front of someone like her, battling it out over who gets to keep the LeCreuset pot collection or the riding lawn mower even though neither of them cooks or cuts their own grass.

Today's battle of the exes was over a crotch-sniffing poodle that somehow had made it into the office and the divorce mediation session. The wife was claiming the dog was her Official Emotional Companion (the words always spoken with utter reverence and implied capitalization by her lawyer) and therefore had to remain with her. Rebecca's client, Anthony, was vibrating with barely leashed anger as he tried to explain through clenched teeth to the mediator that his wife had always hated the dog and that the poodle should remain with him.

Prince Hairy, the fluffy beast in question, didn't seem to care either way. He just wanted to hunt beneath the table and give a filthy how-do-you-do with a wet nose to the private parts of every person in the meeting. Rebecca sent up a silent thank-you that she was wearing a pant-suit, but that hadn't stopped her from feeling slightly assaulted every time the dog moved her way.

A wet tongue licked her ankle, sending a shudder through her, and she gently shooed the dog away, trying to keep her expression unhorrified and professional. But Raul, the other attorney, lifted a knowing brow at her. She had no doubt he'd be telling her later that she owed the dog a drink for all the action.

"Prince Hairy has been with us since he was a puppy," the wife said, tone curt, like she was biting the words in half. "I named him. I take him to the groomer. He's home with me when you're at work. My therapist says that he's part of my recovery. He is my Official Emotional Companion."

"*Emotional companion*," Anthony sneered, his calm breaking. "Come on, Daphne. Your emotional companion was the goddamned contractor you screwed in my bed!"

"Mr. Ames," the mediator said, school-teacher-style warning in her voice. "You both chose mediation to avoid court, but in order for that to work, I need you to keep the accusations—"

Anthony scoffed. "Accusations? They're not accusations if they're true."

Rebecca placed a staying hand on Anthony's arm, silencing him and sending him her own warning message. *I've got this. Calm down.*

Anthony deflated beside her and Rebecca took over. "I think what Mr. Ames is trying to say is that there is no paperwork designating Prince Hairy as an emotional companion. He may, perhaps, be a comfort to Mrs. Ames, but he is not an official therapy dog." He was just Daphne's best bargaining chip because Anthony was ridiculously in love with the canine menace. "Therefore, that should not factor into the decision of where Prince Hairy will live. The dog was adopted under Anthony's name. He is the one to take him for walks and to vet visits. Since Mr. Ames plans to remain in the home, he'll have adequate space for him."

"*What?*" Daphne demanded, her words ripping through the veneer of her pretend calm. "Are you effing kidding me right now? You *are not* getting the house."

Effing. Rebecca smirked. They'd all agreed to no foul language during the mediation. Daphne was apparently willing to fudge on the rules like she'd fudged on her marriage vows.

The mediator sighed the sigh of someone who was questioning why she'd chosen such a career path in the first place. Fridays made one do that anyway, but this one was going for the gold medal of Fridayness. "Mrs. Ames, we all agreed to keep our voices at a reasonable level."

But Daphne was having none of it. Her lips were puckered like she'd sucked a lemon and there was fire brewing in her blue eyes. A fuse ready to blow.

"I'm getting the house," Anthony said simply.

Rebecca smiled inwardly. *And, three, two, one…*

Daphne stood, manicured hands pressed flat against the table and a dark lock of hair slipping out of her French knot. "You will *not* take my house from me, you worthless piece of shit. I just spent two years remodeling it."

"And screwing the contractor."

"Mr. and Mrs.—"

"It's mine!" Her palm slapped the table, which earned a bark from Prince Hairy. "And I slept with Eric because you neglected me and were never home and you...you..." Her gaze zeroed in on him as she found her weapon. "You were *bad in bed!*"

Anthony bristled but Rebecca gripped his arm tighter, praying he'd weather the low blow. When well-prepped, people could deal with a lot of insults in mediation or court, but she'd learned men had a figurative and literal soft spot when their manhood was called into question.

"Mrs. Ames," the mediator admonished.

"Excuse me," Rebecca said, her tone utterly calm, which would only make Daphne look more out of order. "Can we have a minute? I'd like a private word with my client, and I think everyone could use a break."

The mediator's shoulders sagged and she adjusted her glasses. "Five-minute break. Everyone needs to come back ready to be civil or we're going to have to end the mediation and let this go to court."

Daphne huffed and Raul soothed her with gentle words as he offered her a bottle of sparkling water. She took a long sip, her gaze still shooting daggers at Anthony. Raul nodded at Rebecca. "We're going to take a little walk and bring Prince Hairy out for a bathroom break. We'll be back in five."

"Thanks," Rebecca said, knowing that taking the dog

with was their own version of posturing—acting like the dog was Daphne's already—but Rebecca wasn't worried. This was all going exactly as she'd planned.

Once the door to the conference room shut, Anthony turned to her, his perfectly styled brown hair a mess from him raking his fingers through it. "I'm not bad in bed. She's lying."

"Anthony."

"Women always, you know, have a good time, and Daphne always, you know…" A hurt look filled his eyes as he let the sentence trail off.

A pang of sympathy went through Rebecca even though her patience for hand-holding was low on a good day and nearly nonexistent after a court battle this morning and this mediation this afternoon. Anthony's head was no doubt whirling. Was he bad in bed? Had his wife faked her enjoyment? Was that why she'd strayed?

Rebecca reached out and gave his shoulder a gentle squeeze. "Anthony, you know she's just throwing out words to rile you up. I told you she'd say the ugliest things to get you off your game. This is a standard emasculation tactic."

He blinked. "What?"

She blew out a breath. "The easiest way to knock a guy off his game is to insult his penis size or his ability in bed. Men seem to have some inborn need to defend against that type of insult." In her head she called it the Dick Kick, but she couldn't bring herself to say it to a client. "On the other side, men insult the woman by saying she was frigid or ugly, getting fat or old. When cornered, people strike right at the clichéd insecurities. It's completely unoriginal and the tactic of someone who knows she's losing the fight. It means we're winning."

He gave her a you've-got-to-be-kidding-me look. "Winning? She's going to get her therapist to label Prince a therapy dog. Watch. Then, I'll lose Prince, too."

His voice caught and he glanced away, hiding the tears that jumped to his eyes at the thought of losing his dog.

Rebecca frowned. She'd never had a pet because her father had deemed them unsanitary and high maintenance, but she was regularly amazed at how people would throw away everything to keep a pet or some sentimental item. She always preferred to have the client who was less attached to those things. Sentimentality made people irrational. *You can take the eighty-thousand-dollar car as long as I can keep my mother's china.*

Rebecca didn't get it. But, of course, when the mother you worship leaves your family without warning when you're in fourth grade to go start a new family, you learn not to get attached to much.

But Anthony was her client, and he'd told her in no uncertain terms that the dog was the number one priority. He was paying her to get what he wanted, so she would do that because she was good at her job and not there to judge whether a crotch-sniffer trumped a million-dollar home.

Rebecca patted his arm. "I promise. This is going exactly how we want it to."

When the door opened, Raul and Daphne looked smug as they walked the dog back into the office. Prince

Hairy proceeded to duck beneath the table and plop down on Anthony's feet.

The mediator took her seat. "Okay, why don't we start again now that everyone has cooled down?"

Rebecca folded her hands on the table and straightened her back. *Poker time.* "I've talked with my client, and I believe we have a workable compromise. Mr. Ames will give Mrs. Ames the dog, his old records, the Mercedes, and her antique doll collection in exchange for the house and the SUV."

Anthony went tense in his chair, and Rebecca could feel the *what the hell are you doing* vibe coming from him, but she didn't look his way.

Daphne's eyes went comically wide. "My doll collection? That's mine anyway."

"It was acquired during the marriage." Rebecca kept her tone professionally bored.

"The doll collection is off the table," Raul said smoothly.

Rebecca made a note on her legal pad. "Then the record collection is, too."

"Fine." Daphne nodded. "Take your crappy records."

Raul frowned, his sentimental bargaining chip slipping out of reach.

Rebecca nodded. One down. "Okay, Ms. Ames, so you get Prince Hairy and will be solely responsible for his care and vet bills. Mr. Ames will get the house and will buy you out of your half. Agreed?"

"No," Daphne said, glancing at her lawyer with a *do something* look. "I'm not leaving here without the house. I picked every paint color, every tile, chose every piece of furniture. It's *mine*."

"You could move in with your parents, Daph," Anthony said casually, playing his part again. "Until you find another place."

She blanched. "I'd rather kill myself than live with them. I'm not leaving my house."

Anthony propped his chin on his fist as if settling in for a really good movie.

Rebecca tried not to grimace at Daphne's comment. She'd never gotten used to how easily people tossed around those dramatic words. Threats of suicide and murder rolled off people's tongues all the time, especially in divorce mediation. She knew it was just hyperbole, but in high school, two people had made those threats and then carried them through. No one had listened. They'd thought it was an exaggeration. *She'd* thought it was an exaggeration. They'd all been wrong. So very wrong.

Her stomach flipped over and she took a sip of water, trying to shake off the memories that were like the off-key elevator music of her life, never far in the background and always ready to turn up louder. "It seems we're at an impasse."

"Mr. and Mrs. Ames," the mediator said. "If we don't resolve this here, this will have to go to court. Try to remember that compromise isn't losing. Seeking things just for revenge feels satisfying in the short term but will drag this process out, cost you more money with your lawyers, and will create more stress for you. You will be dealing with each other for a long time. If we can resolve this here, you can walk away and not have to see each other again."

"Well, there's a bonus," Anthony muttered.

"I'm not afraid to go to court to get my house," Daphne said, tone frosty.

Rebecca set her pen down and focused her attention on Daphne. "Mrs. Ames, I'm sure your counsel has warned you that if this goes to court, you're going to risk losing more than you will if we can come to an agreement here. Texas allows fault to be shown in divorce. We have proof of your affair. These details will be brought out in court."

Daphne wet her lips and her throat worked.

Rebecca cocked a brow in a way that she hoped conveyed, *Yes, all those dirty details you're replaying in your head right now? That will be displayed in court. And no one is going to side with you after that because no one likes a cheater.*

Rebecca had watched the incriminating video with Anthony at her side since he'd wanted to see the whole thing but didn't want to do it alone. Daphne had forgotten about the security cameras her husband had installed outside by their pool, and she'd put on quite an X-rated show with the contractor one night. The explicitness had made Rebecca feel equal parts uncomfortable and fascinated. She'd never had the urge to literally rip someone's clothes off. Frankly, she hadn't realized people actually did that outside of movies. She couldn't fathom being that…feral with anyone.

But seeing it had made Anthony vomit, and that was when Rebecca had understood the real story.

The man had truly loved his wife, and his world had just been ripped in half.

So Rebecca had no qualms about taking Daphne down. Cheaters deserved what they got. And too bad for Daphne, they were Rebecca's specialty.

"You're trying to scare me," Daphne said finally.

Rebecca leaned back in her chair and crossed her legs, relishing that calm, cool control that filled her veins in these situations. "I'm simply stating the facts, Mrs. Ames. Ask your lawyer if he thinks I'm exaggerating. If we go to court, you will be deemed at fault and the settlement will definitely reflect that."

Raul folded his hands and rested them on the table, his own poker face in place. "We're prepared to go to court if necessary. My client will not bend on the house."

"Mr. Ames, what would it take to compromise on the house?" the mediator asked. "If there's nothing, then we should just move this to court."

Anthony settled back in his chair, arms crossed casually, expression smugly confident. He shrugged. "Sounds like I'd be better off going to court. That way I'll get the house, the ridiculous dolls, the better car, and my dog. You'll end up back home with your parents. You can call Eric and have him remodel your parents' crappy seventies ranch to make your room real nice."

Daphne's jaw flexed, and Raul put a hand on her wrist as if sensing what was about to happen, but it was too late. She was already talking. "Fine. Take the stupid dog! I know that's what you're after. He's a filthy, dumb waste of space anyway."

Prince Hairy lifted his head beneath the table and whimpered, as if he recognized the description and took offense.

Daphne waved a dismissive hand. "Take him and whatever else of your junk you want. Just give me the house, my furniture, and my car. Then, you never have to see me again. I'm done with this crap."

Rebecca gave a *Mona Lisa* smile.

Anthony's chair squeaked as he leaned forward, victory all over his face. "You've got a deal."

Another love story ended with a signature on a dotted line.

Daphne grabbed her purse and stood, her chair rolling behind her and banging against the wall. "You're such a smug asshole, thinking you're so much better than me. If you wouldn't have treated me—"

"That's enough, Mrs. Ames," Rebecca said. "You've said your piece."

Her attention swung Rebecca's way. "And I don't care that you're some famous survivor or whatever. You're a stuck-up, know-it-all bitch!"

"Daphne—" Raul warned.

But Rebecca held on to her polite smile, the words rolling off her like water on a windshield. Let Daphne have her tantrum. People had all kinds of preconceived notions about Rebecca when they figured out she was *the* Rebecca Lindt who'd survived the Long Acre High School prom shooting—that crying redheaded girl who was rolled out bleeding on a stretcher on the nightly news twelve years ago. The notions strangers got of her often involved shining light and singing angels, or like she had some secret sauce recipe on how to live a meaningful life. But she had news for them. Surviving a tragedy didn't make you magical. It made you tough. Not special. Just lucky. "Have a nice day, Mrs. Ames."

Daphne made a disgusted noise and flounced out the door without a goodbye. Her "emotional companion" didn't even lift his head.

—᭞᭞᭞—

When Rebecca shut the door and turned to face her client, Anthony pushed his chair back, let out a whoop of victory, and patted his thigh. "Come here, boy."

The dog scrambled to his feet and leapt into Anthony's lap with glee. The giant poodle was way too big to be a lapdog, but Anthony didn't seem to mind. He buried his face in the dog's copper-colored fur, which really did look like the color of Prince Harry's hair, and let go a litany of mushy endearments.

Prince licked his owner's face and made happy, huffing dog noises. Rebecca crossed her arms and shook her head as she stepped closer, amused. "I could've won you a lot more money *and* the house."

Anthony looked up, absently rubbing the dog's neck. "I know."

"But the dog is worth it?"

Anthony's staid face broke into a slow smile. "Of course he is. He's the best." Anthony cupped Prince's snout. "To be honest, this is all I need. I'd rather be broke than go home to an empty house. There's nothing more depressing than knowing no one is waiting for you at home. That no one cares if you show up or not."

The words pinged through Rebecca, hitting places she'd rather not examine. She forced a smile. "Right." She stepped over to pet the dog, who immediately buried his nose between her legs. "Well, I think this guy will definitely be happy to see you at the end of the day."

"Indeed." Anthony tapped Prince to get him to his feet and stood to shake Rebecca's hand. "Thanks for everything. I won't say it's been fun, but at least it was quick."

Sounds like most of the dates I've had in my life.

"You're welcome. Sorry we had to meet under these circumstances," she said and then walked Anthony out. Those were her standard parting words, but she meant them. People hoped to never need someone like her, and she found it a little depressing to know that this seemingly decent guy who'd loved his wife had ended up here, too.

She paused, rubbing the bridge of her nose. What was with her tonight?

She lived a busy life, was good at her job, had friends. She was comfortable being alone. If she got pent up with sexual frustration sometimes, she knew how to handle things on her own. Frankly, taking care of things solo was more satisfying than the few awkward encounters with men she'd had along the way, and it saved her from having to explain the ugly, pitted scars on her leg— always a fun conversation. Her life worked.

She deserved to be celebrating, not ruminating in the office. A plan formed quickly in her head. She'd pick up her favorite wine from the store down the street, get takeout and dessert from that fancy Italian restaurant that just opened, and rent a new movie with a pretty guy to look at.

She wasn't craving a date. She was just craving a break and a little indulgence. She didn't need anyone else to give her that. She could handle it on her own.

She'd been doing it all her life.

Why stop now?

chapter
TWO

WES GARRETT PEEKED THROUGH THE CRACK IN THE DOOR TO the apartment inside, eyeing the small group of women laughing and drinking champagne. One was wearing a party hat with a big light-up dick on it. He shut the door and leaned against the wall in the hallway. "I can't believe I'm considering this."

Suzie grinned wickedly at him, her lip ring glinting in the light of the hallway. "Don't be such a prude, Garrett. What happened to that wild, try-anything-once guy I used to know?"

His jaw clenched. "Are you really asking me that?"

She waved a dismissive hand. "You know that's not what I mean. I don't want post-apocalyptic you. That sucked."

"Ya think?"

She rolled her eyes. "I'm talking about the you before everything went to shit. You've swung too far in the other direction." She shrugged. "Walking the straight and narrow doesn't mean not having any fun or, you know, a sense of humor."

"Suze…"

"This is a *good* gig." She pinned him with her gaze. "Three hundred bucks for two hours of your time. All you're going to be doing is teaching drunk chicks how to cook simple things. You teach cooking every day. This is no different."

He gave her a droll look. "I teach cooking to teenagers. I get to wear my chef's whites. I don't have to cook naked."

She groaned. "You're not going to be *naked*. That would be a major kitchen hazard. Just…shirtless. And hey, with all your tattoos, you have some added coverage."

Christ. This was what his life had come to? From four-star restaurants to this? He'd thought teaching at an after-school program was a giant tumble down the staircase from his chef dreams, but this was a new level. The basement. At least with the kids he could convince himself he was training future chefs. Here he would be the special of the day. "I don't know."

She reached out and grabbed his hands, face earnest beneath the fringe of bright-pink hair. "Come on, Wes. My other guy called in. Shirtless Chefs is just getting off the ground. If I have chefs no-showing for parties, I'm going to catch hell in the online reviews, and the business will tank before I really get rolling. You've got the skills, you've got the blond bad-boy thing going, which is going to rock their socks off. And once upon a time, you could charm the ladies, so I know you're capable. Plus, you said you needed the extra money. This is easy cash. Win-win."

Wes grimaced. He hated *needing* the money. Hated that he was anywhere close to that place he was so long ago where he'd had to scrape together every damn dime. He'd thought he was far past that and then *boom*, life exploded. But *need* wasn't even the right word. He had enough to live right now with his teaching gig. He knew how to stretch his dollars. What he wanted the money for was a stupid idea. Something he shouldn't be messing with. His family would kick his ass if they even knew he was thinking about it.

Still, he couldn't help closing his eyes and picturing the beat-up school bus his friend Devin had shown him last week. The old bus had looked like it'd been rolled off the side of a rocky cliff and set on fire, but Wes had been able to see the bones beneath, the potential to be converted into a food truck. He'd gotten that itch that he'd tried to ignore since he'd lost everything. The *what ifs?*

Wes had found himself inquiring about a loan at the bank. He'd known the answer before he'd asked, but he'd asked anyway. And he'd put out feelers with his friends, telling them to give him a call if they had any extra catering or temporary cooking gigs.

Of course, Suzie had been the one to call, and Suzie hadn't informed him of exactly how her new private chef business worked until he'd arrived.

But now he was here and she needed his help. And dammit, he wanted the money. He tilted his head back against the wall and closed his eyes. "What am I teaching them to make?"

When she didn't answer immediately, he lifted his head, finding her biting her lip.

"Suze," he said, warning in his voice.

She held up her palms. "Don't hate me, okay? There's a bruschetta recipe and a Bourbon nut brittle that you're going to love. But some of the other stuff is…themed."

His shoulders sagged in acceptance. "I'm making dick-shaped things, aren't I?"

"Um…" Her nose wrinkled. "There may be recipes for Big, Meaty Balls and Eat My Taco Dip."

"I fucking hate you."

She grinned and stepped up to pat him on the cheek. "You're the best, Garrett. If I didn't want to put lipstick on the merchandise, I'd kiss you."

"You say the sweetest things, Suze. I just feel showered by your sweetness and affection."

"Right?" She patted his hip. "Now go in there, be nice, and look pretty."

"Nice. You treat all your employees like cattle?"

She stuck out her tongue. "Only my friends who won't sue me."

He let out a tired breath. "I won't sue you, but if you tell anyone about this…"

"I won't."

"I could lose my job." Not to mention whatever shreds of dignity he had left.

She mimed sealing her lips and tossing the key. "Your secret's safe. I swear."

"Fine. I'll go in."

She did a little celebratory clap, but then her smile sagged a bit. "You sure you're cool with alcohol being at the party? I mean, I know I'm pushing you to do this, but for real, if that part's a problem—"

"I told you on the phone that it's not an issue," he

said, cutting her off, anger trying to surface. "Tonight, that's the least of my worries."

She pressed her lips together and nodded. "Okay. Good."

He ran a hand through his hair, resigned. "Let's get this over with."

"Right." She swept an arm out in front of her. "Godspeed, my friend."

With one last steeling breath, he stepped past her and pushed open the door. All eyes turned his way and the blond woman with the penis hat grinned wide and clapped her hands together. "Ooh, y'all got me a stripper?"

Wes almost reversed his steps right there. Three. Two. One. Right back out the door. But he gritted his teeth and kept moving forward.

"Even better," said a tall, dark-eyed woman at her side. "He doesn't just strip, he cooks for us!"

"Yum!" another of the group said, and Wes couldn't tell if that was about him or his food.

"Hello, ladies." Wes forced a charming smile and then unbuttoned his black chef's coat as a little part of him died inside. "Who's ready to get some hands-on lessons?"

All the women eagerly raised their hands, laughing as they made their way over to the long bar in the kitchen. His ingredients were neatly arranged, his *mise en place* set up by Suzie ahead of time, and the recipe cards were stacked in front of each chair at the bar along with colorful Jell-O shots and glasses of champagne.

He inhaled a deep breath as he took in the festive atmosphere, trying to center himself.

This was a party. Someone was getting married, and this was their fun night with their friends. Maybe the *last* fun night if this chick's marriage went anything like Wes's had. They didn't need some grumpy-ass dude ruining their evening.

He tried to keep that in his head as he laid his chef's coat over a chair and reached back to tug his T-shirt off.

The ladies made appreciative sounds and comments as the cool air hit his bare skin. Their reactions should've stroked his ego. If he'd been his younger self, he'd have rolled around in that kind of attention, would've egged them on and played it up. If he'd been that guy, he would've sidled up to the bar with them and knocked down some of those shots, found a hot single woman in the bunch and charmed her into his bed for the night.

But right now, looking at all the pretty faces and roving gazes, he couldn't find an ounce of interest in anything but the booze. Since his divorce, that part of him had died as well. All he saw when he looked at women now was trouble, drama, and disaster waiting to happen.

No, thanks.

One of the ladies leaned over and poured him a tall glass of champagne. "What's your name, handsome?"

My name is Chef Wesley Garrett. I trained under renowned Chef Amelia St. John, and for a half a second, I owned the restaurant of my dreams and was going to be the next big thing in the city. "Roman."

"Ooh, nice name. You speak Italian?"

"No. Spanish." Because that was what his adoptive mother spoke and was the language of half his former kitchen staff. But he'd be damned if he was going to perform it like some show. "I'm rusty, though."

"That's okay, darling," said an older lady from the far end of the bar. "We didn't hire you to talk."

A few of them laughed, and the muscles in the back of his neck tightened. The light scent of the champagne drifted his way, and though he'd never been a champagne drinker, his throat became parched. He closed his eyes for a second, breathed through the urge, and focused on why he was here.

Money in the bank. Money in the bank.

He picked up a knife, pasted on a smile, and grabbed a bowl of ground beef. "All right, who's ready to handle some balls?"

COMING JUNE 2018

acknowledgments

Every book benefits from having dedicated people behind it, but in the case of this story and series, I needed more than a team…I needed believers. The idea for this book nudged me one day and then *would not leave me alone*. But how was I going to convince anyone that a story about survivors of a school shooting could also be a romance? Those two things aren't supposed to go together. However, this book is in your hands, dear reader, because a.) you're awesome and picked up this book (thank you!), and b.) I had the best group of believers and cheerleaders in my corner.

First, thanks to my husband, Donnie, who always supports my weird ideas and is convinced I can pull off anything. To my kiddo, who keeps me laughing even when the writing gets tough. To the Possum Posse, who keeps me (mostly) sane when I'm writing. To my parents, my original cheerleading team. And to my agent, Sara Megibow, who is always full of encouragement, energy, and thoughtful advice.

Last but not least, huge thanks to Cat Clyne, my editor, Dominique Raccah, and the rest of the talented Sourcebooks team for making me feel so welcome and for having such boundless enthusiasm for this book. I never had to explain why I wanted to write this story— y'all got it from the start. And having people who "get" your vision for a book and are just as excited about it as you are is the best gift an author can receive. Hugs to all!

about the author

Roni wrote her first romance novel at age fifteen, when she discovered writing about boys was way easier than actually talking to them. Since then, her flirting skills haven't improved, but she likes to think her storytelling ability has.

She holds a master's degree in social work and spent years as a mental health counselor, but now she writes full-time from her cozy office in Dallas, Texas, where she puts her characters on the therapy couch instead.

She is a two-time RITA Award winner and a *New York Times* and *USA Today* bestselling author.

WITHDRAWN